Warwickshire County Council

WEL			

This item is to be returned or renewed before the latest date above. It may be borrowed for a further period if not in demand. **To renew your books:**

- **Phone the 24/7 Renewal Line 01926 499273 or**
- **Visit www.warwickshire.gov.uk/libraries**

Discover • Imagine • Learn • *with libraries*

 Warwickshire
County Council

 Working for Warwickshire

The Brook to Cwmdonkin

Dan Farr-Brazier

Printed and bound in Great Britain by:
Book Printing UK, Remus House, Coltsfoot Drive, Woodston,
Peterborough PE2 9BF

Published by Soi Sunset

Dedications

To the twenty crew lost from the SS Geoligist, sunk off Trinidad
July 13th 1955.

To my mother Edna and father Frank who, when streets were
collapsing around us, took our family of seven to a sanctuary in
the Worcestershire countryside.

To my daughter Michelle for her love and companionship when
all seemed dark.

To my son Stephen who has love that I'm sure will bring him to
healthier and lighter days.

To my surviving siblings, Trevor and Diane and the late
Maurice, Audrey and Paul.

To the spirited Welsh.

With thanks to

David Higham and Associates Ltd, Custodians of Dylan Thomas
for the permission to use lines of Dylan Thomas in my book
The Brook to Cwmdonkin.

Contents

Author's Introduction

Back in the 1970s, a poetry and poet enthusiast friend of mine reacted indignantly to my idea of writing a story about a besotted female fan of a famous, late Welsh poet. In his mind, it was as if I was touching on something 'sacred' that ought not be approached. Around that time, as a cartoonist a few of my cartoons involving Shakespeare were published in the district media, including one in the local Stratford Herald. (I wish no other herald, no other speaker of my living actions.) Shakespeare's words beneath its title could have given the historic newspaper a lofty attitude to things Bard related but they used the cartoon as did the other publications submitted to. The cartoons were obviously fictitious, as was my book and apparently, no complaints were forthcoming. Hardly comparable but it made me less cautious about continuing my 'tongue in cheek' tale. Nevertheless, caution, together with domestic problems at that time, persuaded me to shelve the manuscript to gather dust.

Aged 76, I reconsidered the manuscript, pondering what had caused my friend's indignation? Had I perhaps touched on something 'sacred' and what credentials had I to create fiction 'around' the famed poet of whom I too had become quite an admirer? An admiration that had me visiting his childhood haunt, Cwmdonkin Park, in Swansea and also to holiday in those parts of South Wales favoured by himself and while lingering in those places and learning more about the poet, my consideration became complete.

A complex man was the genius it has been said but 'human' and undoubtedly did have admiring female fans who would have kept pictures of him as do I (my own copy of that by Augustus John) in keeping with that admiration. And surely, they'd have attended his recitals whenever possible as was quite evident in the United States where he appeared to have became a forerunner of Brit' pop stars to enrapture especially, young audiences at the many college campuses he visited on tour.

So, why not weave a fictitious tale around this obviously charismatic artiste? My story touches little on the poet's much written about private life which in fact reveals nothing overly scandalous and tells that his wife remained 'the love of his life,' and regarding my fictitious tale, his adoring female fan remains unknown to him throughout.

And so, my indignant friend of yesteryear, while respecting your entitlement to an opinion: something from my research of the 'character' of this Welsh icon, considered I know, by many, as being the twentieth century's greatest Western world poet, tells me that my fictitious tale in which he is but 'spoken' of, would I guess, have been chuckled over by the man himself.

Writing a story or drawing a cartoon I liken to a holiday in the mind and ought to be carried out for any joy it brings to both, creator and reader. Possibly, the only headache from story writing came from the construction of intelligible, flowing grammar but I take comfort in knowing that a reader's enjoyment comes from the story rather than the author's use of grammar.

At school in Crabbs Cross, Worcestershire, I discovered the pleasure of creating stories and the laughter generated on reading them out to the class as I was often asked to do. This pleasure was likely due to my excelling in little else, especially sport which elevated boys in the eyes of their peers. In art I had a secret in that I copied my all-round genius best friend who you'll meet in the story ahead. 'Not bad but cartoon-like' was the deputy head's remark that gave birth to my cartooning hobby. Cartooning causes you to study people and what makes them tick, leaving some individuals curious as to was it them I'd drawn in some journal or other? The enjoyment of my study was to extend it in the form of a book and in my mid twenties, the *'The Brook to Cwmdonkin'* was born and in almost a lifetime, was complete!

Its birth though, wasn't feasible until after my excursions in the Merchant Navy and Army, when I began jotting things down in my 'study'. Well, not a study as such but in the abominable conditions of a Redditch drop-forging factory, HDA, where as a technician, I'd escape reality 'in my breaks', by finding myself on some tropical river or in the throes of some blissful love affair; anywhere rather than that hellish confine of thundering hammers, roasting, belching furnaces and squealing machinery, where I had to make a living because of not sufficiently educating myself.

That I was 'always beavering away?' was a common remark from those who, if had looked closely, would have noticed that my pen was busy 'beneath' the component drawing in front of me and what was being written wasn't remotely akin to a technical report! Next, I took typing lessons and those jottings became a thickening sheaf of a manuscript. What that manuscript pertained to was helped greatly by my experiences in the Merchant Service. One experience in particular initiated the tale I wished to create, while at the same time, troubled me. It was the event of being paid off at the shipping company's London office when one of the ship's officers, on learning what parts I hailed from, asked if, for ten shillings, would I take a letter to an old flame of his residing in the village of Wootton Wawen which was actually a good hour's bike ride from my then home. (There being no direct bus route.) Not in possession of her exact address, he asked me if I'd ask around the village for her whereabouts and personally hand over the letter. Ten shillings was a lot of money in 1955 and the officer had acted good-naturedly towards me at sea, so without hesitation, I said yes, I'd attempt to deliver the letter. What troubled me for years after, however, was that I lost the letter and pondered as to what may have been the outcome of my doing so? Troubled, yes. But surely, there was a story to derive from my carelessness. And isn't it always said that a writer ought only write about what he is familiar with or experienced? The 'motley' crew of the *Roundcape* for example, were well deserving of that description. Their names would be fictitious as would the ship's. The ingredients were there because the voyage itself hadn't exactly been uneventful and combined with the undelivered letter . . .?

3

The 'motley' crew needed a bully and who better suited that the Scot's Second Cook who in reality welcomed the cabin boy aboard by having me collapse on the gangplank with an enormous sack of flour on my back and who punched me unconscious for 'whistling up the wind'. However, once having stamped his authority on his underlings, Jock the Cook showed his more affable side but cast as ship's bully, ship's bully he'd be! Furthermore, not wanting to be seen as castigating that nationality, Scots have turned up in this author's life often to his benefit, such as Billy Ness, from Edinburgh, fellow gunner and friend who served with him in 187 Battery RA, Jordan 1956/7, whom he let down through a tactless decision and has regretted it ever since. Also Ron Reid, a brilliant Scots entrepreneur who revived in me a zest for life by employing me at KAC, his Alcester company for my last working years.

And so the ship, its crew and the factual letter handed over, form the basis of the tale. Its setting, several as the story progresses, include one particularly, thought-inducing memory of a ship battling the well-recorded hurricanes of 1955. Battling wild seas simultaneously with the origins of Rock and Roll being blasted the ship's way from numerous US radio stations: a sound so new and vibrant that told excited young seamen aboard, that something quite different was afoot in the music world! A difference of such magnitude that even they, such fervent enthusiasts of the sound, at that point in time couldn't possibly have perceived!

Rock and Roll and wild hurricanes however, arrive well into the story: a story that begins in Worcestershire, England. The time, early post-Second World War and two boys are making a pact which includes their commandeering a section of brook making it their 'territory'. The Wharrage brook meanders through Hunt-End, a village which then, was not as today, an integral part of the nearby industrial town of Redditch. Hunt-End, so named after its role as being the end of King John's hunting ground in Feckenham Forest. (King John, English Monarch, born 1166, died 1216). These days, the village is more renowned as having been the childhood home of the late John Bonham: drummer of the world famous *Led Zeppelin* group, who, as a toddler, would come out to accept his father's newspaper from this author, the then Hunt-End delivery boy. I'm famous!

Another, while much overlooked famous resident (coincidently, yet another John) and friend of the author's family, was John/Jack Lakin, the second only Caucasian (then reported) to be made an African Chieftain. Appointed so, for his dedicated work in building and running a Leper Colony in mid-twentieth century Africa. John, the iconic drummer, is to have a statue in his memory erected locally. A great and popular idea, while I feel that late John, the missionary, also deserves some form of memorial.

The boys' seemingly nondescript home village, as a travel guide could have described it, did, therefore, have praiseworthy connections. Nondescript however, was an apt description of 1940/50s Hunt-End: its appearance hardly that of a typical English village, its disjointed lay-out consisting of scattered cottages, two rows of stereotype council houses, some older, once grander homes; small groups of modern semi-detached houses, a pub and three shops, plus, the eyesore of Enfield road, a long ugly factory building that once was the home of Royal Enfield Cycles.

Fortunately for our two boys, their homes were where the village thins out along the Walkwood road to become what appears to be, endless and picturesque Worcestershire countryside, a setting much better suited as where to begin a journey which takes our traveller to a mystical Welsh park overlooking wide seas on which he travels a great distance to enter an exotic, tropical river, where, 'love may live?' Then northward to another mighty waterway, so breathtakingly scenic, that travellers could be tempted to linger. A temptation, not his, he being driven by the temptation calling him back to the earlier river. A temptation widely considered as being; the greatest temptation in life.

This story is fictitious while written with a background of factual worldwide events. Accordingly, the names, actions and spoken words of Daniel's friends, associates and characters within the story are also fictitious.

Readers of this book's original draft have posed a question in common regarding what was fact and otherwise, the above paragraph being how I saw fit to answer. Further to that, I will repeat that the event of my being handed a letter following my time aboard a ship out of Cardiff in the summer of 1955, which inspired my writing the tale, was fact. Also fact was that during the voyage I was confined in a strait jacket for my own safety while dangerously intoxicated, an accidental intoxication which brought about a delirious semi-conscious state within which the absurdities and tongue-in-cheek erotica found in the latter part of my book, such as could only be the fevered dreams/nightmares of a teenage youth (obviously fictitious) which, in my staid, senior years, I reconsidered and concluded that what I had written was, as said, tongue-in-cheek humour common to youth, then and now.

Dan Farr-Brazier

Chapter 1

The Brook

The wireless announcement that brought millions rejoicing to their feet, momentarily took Daniel's attention from the large frog poised hesitantly on the brook's opposite bank. The frog it seemed, digested the important news before its lethargic observer and plunged into the cool, sparkling water for a celebration swim. Not in the mood for such exertion, the amphibian was well out of sight downstream before the boy began pondering the significance of his brother's excited cry from the garden above.

Well – yes: winning the war was bound to be generally beneficial. No dads away for long periods and sometimes for ever. And sweet coupons it was said, might well be a thing of the past? On the negative side though, his mention in the local newspaper as being the district's champion foil milk-top collector had made him more enthusiastic about hauling bag after bag to school and how else, if the demand for tin foil ceased as it surely would, might he ever again attract such acclaim?

Okay, accumulating that quantity of milk-tops with his family being the second largest in the village (the Tarvers kept their own cow) hadn't been too difficult to achieve, while the neighbours' and school's praise almost equalled that given to a speech on the wireless from Mr Churchill himself!

The wireless? Heck yes! If Maurice's dad's accumulator was run down, they'll most likely not have heard the news! Perhaps he ought to go over to their cottage and tell them? He'd certainly feel important being the first person to tell the Blooms that we'd won the war! Just imagine the surprise on their faces! They'd be absolutely astounded when they . . .?

Oh no they wouldn't – not the Blooms. There's nothing that could shock the Blooms. The most laid-back folk around were

Maurice's parents. He'd pass on the sensational news and his mother would smile that great big smile and hand him an apple, while his dad, such a small and quiet man for so large a wife, would just grin his permanent grin and carry on with his digging.

Kept themselves to themselves did the Blooms. Unsociable, some folk called them. But 'unsociable' sounded a harsh, unhappy description to Daniel in whose eyes the Blooms deserved anything but such a label. Far from being unhappy, he saw them as possibly the most contented family in the village. To an outsider, their contentment might well have not been immediately obvious. Daniel himself, when first chumming up with Maurice and visited his rudimentary home, suspected their laid-back manner and constant smiles but very soon, he being one of the privileged few to get close enough to study the family, the secret of their apparent contentment became fascinatingly clear to him.

In common with Daniel's own family, the Blooms were not country born. As with his own parents, Maurice's mom and dad had been driven from a war-blitzed Midland city to the sanctuary of the Worcestershire countryside. Their similar stories once there however, changed in that Daniel's family enjoyed the modern comforts of a recently built home within the village, while Mr and Mrs Bloom, Maurice and their teenage daughter's evacuee accommodation was a dilapidated field cottage on its outskirts.

The aged building (so tiny and isolated must surely have been built for a family of reclusive dwarfs) was fronted by an orchard so gnarled and bent that it must have been as old as the cottage itself. These withered trees and a large vegetable patch though, were annually bountiful and of great benefit to the new tenants.

Even their water they took freely from a garden well and the more Daniel studied their simple, unsophisticated mode of life, the more certain was he that through war, the Blooms had stumbled on their earthly paradise. There was little doubt, he perceived, that other than the Blooms having a daughter too,

Maurice's parents were a real life Mr and Mrs Rupert Bear[1] and if their son ever turned up at school wearing yellow checked trousers and matching scarf, it would be time to reveal his, Daniel's, other intriguing discovery concerning the Blooms. That they were raising a son who was nothing less than super-human! A consequence of his discovery had Daniel accepting that while his own skills hardly matched the other's, he'd at least the opportunity to try emulating those of his best friend. In fact, his study of Maurice's outstanding art presentations had their headmaster fooled enough into getting them extra tuition as a twosome. Even in this field, he'd never match the other's superb brushwork but simply being the shadow of one so talented made up for all other of his shortcomings. This offspring of the secretive Bloom's continued through school to live up to all expectations; his sketches and paintings bordering on masterpieces to many an eye. His ability to absorb facts and figures as impressive as his performances on the football pitch when goal after goal he'd take away the opposition's will to continue then afterwards walk home with seemingly nothing more important on his mind than how many eggs might there be now in that coot's nest under the Wharrage bridge?

The bridge became the hub of their dual activities and where their deep understanding of each other was nurtured. While Daniel could in no way, surpass the multi-talented Maurice, it was their mutual fascination with the water flowing beneath the bridge that much influenced their partnership. Three minutes upstream of the bridge, the brook passed through a deep tree lined cutting at the foot of Daniel's garden.

Its constant movement had captured his imagination since infancy. Winter gush or Summer trickles, it never stopped which posed a question in a child's mind. Where did it go to, this perpetual brook?

All brooks and rivers led to the sea his maritime-obsessed older brothers told him, happy to talk about where they were eventually bound. But the sea in Daniel's mind was a cold,

[1] Rupert Bear. Cartoon character of Daily Express

inhospitable place to where the brook, except while in flood, seemed in no hurry to reach, he observed. Yet its meandering route kept him curious, a curiosity which, on one of his braver days, had him following its downstream course way beyond the village outskirts.

Alone on that occasion, the unfamiliar surroundings and the sound of what he swore to his brothers was surely the sea, he'd lost his nerve and turned back. His brothers had scoffed and called him an idiot because the seas was a hundred miles away and he could hardly have been out of the village! What was it really that had scared him, they'd teased causing him to tell the *truth* about why he'd turned back.

"There was something or somebody coming towards me upstream! I couldn't make out what because the overhanging trees made it dark and gloomy at that point! But I'll swear that there was something coming towards me grunting and sort of cursing, getting closer by the minute so I ran for it! Scared to death I was cos I felt it was after me, I'll swear to it!"

"You imagined it, you twerp!" his brothers had teased. "You're always imagining things!"

He swore again that this experience was true, embroidering the tale with every telling.

On the day that he and Maurice mischievously tipped two sacks of milk-tops into the water off the Wharrage bridge reasoning that they'd likely reach Mr Churchill's navy more quickly than via the school, the story of his unnerving venture downstream was given yet another airing. While a tad sceptical, Maurice at least didn't scoff and being the plucky type that he was, offered to investigate himself.

Upstream was of no matter, the brook's source less than one mile distant and well charted. Downstream was the challenge and while Maurice dared venture even further than where his chum had ran into trouble, he did confess to feeling just a little uncomfortable. During his wade though, he'd not seen or heard anything that would help make the other's story more credible

10

but did maintain that his feeling of discomfort had bordered on fear. Fear of the unknown!

Their thoughts and resulting agreement were thus: Even though the brook was supposed to eventually reach the sea, they'd no definite proof that it did? And even if it did the seas that they'd never seen were said to be so vast that to them, they seemed infinite! Infinity, they concluded, was inexplicable and made them uncomfortable... therefore, the point along the brook where they'd began to feel uncomfortable must be the beginning of infinity. They would mark it and never travel beyond it.

This pact sealed their relationship once and for all. They claimed the bridge section of the brook as their very own. Discovering new aspects of it made their imaginations soar. The water babbling over pebbles in the shallows was actually speaking to them.

"Hello boys," it would greet them. "Come and have fun with me; I'm so glad of your company."

So then it was a threesome and eventually Daniel one day so excitedly discovered, they were four!

"A girl's face? A girl's face in the water, you say?"

Maurice in this instance sounded disbelieving causing Daniel to try proving what he'd discovered.

"Look for yourself then," he challenged, pointing into the water. "Those two stones are eyes and that one and that one nose and mouth and the deflected water is creating long hair being blown around her smiling face."

The formation remained long enough for Maurice to just make it out but his attitude on this occasion wasn't exactly in unison with Daniel making the latter troubled as to whether he'd for once been too imaginative? In mind of this he decided to tread carefully in future and when the same girl continued to appear in water and then in his dreams, it remained the one pleasure not imparted to Maurice. Likewise, even when the vision appeared to him from a mountain stream while holidaying with his parents in distant Wales, on returning home and tempted to mention this, the most perfect of her appearances to date, he

11

said nothing. In fact the event of his dad inheriting his father's Austin Seven, enabling the Brazier family to holiday for the very first time, was something he'd hesitated from telling Maurice, the Blooms appearing not to have the means to emulate such an experience. In truth however, cars and travel Daniel suspected, were not something that this proud, self-sufficient family would have found desirable enough to envy. As expected, Maurice didn't appear to be the slightest bit jealous in common with his mother whom, he said, told him that Wales, she'd heard, was the wettest part of the British Isles and she'd no wish to visit anywhere with an umbrella in hand.

Daniel's experience of Wales though had been memorable not only for the event of the girl smiling up at him from the stream where he'd be filling up a camping kettle to top up the Austin's overheated radiator but also through feeling, a belonging to this ruggedly beautiful country where it was said some of his ancestors had hailed from. The girl too he felt, was in some way connected to this part of the world, a feeling which would eventually prove correct when in the most extraordinary of circumstances, she'd return and reveal her identity to him.

And so with little effort, things resumed as before, the boys remaining inseparable within their pact, not seeking change until one day in the most natural of ways in their early teens, fate intervened.

Girls! Their domain around the Wharrage bridge became a magnet for blossoming girls! This threat to their male world had to be dealt with and the solution reached was not to over-encourage them. A total ban had been considered but Angela Treadgold had proved useful in gathering wood for their bonfire in the cooler months and it also couldn't be denied that she and Bernice Foreman had appeared attractively 'grown up' while taking a scantily-clothed dip in the brook on one exceptionally hot Summer's day. Nevertheless, girls it seemed were generally serious creatures and the mainstay of their long union had undoubtedly been 'humour', seeing themselves alike to their film idols Abbott and Costello, their proposed journey through

12

life similarly one endless laugh. 'Nothing' would part them! When the time came, they'd seek employment together and should they be called up, they'd insist on doing National Service together and to cap the deal they'd one day renovate that derelict cottage in the field next to Maurice's and grow old together.

The brook was a snaking ribbon of ice. Must get Maurice to help break it open to prove that it's still on the move. They'd always found at least an inch of water still flowing. Yes – must get Maurice.

The field in which they'd enjoyed each other's company for one long, carefree decade was thick with snow. Nearing the cottage he saw that its tiny windows were thickly coated with frost and no smoke curled from its crooked chimney. His anxious knock on the rickety front door echoed about a still interior bringing a fine shower of snow cascading from the trellis surround. Looking about him, he saw that the fruit trees he'd witnessed defying time through seasons of copious fruition now sagged wearily under a mantle of snow. At the spot where he'd last seen Mr Bloom tidying up his vegetable patch, a garden fork stood conspicuously alone and next to the well that had echoed their boyhood yells, Mrs Bloom's bucket peeped out of the snow.

Hammering on the door again, a solitary crow laughed down at him from one of the towering poplars beyond the cottage. Looking back up the field he saw that his were the only footprints in the snow and the last fall had been more than a day ago. His fingers raked frantically at the iced windowpanes! The cottage was bare of all furnishings! Bare of all life! The Blooms – Maurice, his pal, had gone!

"Mauriiiiiice!" A voice he hardly recognized as his own rang out across the silent field.

The field where they'd romped in long Summer grass; sped down its steep central path on a homemade trolley and made plans, laughed and played from knee-length trousers to first long, grey flannels, was silent.

"*Mauriiiiiice!*" His cry once again cracked the sharp Winter air.

"Gone! Gone! Gone!" laughed back the crow.

It was said around the village of Hunt-End that the Blooms had finished their game in the insular manner that they'd played it; a view that proved to Daniel just what a blinkered lot the villagers really were! Nevertheless, for Maurice at least to have departed without so much as a goodbye was definitely strange and there just had to be a logical explanation? Okay, things hadn't been quite the same between them since his, Daniel's, preoccupation with the angelic-faced Patsy Harding who would surely soon become aware of her latest admirer. Not that Maurice had appeared rejected: he'd been too busy chasing that bit of leather around the football pitch to have been aware of another's distractions. He'd even found an excuse not to accompany his old chum to be interviewed for vacancies on offer for trainee fish-hook pointers in nearby Redditch. On being accepted, Daniel's demeanour during the first week of boring toil at the grindstone was hardly helped by him brooding over his friend's sudden absence until finally he found himself admitting that only a mindless fool would call such drudgery 'a trade for life' and Maurice was neither mindless or a fool.

"*Sorry not to have had the chance to say something,*" Maurice eventually wrote. "*But me mother suddenly got offered this house back in Coventry and before I knew what was happening, the lino was rolled up and the furniture van had arrived. You are welcome to visit just as soon as we've settled in, me mother says,*" concluded the letter from his 'pal for life' chum. "*Look forward to seeing you.*"

"*As soon as I'm old enough for a licence and I've got the money together for the deposit on a motorbike, I'll probably do just that,*" Daniel wrote back while really wanting to say,

"There'll be a few things I'll be wanting to get off me chest to that mother of yours when I step inside her Coventry council house, you pathetic mother's boy, you! And if that Patsy Harding at work flashes just one more smile at me when she passes me grindstone, I'll likely bring her along to blooming-well listen to me say 'em!"

This promise became Daniel's obsession and eighteen months later the bike was his. And Patsy Harding . . . ? Patsy Harding's smiles, he learned to his embarrassment, had been grimaces of displeasure at being showered with sparks as she'd ducked and weaved her way past the besotted twerp's grindstone, so her soon-to-be fiancé from the same office took pleasure in telling every piss-taking sod in the factory!

Time cools and the promised tongue-lashing during his Coventry visit was reduced to a feeble, "I'll bet you're missing the Worcestershire countryside in springtime, eh, Mrs Bloom?" which was either too feeble or completely failed to penetrate her brain as she handed him tea and biscuits while awaiting her son's return from his place of work.

"He'll be home any minute now," she said while proudly bustling about her suburban semi. "Time and a half on Saturday morning is his rate and he'll not miss out on that while it's on offer. Do you get any overtime at your works, Daniel?" she asked while he was wondering if the sad woman had ever been remotely aware of her factory-working son's genius?

"Overtime . . . ? Er – yes but – but I'm not working any now like. While – while I'm waiting for me papers to come from the navy, Mrs Bloom. They should be arriving any day now and then I'll be off," he lied spontaneously.

"Oooooh! You ought to be working overtime while it's on offer," she insisted, completely ignoring his important disclosure and making him want to scream, *"Overtime, Mrs Bloom? What has blooming overtime got to do with anything? How can overtime help Maurice make use of his mathematical mind, his artistic and athletic skills which stunned his teachers all of those years? And you, Mrs Bloom? What about your little cottage standing cold and empty in an overgrown wilderness that was once your paradise on Earth? The haven where you raised your genius son to excel in skills far removed from the industrial drudgery he's now been put to? If only you'd stayed, Mrs Bloom, his and your futures would have been far better than that you're heading for. Your cottage could have been renovated and you'd have continued life even more contented than how I remembered you! Oh why, oh why, Mrs Bloom, go and spoil everything by swapping all that for dismal this?"*

"Because she wanted gas and electric and water from a tap the same as your mother has," Maurice explained later as they walked the drab city streets, finishing up out of sheer boredom watching their old favourites Abbot and Costello at a local cinema. The film hardly drew a chuckle and words were hard to find on the way back. Maurice did condescend to point out the factory where he now worked as an Apprentice toolmaker but his mood was as dull as the building was drab and Daniel was beginning to regret his trip.

They were almost back at Maurice's new home when he unexpectedly enquired about something in their past. Something which had become taboo at the time and accordingly, long out of mind.

"The er – girl . . . ? The girl that you reckoned you'd seen in the brook that time, remember?" he began, almost as if for the sake of not wishing to appear totally unsociable. "Your, er – *vision* that time? Did – did you ever see it . . . her again?"

"Naah," lied Daniel, if only not to appear the over-imaginative adolescent of yesteryear. "Well – that is except for one time I – er – thought I'd seen something in a stream in Wales like. But – but we were both a couple of dreamers in those days, weren't we? What, er - ? What made you bring that up of all things, Maurice? It – it was only our little game that we had fun with those days as I recall?"

"Yeah, I suppose it was but – but it was just something I saw, or *imagined* I saw around about that time but forget that I mentioned it cos as you said, we were both a couple dreamers

16

those days, weren't we? I thought it best not to mention, er – her. She – she could have been anybody like, so I thought I'd sound daft . . ."

Daniel's curiosity was such that he had to know more!

"Are you telling me that you saw her apart from that time when I showed you that face in the brook when you . . .?"

"No – not in the brook, an' – and I never did go along with you that time if you remember? It – seemed childish and I'm not even suggesting that what I saw was in any way connected to what you thought you saw and – and . . ."

Maurice paused and, looking serious again, said, "Let's just forget that I even brought it up, shall we?"

"No! I'm *really* interested in what you saw or think you saw. Just out with it and then we'll forget it!" compromised Daniel.

"Okay – okay then . . ." Maurice appeared distinctly regretful for having mentioned his experience but continued. "It – it was one afternoon, er – back at our cottage like, when you were walking back up the field towards the road at around teatime when I, er – noticed this girl, a young woman walking a few feet behind you. She glanced back and I put her at about the same age as our Dinah and your oldest sister and before she'd turned, I thought it might have been one of them larking about cos she was about the same build as our sisters and had black hair, only hers was much longer, right down her back so that ruled out both of them, our sisters like, who wouldn't possibly have had the nerve to go walking about in the, er – in the . . ."

"Walking about in the what?" asked Daniel, frustrated by the other's hesitation but his question was eluded by Maurice who then went on to say, "So – so I thought I'd get a closer look and dogged you both up the field to the gate and she followed you through even though you didn't seem to know that she was right behind you. But – but when I got into the road, there was only you heading home and – and she was nowhere in sight! She – she'd completely vanished!"

Daniel studied his old chum's face, awaiting the sudden grin that would reveal it had all been a joke.

Not even a hint of a smile led him to ask, "Why – why on earth didn't you tell me about what you saw? We always used to tell each other *everything*. You knew that she couldn't have been one of our sisters and if she'd been a local girl, we'd probably have worked out who from what she was wearing or something. And – and thinking about it, one of the Tarver girls had been tailing me on and off for years. Me brothers never stopped taking the Mickey over it. Yes – that's who it likely was! Ivy Tarver! She's more than likely got through the hedge from her place into your field, followed me into the road then nipped smartly through their cottage gate when she realized you were tailing her. It – it likely was as simple as that and if me memory serves me right, she'd have been wearing the same pink, chequered dress that she'd worn for years? A hand-down that at first had been much too long for her but she didn't half start to fill it later on we all noticed. Yes – I'm betting that it would have been Ivy Tarver."

Maurice's expression told him that it couldn't be quite so simply explained and, drawing a breath, began to tell why.

"As – as I said, I thought it best to keep it to meself and besides, you were away on holiday to Wales the next day and by the time you'd come back, I . . ."

"Just tell me if she was wearing a pink, chequered dress?" interrupted Daniel impatiently.

"Er – that's just it," replied Maurice. "I'd have looked an idiot telling what I'd seen. That's why I decided not to say anything."

"You've lost me completely now, Maurice. What exactly did you see?"

"Well – your's and my sister's or Ivy Tarver for that matter wouldn't have been seen dead without any clothes, would they?"

"I – I suppose not but – but are you saying that the girl you saw was . . .?"

"Yes – she was naked," completed Maurice. "As naked as on the day she was born!"

Maurice's revelation had saved an otherwise disappointing day from being a total disaster but when seated later around Mrs Bloom's table, the awkward silence between the pair had resumed.

"I – I've heard they'll soon be bulldozing your cottage into the ground, Mrs Bloom," announced Daniel mischievously.

"And not before its time," replied the ever-complacent Mrs Bloom while Mr Bloom simply grinned into his teacup.

"Did – did you know you'd left your garden fork behind, Mr Bloom?" asked their visitor pointlessly. "And – and your bucket, Mrs Bloom?"

"The fork's handle was split and my bucket had a hole in it," smiled Maurice's mother, adding, "so they might as well go on to the demolition wagon along with everything else."

It was a despondent Daniel who bid a now indifferent old pal goodbye that evening.

"So you're going to follow your brothers into the navy, are you?" asked a yawning Maurice.

"Yes – me papers should be arriving any day now and with luck, I'll be off by me seventeenth birthday," replied the other, making capital out of the decision he'd arrived at over Mrs Bloom's apple pie.

"And to think you were once too scared to go more than half a mile down our brook," remarked Maurice with another yawn that told he really couldn't care a sod about his once bosom friend's new career.

The bike at full throttle helped little in pacifying the youth as he rode home. Even Maurice's absurd story had likely been a pathetic attempt to apologize for something broken that could never be fixed!

"So you'll be travelling off down the brook without me, eh?"

His last feeble attempt to show that they were once united by humour was as pathetically concocted as his absurd fabrication about he, Daniel, being stalked by a naked girl in broad daylight! And he'd thought him so naive as to be taken in by such nonsense! A tale as nonsensical as him presently imagining the face of a girl smiling at him through the bike's rain-spattered windshield causing him to lose concentration on that sharp bend two miles out of Leamington.

"Yeah!" he promised apathetic Maurice just seconds before colliding head-on with the Ford Anglia. "You bet I'm travelling off down the brook without you! You bet I am!"

Chapter 2

Letter to Heloise

Darling. Fanciful heading
address now vacated!
Yours, I W.

Third Officer
Ivor Williams,
The bandstand,
Cwmdonkin Park,
Uplands,
Swansea
16th June 1955

My darling Heloise,
Yes! It has finally happened, my love. Oh, sorry,
my sweet Lise! How does my letter find you? In the
best of health I hope. As for your Ivor, if you detect a
touch of euphoria in my writing, then your senses
are serving you well.
What has happened? You will already have
guessed, my love, that the pool doc' in Cardiff has
passed me fit and I'm packed and ready to go! My
first ship in two years and it all came about in a
matter of hours! From the doc's I wasted no time
and went straight over to the nearby pool office from
where, with little fuss, they told me to get myself
over to Bute dock for assignment, okay, she's not
quite the Lizzie (a London Greek tramp if that means
anything to you?) but her Master was happy to see
me, having just received orders and urgently in need
of a Third mate,Cook and catering boy. So he
immediately put me to work in the pantry! No, joking
apart, my darling, although my papers were in
order, I'd expected him to at least want to go into
more detail re my two years ashore but getting
underway was obviously his priority, so if he's later

adversely informed, it'll be information too late when we're days out to sea.

Also of interest to you, sweet Lise, *is that I didn't travel to Cardiff in complete ignorance of the outcome; my family GP having told me he'd forwarded a good bill of health to the pool doc' and his response had been favourable. So, darling, the aforementioned euphoria having already set in, I decided to celebrate by taking one last stroll up Cwmdonkin Drive where on arrival, even the sun must have known that this was no ordinary day, choosing to emerge from behind a great mass of cloud and alerting every bird in the park to join in the celebration!*

Springtime in Wales has been just as you would have liked it, darling. What's the weather been like in New York? After all this time, you must long for a sunny day on the Gower. If I'd had the time, it being this time of the year, I might even have taken myself down there to relive those memorable outings of ours. But our spiritual home, the park, well sufficed, weather-wise very similar as on the day we first met there (I'll not apologize for the above address because I know you'll appreciate the sentimental thought behind it) and, oh yes! While there, I, being the loquacious soul I am, got chatting to a couple of young tourists who were taking snaps of his boyhood haunt and when I explained its relevance, they took some of the bandstand too.

I'd actually accompanied these young ladies up the drive and they'd graciously asked me to snap them with the Thomas home in the background which had me tempted to rouse their American curiosity (American or Canadian?) by telling them about our own 'camera excursions into poet country'. But even with the time, how would one even begin telling complete strangers about the lengths we'd go to in order to get something to prize for your precious album?

Which reminds me, dear Lise. On getting my suitcase out last night, I found the duplicated snap that you called 'your scoop'. Remember? The one with you virtually alongside him as he left Browns Hotel in Laugharne? The occasion that brought on one of my possessive moments because as you overtook him, I swore that his eyes were fixed on the most shapely backside in Wales! And, darling, I kept that observation to myself at the time lest a tiff should dash my hopes of spreading the car rug on Pendine Sands later that day. Where was I? Oh yes, those young tourists? How absurd it would have sounded, my telling them that on one particular visit to Laugharne, my lady friend had childishly thrown pebbles at the door of the poet's studio (driveway shed) and then had reproached herself for maybe having interrupted the flow of some inspired verse? Oh why, oh why, darling, did I not fall in love with someone whose infatuation was for some run-of-the-mill celluloid movie star? 'Because,' I can hear you remind me, 'his commanding presence and the aura given out at his recitals in America and elsewhere touched his fans in a way that artificial screen stars with their groomed looks and obvious vanity could never do!' To which I have to add from the viewpoint of a male that his inimitable deliveries compared well to the best of orators and most definitely appealed to those fans of the 'weaker' sex. And after you've reproved me for 'weaker', you'll also remind me 'that while his deliveries were awesome, it was the content of his poems that ultimately captivated both male and female factions of his audiences.'

23

So, darling, we've once again found ourselves agreeing to agree, in the process of which I've reminded myself to thank you again for your so thoughtful a gift which I'm also taking aboard (oh and it being a typewriter might well have something to do with my illegible handwriting which I assure you was always to do with the ship's motion) and as long as I'm able to replace its ribbons, will be used in my continuing correspondence to sweet you. Plenty of ribbon at this precise moment and I just have to continue with referring back to those young tourists who were part way up Cwmdonkin Drive as I entered it and suddenly, you were back! Yes, darling, one of the girls was of your build and had long, black hair and you'd returned as I'd so often anticipated without warning, completely out of the blue to give me so pleasant a surprise in the place promised to each other as the rendezvous for our eventual reunion. That it was not exactly 'in' the park was hardly a disappointment but what did greatly disappoint me was finding that the face that suddenly turned to see me following while strikingly pretty, was not yours! And there's me stupidly convinced otherwise and about to embrace you showing that stupidity as she smiles and politely asks if I'd mind taking a few photos of them together, to which I naturally reply 'of course I wouldn't mind' and within seconds, I'm snapping away and answering their questions as if the local tourist guide! They expressed their gratitude to me for engaging with them in the subject they were there to learn more about and spoke of a less gratifying experience when visiting the Mermaid in Oystermouth the previous evening where the locals had appeared apathetic towards the famous poet who'd frequented and written about their bayside

24

pub. A reaction, I assured them, quite untypical of the Welsh who are usually more likely to heap praises on anything outstanding in their culture. Why did their experience so sadden me I ask myself? Is it because I've been totally brainwashed in all things Dylan by his greatest admirer who also happens to be the love of my life? Probably so, because love influences so much in one's character and you, darling, could influence me to try walking on the sea!

Mentioning the sea brings me to things more pertinent so I'll start with the ship I've been assigned to. She's the Roundcape: dry-docked for an overhaul which has been sped up, her owners wanting her underway by the end of the week. Where to, I can't tell you at this precise moment? Her Master says he's waiting for clarification of orders which usually means he knows but won't be telling until underway because some crews can play up over unhealthy cargoes which can often be guessed from the given destination. Cargo, destination? They're of little matter to me after so long ashore, my sweet. Unless that is, if our orders just happened to be, say, New York which would send my present good mood soaring with the thought of passing the Statue of Liberty knowing that you'd soon, God willing, be in my arms once again! Well, one cannot be blamed for glimpsing a fairytale ending however unlikely, eh, Lise? (You never did quite take to my shortening Heloise to Lise, did you?) Where was I? well, where I'm literally due in a moment is out on deck supervising the loading of stores, so I'll finish by promising you that despite soon being at sea, I'll do my utmost to keep in touch via Megan whose address she welcomes you to use for all future correspondence. (Whatever became of your letters to date remains a mystery.) Yes, Megan has been a gem of a sister these last two years and has promised once in receipt of your address, to post on my letters to you which, in the circumstances, darling, is quite the best arrangement.

Bows north, south, west or east,
my letters of love will never cease,
to keep alive our hopes and dreams,
'till we linger again, 'neath Cwmdonkin's[2] trees.

An off-the-cuff message with which to end, my darling Lise. To our early reunion,
                    Yours Ivor.

PS. Should you still be reproaching yourself for that mischievous assault on his studio door? I now feel a touch of guilt for my, as mischievous failure, to ease your conscience by telling you that I knew he was broadcasting live from London that day!

Oh! Reading through this letter has reminded me to mention my happiness on knowing that you would have at last attended one of his US performances. So happy. x

---

[2] Cwmdonkin Drive Swansea. Where Dylan Thomas was raised and wrote about the adjacent Cwmdonkin Park.

Chapter 3

Shipmates

The year 1955 began like a dull, wet Sunday. On the day of June 11th, the drizzle breaks into a storm. Eighty-two people are killed at Le Mans in the worst motor racing accident to date. The storm becomes angrier when in August and September, hurricanes Connie, Diane and Janet leave trails of destruction from the north-eastern states of America down to the sun-kissed isles of the West Indies. Undeterred by disasters resulting from the haste of man and nature, Donald Campbell continues his pursuit of speed records and in November, churns up the waters of Lake Nevada in *Bluebird* to beat his own world water record at an incredible 216 miles per hour.

In September, 'speed' robs the United States of its 'first teenager', when James Dean, film star and youth idol is killed in a car crash. Millions of fans go into mourning but their lament fails to quell the blustering year, which, from so mild a beginning climaxes in a thunderous fanfare of drums, saxophones and guitars. The mid-century doldrums were over. 'Rock and Roll' had arrived.

The pulsating sounds to be enjoyed on the indistinct wavelength of Radio Luxembourg[3] were far from Daniel's mind as he looked down on the dry-docked *MV Roundcape* on that June afternoon. The ocean-ravaged old freighter was as formidable a sight as had been the prison-like structure of the sea training school some weeks earlier when a couple of would-be recruits accompanying him had fled back to Gravesend railway station. He too had been tempted to run but dreaded giving those

---

[3] Radio Luxembourg. A British teenager's only way of listening to American Rock sound in 1955.

back home so early an opportunity to scoff. After all of his bragging about being finished with dreary factories and hick town life, there could be no running back despite the nagging thought of having disregarded his father's passed on opinion.

"How does he blooming well know I'm not cut out for it?" he'd protested to his mother. "It might seem like a sudden whim but the more I think about that big world out there, the more I want to go!"

Little else was said about his 'suitability' but he quietly worried about this father's comments knowing full well that he never voiced an opinion lightly. Driven by sheer stubbornness however, he'd gone ahead with his blind pursuit; a pursuit that had brought him on this warm, Summer's day, to the heart of the Cardiff dockland.

The ship below him bustled with activity. Men scurried about its decks and on the adjacent quay. A shrill Welsh voice guided a net full of sacks aboard, the crane driver then turning his attention to other supplies arriving alongside the ship by way of an incline at the open end of the dry dock. Clutching his sea bag nervously, Daniel made for the top of the incline where he paused once again to take in the scene before him.

Should he simply turn about and rid himself of the fear of meeting these people of the sea, he asked himself, recalling his brothers unsettling accounts of first boarding? He turned his gaze back towards the dock entrance then back towards the ship. People down there were studying his unease, he sensed, suddenly feeling conspicuous in his blue serge training school garb, knowing that only officers wore uniforms on workaday freighters. The whole outfit, including plastic tie and beret, had cost only four pounds but with the *MERCHANT NAVY* shoulder flashes, he'd strolled about with pride back home, factory-hand turned sailor. Well – not 'sailor' in seagoing terms but the word 'Steward' lacked the masculine ring so important in promoting his new image. His training had included learning to tie a few knots and an hour or two of lifeboat drill but the art of laying a table had been much higher on the curriculum than he'd cared to reveal. Whatever the nature of his duties, it was now or never to find out together with all the other uncertainties that so troubled him, he knew. Trying to look confident while belching with fears, he descended the incline towards the *Roundcape*.

Assistant Cook Jock McLaughlin took a break from loading stores. Making himself comfortable on the sacked flour, he lit up a cigarette and studied the youth's hesitant approach.

"Every ship is lumbered wi' one an' this is fuckin' ours," he muttered to Reno, his short, stubby Maltese companion.

"Looks like we get them straight from kindergarten now, eh, Jock?" grinned Reno, keen to side with his fiery cabin mate.

"A fuckin' nappy wouldnae be out o' place on this bastard," growled back the Scot. "Looks like he's about to shite himself any minute now."

During his fourteen years at sea, McLaughlin had made it his business to knock first-trippers into shape. It was wise to take them in hand from day one. Always inoffensive initially but once over their first bouts of seasickness, they'd be strutting about the ship mouthing their cheek without a shred of respect for any man if allowed? Show 'em their status aboard from the word go, convincing 'em wi' a walloping and you'd have nipped it in the bud. Christ! But for the risk of his being spotted from up top, he'd like to kick this uniformed wee prat in the guts before he got a foot on the gangplank!

"What you want, sonny?" But for his dark, swarthy complexion, Daniel's questioner bore a passing resemblance to Lou Costello[4].

"What you want?" Reno asked again. "You joining us, sonny?"

"I – er . . . I – . . ." Daniel found the man's grin and his seated companion's narrow-eyed scrutiny uncomfortable.

"I – I . . . I'm the new Steward."

"We already got a Steward, sonny. In't that right, Jock?"

"Aye, we have that, Reno."

The seated man's tone was as mean as his looks.

---

[4] Lou Costello, of Abbott and Costello, famed comics of American films in the 1950s.

"The Chief Steward's aboard sure enough. What ship have you been assigned to, sir?"

The burly man's *sir* increased Daniel's discomfort.

"The, er . . . the *Roundcape* in Bute dock they told me at the shipping office," he replied, glancing up at the ship's name.

The Scot drew on his cigarette, appearing puzzled.

"Ay, laddie. 'is the *Roundcape* sure enough. But apart frae Chief Cook an' Cabin Boy, we've a full complement. You wouldnae be either o' them by any chance, would you?"

Daniel reddened on realizing his mistake. The term 'cabin boy' was rarely used at the school. He'd been trained to be a 'Steward' and assumed that to be his title. Before he could explain, an unsettling smirk spread across his questioner's scarred face.

"Och now! So you are the Chief Cook, are you?" he asked, mischievously. "Allow me to introduce myself. I'm your understudy, sir. An' a more obliging understudy as a Chief-cook could wish to have, I assure you. Kindly allow me to carry your gear aboard, sir. Then I'll arrange your bunk an' rustle up some grub an' a wee tot o' somethin' to celebrate your arrival!"

"How long've you been a Cook, sonny?" joined in his companion. "Five or more years, I'm thinking?"

"Congratulations on achieving such status so early in your career!" echoed the other, reaching out to give a bone-crushing handshake.

"I – I, er . . ." began Daniel, wincing before getting his hand released. "The, er – training school didn't tell me that . . ."

"Nae need to explain what they did or didnae tell you at the training school, sir. As long as you can cook, there's little else you've to concern yourself about. Now – let's be havin' that bag o' yours. The old man'll be as pleased as Punch to see you board," the Scot continued to bait.

"No – it – it's alright, thanks. I – I haven't got anything else to carry. I can manage meself . . ."

"Oh yes, you fuckin' well have, laddie!" erupted the Assistant Cook indicating that the pretence was over as he heaved his muscular form off the sacks and extinguished his cigarette beneath a size ten boot. "You, laddie, have been on the company's payroll since signing on at yon' shipping office, an' as yet have nae done a stroke for your fuckin' keep!"

Daniel stared dumbly back hoping that this was some kind of initiation jape but saw nothing in the man's expression to confirm it. He recalled the training school Scots, most of them amiable but some who spat out their raw dialect and smacked you just for being English. The Glaswegians especially, he'd quickly learned, were better on your side and there was no mistaking his present tormentor's twang!

"I – I'm willing to – to do me bit," he stammered.

"Right, laddie! If you're goin' on board, take one of these wi' you!" barked the Cook, beckoning to the Maltese to help drag one of the bulging sacks off the pile.

"Bend down, laddie and brace yourself to take this on your back!"

Stooping, Daniel watched as the two men lifted the sack and sidled towards him.

"Ready, laddie? One! Two! Up!"

The sudden weight on his back caused him to lurch forward and after two feeble steps, his buckling legs sent him face first onto the quay.

"On your feet, laddie! An' this time fuckin'-well brace yourself!"

"Don't attempt it, boyo. The crane's about to lift the pallet on board any minute," intervened one of the two dockers who then unburdened the prostrate youth and helped him to his feet. "Have you got a hanky, boyo? You've split your lip."

The Welshman offered his own handkerchief but was brushed aside as the Cook and his still-grinning companion continued the welcoming ceremony of the now flour-covered Cabin Boy. This time, Daniel, more prepared, accepted the load and began a cautious shuffle towards the ship.

"Steady!" bawled the Scot as the youth almost collapsed while attempting to place a foot on the gangplank. "If you drop it I'll have you fuckin'-well logged!"

Logged? Some kind of naval punishment and he wasn't even on board yet! Daniel tried once again to get a foothold on the wooden incline.

"Dinnae just stand there, laddie! Get up the bastard!"

The order went over his head. A couple of feet up the gangplank was enough as the gaping chasm beneath him took his breath away. If there'd been water below, his desire to prove himself at that moment might have superseded his fear of drowning. Even a non-swimmer had a small chance of survival in water but the long drop to solid concrete he stared into meant certain death! Distant figures moving about down there worsened his nausea, causing him to stagger backwards and lose what small hold he had on the sack which slipped sideways from his back and into the void.

"Take the useless bastard up top an' get him logged!" yelled the cook.

"Come with me, sonny," smirked the Maltese. "Lucky for you nobody got killed down there," he added, indicating to Daniel to follow him aboard.

"Get him out of my fuckin' sight!" bellowed the Glaswegian, his vociferation and laughter from observers aboard ringing in the bewildered newcomer's ears as he climbed the gangplank, averting his eyes from the terrifying drop by fixing them on the leading Maltese's broad rump until it disappeared over the top of the incline. His calamitous reception and the threatened 'logging' were momentarily forgotten as he stepped onto the *Roundcape's* deck.

He'd only a vague idea of what an oceangoing ship would look like at close quarters. The impressive passenger liners leaving Tilbury had sparkled as they swept majestically past the Gravesend training school and 'the decks of super tankers were fit to eat your dinner off,' his brother had told him, 'but avoid them clapped-out old tramps cos conditions are so bad that you'll regret the day you ever signed up!'

From the moment of stepping aboard, Daniel knew that the *Roundcape* was exactly that. 'A clapped-out old tramp'. Years of weathering the oceans had left its mark on this ugly hulk which incredibly was still traversing the globe. He'd somehow expected the decks to be wooden but everything, except for the hatch coverings and the lifeboats, was steel. Buckled, rusty solid steel, made even more unsightly by the scrape and paint job now in progress. Hatch timbers, dismantled deck mechanism, hawsers and chains and provisions waiting to be stored contributed to the general disarray of the ship. The urgent activity he'd witnessed looking down on the vessel appeared to have ceased. Everybody was looking at him and he was relieved when the Maltese appeared at an entrance to the bridge to call him inside and away from the uncomfortable scrutiny. Before he entered however, somebody called out to him.

"Yours, boyo, I believe?" The man handing him his sea bag which he'd left behind in the confusion, wore a white boiler suit and an officer's cap. "It's not my place carrying for you but I think you were a little bit preoccupied down there," he added.

"Er – thanks . . . thank you, sir . . ." but the officer was halfway up the outer bridge stairway and probably failed to catch Daniel's stuttered appreciation.

"Skipper will see you now," said Reno, reappearing. "Mind your manners and don't get staring at his missus," he warned without the usual grin before turning to lead the youth up an inner stairway.

"Poor little bugger," chuckled big Ianto, waving his dripping paintbrush under Martyn's nose. "Think yourself lucky we deckies didn't initiate you. But there's still plenty of time for you to find out what can happen to first-trippers, boyo!"

Martyn couldn't help but share Ianto's pity for the Cabin Boy after watching his boarding ceremony. Despite the newcomer's smaller stature, he guessed his age to be about his own. Seventeen and fresh out of training school himself, he was thankful for having left his uniform at home. dungarees and T-shirt were less conspicuous in this rough and ready environment and he'd been treated fine, so far. Ianto and his fellow Cardiffians did rag him about being a 'valley boy' but it was only light-hearted piss-taking. His father had been concerned about his welfare and had been pleased to know that two-thirds of the ship's crew were southern Welsh and even her Somali firemen and greasers had homes and families in the Cardiff area.

"I see they've hoisted the Cabin Boy's boarding flag," smiled Ianto, pointing aloft with his paintbrush.

"Where?" enquired Martyn, looking up. "Ooooh! You bastard!" he yelled, reaching to wipe the paint off his nose.

"You see! When her eyes meet mine!" sighed Reno about to knock on the Captain's door. "She's infatuated with my Latin looks!"

Whatever her reaction to the vain Maltese, Captain Robert's young wife, recumbent on her bunk was too scantily dressed in brief shorts and halter for Daniel to give her more than a glance on entry lest the Skipper think he'd hired some kind of sexual deviant. Reno however, showed no such restraint and to Daniel's embarrassment appeared to be literally drooling over the attractive blonde whose youthful looks and demeanour put her age at around half that of her husband, a slim, dapper man in his mid to late forties. The latter began the meeting by outlining the duties of 'catering boy' and what was expected of him in his role aboard. His softly-spoken manner with just a hint of a Welsh accent and his large, hazel eyes flickering in co-ordination with effeminate hand gestures, had an hypnotic effect on Daniel who replied with whispered 'yes sirs' and 'no sirs', until the interview was over with the spellbound Reno being instructed to "show the lad his bunk and get him something to eat."

"Oh. And has he met the Steward yet?"

"The, er - ? The Chief Steward? Er – no, sir . . ." replied the Maltese coming out of his trance.

"I told you, that woman has got the hots for me!" sighed Reno, leading the way back down the stairs and along an alleyway to a door bearing the title *CHIEF STEWARD*. A scarcely audible grunt answered his knock and displaying somewhat more caution than on their visit to the Skipper's accommodation, he ushered the youth inside.

The cabin was much smaller than the Captain's and its dark interior became even gloomier as Reno closed the door behind them. As his eyes adjusted to the poor light provided by just one porthole, Daniel began to make out the forms of two, very large people seated at a small central table.

"The old man's seen him, has he?" enquired the Chief Steward in a low, rumbling tone, the small porcelain teacup he sipped from looking inadequate for such a large, bloated face.

"Yes, Chief," replied Reno. "He's told me to feed him."

"Hard luck," came the blunt reply. "We've only one Cook aboard and he's loading stores and I've just locked up the pantry. Show him his bunk and put him to work."

The situation explained, the Chief resumed sipping tea as if indicating the interview over. During the brief exchange, his wife had stared blankly up at Daniel. Anticipating a few words of motherly assurance, he'd made eye contact but in vain.

His bunk was strewn with timber and Carpenter's tools. Jock was there to greet him.

"Your pit's under there somewhere!" he guffawed, kicking out at a locker at the end of the bunk. "An' that's where you'll stow that smart uniform an' your tropical whites if yon fuckin' training school were kind enough to kit you wi'?" he teased as the locker door creaked open on a single hinge.

A youth sprawled upon an opposite top bunk (the cabin had four in all, Jock's being above Daniel's and Reno and the youth in the other pair) was thoroughly enjoying the torment. While not happy with his lack of sympathy, Daniel was at least grateful to find he'd a cabin mate nearer his own age. Jock and Reno he put at around thirty; the youth around ten years their junior. His long, narrow face matched his wiry physique and a quiff of

35

straight hair was trained over his brow in the current Teddy Boy fashion. His laughter ceased on meeting the newcomer's stare and, swinging his legs out of the bunk, he sat up and stared contemptuously back.

Training school experiences had developed in Daniel the habit of judging an individual's toughness by his accent, the youth's tough-guy pose falling flat when in a broad West Country accent, he muttered, "Yer'll 'ave to get used to the piss-takin', mate."

"If he's your *mate*, Billy," intervened Jock, "you'll nae mind getting stuck in wi' him an' clear this junk up! I'm due in the galley!"

As the Scot left, Billy climbed down from his bunk and begrudgingly began helping Daniel move in.

"Used our cabin to store their fucking junk an' never so much as knocked a fuckin' nail in, them chippies," he began his grumble.

The state of the ship, he explained, was due to the overhaul she'd been dry-docked for. But only today, her owners had sent orders for her to be made seaworthy as soon as possible and any unfinished work on accommodation to be completed by her crew once at sea.

"The fuckin' union should be called in!" he ranted on. "No time though and at any rate, a good part of the crew are the dregs of the pool and were only too grateful to be signed on according to Jock. In other words, as long as the fuckin' thing floats; bollocks to the Cabin Boy's pit! He'll more than likely be sharin' the old man's bunk once past Lands End if there's any truth in the gossip about 'im up top being none to choosy," he chuckled, winking at Daniel.

Next came a breakdown of who was who aboard? He, Billy and Reno were Assistant Stewards. Jock, who'd 'welcomed' him aboard was Assistant Cook, the Chief Cook still not having boarded. He, Daniel, was 'shit of the ship' as Cabin Boy and the five of them answered to old fat guts Mr Bond, the Chief Steward who was a raving alcoholic who'd reveal as much once his wife had gone ashore because the booze he'd helped stow away in his cabin's every conceivable hiding place that very morning, was proof enough. Furthermore the chances of them still being afloat or at least escaped a collision before clear of the docks was slim, due to their officers, Engineers and sailors being largely pissy-arsed Taffs who'd not be fit enough to crew a blow-up dinghy after their last night ashore. This didn't bother him however, because there still being no sign of the Chief Cook, he'd be on the next train back to Bristol if it looked like they'd be sailing with Jock in sole charge of the galley.

"Er – why's that?" ventured Daniel.

"Because old fat guts, the Steward'll be lookin' for some poor twat to 'elp that great 'airy 'aggis! And after a night on the piss, I wouldn't want to be around old Jock with a fuckin' carving knife in 'is 'and!"

The reference to violence seemed to stimulate Billy's conversation and he began to ask Daniel about the 'Ted' scene in his neck of the woods.

"The Teds[5] are stirring things up in Brum but locally, they don't allow it," he answered.

"Don't fuckin' well allow it? Who don't allow it?"

"Er – the police and dance halls, like. No Edwardian dress allowed. There's notices everywhere. They're really clamping down on the Teddy Boys."

"An' they take notice of a few poxy notices? Are they gutless or what? We've been causin' 'avoc in Bristol! The old town'll never be the same again! 'ad to cut short me leave else I'd 'ave been nicked! 'ere! What yer think of this then?" he continued excitedly, flinging open a locker door to reveal a shocking-red Teddy Boy suit, complete with leopard skin lapels and cuffs.

"Some suit, eh, me old acker?" he gushed with pride while carefully taking down the neatly-hung outfit to show it off. "Tightest drainpipes in Bristol town! Grips me ankles like a second skin they do! An' leopard skin trimming's unmistakable

---

[5] Teds. 'Teddy Boys'. Gangs of troublesome youths dressed Edwardian style in 1950s Britain.

from the real thing, so me tailor reckons! The Cardiff bints'll be swoonin' all over this Ted if we gets shore leave tonight, don't yer think?"

Not waiting for an answer, he grabbed Daniel's sea bag and began delving inside.

"You fuckin' square!" he jeered, withdrawing a chequered sports jacket followed by grey flannel trousers. "Borrow 'em from yer dad, did yer? An' don't think yer'll be coming' ashore with me in that fuckin' clobber!" he added seriously.

"I, er . . . I left me best gear at home," lied Daniel. "Didn't want to get it spoiled like."

"Not everybody's got dress sense," resumed Billy, in a softer tone. "Me mam would've burned this if she'd got 'er 'ands on it. Clueless about the youth revolution are the older generation. She'd 'ave robbed Bristol of its peacock she would 'ave. We Teds 'ave given the world what men 'ave been lackin' since the war. Colour an' fashion! An' I'll wear this in New York city, given the fuckin' chance!"

"Is – is that where we're going then? New York you reckon?" asked Daniel.

"Wouldn't be surprised. 'eard the Third Mate mention it at breakfast this mornin'. You know 'im? The officer you're next in line after the Skipper to bed with if anythin' can be read out of 'is carryin' your gear aboard. But then again, 'e might save 'is strength for the bint 'e reckons is waitin' for 'im in New York, unless of course, 'e's just another bullshitting Taffy? There's a few of them aboard, you'll find out.

"Chief Steward wants you in the pantry, sonny!" interrupted Reno through an open porthole. "Get your working gear on and make it snappy!"

Clad in training school issue, shirt and dungarees, Daniel, following Billy's directions made his way for'ard to the pantry, an integral part of the bridge structure. The cabin which he was to share with Billy, Jock and Reno was at the for'ard end of a row of four midships starboard. The adjoining three were single berth cabins housing the Chief Cook and two Engineers. The

Chief Engineer and the remainder of his understudies were housed in an identical row on the portside. Access to these cabins was off two parallel alleyways between which lay the engine room, the ship's single funnel crowning this midship superstructure.

As Daniel proceeded along the alleyway leading from his accommodation, his passage was momentarily blocked by an elderly man clad in a greasy boiler suit emerging from the engine room. This old, bent and weary-looking character reminded him of the near pensionable old-stagers he's worked alongside in grimy workshops back home. Oblivious to his presence, he studied the old man as he coughed and wheezed his way ahead of him until entering the end cabin with what seemed to be a loud sigh of relief.

To celebrate the completion of another arduous shift made more difficult by a hot-tempered Chief Engineer who seemed hell-bent on bullying his staff into making worn-out engines perform as new, Fourth Engineer Edgar Reece collapsed on his bunk and lit up a cigarette. Smoking, he'd been told, had contributed to his general poor health and his prematurely old appearance, a warning that up until the events of his last shore leave just eight weeks ago, had persuaded him to quit the habit for a record six months. But then the death of his brother, two years his junior at age fifty-eight followed closely by his wife leaving him for another man after thirty-six years of marriage, he'd thought reason enough to chance further damage to his health and appearance in order to enjoy the small pleasure of tobacco.

"Senile and incompetent," the Chief had called him behind his back. But with the ship being prepared to sail within twenty-four hours, there was little chance of him being replaced as well they both knew. The fact of his being on board at all was only due to fate intervening so cruelly. His last trip was to have been exactly that, because with an ample nest-egg and a small pension, he'd been about to do what Terence, his brother, had been urging him to do for many years.

"She's had her fill of a twice-home-a-year spouse!" he'd warned. "She's not been seen at Pontyvale bingo for yonks and Crusty Lightfoot's bread van has got the curtains twitching the length of your blessed street, so I'm informed by those who pretend to mean well look you. The rosy retirement you've been saving for'll not be so rosy when you're sitting in the club bar with just a pint for company, Edgar."

But Crusty had been a friend of both his and Cynthia's since schooldays and their keeping each other company had had his full blessing. Nothing to be read out of that and the curtains in their street would move at the coo of a pigeon, he'd replied with sarcasm that convinced only himself and goaded Terence into being more explicit about local ridicule.

'Freshest bread in the district until you're at home!' was the latest snigger to circulate and his last attempt to shock his brother into believing him only hours before the shock of a Tory die-hard moving into the house next door had triggered off the heart attack that killed him.

Coal dust and forty cigs a day. A lethal combination which Terence's GP had witnessed send too many men to an early grave. That Edgar had chosen the sea rather than the pit had been most wise, he'd said while giving him an examination that resulted in his being advised that his own ticker was no longer engine room fit!

"Stay home if possible and let that little lady of yours pamper you some," he'd recommended, proving that GPs are the least likely recipients of local gossip.

He'd reported to the Cardiff shipping office the very next day. With Cynthia resolute in her decision and Terence's demise leaving him with no close family: one last trip would give him time to think away from the place where his world had suddenly collapsed. Today had been hard but once at sea he'd recover sufficiently enough to tackle the job which normally was second nature to him. Furthermore and while not generally given to sharing his woes with others; seamen, because of the nature of their lifestyle, were more inclined to lend a sympathetic ear and give advice where required. Their present Third Mate, for instance. A fellow Welshman whom he'd never met before until sharing a saloon table at breakfast that very morning, while considerably younger than himself at thirty-eight, had listened intently and declared his full understanding, having recently experienced what he called 'mental hell' himself. The loss of someone close had figured in his misfortune too, he'd began to explain before their respective senior officers had intervened to get them back to work. They must talk again when things were quieter, his new friend had said after beginning to reveal that the person lost to him wasn't exactly *lost* in the eternal sense; a revelation which suggested that his 'mental hell' could hardly have compared with his own but whatever some eventual clarification, he'd nevertheless show Mr Williams the same sympathy and understanding as that morning, he'd shown himself. Reluctance for further such chats did arise however, when on their next meeting he appeared to be strangely deluding himself when talking about a sudden new development regarding his lost lady friend who was mysteriously 'no longer lost' and within ten days, they'd be reunited soon after docking in New York.

How ever, over-imaginative this Third Mate character might be, their initial chat had lightened Edgar and provided some respite from his own self-pity. He'd even managed to chuckle to himself when realizing how wrong was his stated first port of call.

New York? Why New York when it was common knowledge aboard that their Skipper had confided their destination to his senior officers which inevitably was leaked to fellow crew such as he and it most certainly wasn't Yonkers! While his depression was hardly lifted, Edgar's curiosity was growing!

"What kept you, boy?" grumbled the Chief Steward, his large frame blocking the pantry's external doorway. "Get stuck into that lot," he indicated, leading Daniel to a sink full of used tableware and cooking utensils. Billy's 'shit of the ship' reference began to make sense as he tackled the huge pile, obviously left untouched in anticipation of his arrival. Through an internal doorway, he spotted Reno preparing tables in what he took to be the officers' dining saloon, the job he'd envisaged doing himself, he reflected, recalling the rap on the knuckles for misplacing a fruit fork or serving soup at the wrong level.

"She's listing at forty degrees and the Mate wants it on the table in front of him! Not down the front of his dinner jacket!" the instructor had yelled.

"How you taking to sea life, sonny?" enquired the ever-smirking Reno, walking in and catching his glum expression. "Better leave the washing up for now and get over to the galley to see if your friend Jock has got anything for me to serve up?"

The galley, about ten yards aft and visible from the pantry, adjoined the midship cabin section and had entrances port and starboard. Skirting a hatch, Daniel entered on the starboard side to see the grumbling Jock shovelling coal into the cooking range.

"The miserly bastards could at least have converted it to oil!" he moaned, glancing up at Daniel. "An' you can fuck off!" he snapped. "There's fuck-all ready for you!"

Turning to make a hasty retreat, the youth almost collided with a giant of a man standing behind him.

"Yours is ready, Paddy," groaned the Scot. "Yon fuckin' officers'll be waitin' forever if we put to sea wi' only one Cook!"

Strictly observed hygiene standards aboard ships of the British Merchant Fleet was just more training school bunkum, mused Daniel as Jock reached for the big man's food containers with coal-blackened hands.

"You'll be sinking a few jars tonight, eh, Paddy?" enquired Jock.

"I'll be doing just that," replied the other, folding huge tattooed arms across a broad chest.

Daniel studied the two men. Stripped to the waist in the heat of the day, their physiques were as impressive as many of the bodybuilding fanatics he'd seen posing in the current *Charles Atlas* ads.

The shorter in height Scot, carried not an ounce of surplus fat, his solid chest tapering to a narrow waist and hips giving him the appearance of an athlete in his prime rather than a ship's cook. With thick, black, curly hair and well-proportioned features, he would have been considered handsome but for the deep scar curving down his right cheek to beneath his bottom lip together with dark, unsmiling eyes, giving him the appearance of man one would be foolish to mess with.

The sound of foreign chatter interrupted the youth's perusal as a group of Somalis formed alongside him. 'To keep his arse to the rail when them greasers and donkeymen were about', had been another piece of Billy's 'first-tripper' advice. Jock appeared to read his thoughts.

"Dinnae get stooping to do up your bootlaces, laddie," he said with a wry smile, his tone still mischievous as he greeted the Somalis by presenting them with a sizzling joint of pork.

"Evening, Abduls! An' look what I've rustled up 'specially for you! Pork! Pork! Delicious pork!" he teased, thrusting the meat towards the Arabs who reacted with loud wails as they turned their faces to the immediate bulkheads.

"'Tis vile in their religion is pork," the Irishman muttered into Daniel's ear, suggesting that he didn't approve of such teasing.

The disturbance was broken up by the Chief Steward, anxious about a saloon full of hungry officers. The Cabin Boy was handed a container of soup which was quickly snatched from him by Reno on his return to the pantry.

"That heavenly creature can't take her eyes off me!" he sighed, smoothing down his oily hair and gesturing to where the Captain's wife was seated in the saloon.

"She can't take her eyes off you cos she's just asked me how much longer has she and the old man got to wait!" grumbled the Chief Steward entering with the pork earlier thrust upon the Somalis. "So, when you've done drooling over a lady far above your station," he thundered at the shrinking Maltese, "bloody-well get carving this! And you, son," he completed, turning to Daniel, "get back to the galley for the gravy."

Daniel found a calmer Jock relaxing on a stool, bottle of Scotch in hand.

"Gravy's over yonder, laddie," he grunted. "Gi' it over here a mo'."

Handing over the gravy container, the youth watched curiously as the Cook peered inside it.

"Lost a fag-end just now," he muttered. "Keep your eyes skinned when they're pourin' it," he added without the hint of a smile to suggest that this was just more of his peculiar jesting.

The evening meal finished with a commotion involving the Skipper's wife whom Daniel observed, still clad in the afternoon's scanty attire, leaving the saloon in a huff.

"Too busy nosin' down 'er cleavage to see where you were fuckin' pourin' the wine!" Billy teased a very deflated Reno as he, Jock, Daniel and the Maltese sat down in the saloon to have their own meal after the officers had left, as turned out to be the practise.

"Two small drops on her legs and she's almost in tears!" whined Reno. "But I think it's this thing between us that's causing her to be so emotional," he continued wistfully. "I saw it when our eyes met."

"It were you on your knees dabbing away with your tea towel an' your fuckin' tongue 'angin' out that got 'er blartin'," pursued Billy, "an' if you've still got this hankerin' for moist and musty places, I'll take you on a tour of Wookey 'ole when we get back?"

"What a vile mind you have!" erupted the Maltese. "I only work with you a couple of days and I know already that you are nothing more than an uncouth, foul-mouthed Teddy Boy! You have no idea about the chemistry that flows between us every time I go into the Skipper's quarters!"

"The Skipper's been flashin' those big, sexy eyes at you as well then?" taunted on Billy, clearly enjoying Reno's discomfort.

"I'm not speaking about the Captain and well you know it, you vile-mouthed . . .!"

"You're both wasting your time if it's the old man's affections you're squabblin' over!" cut in Jock, his eyes falling on Daniel. "I'll wager it'll be the lad here who'll be knockin' on his door, Vaseline in 'and afore we're clear o' the Channel. You'll be happy to wait on his pleasure once his missus is ashore, will you, laddie?"

"I – er . . ." began a reddening Daniel. "I – I thought that Billy here was the, er – Captain's Steward?"

"Aye. He is that, laddie. But his lordship'll nae be content wi' this weed o' a Teddy Boy for long, that's for sure."

"And if the old man don't fancy him, the Third Mate's already got his eyes on him," joined in Reno, relieved at having the attention drawn away from himself. "Carried his gear aboard for him this afternoon, he did. How's that for favouritism with a means to an end? And we all know which end the Third will be after, don't we?"

"Eh? What were that bit about a *weed of a Teddy Boy*, Jock?" cut in Billy, as if Reno hadn't spoken. "One of the 'ardest knocks in Bristol, this kid, I'll 'ave you know."

"Dinnae make claims you may have to prove, Billy," warned the Scot. "If I say you're a weed, you're a fuckin' weed!"

"*Ouch!*" Billy was suddenly out of his chair and hopping about the saloon in obvious pain. "You! You fuckin' kicked me, Jock! You fuckin' kicked me!"

The Cook's under-table kick had connected painfully with his shin and he was furious.

"There was no need for that!" he gasped, as the Chief Steward made an authoritative entry.

45

"And there's no need for such loutish behaviour!" he thundered. "You'll learn to dine like gentlemen in the officers mess or you'll eat astern where they don't know any better!"

No-one, not even Jock, it became clear, would question the Chief Steward's word and all four quietly filed out of the saloon to recommence their respective duties.

That he would be sharing a cabin with the likes of that trio, was the daunting thought in Daniel's mind as he tackled an even larger stack of washing up.

And those innuendos about the Captain and Third Mate? The training school had kept quiet about many things it appeared! Unless of course, it was as he half suspected, all part of introducing naive first-trippers? Whatever the truth, as he watched through the pantry door, the maintenance crew leaving the ship for their homes, he wished that he too, was leaving the factory to cycle home for his tea. Afterwards, maybe, ride into the village to join other lads in their nightly tease of the local girls; prolonging the banter perhaps until dark, in the hope of more intimate liaisons.

Patsy Harding would about now be pushing her bike up the long hill out of Redditch town. Had she missed his helping hand on the steepest part of the hill? he wondered, recalling his eagerness to help in any way that might gain her friendship. And the little things he'd done unknown to her like pumping up her bike tyres and adjusting its brakes during his dinner break, secretly demonstrating his feelings for a girl who hardly acknowledged his existence. While buying the motorbike had been important in reuniting him with Maurice, he'd quietly hoped that it might also serve to raise his esteem in Patsy's eyes and perhaps even tempt her away from her ill-chosen fiancé. In retrospect, its failure to achieve either of these had led to this foolhardy venture which, scarcely before it had begun, looked to have been a poor decision.

His father too, was suffering from his hasty action by taking on the instalments for his wrecked bike on the promise he'd settle with his first pay off. This, despite his reluctance to sign yet another son over to the 'British Shipping Federation'.

"Perhaps it'll bring you out of your shell?" were the only words directly to him on the matter until wishing him a solemn 'good luck' at the railway station. Had he been glad to see the back of him? It must have been a headache carting him for treatment at Outpatients several times a week following the accident. He felt sudden guilt at the thought. If anything could be read out of his father's telling silence as he'd pushed a ten shilling note into his palm at the station, it would have been, "Best let you find out for yourself, you headstrong young fool, you."

His brooding was interrupted by the Chief Steward arriving to show him how to lock up every evening, a duty which would include securing the hatch in the pantry floor which led to the store and bond rooms.

"There's a thief on every ship, son," he said. "So be vigilant and security conscious. And, oh yes, before you knock off there's one little job I'd like you to do especially for me," he added, before striding off in the direction of his cabin and reappearing moments later with a tray of delicate china.

"I'd like you to wash and dry these and return them to my cabin when you're done. Wife's pressy from me," he announced proudly while carefully handling the porcelain to demonstrate its perfection. "All the way from Japan, this tea service and she's taking it ashore with her. So take the utmost care, son. The utmost care."

Daniel washed and dried every piece meticulously and on completion, rearranged them on the silver tray and set off for the Chief's cabin. On arrival, he found the door open but a curtain drawn across the entrance.

"Come in, son!" called out the Chief on hearing the tinkle of china. The tray, followed by Daniel's head and shoulders accepted the invitation but the door combing, a feature of ship's doorways with which he was not yet fully acquainted, prevented his feet from following suit. The result was a spectacular dive ending at the feet of the Chief and his wife, who, when eyes eventually met, simply scowled down in a telling silence at the youth, prostrate amidst the remnants of their parting gift.

"You'll have to get used to the roll of the ship, son," was how the Chief Steward eventually broke the uncomfortable silence, while his wife, other than continuing to glare, reacted neither to the unfortunate breakage or to her husband's sarcasm. Probably, Daniel told himself later, she was as slow as himself in realizing that ships simply don't roll in dry dock?

After clearing up the fragments and being dismissed with several grunts which conveyed to him that he was the most inadequate prat of a Cabin Boy ever to step aboard a merchant vessel, he miserably made his way back to his shared accommodation where his cabin mates were preparing for their last night ashore. Jock and Reno wore conventional trousers and open-necked shirts, while Billy was dressed in the full 'Ted' regalia from bootlace tie down to bulky, thick-soled shoes protruding conspicuously from the bottoms of his skin-tight drainpipe trousers.

"Aye! You're a fetching sight in red, Billy!" Jock was taunting. "But dinnae get standin' round on street corners wi' your gob open or some poor-sighted fucker'll mebbe mistake you for a post-box!"

"You're not with it, Jock!" retorted Billy. "I were reading only the other day that our gear represents a youth revolution the likes of 'as never been seen before! We're breakin' away from the image of our dads an' doin' our own thing! Take the piss as much as you like but it's *our* world out there!"

"Like Jock says," chuckled Reno, "take care that nobody tries to post a letter!"

His copycat humour however, was lost on the Cook who's attention was now directed towards the recumbent Daniel.

"Laddie, wi' your unpackin' an' such, you'll nae likely have the time to come out wi' your shipmates, I'm thinkin'."

His tone was suspiciously more friendly.

"Er, no – I – don't think I'll bother."

"Then you'll have nae use for any spare cash you'll mebbe be carryin' is what I'm sayin'. So could you mebbe see your way clear to loanin' us lads a bob or two?"

'Watch out for spongers!' his brother had warned. 'It's all subs and borrowing and the borrowed is never returned.'

But, keen to ingratiate himself, Daniel began fishing for coins in his pockets. With the odd change he found was his father's crumpled ten shilling note which Jock immediately snatched from him.

"Good on you, laddie! I'll see you get it back."

Billy grabbed the remaining coins and all three made for the door. Thinking they'd gone, Daniel sank back down on his bunk but was startled by Billy returning carrying a cardboard box. Sheepishly, he placed it on the cabin table, saying quietly, "Look, there's a couple of dozen empty bottles in 'ere I've collected so if you do 'appen to go ashore later, there'll be a few coppers return money for you to pocket like."

The garishly-dressed Assistant Steward departed once again, his gesture having done little to cheer up the other. His father's ten shilling note had remained clutched in his palm well into the journey earlier that day, his forlorn expression as he'd handed it over filling him with guilt for having ignored his wise advice. Perhaps at that moment he'd been thinking bout the letter amongst the Christmas cards just a few years back? A letter telling him that his oldest son had been taken from an oil tanker in Falmouth, for observation in hospital. Poliomyelitis, it had turned out to be and all of the way back from the West Indies where he'd fallen ill, they'd been treating him for malaria. No wonder his dad had looked so miserable. The life of his first son saved only by his desire to get back to sea. a desire never fulfilled but a significant factor in his fight to recover the doctors had said.

No, the concern etched on his father's face wasn't due to the loss of another contribution to the family budget, or taking on the payments for his bike but he'd more than settle up with him when he got his first pay off, depending of course, he ever got one? In his present mood, he'd be making the payments himself from a wage earned ashore, even if that meant suffering the inevitable ridicule from family and mates. Being accused of not having the bottle would be a hard pill to swallow. But could that be worse than what might lie ahead? But then it did appear that he was slowly being accepted by some aboard and even the Chief Steward's reaction to the loss of his wife's tea service could have been much stiffer, unless of course, he'd got some kind of punishment up his sleeve which he'd dispense once his missus had gone ashore. And the loathsome Assistant Cook? Well, even he had seemed impressed by the ten bob loan: a move that could lead to less hassle once at sea. Billy too, had appeared human by presenting him with the empties so that he'd not be without a little cash. And even if he was being over-hopeful his welfare aboard might well be assured from an unlikely quarter. Had not that Third Mate character gone out of his way to acknowledge him again as he'd left the pantry? An officer on his side and there'd be little to fear! What! He'd likely be ship's favourite before the trip was over and, with luck, it might only be a matter of weeks until he was back home recounting his adventures to those who'd seen fit to doubt him!

A ray of evening sunshine filtered through a grimy porthole. He began to unpack.

Chapter 4

Hilary

Yes, he was certain now. The girl on the bike had been tailing him since his exiting the docks. She's studied his passing with a haughty stare that he'd found uncomfortable. The tinkling bottles in his cardboard box had also attracted a following of children.

"Give us a swig of pop, Mr Sailor-man!" they yelled, making him wish he'd donned his civvy clothes rather than the training school rigout for his walkabout. On the plus side though, it was commonly known that girls were attracted by uniforms and the girl on the bike was still behind him.

At first sight, Tiger Bay was hardly the inhospitable place he'd envisaged. The street he eventually slipped into in hope of shaking off the kids was, though, definitely more slum-like and to his relief, only the girl now followed. Such rundown areas he knew, were commonplace across Britain and during a visit to Birmingham, his birthplace, he'd quietly thanked Hitler's bombs for taking him away from such an environment and to the rural quiet of Worcestershire. He'd visited relatives in the city but there'd been a personal reason for his trip which revolved around his growing search for an identity: a search that had come to the fore during his time at the training school. Londoners, Glaswegians, Scousers, Tynesiders and the Cardiff lads all had distinctive identities, while the only two Brummie lads were more introverted than himself. A chat with a Liverpool trainee however, helped give him a, if vague, form of identity amongst his peers. The inner-city lad confessed to not having seen a field of cows until his recent train journey south and took interest when Daniel revealed a lifestyle that included such things as walking across meadows to get to school (there'd been an alternative route but he and Maurice preferred the pastoral one) and then escalated his rural background by telling his listener that the radio serial *The Archers*, an every everyday story of [6]country folk, was often recorded in the nearby villages of Inkberrow and Hanbury and that such places *swarmed* with BBC actors and crew, an exaggeration which, in truth, didn't overly impress anybody while in *his* mind, did single him out to be at least *different* to the mostly-city lads. Those somewhat hollow boasts had resurfaced when earlier he'd been making his way out of the docks, the strains of *Barwick Green*, the signature tune of *The Archers* resounded from the open porthole of a berthed vessel, reminding him of the doubts he'd felt while skivvying aboard the ship that late afternoon. *Barwick Green* rekindled those doubts and reminded him of the patchwork-quilt landscape of Worcestershire rolling west towards the thirty-mile distant undulation of the Malvern Hills as viewed from the playground of his hilltop school. Yes – he'd still time to abandon his venture but returning home wouldn't exactly resolve the problems which had contributed towards his planning it. Maurice definitely wouldn't be returning: he'd likely return to factory life with little more than farm work available and Patsy Harding had never really been within reach.

'Patsy Harding?' Why brood over the unobtainable when a girl only lacking make-up and perhaps more sophisticated attire was, at this very moment, seemingly stalking him as he'd hopelessly stalked Patsy!

"You can easy get lost around here you know?"

It was as if she'd read his thoughts. She overtook him, turning in the saddle.

"Looking for anywhere special are you?"

She was almost at a standstill, waiting for him to catch up.

"Do you . . . do you, er – know anywhere that takes empties?" he stammered, surprised at her boldness.

"I might and I mightn't. It depends on whether you'll do me a big favour?" she replied mysteriously.

---

[6] The Archers. Debuted Jan 1951. Longest running radio serial on British radio. 'An everyday story of countryfolk'.

"Please yourself," he returned, taking the opportunity to study her more closely as she pedalled alongside him. Her approach was that of a juvenile but her build suggested sixteen, even seventeen?

"Got your eyeful, have you?" she asked with a hint of embarrassment, almost losing her balance as she attempted to brush a wisp of long, red hair away from her eyes.

Despite this sudden shyness, he continued to look her over. 'Pretty', she was 'pretty'. Up until recently, that the girl had a pretty face was enough to grab his attention. Lately, he felt guilt for the compulsion that urged him to look for more than just facial perfection. He felt guilt now as his gaze dropped from the fresh bloom of her face to freckled knees innocently exposed as she pedalled. Her carelessly draped cotton dress which he ought tell her could easily get caught up in her rear wheel, was only serving to give him salacious thoughts as how more mature girls tended to wrap their skirts beneath their bottoms when cycling in order, it was joked, to avoid too intimate a contact with the saddle. Or had perhaps the old playground theory as to why certain girls took up horse riding corrupted his thoughts and such vulgar notions were leading him into becoming as vulgar-minded as the lads who seemed to talk about little else?

"You – you'll be off that blooming bike if you're not careful," he warned, vainly attempting to appear more concerned about her safety than with her bare thighs. She appeared puzzled.

"What was that you said? You speak funny. Off the ships are you? A trainee officer or something? The uniform and all that I mean?"

Her grin suggested that she was teasing him. That's all he wanted to cap the day. A slip of a girl taking the piss. She paused behind him as he turned to answer.

"Yes! I'm off the ships and *no*, I'm not an officer! I'm a trainee Steward! Now – where can I get rid of these empties?" he asked, his tone becoming less sharp as her eyes met his while arriving alongside again.

"For your temper, I'll only show you where to get rid of them if you promise to do me this favour!" she replied quietly but sternly.

"What blooming favour? I've only just met you and you want me to do you a favour?"

Her grin was back and he suddenly reddened with improper thoughts as to what this 'favour' might be? Still eyeing him mischievously, she turned and braked in his path. Lost for words, he stopped and returned her stare. Brazen-faced girls had always made him feel uncomfortable but this red-headed teenager's suggestive smile quite appealed to him and with a touch of lipstick and a pair of stiletto-heeled shoes, she'd compare well with Patsy Harding. She now appeared less bothered by his scrutiny, even unfastening the top buttons of her dress to expose a little cleavage, sighing, "God – it's bloody hot tonight!"

He too was perspiring. The thick serge outfit had definitely been a mistake and her increasingly provocative manner wasn't helping.

"Come on then! Show me where to get rid of these empties!" he blurted, trying to disguise his unease and almost losing his grip on the box while stumbling off the kerb as he went to push past.

"Almost lost your precious empties!" she teased, increasing his embarrassment. "Come on then. The nearest pub is down that street over there look you!"

"Oh alright," he groaned. "Better not be too far though. They'll be waiting for me back on board," he added, the 'back onboard' bit helping to restore some self-esteem as he trailed behind her.

"How much blooming further is it?" he grumbled, following her into the street.

She turned and waited for him, grinning again. With her left foot raised at top pedal, she began rubbing a grazed knee, precociously daring him to look.

"Not far now," she smiled invitingly as he approached, her hitched-up skirt all part of the bait.

"Do you know what a French kiss is, sailor-boy?"

She was throwing herself at him and he didn't know how to react! He walked on.

"You – you'll get yourself into trouble, you will."

His words were stumbled, almost inaudible. She raced past him giggling.

They entered another street and his escort was halfway across it having ignored a pub a few houses to her left.

"Eh! What's that, then? The blooming Salvation Army?"

She appeared oblivious to him, having stopped to talk to a middle-aged man.

"You're too trusting, Hilary!" said the man sharply, glancing towards Daniel. "Just you get back to your auntie's before dark look you!" he added before moving off.

"Alright! Alright! Don't go on so!"

She was pulling a face at the man's back as Daniel joined her.

"Gets on my nerves does my dad," she muttered sulkily. "Oh no!" she gasped as her father, with a glance back, entered the pub. "Why doesn't he just go to his nightshift and leave me alone? I'm sixteen coming on seventeen for God's sake!"

"Having a drink before he goes by the looks," murmured Daniel. "Might as well nip in meself and unload these bottles."

He started to move off.

"Wait!" hissed the girl. "Oh Christ! What's the matter with the mun? He knows I can look after myself!"

Her father was back on the pavement outside the pub and a gang of youths were filing out of the building, their eyes fixed maliciously on Daniel!

"Oh why couldn't he just go to work and not be so bloody-well interfering all the time?" she groaned.

Daniel went to move off in the direction they'd come but she grabbed his arm and, wheeling her bike, tugged him to follow her into a cutting between the houses.

"Where – where now?" he gulped, a backward glance telling him that the gang was bearing down on them. After a few yards he pulled himself free.

"Look, er . . . I'm off. I'll – I'll see you, er – sometime . . ."

As he turned, the gang was sauntering into the cutting. He paused and they did likewise. He looked towards the only gap in their ranks and they filled it.

Most of them wore the full Ted rigout. Garishly-coloured jacket, skin-tight drainpipe trousers and the trademark bulky footwear. Never had he seen such a formidable bunch and every man jack of them bent on doing him harm! Dragging on cigarettes and swigging from bottles of beer, their piercing eyes never left him. One of them withdrew something shiny from his pocket and slipped it on his fingers. A knuckleduster! They were going to give him a good belting! The girl's father had departed and it would be a waste of breath appealing to this bunch of thugs! God! A bicycle chain! One of them began moving towards him, bicycle chain held aloft!

"Piss off, Gareth! He's done you no harm!"

Hilary was tugging at his arm again, this time more urgently. He backed away with her as she wheeled her bike through a gateway and into a back yard.

"It's only my cousin acting Mr Big look you," she murmured, closing the gate on the approaching gang. "They'll not dare touch you while I'm around. Come on inside; there's nobody home. My mam's at work and all, see."

Wouldn't have *touched* him! They'd have slaughtered him! He followed her uneasily into a back kitchen, cursing himself for getting into such a situation. He'd only intended strolling as far as the dock gates but had picked up the empties at the last minute lest Billy might think he'd snubbed his gesture. He should have just ignored her! Just walked on as if . . . God! She was doing it again! One foot on a chair, skirt thrown back, unconcerned that he . . .!

"Bloody sore this knee! Came off my bike earlier and it didn't half hurt. Got dirt in it by the looks. Needs cleaning don't you think?"

She was grinning that grin again and it wasn't just her knee she was showing him! Just how was he supposed to react to . . .?

"Fancy a tot of whisky do you? Always top the bottle up with water I do. Dad never knows the difference, daft bugger."

Ceasing to exhibit herself, she produced a bottle of *Bell's* whisky and began filling a tumbler.

"I – I don't want that much!" he blurted.

"Get it down you now," she replied, thrusting the tumbler into his hands. "You looked white as a ghost out there."

"Ugh! It blooming-well burns!"

She topped his drink up with orange to make it more palatable. He sipped at it again, found it much better and, being thirsty, drained the tumbler. He began to cough: she patted his back and he suddenly enjoyed the nearness of her. In fact he was feeling increasingly relaxed as she began massaging his back and shoulders and the sweet odour from her young breasts as they brushed against him was tempting him to reach out and . . .!

But it was too early in the game, she decided and had moved to sit at the kitchen table and continued to eye him with a teasing smile.

"I don't give in that easy, sailor-boy," she chuckled. "You're not so shy after all. Or is it the drink that's got you randy?"

"I, er . . . I was trying to push you away," he lied, unconvincingly.

"Pull the other one," she returned. "Look now, about that favour," she continued, "and you owe me one since I saved you from getting a beating."

"I – I've no time for favours. As I said, I've got to get back to me ship or I'll be in trouble. Er – could you show me which way I, er . . .?"

His voice faltered as she reached behind to undo a couple of buttons and slipped out of her dress.

"Don't get any ideas look you. I'm just bloody hot, that's all," she said, noting his look of disbelief as she stood up clad only in white panties and bra. "But if you do this little favour for me, I might just give you a thank-you kiss," she added, posing seductively and looking pleased with his wide-eyed reaction.

"The favour I'm begging of you? I'll show you. It's in my bedroom if you'll come up?" she asked quite seriously. "Come up and tell me what you think?"

She skipped across the kitchen and opened a door leading to a stairway.

"Come on now! You've only got to give me a yes or no!" she called, clambering out of sight.

So soon! Could this really be happening? Not even one day of his seagoing venture under his belt and it was seemingly being thrown at him! The training school dormitory banter, which he'd thought over-imaginative, about dusky maidens waiting on the quayside in foreign ports had kept tiered bunks swaying and creaking well after lights-out. and he'd had good reason to pour scorn on their optimism, for while his eldest brother hadn't breathed one word about such goings-on, the younger one had had to wait until Japan before any such experience. Best be cautious then. The whisky was definitely affecting his judgement. Sober, he'd never had made a grab for her. Whisky wasn't meant to be downed by the tumblerful and her simply removing her dress could well have been due to the heat rather than some kind of enticement. She'd seen him as some kind of immature dimwit who'd not have a clue as to how to perform and so felt safe being partially undressed in his company. It was as simple as that.

She'd guessed his inexperience and therefore felt okay. But why then, when she'd noted that his eyes were fixed on her backside on leaving the room, she'd then beckoned him to follow? Was it maybe her intention to disclose the 'favour' and then reward him . . .? But should her father return with the Teds while they were . . .? And to slip out now with at least her voiced protection with the gang likely still about . . .? Yes – better to stay around awhile, there having been no mention of how long he could stay ashore and he wasn't exactly eager to be back with his 'shipmates' so soon. Also, should anything come of this encounter, he'd relate the story to them, even embroider it a little, just to see their change of attitude towards the naive young Cabin Boy they'd left sulking aboard.

"Come on up then! What's keeping you, sailor-boy?"

Oh God! Not a hint of doubt in her voice! This was it then . . . but what if her allure proved too much for him to resist and he launched himself onto an innocent young girl? Okay – she was sixteen coming on seventeen and her body was certainly that of a mature young woman: but that was hardly reason enough for allowing himself to be led on by her precocity and risk getting it wrong. His lust, heightened by the alcohol still warm in his belly could well be his undoing and that 'cell-like' cabin back on board might well be exchanged for the real thing ashore!

So why then, with such doubts was he moving, *staggering*, towards that stairway? Because, he reasoned with himself, even tipsy, he'd have the willpower to simply take just one more look at that exquisite, scantily-clad young body and, if offered, decline even so much as her 'French kiss' whatever it might be and be on his way.

"Come on then!" she called out again. "Or have I got to come down there and get you?"

Gingerly, he made his unsteady way up the stairs and arrived on a small landing with the choice of two doors off. Still he hesitated. This time perhaps because her last call seemed to have a 'womanly' insistence about it and he was suddenly doubting himself again. Not just morally but also, should this invitation be about what he was now almost certain it to be: doubts about his own ability?

This might well turn out to be much more than just some clumsy groping performance as had been his only one previous experience. He could make a real fool of himself should she be 'begging for it', as he'd heard some over-eager girls did. The explicitly graphic magazines he'd pawed over in factory lavatories had given him the basics of how to go about it when the time came. Perhaps another good swig of whisky was what he really needed before attempting to twist his frame into those amazing positions as portrayed in the pornography? The so-called 'missionary position' wouldn't perhaps satisfy an experienced girl as he was now guessing Hilary to be: and even summoning up the nerve to try even that would definitely need a drop more of that tension-relieving liquor downstairs.

But, evidently, she could wait no longer as the door immediately in front of him flew open and he found himself being dragged towards where his initiation would occur on her untidily-made single bed! But all wasn't as it appeared he gathered, somewhat relieved, as she suddenly let go of him and flung herself face down on the bed and began delving beneath the pillows.

"Come on, you little bugger!"

His eyes, riveted on her upright bottom, many seconds passed before Daniel's lustful thoughts cleared enough to comprehend that he wasn't the 'little bugger' in question when, from beneath the pillows, she withdrew a struggling black and white kitten.

"You'll take him with you, will you? My dad's drowned the rest but I revived this one but I know he'll drown it if he finds it, I know he will!"

Daniel stared in disbelief as she offered him the kitten.

"I – I can't . . . they – they're not allowed on board," he stammered.

"Oh yes, they do allow! Most ships have a cat! Keeps down the vermin, see!"

"I – I can't! I – I don't even know whether I'm going back on board meself yet!"

"Why's that? Are you in trouble or something?"

"Not half as much as I'll be if I take that blooming thing back with me!"

"I reckon you're in some kind of trouble."

"I will be if I don't get back soon. Er – thanks for the drink. I – I'd best be on me way."

Instead of leaving, he sank down on the end of the bed, his head in his hands.

"Are you alright now?"

She let go of the kitten and rose to put a comforting arm around his slumped shoulders.

"It – it's the drink. I'm not really used to it." He pulled himself free and made for the door. "I'll be okay. I'll walk it off."

"Aren't you even going to give me a peck goodbye?"

Sitting on the end of the bed, her eyes were closed, her lips puckered. He stood there, staring blankly at her.

"Don't you fancy me one bit then?"

Even forlorn, she was definitely a very pretty girl. He moved back to her and kissed her on the cheek.

"I'd best be off then," he murmured.

"That's not a kiss!" she erupted, wrapping her arms around his neck, her lips seeking his.

Even in surprise, he found himself enjoying the intimacy of her moist, sweet mouth against his own and instinctively reached out to clasp her bare midriff as she stood up to respond to his sudden fervour. It was she who broke the embrace perhaps a little concerned by his eagerness?

"Thought you were on your way a minute ago?" she smiled.

"Er . . . I . . ."

He began a stumbled apology but she cut in with, "Have you got a girl back home . . .? A steady, like?"

"Er . . . no . . . well, there was this one girl who I sort of fancied but she . . ."

"But she didn't fancy you so you got arsy and joined up, eh?" she teased, then continued before he could reply. "Would you write to me? When you're at sea, like?"

"Er . . . could do, I suppose . . . that's if I go, like. It's as I said just now. I'm having second thoughts about going back on board. I've got some thinking to do."

She queried his doubts and he told her about the ship and why he now had so many misgivings.

"You'll be alright," she assured him. "If I was a boy, I'd be off to sea myself look you. My uncle's a policeman in the docks. You likely saw him on the gate this evening. He turns a blind eye whenever I'm at a loose end and fancy seeing what ships are in or when there's one sailing. That's what I like best, see. When there's one sailing. It gets me right here!" She placed a hand on her bosom. "It's a lovely feeling. Romantic like: all those sailors waving and calling to me cos I'm the last female they'll likely see for yonks. Some shout rude things too but I feel safe cos there's nothing the randy buggers can do about it so it's all just a giggle really. Most of them just blow kisses till they're just tiny specks hanging over the rail and . . . and I cry at the wonder of it."

She picked up the kitten and lay back on the bed, her eyes looking pensively into Daniel's. He felt moved to lie with her and kiss her again but his naive self had returned and prevented him. About to rise and bid her a positive goodbye, Hilary's wide, refocused eyes told him he was in trouble!

"Gareth! I told you to piss off! He's doing me no harm!"

Daniel recognized the scowling Ted in the doorway as the one with the chain.

"Doin' no harm but it didn't take him long to get your frock off, you silly bitch!" came the snarled reply. "I've been asked to look out for you and that's what I'm doin'."

"I'll look out for myself if you don't mind!" spat back Hilary. "So piss off!"

"Not 'til sailor-boy's out of this fuckin' house!" He glared at Daniel and produced a flick knife. "On your way, bastard, and quick about it!"

As the blade sprang out, Daniel made to leave but Hilary leaped from the bed and positioned herself between him and the intruder.

"He's staying!" she screamed.

"We'll see about that!" barked Gareth, pushing her aside to lunge at Daniel and would have reached him had Hilary not grabbed his sleeve, giving the Cabin Boy a split second to make a hasty exit.

"There's no need to go!" she cried after him. "He'll not harm you!"

"I fuckin'-well will!" echoed Gareth.

Acutely aware of the young thug being hard on his heels, Daniel descended the stairs three steps at a time, his pursuer catching up halfway but hurtling uncontrollably past, his arms and legs flailing about in a desperate attempt to save himself. A wail went up with a sickening thud that ended his headlong fall.

"I – I was only trying to stop him!"

From the middle of the stairs, Daniel turned to see Hilary looking ill-at-ease to where her cousin was painfully attempting to get on his feet below.

"You – you fuckin' evil little bitch! You pushed me! You pushed me!" he groaned. "Well, that's it then! There'll be no second chance for your randy little sailor cos I'm gonna cut his balls off once he's outside this house! You see if I don't!"

His groaned threats continued as he limped out of the house, slamming the door behind him.

"Idle threats," scoffed Hilary, joining Daniel as he peered nervously out of the kitchen window. "Never means what he says, our Gareth," she added scornfully.

"Sounded like he meant it to me and I'm not hanging about to find out," he replied decisively. "Which way will he have gone cos I'm taking the opposite."

"More than likely back in the pub bragging about the beating he gave you if I know him."

"More likely he's gone back to get his mates, so I'm away before he gets back!"

"I'll not let them in, don't you worry!"

But Daniel *was* worried and he didn't even pause to receive her goodbye kiss as she let him out of the back gate. Exiting, he went left so as to avoid entering the street with the pub and, once out of the girl's sight, his stride became a sprint that almost sent him flying as he stumbled over bricks and stones and into the many potholes in the falling dusk. Eventually, he entered a street which, after a few minutes, brought him into a main thoroughfare where he joined the sanctuary of a bus queue.

City Centre, read the first bus's destination and, despite knowing that this was the opposite direction to the docks, he hopped on and rode into Cardiff.

The relief he felt during that ride was not simply because he was widening the gap between himself and the Teds but that he was also, with every passing second, distancing himself from the ship. The impulse to catch a train and put it all behind him was however, impracticable. Even if he abandoned his few belongings aboard the little money that he carried would only cover his fare back to the docks. And so, with no option, after an hour or so of wandering city streets, he reboarded a bus and despondently headed back to the *Roundcape*.

He alighted at a junction but a short walk to the dock entrance and at about the spot where he'd first noticed the petite, young redhead. The light in the gate policeman's hut was well in view when he heard her call. Without stopping, he glanced anxiously back to see if she was accompanied.

"Hang on a sec!" she cried. "You left your box, see!"

He paused, grateful that she was alone as she caught up with him and pushed the box towards him. He'd no use for the empties now, he told her, refusing to take hold of it.

"You shouldn't have bothered to come all this way with a few bottles," he chided.

It was no bother, she explained. She was sleeping at her Auntie's just a few houses back and had to come this way.

"And I've cashed your precious bottles," she continued, placing the box onto the pavement and pushing a few coins into his palm.

"So . . . so why bring a blooming empty box . . . all this way?"

Her mischievous smile told him what it contained, causing him to reconfirm that no way was he taking a cat on board! No way!

"But your mates'll be glad of it! Something to fuss and it'll more than likely put you in their good books!" she reasoned. "But, okay . . . if it worries you that much I'll take it back for me dad to drown," she added with a sigh. "But let's not fall out over this. I haven't been waiting around just to give you the blessed kitten. I – I still want to know if you'll write to me cos I just love getting letters from somebody in my heart. Will you. . .? Will you write to me?"

Daniel was the first to break the embarrassing silence.

"We – we hardly know each other . . . it – it's only been a couple of hours since we met . . ."

"Makes it more romantic, don't you think?"

She reached out to grip his arms, gazing into his eyes wistfully as if the love of her life was about to depart.

"Yeah . . . yeah, if that's what you want?" he murmured, her face so miserably lovely, that he'd promise her anything.

"And when you sail, can I come and see you off?" she asked, suddenly her bubbly-self.

"If you want. That – that's if I sail of course. I might just nip down to Cornwall first and have a word with me brother: get his advice like. He caught polio at sea and he's just learning to get about again. Got his legs it did. But he'll be okay."

"Terrible that is. Hope you don't catch anything like that."

She placed his arms around her waist, coaxing him to embrace her.

"Already got a gammy leg. Smashed me motorbike up, I did. Lucky to pass the medical I was."

He liked the scent and feel of her but couldn't relax.

"They – they'll more than likely turf me off when they see how bad me limp is tomorrow."

"Why don't you stay around and get a job in the docks? We could see each other every day then."

"What? And get done over by your cousin's mob? Not blooming likely!"

"Why don't you swear? Never met a boy who doesn't swear. Is it because you're with me like?"

"Well – I certainly don't go effing and blinding in front of girls but that doesn't make me some kind of sissy. It's just that I was brought up to . . ."

She shut him up with a kiss on the mouth and, taking his hands, leaned back and willed him to look into her smiling eyes.

"I fancy you," she whispered. "I fancied you the minute I set eyes on you. There is some girl back home you're missing is my guess, eh?"

He thought of Patsy Harding and then looked hard at the pretty Welsh girl and wondered what working on the docks might be like?

"There's . . . there's something nice about you," he said eventually.

"Then why didn't you do something about it earlier?" she chuckled. "I don't take my frock off for any Tom, Dick or Harry. You are a slow one, aren't you?"

Her words surprised him and he was lost as to how to reply.

"I thought it was the heat . . . I – I thought you said you were too hot. I didn't think you were wanting me to, er . . .?" he spluttered eventually.

"Of course I didn't!" she teased. "You away in the morning and me with something growing in my tummy! I fancy you but I'm not that daft. I – I really don't know why I did it. Just a feeling that came over me, that's all. You know? To sort of tease some reaction out of you but I'm glad you didn't . . . react, I mean. Heaven only knows what I'd have done if you had? Probably have screamed the place down . . . see – I've . . . I've never . . ."

She slipped out of the embrace and he thought that she was leaving but instead she stooped to pick up the cardboard box and offered it to him again.

"Pleeease? Take it with you?"

He accepted the box more out of reaction than willingly and she was still thanking him, as they arrived at the dock gates.

"Hi, Uncle Bryn!" Hilary called out to the duty policeman.

Uncle Bryn acknowledged her greeting with a smile but seemed more interested in Daniel's box than his niece.

"Not big enough for the crown jewels, boyo but big enough for a small bomb I'm thinking?"

Taking the box from the youth, he carried it into the lit gatehouse where he opened it with, "Oh dear!"

"A problem?" asked Daniel quietly, hoping that it would be.

"There's regulations about the import and export of live animals, didn't you know, boyo?"

"It followed him out so he's taking it back, Uncle," lied Hilary. "Please believe me."

"Oh . . . that's okay," replied uncle hesitantly, "but I never clapped eyes on it, remember? But you don't belong on the quayside at this time of night, young lady," he added protectively.

"I'll come and see you off tomorrow then, okay?" said Hilary, giving Daniel a quick peck on the cheek. "What time do you sail?" she asked, handing over the box for the last time.

"Haven't got a clue but I'll look out for you," he replied, moving off.

Walking towards the scattered ship's lights, he turned to see her waving from the gate. His hold on the box prevented him from waving back but he glanced over his shoulder a couple of times until suddenly, he was alone in the darkness searching for the *Roundcape*. When at last he found her sitting in the gloom, she appeared even more forbidding than on his first sighting. Drawing alongside, Somali jabbering echoed from a solitary lit porthole astern. The only other light was a lamp at the head of the gangplank. He made for the incline recalling his arrival hours earlier. Reaching it, he paused to consider letting the cat go, but then with the box still under his arm, proceeded to board.

Arriving on deck, he turned to look at where the glow of Cardiff merged with the night sky.

"Mom!" he said under his breath. "Oh Mom!"

Chapter 5

Underway

"What the fuck . . .? Who brought that bastard fleabag on board?"

Daniel had been expecting this ever since Billy had deposited the kitten on Jock's bunk with a whispered, "Cat lover is old Jock," before leaving for the pantry. He turned from the cabin wash basin just in time to see the petrified animal come hurtling down from the bunk above.

"Fleabag yours, laddie? You bring the fuckin' thing on board did you?"

"Somebody, er – gave it to me but I . . ."

"Then you'll just have to give the bastard back, laddie! I'll nae suffer cats sniffin' around' yon galley, I'll tell you for nothin'!"

"I – I'll put it on the quay in a minute," offered the Cabin Boy resuming his wash.

"Sure you will," returned the Cook. "Hand me a beer up, laddie."

He was pointing at a crate of beer on the cabin table. Daniel handed him a bottle which, after removing its top with his teeth, he began gulping from.

"Pass me my fags an' matches."

His bemused look as he handed up the cigarettes and matches apparently annoyed the man who belched loudly into his face and rasped, "You've nae seen a man havin' a drink o' beer afore, laddie?"

"Er, well . . . not first thing . . . in bed like," he replied with a nervous chuckle.

The Scot, naked except for his socks, swung his legs over the side of his bunk and glared down at him.

"Christ, laddie! You've a lot to learn I'm thinkin'!"

"I might be off home today," said Daniel, pulling on his shirt.

"Did I hear correct, laddie? You might be off where?"

"It's this gammy leg, you see? I never told anybody about it at me medical and . . ."

"See here, laddie!" Jock looked about to explode. "You've signed for the roun' trip and by fuck you'll do the roun' trip!"

"I – I'm in me rights. It's not the Royal. The Merchant Navy's just like any other civvy job so I can walk off when I want," replied Daniel in as brave a voice he could muster.

"I'll show you if you can fuckin' walk off or nae!" roared the Cook, dropping from his bunk and slamming his beer bottle onto the table. "I'll tell you exactly what you can or cannae do, laddie!"

The man's nudity tended to make his threatening approach comical but a non-smiling Daniel backed swiftly away saying, "Okay! Okay! I was only just saying . . .! Me brothers would give me hell if I quit now they would!"

He wished the younger of his brothers, a strapping six-footer was there at that very moment. That moment however, belonged to the *Roundcape's* Second Cook and he was intent on having his say.

"Listen you here, laddie!" His right hand was a raised clenched fist while he scratched his testicles with the other. "Dinnae ever gi' lip to a Sea Cook! You can choose to cross any man aboard from the Peggy aft to the Skipper up top! But never, laddie . . .!"

The ball-scratching fingers were now prodding the youth's chest.

"Never, I'm tellin' you! Never cross a ship's Cook or you'll sail into a livin' hell that'll have you regret the day you climbed aboard"

He paused to belch rancid, beery breath into the other's face.

"Och aye! You think I'm shootin' the shit but let me tell you now, when you've been weeks out yonder an' bored out o' your skull wi' nae booze an' nae women, it's *grub*, laddie, that'll stop you frae goin' fuckin' insane. An after a while you get to worship the stuff an' the man who fills that cravin' becomes God

69

an' the galley, the holy o' holies an' you'll find yourself crawlin' in there on your fuckin' hands an' knees every opportunity you get!"

His lecture was interrupted by Billy appearing at an open porthole. 'Food', was the subject of Billy's urgent enquiry.

"I've got the nosh up from below Jock, but the Steward's found the galley stove's gone out again an' wants to know where you've got to?"

"A quick shower an' I'll be wi' you, Billy!"

Jock picked up a towel and made for the door.

"An' that's another thing, laddie!" he snapped at Daniel. "A ship's caterin' staff *shower* on wakin' nae just splash a few drops o' water on the'selves as you seemed accustomed. See you follow me in!"

The youth's mind was made up! He was leaving! As absurd as he took the Scot's lecture to be, his threats couldn't be taken lightly. His huge knuckles he'd observed during his browbeating, were badly lacerated after a fight that he, Billy and the big Irish decky had been involved in the previous night. He'd been woken by the three of them (Reno was already in his bunk) as they'd revelled in an account of how they'd sorted out a group of locals ashore. He'd lay there terrified, pretending to be asleep and decided that this certainly wasn't an environment for a quiet country lad!

Now, with Jock out of the way, he hurriedly stuffed his clothes into his sea bag and concealed it in his locker. When the opportunity came he'd seize it, nip back for his gear and be away! On his way out a strangled Scottish air echoed from the shower room. Darting past, he pushed open the alleyway door and stepped out to the pandemonium of the decks.

The urgency of sailing greeted him from every quarter. The gaping holds, now sealed with massive timbers, were being draped with weatherproofing tarpaulins. The removal of refit tools and debris had begun to reveal the contours of the ship, reminding him of the cliché *shipshape and Bristol fashion* often used in seagoing stories. The upper part of the bridge, one of the first parts of the ship to get a final coat of paint, gleamed white against a clear blue morning sky. Two officers climbed its outer stairway, the gold braid of their uniforms glittering in the morning sunshine. One of them he recognized as the man who'd carried his gear aboard the previous day. At the top of the stairs, the officer looked back down and seemed to acknowledge him before entering the wheelhouse.

"Mind your back, boyo!" shouted one of two sailors lumbering towards him carrying a huge piece of winch mechanism.

"Rest awhile, Peggy, if you're knackered?" he called out to his companion in a shrill Welsh voice that hardly suited his rugged looks.

They lowered their burden and leaned against the rail.

"Dick Whittington, is it your name?" the big sailor enquired of Daniel with a smile.

He began nudging and winking at his companion, a youth of about Daniel's age. The Cabin Boy followed their grins to where the kitten was engaged happily rolling about the deck with a length of rope having obviously followed him from his cabin and appeared completely at ease in its new surroundings.

The younger sailor smiled at Daniel, saying, "Take no notice of Ianto, he's always kidding around look you."

The youth, fair-haired, even-featured and slim, a couple of inches taller than himself also spoke in the regional accent.

"Where'd you do your training?" he asked. "I can't remember you from Sharpness."

"Gravesend," answered Daniel. "Me brothers went to Sharpness a few years ago though."

"Turn 'em out military like do they now, boyo?" grinned Ianto, snapping to attention while adjusting the small black beret perched on his large, square head.

"He's poking fun at the uniform you came aboard in," chuckled the youth. "I'm glad I left mine at home. They're a piss-taking lot."

"No time for jawing!" shouted an officer from the bridge walk.

As Daniel looked up, the man threw down a bundle of red cloth.

"Get this dhobied, Cabin Boy!"

Pushing Daniel aside, Ianto caught the bundle himself and chuckling, spread out the flag of the British Merchant Navy on an adjacent hatch.

"What's this, matey?" he screeched back to the officer, pointing at the Union Jack in the 'duster's'[7] top left-hand corner. "We were promised the Welsh Dragon on signing!"

The officer scowled and walked back into the wheelhouse.

"Gone to jot my name down for a keel hauling I shouldn't wonder!" laughed Ianto.. "Come on, Peggy, before he jots you down an' all!"

"What's your name then?" the youth asked Daniel before moving off.

"I'm Martyn by the way."

Before the Cabin Boy could reply he was being propelled into the pantry by his ear.

"You're twenty minutes late, son!" thundered the Chief Steward, thrusting him towards yet another stack of washing-up.

Billy was in the pantry bragging to a sceptical Reno another account of the previous night's fight.

"Think you would have better things to do!" snorted the Maltese. "I went to the cinema to see Jane Russell in *Fire Down Below*. Oh Mary! She reminded me of her up top! She was . . ."

"Flashin' them big tits and you got a fire down below!" completed Billy.

"You crude little Teddy Boy! You know nothing about charm and beauty and you're jealous cos she aboard, who is comparable to any film star, has the hots for me and ignores you!" yelled Reno. "A woman like her wouldn't give scum like you a second glance!"

---

[7] 'Duster'. Red-duster, nickname for flag of British Merchant Navy.

"Then why did she ask Jock if it were 'is cookin' oil that you saturate your wavy locks with?" countered Billy with alarming results.

"I kill you! I kill you!" shrieked the Maltese, his pudgy fists flailing the air as his tormentor backed agilely out of reach.

"A joke! A bleedin' joke!" laughed Billy, pretending to cower against a bulkhead. "Can't you take a bleedin' joke?"

"Okay! Okay!" warned the Maltese, shaking his fist under the Assistant Steward's nose. "But one more such joke and you will be in serious trouble! It might be a long trip and I want you to remember who is Senior Assistant Steward aboard! And that goes for you too, sonny!" he shouted at Daniel in the same superior tone as he swaggered out of the pantry and into the saloon.

"An' that goes for you too, sonny!" mocked Billy as soon as he was out of earshot.

He handed Daniel a stack of containers saying, "Get yourself over to the galley, *sonny*. Looks like Jock's got the range going," he added, pointing to a plume of smoke rising from the galley stack.

On arrival, Daniel met up with Martyn the Deck Boy again, waiting with a group of Somalis.

"Breakfast gets later every day," said Martyn, unaware that Jock had walked over with the Somali's containers which were filled with a curry-like substance.

"An' fuckin' breakfast'll be later still in future if yon Cook dinnae turn up soon!" he barked, slamming down the containers on the serving hatch. "An' there'll be nae time to waste fuckin' about wi' fancy dishes for you lot," he grumbled at the wide-eyed Somalis. "You'll eat good, wholesome *pig* like the rest o' us!"

As the jabbering Somalis retreated with their food, Jock slammed Martyn's containers onto the hatch shelf with such force that several rashers of bacon spilled out. The Deck Boy quickly scooped one up and stuffed it in his mouth and as Daniel reached out to do likewise, his own containers came crashing

73

down, narrowly missing his fingers. Under a murderous glare, the youth picked them up and made a hasty exit.

"Where did that come from, son?" the Chief Steward asked the still-trembling Cabin Boy on his return, pointing to where he'd dumped the flag on the pantry floor.

"Er – somebody asked me to dhobi it."

The Chief was still pointing into the dark corner where Daniel then made out the kitten curled up snugly amidst the folded material. The Chief shook his head and laid a huge hand on his shoulder.

"Look, son. Either you're green or just plain stupid. You don't wash cats, they wash themselves. Whoever *somebody* is, he's having you on. My wife's best china I'll do my best to forget. But idiocy and insolence I've no bloody time for. So, I'll ask you second time. Where did that moggy come from?"

"I, er – thought you meant the flag. Some, er – officer gave it to me . . . and the, er – cat . . ."

Ignoring him, the Steward stopped to fuss the slumbering kitten.

"Came aboard in Tiger Bay, did you? We'll call you Tiger. No, you're a bit too cute for Tiger. 'Tiggy' sounds better. We'll called you 'Tiggy'."

After the officers had left the saloon, the Chief told his staff to move in and have their own breakfast. Not having eaten since the previous morning, Daniel ate ravenously and only when he'd finished did he begin to study his surroundings. The saloon had that touch of luxury that he was soon to identify with 'officer only' status, the maritime equivalent of management dining room as opposed to shop floor canteen, he reflected while studying the landscape reproductions fixed to the gleaming white bulkheads. Despite their tatty condition, the faded red carpet and matching red curtains, contributed to the aura of respectability that set this area aloof from the rest of the ship.

"Think yourself honoured, laddie but the next time you skip a fuckin' shower, you'll eat alone in yon pantry!"

Jock had evidently noted his perusal but the other's attention was suddenly directed towards the Captain's wife at the door saying her goodbyes.

"Have a good trip, boys!" she cooed with a pearly smile.

"Thank you, madam!" chorused Reno and Billy (Jock condescended to nod his head) as the woman made a theatrical exit blowing kisses.

"Oh Mary!" whimpered Reno, sniffing at her lingering perfume. "The woman of my life gone and nothing left for me but the sweet fragrance of her wonderful self!"

"If it's summat to sniff at you're wantin'," smirked Billy, "there's a pair of her dirty drawers still in the laundry bag!"

"That's it! I had my fill of you!" screamed the Maltese. "I go and tell the Steward it is impossible I work with such dirty-minded scum! I go and see him this very minute!"

"Bollocks!" retorted the Bristolian. "You can go and see whoever you . . .!"

He stopped abruptly as the tableware began to tinkle and move about. Daniel felt a shudder that seemed to spring from somewhere far beneath him. The ship was suddenly creaking and groaning as if under great stress.

"We're afloat!" whooped Billy. "The old tub's afloat!" he yelled, sprinting out of the saloon.

"Anybody'd think he never go to sea before!" remarked Reno scathingly as he followed him out.

Jock sipped his coffee and eyed Daniel with a derisory smirk.

"You wouldnae by any chance be feeling seasick, would you, laddie?" he cackled.

Oddly enough, as the youth pushed back his chair and stood up, he did experience a momentary unbalanced sensation. 'Imagination,' he reassured himself, walking unsteadily out of the saloon, Jock's raucous laughter ringing in his ears.

Out on deck, he joined Billy and Reno on the rail for'ard of the bridge watching the murky water surging into the dry dock to swirl and froth around the freshly-painted hull. From the bridge, an officer dictated orders to sailors labouring with hawsers that linked ship to quay.

"Looks like it then!" said the Deck Boy excitedly, appearing at Daniel's side. "Look you, there's the tug boats waiting to take us out into the Channel! Ianto reckons we'll be out there by midday cos of the tides. Could be well out to sea this afternoon I reckon!"

"Could we bollocks!" spouted Billy. "She'll weigh anchor out there and wait for the Cook!"

"Ianto reckons they'll make do with the Second Cook," replied Martyn.

"Will they fuck! No ship sails without its cook!" Billy emphatically informed them. "Do either of you two first-trippers know who the Cook is aboard?"

"Er – God?" ventured Daniel.

"Learnin' quick, aren't we?" returned Billy, sounding a little upstaged. "At any rate," he muttered, glancing over his shoulder, "here comes the son of God!"

Jock led the Cabin Boy to the head of the gangplank.

"See yon sacks o' spuds down there?" he said, pointing to the quay. "I'll be directin' yon crane to pick 'em up, so away down wi' you an' fix the hook to the nettin' they're laid on."

The gangplank, Daniel noted with dismay, was suspended by a winch hawser that adjusted its height as the ship rose in the dock and was now at its maximum angle leaving an ever-increasing gap between it and quay.

"Dinnae just stand there!" bellowed the Scot, giving him a shove that sent him careering down the incline so fast that his feet hardly touched the woodwork. He made a hard landing but was grateful for the mercy of it being a dry one. Following Jock's screamed instructions, he climbed on top of the sacked potatoes, pulled the netting around him and looped it over the crane's hook. His task completed, he went to climb out of the encirclement.

"You'll have to come up wi' them!" bellowed Jock, pointing to the suspended gangplank. The netting tightened and suddenly he was on his way up! Within seconds, the swaying rope cage was level with the grinning Cook who beckoned to the crane operator to proceed.

"See if the stack needs cleanin' while you're up there!" yelled Billy, crying with mirth as the Cabin Boy, his ashen face staring grimly out of his rope imprisonment swept up past the bridge from where a solemn-faced First Officer followed his ascent until the crane stopped, leaving Daniel and potatoes suspended above the *Roundcape's* single funnel.

"A smoko!" decided a beaming Jock and even the smiling crane operator sat back and lit up a cigarette.

Far above, once confident that he was quite safe, Daniel relaxed and began to take in the view.

From above the ship looked tidier and much less forbidding, her crew less threatening.

Lined with sleeping ships, the adjacent waterways glistened for silvery stretches all leading to the vast expanse of the Bristol Channel and the sea beyond. Suddenly, his heart was in his mouth as the *Roundcape's* siren emitted a thunderous blast; the pair of tugs off her bows answering in resounding union, the water at their sterns becoming a white froth; the linking hawsers tautening.

Suspended above, the *Roundcape* was moving off without him!

No such luck! He turned to see the crane operator throw a lever and he was descending. And then he saw her! Hilary! Hilary was peering over the dock wall at about the same point he'd first viewed the ship the previous day. His hand was quickly through the ropes waving frantically. She'd not seen him yet but was acknowledging bawdy calls from the rail! As the potatoes thudded down onto the deck, he leaped out but could hardly penetrate the rowdy throng but once through, their eyes met, their gestures to each other quickly noted by those around him who ruffled his hair and almost lifted him over the rail.

Boooooom! Boooooom!

The deafening siren drowned all goodbyes and the little Welsh girl had gone out of his life forever but maybe not quite . . .?

Under the Chief Steward's orders, he miserably fell in with others stowing away the potatoes.

Underway, his misery lightened briefly as they slipped past moored ships with curious names and home ports on their jutting sterns inducing thoughts of distant places and different people, while above drooped their national flags soon to fly proud with ocean winds.

"Get a move on, you slackers!" and then naval language as in films.

"Starboard a little."

"Starboard a little, sir,"

Too late now to escape the reality of what he'd blindly committed himself to but early enough to recognize the symptoms of *seasickness*! Symptoms that only eased on dropping anchor well clear of the harbour to await the Cook. Another smoko was declared and while a non-smoker, Daniel accepted a cigarette on Billy's advice.

"Lookin' a bit green round the gills, me old acker. A fag'll 'elp with yer gettin' yer sea legs no end!"

Two drags later and a much 'greener' Cabin Boy was clutching the rail.

"'ave another when we're down channel some!" teased Billy to a chorus of laughter which suddenly escalated to loud cheering as a launch arrived alongside carrying the Chief Cook. Standing up somewhat unsteadily, the Cook, a stout, balding, middle-aged man responded to his welcome in what Daniel recognized as a Birmingham accent.

"Get the bloody kettle on and lace it with a drop of the hard stuff!" he yelled good-naturedly.

A rope ladder was lowered and the Cook, with surprising agility for a man whose size compared well with that of the greeting Chief Steward, clambered up. Once on deck, he shook the Chief's hand then turned his round, spectacled face up towards the wheelhouse.

"Grub up by Lands End so get that bloody anchor up, lads!" he shouted comically.

"His holiness himself," muttered Jock into Daniel's ear. "His holiness himself."

The Skipper glared indignantly back but within minutes the anchor winch had completed its task and they were underway again. Daniel watched as the tugs made a wide sweep and headed back to Cardiff. The launch that had brought the Cook followed the *Roundcape* for a short distance before taking off the Pilot and making for home herself.

Paaaaaaarp! Paaaaaaarp! she goodbyed, her propeller whisking up a creamy wake.

Boooooom! Boooooom! answered the *Roundcape*, getting up steam.

The crew resumed their various tasks with a new topic of conversation.

"Sailed with old Brumpud myself a few years back," a scrawny, pipe-smoking Cardiffian who reminded Daniel of Popeye The Sailor and in fact turned out to be the Bo'sun, was saying. "Eccentric by any standards and his cooking's nothing to write home about you'll find. There's one tale I recall him telling about being sunk off Norway during the war and getting picked up by the German destroyer responsible see? Says they were short-staffed on the catering side and it being around Christmas to boot, they puts him to work in their galley where he uses his own special recipe to rustle up some monster Christmas puds. Consequently he has it, he gets blamed for a bout of tummy disorder that has the Krauts sheltering up a fjord for a week."

"Poison 'em did 'e, Bo'sun?" asked a sailor.

"No, that's the worrying part of his tale," came the reply. "Old Brumpud swears he didn't tamper with them puds and he's been stuck with that name to this day."

The decks were alive with anecdotes by those who knew or had had heard tales about the Cook which, on airing, sent Daniel heaving to the rail, the detailed description of inedible food causing it to be several vomits later before noticing the elderly Engineer who'd crossed his path in the alleyway the previous afternoon. Standing a few feet away, oily, gnarled hands also clutching the rail as he gazed mistily towards the Welsh coast, his stooped form looking pathetically out of place on this ship of large and active men, an observation which became even more apparent as the broad-backed Ianto sidled up to him.

"You'll not see 'ome from here, old timer," he joked, placing a friendly hand on the Engineer's shoulder. "Might spot the funfair at Porthcawl with a pair of binoculars though. Met a valley girl at Porthcawl on leave one time. Cost me a bomb she did but she was well worth it if you get my drift?" he chuckled. "Can't beat a valley girl, in't that right, Dai?"

"You're a valley-man are you?" enquired the Engineer distantly.

"Noo," replied Ianto. "Cardiff bred and battered that's me. Sailed with a couple of lads from up your way though. Ever hear tell of old Alun . . .?"

"Not too well acquainted with many folk back home these days," cut in the Engineer. "Too long at sea, you know how it is."

"Too bloody right I do, old timer!" moaned Ianto, raising his voice and smiling towards Daniel. "Deprived, that's what we are at sea. All those sexy creatures we once knew and now all we've got is the training school's latest output to share between the lot of us!"

His wit, seemingly lost on the solemn-faced Engineer, Ianto turned his attention to Daniel.

"And what are you doing over this side, Cabin Boy?" he asked jovially. "Oughtn't you be on the port side saying your goodbyes to England? Couldn't get a look in with all them bloody greasers craning their necks towards Mecca I'll be bound. Best get old Jock to scatter 'em with a few bacon rinds! He'll be wanting a good spot to feast his eyes on the last distillery I'm thinkin'. Hear he mixed it with the Tiger Bay boyos last night," he chuckled, moving alongside the youth. "Found better things to do with your time ashore if that young filly on the quay was the one I hear tell you were spotted with last night, eh, boyo?"

"One night on the tiles and he's too bloody knackered to earn his keep!" bellowed the Chief Steward arriving to escort the sickly Cabin Boy back to the pantry from where he was immediately despatched to the wheelhouse with three cups of coffee. Two were for the Mate and Helmsman, the remaining cup for someone standing outside on the starboard bridge walk, indicated the Chief Officer. As the person referred to lowered his binoculars to receive the coffee, Daniel recognized him as being the officer who'd carried his sea bag aboard during his unhappy arrival.

"Thanks, boyo. It's just what I needed."

His voice was almost whisper; his expression as grim as that of the old Engineer still clutching the rail directly beneath them.

"Swansea that'll be look you there."

About to descend the bridge stairs, a still-queasy Daniel turned to find that the pointing officer was speaking to him.

"Hardly visible to the naked eye but I'm very familiar with that stretch of coastline."

The face that turned momentarily towards him and then back landwards was gaunt and pale.

"That height about there . . .!" he continued and about to offer Daniel the binoculars, glanced within and changed his mind. "The Uplands that'll be! The Uplands!"

He choked on his coffee as he nodded to where Daniel should be looking.

"Oh, er – yes . . ." but the Cabin Boy saw nothing but an indistinct coastline.

"And about here, do you see?"

The officer had suddenly drained and placed his cup back on the tray and was pointing again.

"About there, boyo! About there are the treetops of Cwmdonkin Park!"

Third Officer Ivor Williams,
MV Roundcape
(one hour out of Cardiff)
June 18th 1955

Dear Heloise,

Typing the above address was most pleasurable! Because, my darling, as useless as the previous one will be to you, IT'S FOR REAL! And I hope conveys my elation at being back at sea to your sweet self.

And so begins this new chapter in my life which should, God willing, lead to our reunion.

Cardiff being my pool, sailing from that port was highly likely and to my joy we soon and unexpectedly took a north westerly course for Swansea (also inexplicably changed at the last minute) but so close to shore that after the port, the Gower[8] came evocatively into view. Oh, what treasured memories of our times in what many now call Dylan Country, came flooding back during those minutes at the rail.

But, my 'Flower of the Gower', as I've intimated in previous correspondence and especially now, while I'm undertaking a fresh start, as wonderful as those memories are, we should both now look forward to reuniting and begin to make new ones!

In the meantime, darling, my spare time will be used keeping you up to date (diary fashion) about everyday life at sea but promising to put some cheer into the dullest of days (we're not a fun and games ocean liner) so that you know my newfound optimism is as permanent as our love which even the

---

[8] The Gower Peninsula. Area of outstanding natural beauty, adjacent to Swansea, South Wales

worst of storms cannot extinguish! Oh dear: seeing the Gower lit up in the afternoon sunshine has affected this 'diary' entry so predictably! So Heloise! Everyday life at sea?

I'll begin by saying that if the ship has seen better days, then her crew could be described similarly but lest someone chooses to include myself in that description, I'd best change first impressions and describe my fellow shipmates as being a 'colourful' assembly of lads who'll surely help spice up my diary in the coming weeks!

Hastily recruited, most aboard hail from the Cardiff area while our Skipper, despite his somewhat affected accent, is from Merthyr way. He's mid-fortyish, has a wife half his age whom many were willing to stay aboard for 'decorative' purposes but who went ashore just before sailing. The wags aboard have it that she'd apparently found somewhere to sunbathe amidst the pre-sailing chaos which I'm told, was hardly a discreet situation! Something that I'm purposely mentioning if only to forewarn one sun-worshipping young lady who's often expressed a desire to sail with her future husband! Yes, who else but you, darling, which brings to mind the Gower and its heavenly, secluded coves and I find myself wishing that I'd used my camera more to capture those times and if I dare say it, those 'temptress' poses? Poses that could never be recreated on the open decks of a merchant ship, if only because those poses belonged to 'possessive' me! But would you heed such jealousy-driven advice, young lady? I think not but which reminds me to tell you that I've become something of a counsellor onboard! That is, at least, in respect of one man, namely our Fourth Engineer *who'd mistakenly learned that my two years ashore were to do with 'marital problems' and he'd needed a friendly soul to hear out his own experience. Being told that he'd been fed misleading gossip and that my personal life had never been so promising, seemed not what he wanted to hear (people down on their luck seem to benefit from tales of woe far worse than their own) but on finding that one amongst the crew sympathised rather than made fun of the poor old boy's tale which, in all honesty could, as related, be the script of some music hall farce to a less sympathetic ear, so having gained his confidence, he's taken my advice (Edgar's from Pontypridd and out of frustration was about to return there) to use this trip as a cooling off period in which he might begin to accept his circumstances because I told him from experience, wait long enough and life has a way of dealing one a better hand. (What philosophy! And me not even a card player!)*

To finish in this optimistic mood, my darling, I'll reveal to you that there's a rumour aboard that when our old man gets final orders, the States (even New York) could well be our destination, which could mean that the largest sapphire ring to be found in Durban could be on your finger within weeks. But until those orders (usually off Lands End) I'll stay optimistic and pray that I'll not be finishing this letter by deleting this final paragraph.

Chapter 6

Whistling Up The Wind

When at times, Daniel lifted his trance-like stare from the rushing, spuming water below, the sheer magnitude of the ocean and their isolation upon it, he found awesome.

In every direction lay the same aqueous horizon topped by a cloudless blue sky inhabited only by the dazzling orb of the sun which, when he closed his eyes, temporarily eased his condition with a soothing warmth. On opening them, this relief continued for a few seconds when he found that the rail he clutched had become the playground rail of his old hilltop school and he was once again looking out over the rolling pastures of Worcestershire, the Atlantic horizon becoming the distant undulation of the Malvern Hills and in the valley below, the houses and cottages of Hunt-End just visible through the wooded fringe of the sloping field across which he and Maurice would shortly be fooling their way home. He was halfway across that field when Billy arrived with 'sympathetic' advice from Jock.

The Cook awaited them inside the galley with a large chunk of animal fat dangling on the end of a length of cord.

"Get this down your gullet an' slowly withdraw it, then repeat the . . ." was his remedy that before he'd finished sent Daniel staggering back to the rail where, seconds later, the First Mate arrived to order him back to the lower bridge to perform a task so unpleasant that suicide by drowning would surely have been the better option?

Hardly aware of the drama unfolding just four hours out of Cardiff, Daniel suddenly learned that the Chief Steward had become *indisposed* after locking himself inside his accommodation to partake in a large amount of alcohol before shooting himself with a pistol taken from the bond-store. The AB, lowered over the side to look into the Chief's porthole, described him as appearing very inebriated and 'tinkering' with the gun, a situation of grave concern aboard including, not least, Billy, who'd predicted such an event after helping store the alcohol. His concern, though rather sympathetic, was more to do with possible staff rearrangement, 'should old fat guts blow 'is fuckin' brains out'. They'll likely make Reno Chief an' with that prat of a Cabin Boy under lock and key for mutiny, I'll be doin' the work of three!" he moaned, the reference to 'mutiny' having arisen after Daniel finding that the task he'd been led to was a badly soiled lower-bridge toilet where the Chief, after a frantic dash from his cabin had literally 'exploded' before heading back to resume his binge.

"Whoever blooming-well did it should blooming-well clean it!" the Cabin Boy had told an aghast Mr Purdoe, the First Officer no less, before vomiting his way back to the rail.

Whoever's task it became, Daniel neither learned or cared about. Even the reason for the Chief's disgraceful behaviour was never revealed, certainly not to lower ranks, he remaining *indisposed* for a further twenty-four hours after which he emerged to continue his role as if nothing had occurred. 'Depression' was a word briefly mentioned which had the ship's Cabin Boy wondering if perhaps the loss of a china tea service had somehow contributed to the man's said malaise? Eventually however, he was to discover, bouts of drunkenness aboard when alcohol became available, was part and parcel of sea life and while frowned on, seemed to generally go unpunished. Abstainers aboard though (except for one rebel) were the Somalis, one of whom that afternoon, joined the defiant Cabin Boy on the rail.

"Good for you, son," sympathised the elderly Abu, his mouth barely visible through profuse, white facial hair. "I can't advise disobedience aboard but what I've heard they asked of you, especially while sick, was most unkind."

His tone was warm, his eyes moist and veined, smiled with genuine compassion.

"Let's hope that your stand makes them think," he added before moving away.

This meeting was the first of several, the ageing greaser becoming the youth's father-figure aboard. He was soon to gain another, if stranger friend, but when troubled, it would be the kindly Abu Shalaan he would turn to for advice and consolation. Following their brief encounter, Daniel's weakness through lack of food persuaded him that lying prostrate on his bunk might be beneficial. On returning to his cabin he quickly realized that while inebriation was strangely acceptable aboard 'mutiny' was most definitely not and his cabin mates were about to confirm as much!

"Are you aware o' the consequences for mutiny on the high seas, laddie?" growled Jock as he entered. "When the old man gets to hear o' your insubordination, I'd nae be in your shoes for all the whisky in Scotland!"

"Jock's right, Danny boy," grinned Billy.

He'd hastened back to the cabin with news about the 'mutiny' and was now sprawled on his bunk thoroughly enjoying Jock's lecture.

"If it's walkin' the plank, old Abu'll likely walk 'im to the end. Seems to 'ave taken 'im under 'is wing 'as old Abu," sniggered the Bristolian.

"It's nae laughin' matter!" barked the Scot, glaring at Billy and Daniel in turn. "The lad's shite his nest good an' proper this time an' I wouldnae mind betting he'll get nae shore leave an'll be fined half o' his pay into the bargain."

"Who do you think will clean the mess up?" joined in Reno. "The Skipper maybe?"

"I've already said that whoever makes a blooming mess ought to clean it up!" responded Daniel positively, inducing a further barrage of abuse from the bunk above.

"When the Chief's properly back on his pins, he'll show you whose job it is to clean up shite aboard, you cheeky wee upstart you! An' any more o' your backchat an' you'll get a fuckin' belt aroun' the heed afore I jam it down that fuckin' lavatory!"

As the ranting continued, Daniel slipped from his bunk and made for the door.

"I reckon the Skipper's got your cards ready if that's where you're off to?" quipped Billy. "An' I hear tell 'e's transferrin' you to the first Blighty-bound ship along!"

"An' if one doesnae come along, he'd best sling the immature wee twat over the fuckin' side an' make him swim home! *Immature*, laddie, do you hear? You're too fuckin'-well *immature* for this game!" was the Cook's final and stinging remark as Daniel exited.

Out on deck he made for aft, finding the going increasingly difficult due to wind and rougher seas now being encountered. Near to tears, he cursed the ship, its crew and the ceaselessly shifting ocean. While hardly fit for socializing, he hoped to find Martyn, the Deck Boy: discover how he was faring, and perhaps gain some sort of consolation by sharing their misery. It was mid-afternoon, the customary time for those not on duty to take to their bunks. Martyn however, was too ill to talk, being doubled over the rail in the company of a Somali youth who worsened Daniel's mood with the boast that although a first-tripper too, was suffering no ill effects whatsoever. Martyn, like Daniel, was obviously less fortunate. Seasickness had stifled his friendly nature and after a brief groan about the hell of it all, shuffled off below with his friend Hassan.

Astern for the first time since boarding, Daniel discovered in the form of the vessel's frothing white wake, the long, aqueous road home. Spellbound by this ocean highway, he derived a measure of comfort from knowing that the molecules of water forming this road would, in an unbroken chain, lead back to the very brook flowing at the foot of his garden back home.

Immature. Jock's inference had hurt while he knew contained some truth because here was he, childishly reflecting on the past; a past he'd petulantly dismissed but was now bringing to mind with longing. The brook, while not exactly having dominated his growing up had, in a form of escapism, contributed much to it. In fact when in his last year at school, the headmaster had asked his class to write an essay about anything that might have influenced their young lives so far, a popular choice being parents, while he, getting wind of it and wishing to appear creative, chose by way of maps and memories, to write about his childhood brook: an effort, while not an outright winner, did please himself. Surprisingly, he remembered it almost word by word.

He wrote as himself travelling upstream from the confluence of Bow brook with the River Severn, a little west of the solitary dome of Bredon Hill. His description of this first long stretch of brook was, not having travelled its course that far, imaginary.

'From the shallow, meandering stretches of water, overhanging trees, bushes and wild flowers are at my fingertips, blackbirds screech at the intruder's approach while sparrows and tits sing welcoming songs. Rabbits scuttle into ripening fields of corn awaiting the harvester. Amphibians and rodents of the brook dive for cover or secrete themselves underground until danger has passed. Minnows and tadpoles playing around my feet, vanishing along with the red soldier I've stooped to tickle.

Nothing there but with curiosity and time to spare are back to investigate as do I, climbing banks to survey the landscape for anything familiar, then back to the water which passes through and round villages and hamlets with names like Drake's Broughton, Peopleton, Upton Snodsbury, Himbleton, Bradley and Feckenham. Minutes upstream of Feckenham, a leaning signpost just visible above a crumbling bridge parapet, reads HUNT-END 1.

Passing under the bridge, moorhens scatter for cover as a small pool is approached where I leave Bow brook and seek beneath a clump of bushes, the outlet of another brook, the Wharrage brook, just one of many confluences across this low-lying land. But the Wharrage brook flows through home territory and, following it, the rise and fall of the landscape, its meadows, copses and scattered cottages are familiar; instilling an urge to quickly move on. Skirting the village, my temptation to visit Hunt-End's tiniest shop to exchange sixpence and one ration coupon for a quarter-pound of chocolate caramels is avoided.

Must press on to where vegetation arching from the brook's steepening banks forms a shadowy tunnel leading to Wharrage bridge where at dusk, girls shriek at the teasing boys to stop, then appear rejected when they do. Not a soul about so it's under the bridge to where Mrs Bennet keeps her sow and threatening geese, then in less than a minute arrive at a spot where tattered comics lie scattered around the ruin of yesteryear's camp.

No boyhood laughter now, only the sound of water babbling over glistening pebbles; the bark of a dog and clucking hens telling that the journey along the brook is over at the place where memories are formed and plans for the future are made to continue. To continue the journey of life itself.'

"Thinkin' of swimming back home, eh, Cabin Boy?" quipped Ianto, joining the deep-in-thought youth. "What brings you aft then, boyo? Pining for your little Cardiff bint I'll wager. Or is it that nasty smell amidships you've come to be away from?" he teased, getting a laugh from a group of sailors emerging from below.

"He'll not miss her from Cardiff once the Third Mate has introduced him to the alternative," joked one of the group. "Hear tell he carried his gear aboard," he chuckled. "Got your card marked, eh, son? There are rumours about the Third quite disturbin' like and I . . ."

"I'll have no slanging our seniors aboard!" intervened the Bo'sun from their midst. "A tad eccentric maybe but I've heard that Mr Williams has had a bad time of late, so no more of your tittle-tattle or I'll be reporting you for . . .!"

"It's the *Mary!*" was the cry that curtailed the Bo'sun's rebuke and sent men scrambling to the rail to see the *Queen Mary*, presently about half a mile off their starboard bow and approaching fast. His troubles momentarily forgotten, Daniel viewed the passing queen with awe. With only the odd distant vessel glimpsed since Cardiff, now, drawing closer every second, her two for'ard stacks trailing identical ribbons of black smoke across a pale, Atlantic sky, the world's second largest liner!

"Give 'em a wave, boyo!"

Ianto had led him to a good vantage point just as the *Mary* was at her closest.

"She'll likely give us a blast when they make out our registration!"

Sighting the *Mary* was certainly the high point of Daniel's first long, miserable hours at sea. Sickness and teasing having been incessant, he seized every opportunity to lie prostrate on his bunk where he found the greatest relief from his malady: the rhythmic beat from the engine room far below, he found soothing and dreaded the moment when he'd next be disturbed for pantry chores and cabin tidy-ups. He'd also be disturbed for the sheer hell of it!

"If you're intendin' to spend the rest o' the trip on your back, laddie, I'm goin' to get the Bo'sun to disinfect this cabin cos it's beginnin' to reek like a fuckin' Egyptian whorehouse!"

Wonder if Jock got that scar from being glassed by his mother for not drinking his milk? Or had he been born with that attitude which was contributing to a certain Cabin Boy's premature demise?

Demise? Or at least, approaching demise? It was worth trying and so later that morning the Chief Steward, now up and about, had found him 'unconscious 'on the pantry floor. Next in attendance was no other than Jock, who, from the galley had witnessed his collapse through the open pantry doors.

"He kinda just dropped, Chief. A good three minutes he took to avoid hurtin' himself. Will you be in need o' the fat poultice to keep his windpipe open?"

"That'll not be necessary, McLaughlin. Best rest him up in the hospital awhile."

Hospital. Despite Jock's sarcasm, he'd fooled the Chief and, just as Billy had predicted, he'd be transferred to a homeward-bound ship for hospital treatment ashore. So why then were they lumping him, into the Bo'sun's store? This was hardly a hospital. But the Bo'sun's store was multi-purpose, it was later explained. Sick men were installed there to die amongst tins of paint, coils of rope and other tack with not a nurse in sight! Surprisingly though, his hour stay plus medication worked wonders because by the very next morning (or was he at last finding his sea legs?) an improvement was such that he'd even began whistling while performing breakfast chores without so much as a belch! Once again, Jock had observed, or more like heard something, that by his frown as he entered the pantry, clearly annoyed him!

"Was that you I heard whistlin' just now, laddie?"

His tone was especially mean as he moved the cat away with his boot.

"Whistling? Er, yes – it was. Why, er – do you ask?"

"Because, laddie, whistlin' at sea summons the wind! Storm winds, didnae you know?"

"That's blooming daft superstition," grinned back Daniel in the same split second of regretting it.

"Christ, Danny boy!" taunted Billy. "Don Cockell lasted nine rounds with Marciano in their last fight an' Reno tells me you never even 'eard the first bell! Should 'ave warned you, old Jock's got a left 'ook like the kick of a mule! Seen 'im in action that last night in Cardiff. It were a great night 'cept for gettin' me suit grubby. Pity you 'adn't come along. You'd 'ave known what to expect before givin' 'im lip."

Still too shocked to comment, Daniel hadn't needed to fake unconsciousness that time, which he swore put getting his sea legs back at least a week which Billy found hilarious, only until the Assistant Steward discovered that Jock had done him a favour by putting his prized suit in the wash resulting in its 'genuine' leopard skin trimmings becoming slightly pink after merging with the outfit's red dye.

"Well, you've been moanin' about the state o' it since Cardiff an' now I've done you a favour an' cleaned it up, still you fuckin' moan!" offered the Cook, hardly able to hide his smirk. "So stop your blubberin', Billy, else I'll get to thinkin' I socked the wrong guy."

When Billy eventually took down his Teddy Boy suit from a line rigged between galley and pantry, Daniel couldn't help but pity him as he ironed away for hours attempting to restore it to its former glory. Further humiliation came when he came to putting it on and finding that it had shrunk somewhat.

"Bit difficult doin' the jacket buttons up," was his only complaint in Jock's presence, "but shorter trousers'll show off me luminous socks a treat don't you think?"

Daniel nodded his agreement while under his breath, cursed Jock and swore that he'd somehow avenge Billy and himself.

"I'll whistle up something much worse that the fucking wind," he vowed, his escalating use of swear words boosting his resolve.

"Much worse than the fucking wind!"

Chapter 7

First Conversation

"I'm hardly the person to ask whether or not he resembles the mun?" muttered the Fourth Engineer, appearing more interested in spreading his marmalade than the question poised by the Third Mate. "In fact I can't even recall seeing a photo or whatever of this poet fellow you're suggesting the lad resembles."

"Just a passing thought, Edgar," replied the Third. "And any similarity was only when he was about the boy's age you see. I've got a newspaper cutting somewhere if you'd like to see . . .?"

His approach faltered on noting his companion's interest was definitely with his breakfast rather than his idle chatter so returned his unsettling stare towards Daniel, causing the embarrassed Cabin Boy to increase his mopping pace in order to distance himself from the two late diners.

His indifference to 'any likeness' established, 'Edgar the Silent', aptly named by no other than Billy, finished his breakfast without a further word. Despite his generally uncommunicative manner, the old Engineer's matrimonial problems were, by way of his probing fellow diners and over-attentive Bristolian Table Steward, common knowledge aboard. Equally aired by the inquisitive, scandal-mongering Billy, was the Third Mate's said *interest* in Daniel; unfounded gossip that was already bringing about much jocular comment.

'Bet 'e can't wait to run 'is fingers through those silky curls of yours,' and 'mind you don't get stooping with your dustpan an' brush while 'e's around,' were typical of the jibes resulting from the Second Steward's mischievous whispers: whispers, in Daniel's opinion, put about to divert attention away from his own ragging about the Captain's rumoured interest in himself.

Such teasing, the Cabin Boy was fast beginning to accept, was part and parcel of life aboard. Nevertheless and however much he tried to dismiss it as teasing, the Third Mate's rumoured fascination with him even while they'd hardly spoken to each other since the officer had pointed out some distant park not long out of Cardiff, was unsettling enough for the boy to avoid the man as much as was possible. Complete avoidance however, since he was the Third's Cabin Steward (cleaner) was difficult and the inevitable moment would soon arrive when the unlikely relationship of Cabin Boy and officer would begin.

The first of the many conversations (largely dominated by the senior) between the pair occurred six days into the trip: six days of abject misery Daniel would recall, he still being sensitive to the mildest of swells right up to the day of the encounter and consequently, even more reluctant to fraternize.

Still bitter at being exposed as a fraud while attempting evacuation, the best he could now hope for was continued calm seas and an immediate return home from wherever they were bound. With this in mind, he had steeled himself to go about his duties, duties that had sent him armed with cleaning utensils to the Third's cabin on that particular morning.

The size of the cabins on his daily rota varied with the status of their occupants but were all similarly furnished consisting of a single bunk, locker, bureau and one, sometimes two, chairs according to the floor space available. 'Doing' for the First and Second Mates was no problem. These officers were meticulously tidy but the Third's accommodation with balls of screwed-up paper scattered about, an overflowing waste bin and ever-full ash trays doubled his work. An obviously restless sleeper, his untidy bunk together with strewn clothes which had to be sorted for dhobi or re-hanging in an impossibly full locker contributed to his irritation.

The source of the scattered paper, he observed, was a portable typewriter on the bureau always loaded with a new sheet of paper likely waiting to be screwed up and tossed aside with the rest. Above the typewriter, fixed to the bureau mirror was something that had intrigued Daniel from the first day of his entering the cabin.

Meaningful to the officer those ink-black words printed within a light veneer frame, he guessed? A homemade assembly but properly glazed which probably accounted for the generous amount of adhesive tape securing it to the mirror.

That morning, as on every morning since his health had begun to improve, on arriving in the cabin, he inexplicably found himself reciting the bold, black words under his breath. *'AND DEATH SHALL HAVE NO DOMINION'*[9] repeating the sentence as he worked, ignorant as to its meaning, yet strangely moved by its dramatic ring.

"And death shall have no dominion!" he growled, kicking out after a ball of paper, frustrated at having to tidy up after someone who'd create the same mess well in time for his next visit. After re-hanging a jacket and shirt, he found that the locker door refused to close properly so began slamming it repetitively.

"Getting something out of your system, eh, boyo?"

The Third had entered unnoticed and stood there grinning at him. Daniel spun to face him, embarrassed that his madness had been witnessed.

"I – I'm, er . . . I'm . . . I'm nearly finished, sir," he stuttered.

Removing his cap, the officer smoothed back his fine, sun-bleached hair and closed the door behind him.

"No hurry, boyo! No hurry! We work to the beat of the engine these days, not the speed of the wind," he said good-naturedly while easing himself into his bureau chair. "Oh – and while I think of it," he added, his eyes fixed on the typewriter in front of him, "see that you don't touch anything other than the ashtray on my desk here would you please?"

"I – I never touch anything valuable or, er – personal, sir," Daniel answered politely.

"Good . . . good. That's what I like to hear, boyo. Use your loaf about these things, do you?"

The officer turned in his chair and was grinning at him again.

---

[9] The collected poems of Dylan Thomas. The new centenary edition.

"Training school, sir . . ." replied the youth, trying to push Billy's taunts to the back of his mind. "They told us about other people's belongings like . . . and – and . . . I – I've got two brothers at sea . . . well – er . . . one that is now . . . and they told me how to go about things like."

"Seafaring family, eh?" enquired the officer. "Whole blessed family got the call, did they? What parts are you from, boyo? You weren't born by the sea with that accent I'm thinking?"

"No, sir. I – I'm from Worcestershire . . . er – near Redditch if you've heard of it? A village just a couple of miles from the town like."

"Not too familiar with the Midlands," replied the Third. "What was it that persuaded three brothers to go to sea? Lack of work in that area?"

Before Daniel could answer, he turned in his chair and gestured towards the cabin's single porthole.

"It called you, eh?" he said quietly. "It calls you does the sea. It's the sense of adventure that's in most of us in our early years. The idea that going to sea will somehow change things for the better until you comprehend that the emptiness of the sea betters nothing!"

His look was distant as he turned back to Daniel.

"And if my observation is correct, that's about the point you've arrived at, eh, boyo? he asked, the hint of a smile suggesting he ought not be taken too seriously.

"Er – yes . . . I – I suppose you're right. I – I'm not too happy with . . ."

"Disappointed aren't you now? Downright pissed off is my guess if your glum expression is anything to go by?" interrupted the officer, leaning back to await the other's confirmation.

"It's not turning out as you'd hoped is it, boyo? It's early days but you're already thinking you've made a mistake, eh? It's an unnatural way of life is seagoing. Like the chapters of a book: some grab you, others a complete waste of your precious time but you continue to read because in truth, time is plentiful at sea and that interesting chapter you're coming to is the next docking or home leave when you really start living again."

His voice was now low and distant, his preacher-like manner causing Daniel to feel ill at ease.

"The dull chapters are too long, you see," he continued mournfully, "and when you arrive at where you hoped the author would compensate you for having stuck with him through the doldrums, he lets you down so badly that you vow never to read another word that he . . ."

Daniel's vacant stare caused him to pause.

"You do get my meaning, boyo? About what you've let yourself in for that is?" he began to apologize. "Of course you don't. I'm doing what I've fallen into doing of late. I'm talking as if I'm writing . . ."

He pointed towards his waste bin.

"All this that you clear up every day: it's what I do see? To ease the monotony. Some of it poetry which is why I embroidered what should have been a simple explanation of life at sea and finished up giving you a bloody headache I shouldn't wonder? I apologize for that and don't get taking Ivor Williams too seriously will you, boyo?"

"Er – no . . . I – I . . . I'd best be on me way now," replied the youth, using his apology as an excuse to leave while anxious not to appear ungrateful for the officer's friendliness towards one so low in rank. Such fraternization was hardly the norm on recalling how training school officers would lord it over subordinates. The Third's intimate chatter was not over yet it seemed, as he ignored his visitor's continued attempts to excuse himself.

"Remember, boyo!" he resumed in a tutor-like tone. "Remember that the last trip was the best and that every trip is the last!"

He smiled while waiting for his words be digested but appeared hesitant before continuing.

"Sorry, boyo, it's not my job to philosophize to you or any other aboard and all you need is experience to overcome your present concerns. It's just that of late I'm finding that advising others helps diminish one's own problems and in fact, every crew has someone in need of a psychiatrist rather than a philosopher and already on this trip I'm, er . . ."

Daniel's expression caused him to pause and apologize once more.

"Take no notice of my rambling now. I'm talking to myself really. The problems of old hands aren't of interest to first-trippers such as yourself and I ought know better than to broach them so let's start again shall we? I expect you've a few problems of your own you'd like to get off your chest, eh? Well – I'm always ready to listen but I can't promise to help you jump ship or anything drastic," he chuckled. "And of course, any serious matter should be addressed to the head of your department. I'm sure the Chief Steward'll give you a sympathetic hearing as long as you work hard and don't mention the word 'home'. He'll only jump down your throat and tell you what anybody else aboard would. That home's only talked about when you're experiencing the *channels* as they say. A term used when you're in home waters and looking forward to being paid off. We all want to go home to our nearest and dearest do we not?"

The Third was once again staring vacantly in some private thought causing Daniel to feel he should say something to break the awkward silence.

"Where – whereabouts is your home, sir?" he asked politely.

"My home, boyo . . .? Whereabouts is my home . . ?" came the eventual reply. "I pointed out my home town to you not long out of Cardiff if you recall? Raised by the water me. The sight, sound and tang of the sea formed my very being as it were. Have you ever been Swansea way?"

"Er – no . . . Me dad used to take us camping up North Wales, Barmouth and thereabouts. I think Swansea's more south isn't it? Me geography's never been up to much."

"What! You've never seen Swansea Bay and the beautiful Gower Peninsula?"

"Well – me dad only had an old Austin Seven and we used to chance it just on an afternoon trip to Stratford on Avon; what with gaskets blowing and punctures and everything. Although – we had used to cram up to five in it after me brothers went off to sea; that's with luggage on the roof rack and all."

"You only saw the ocean once a year," chuckled the officer, "and yet you and your brothers chose to go to sea as soon as you were able!"

Fingering the bump on the bridge of his nose, a feature that took nothing away from his maturing good looks, he then enquired, "You followed your brothers to sea just to be their equal, eh?"

His teeth were surprisingly white considering the evidence of his heavy smoking, Daniel found himself thinking while searching for an answer other than that he was shadowing his brothers but the Third Mate beat him to it.

"You spent your boyhood in rural surroundings; never so much as got your feet wet and yet the sea called you, eh, boyo?"

His questioner was trying to tease an answer from him and the only one Daniel could think of sounded absurd even as he began.

"Er – the brook, sir . . . the brook at the bottom of our garden. It was always my ambition to find out where it led to . . .? And – and . . . well – here I am."

The Third's broad grin suggested he thought his answer absurd too but, surprisingly, his next words contained no hint of ridicule.

"I like that, boyo. Very well put," he said quietly. "I'll have to remember that for my next letter. She'll appreciate that will Heloise. She'll appreciate that."

Whoever Heloise was, was left for another day because the Third Mate's interest in Daniel at that particular moment ceased as abruptly as his chatter as he swung to face his bureau mirror.

"I – I'll be off then, sir," said the Cabin Boy almost with relief.

But the pained reflection in the mirror showed no sign of acknowledgement.

"Barmy! The Third Mate's as barmy as they come an' schemin' to boot!"

Billy was never hesitant to condemn and on hearing Daniel's account of his prolonged stay in the officer's quarters, was only too eager to offer his opinion.

"Any officer who finds time for idle chat with the shit of the ship 'as got an ulterior motive!" he spat. "Come on, Danny! What really did 'appen in there? Come on! Out with it!" he badgered until Daniel finally exploded.

"Nothing worse than what you and the Skipper get up to when you take him his morning cuppa if Jock's guess is right?" he retorted only to find himself gripped by the throat after descending the storeroom ladder with the Assistant Steward.

"An' just what's that fuckin' load of crap supposed to mean?" snarled Billy, tightening his grip.

"Well . . . er – you know Jock," gasped Daniel appealingly. "Never a good word for anybody and I didn't really take him seriously, honest."

What's 'e 'ave to say about me an' the Skipper? Come on, let's 'ave it?"

"Er – only some rubbish about you dolling yourself up when you go upstairs."

"What's 'e mean? Dollin' meself up?"

"Well – the neckerchief and Reno's poncy hair oil you've been using and . . . and . . ."

"An' what? An' what else 'as the Scotch arse'ole been sayin'?"

"Er – and he's been joking about you putting scent on your privates but I don't believe a word of it, Billy. Not a word."

"I only 'ope you don't believe a fuckin' word of it!" growled Billy, letting go only to grab his captive between the legs. "Else you'll 'ave no privates to do fuck-all with when I'm finished with you!"

"You know whose side I'm on, Billy," returned Daniel, managing to squirm out of the painful grip. "You know what I think about old bully boy."

"An' don't come that James Dean[10], big man stuff with me again if you ain't got the spunk to back it up!" warned Billy finally. "Besides – we've got enough fuckin' film stars aboard without you tryin' to be one," he added, grinning in thought.

"Film stars? Oh yeah . . . the film stars aboard . . ."

Daniel was puzzled but anxious to maintain Billy's cooling mood with the change of subject.

"The fuckin' Bo'sun? Popeye the Sailorman, pipe and all. Popeye's fuckin' twin wouldn't you say?" cracked the Assistant Steward.

"Er – yeah . . . he does come to think of it," agreed Daniel, catching on. "And – and Reno, your mate: spitting image of Lou Costello, don't you think?"

"'e's no fuckin' mate of mine just cos we're Stewards. But yeah, I can see the likeness an' 'e's fuckin' well as daft as Lou Costello that's for sure! An' what about that big Taff sailor Ianto? Dead ringer for Bill 'aley[11] don't you reckon?"

"Er – who'd you say?"

"Bill 'aley? Christ almighty, Danny boy! Are you still usin' crystal sets in the fuckin' Midlands?"

"Er – oh yeah . . . of course I've blooming-well heard of him . . ."

"What's the name of 'is band then?"

"I – I can't bring it to mind at the, er – moment."

"The Comets, you twat! Bill 'aley and the Comets! You 'aven't got a fuckin' clue about rock an' roll 'ave you? But at any rate, you can forget about 'aley as brilliant as 'e is. There's another Yank who's takin' the rock scene by storm accordin' to those southern Yankee stations I've been pickin' up on Jock's

---

[10] American James Dean. Film idol of the 1950s.

[11] American Bill Haley. Considered first of the rock stars.

wireless. That's when I've retuned it from the fuckin' BBC. Jock were in 'is element this mornin'. 'e got Victor Sylvester with an echo because 'e reckons because the BBC 'as got the most powerful transmitters in the world and we're gettin' reception from both directions aroun' the globe."

"These – these Yankee stations . . .?" asked Daniel. "Does that mean we're going to America?"

"I fuckin'-well wish we were," replied Billy miserably. "The music's fantastic. They're far ahead of us an' what little I've been able to pick up about this bloke from Tennessee, 'e's gonna turn the rock scene on its 'ead. Naa, we're 'eadin' for the Caribbean area so the Bo'sun reckons; calypso music an' all that square stuff. But mind you, Danny boy, me old acker!" he added, his face lighting up, "the birds are worth shaggin' 'e tells. Just imagine, Danny boy? Could likely lose your virginity, that's if you didn't lose it in Cardiff? Could well be gettin' your end away for the first time stuck into some dusky, young maiden? Just imagine that, Danny boy! Just imagine that!"

Exactly what Daniel's involvement with the little redhead who'd conspicuously waved her goodbyes to him from that Cardiff quay had amounted to, had been very much debated by his teasing cabin mates. Billy especially, was determined to find out whether he had or hadn't. But Daniel was equally determined to keep them guessing, knowing that the truth would be more ammunition with which to belittle him while his brief mention about being invited to her bedroom during his stay, gave away nothing about the reality of the experience, they, wanting to hear an explicit sexual account and not what he now recalled as being an innocently 'romantic' happening.

Romantic. He'd never dare use that term in front of the vulgar threesome who'd have a field day should he reveal that even though Hilary had partially undressed prior to inviting him upstairs, he'd still not taken advantage. So why now, while daydreaming about the experience was his imagination straying to questions such as should she have slipped down those brief white panties, would her pubic hair have been as vividly red as that on her head? Was such lewd pondering something he ought feel guilt about or was it just natural curiosity regards sex? Surely his present insomnia was down to the claustrophobic conditions he was supposed to sleep in and nothing whatsoever to do with flashbacks of her upturned rump as she'd probed for the kitten? Yes – he'd keep those memories of the friendly young Welsh girl pure. There would apparently, be opportunities enough to indulge with less innocent and more experienced females very soon if shipboard talk was anything to go by. He'd take his time though. As anxious as he was to experience this said, sublime act of nature that just had to be ecstatic beyond comprehension as about ninety per cent of the crew were suddenly talking about little else! Well – ninety per cent was a bit of an exaggeration and a probable slight on their Somali crew members who, it was anybody's guess as to what they might be jabbering about in their own language but more than likely to be about religion or their families than anticipation of lustful liaisons ashore.

Oh – and there was one other character aboard whom he could hardly picture in the joked-about queue for condoms outside the Chief Steward's door. No, the Third Mate definitely didn't belong in the 'shag-happy' category. Obviously, his *seen* behaviour as an officer ought be beyond reproach but Daniel instinctively knew that he was a person of good morals and in fact, if the typed poem he'd salvaged from his waste bin and read several times was an indication as to the man's nature then he was as romantic as himself.

Chapter 8

Heloise

Ne're again to linger o'er scattered sea town lights,
or wend the paths hand in hand upon Cwmdonkin's heights.
Ne'er to trace with arms entwined, the hunchback's route
immortal from the poet's mind.

Gone life's sweet warmth from my side,
ne'er again to hold and thoughts confide.
Lost as the sea wind switherin' 'bout my face,
which tomorrow may blast that empty place.

Oh switherin' wind perchance your landward breeze
should kiss dark tresses 'neath Cwmdonkin's trees
Kiss too those lips which now it seems,
belong to the hunchback and poet of but dreams.

"If this crap don't prove that the Third's lost 'is marbles, then nothing' fuckin' will!" was Billy's opinion of the poem salvaged from the Third's waste bin.

"Give it back! It's not meant for *anybody* to read!" pleaded Daniel, attempting to snatch back the typed poem held aloft by a tormenting Billy, their antics disrupting the galley queue.

"What do you reckon, Jock? Doesn't this sentimental twaddle prove what I've been sayin' all along? That the Third's a fuckin' nutcase?"

Jock, not the easiest man to seek agreement with, strongly rejected Billy's criticism.

"Sheer Sassenach pig ignorance to ridicule a man for passin' away his spare time in contemplation of his life or whatever!" he bellowed. "We Celts have a side to us that's envied throughout the literary world I'll have you know! Men such as Robbie Burns, probably Scotland's most celebrated poet was brought to all of your attentions at some point in your schoolin' nae doubt? But you'll have paid him as little attention as you did your own fuckin' Shakespeare I'll bet. You English give more praise to your Stanley Mathews than your Shakespeares an' your Wordsworths, while the Scots, Welsh an' the Irish have inspired the intellectual world wi' their poems, sonnets an' so forth."

"It's right enough," agreed Brumpud, dipping a tasting finger into the mutton stew. "Once had a galley boy from Dundee way who was gifted poetically like. Could certainly knock up some verses could that one."

"Good o' you to back me up," nodded Jock, "but with all respect I wouldnae have thought poetry was exactly your cup o' tea?"

"And you'd be right, our kid," replied Brumpud, licking his finger clean. "But until the Bo'sun made him paint 'em out, it was something to chuckle over while havin' a shit."

Brumpud, not the most loquacious of men seemed to enjoy making fun out of something another found serious and was the one man aboard uncaring enough to be flippant even with the opinionated Jock. Surprisingly, Jock never retaliated against his senior, even showing a quiet respect for the man who after all, according to the Scot, was 'God' aboard.

Later that day, Daniel went aft to swap experiences with Martyn who too was over the worst throes of seasickness. The Cabin Boy's story of his encounter with the poetry-writing Third Mate however, sounded dull compared to an almost daily experience of Martyn's whose duties he said, involved waking up sailors and petty officers for their respective watches. Included was a Somali in charge of the greasers whose status entitled him to his own cabin which was located above Daniel's amidships.

"Lies there on his bunk with just a vest on he does!" chuckled the Deck Boy. "He's only a skinny little runt but you'd never believe your eyes, mun! It's *huge* it is! Stands up like a totem pole all black and shiny like pig's pudding! Must be ten inches long and nigh on as thick as my wrist! Pretends he's asleep he does but I know he's not cos I've seen him playin' with himself through his mirror!"

"Christ!" exclaimed Daniel. "Why don't you tell the Bo'sun or somebody?"

"Cos they'd only take the piss, mun! Besides, everybody knows about the perverted Yussef Rashid. Ianto thinks it's hilarious.; says he'll be up on the boat deck burning paint off in a couple of days and on the given signal he'll nip in with his blow torch and give his taters a blast. Burn it off at the roots so to speak, he says."

"I know the shifty-eyed little sod," frowned Daniel. "He keeps giving me funny looks as well. Trouble is, you don't know who's kidding and who isn't, do you?"

Their thoughts were mutual over that matter and they began listing who most concerned them. Yussef, the Head Greaser topped the list which even, due to the many inferences voiced in Daniel's quarters, included the Skipper himself.

"But don't mention a word about what I've said, especially in front of Billy because it's a touchy subject at present," advised Daniel. "Besides, Reno says the old man wouldn't risk his reputation even though he reckons he is a bit that way inclined. But he's one to talk because he's already admitted to Jock that watching me undress turns him on, the fat creep! But then Jock had a go at him and said that all males born Med' and Middle East way suffer with confused gender and that's why their mothers encourage them to grow moustaches as soon as they're in their teens."

"I've never heard about that!" chuckled Martyn.

"Nor has anybody else," replied Daniel. "And Billy really got himself into trouble by asking Jock if the Scots originated from that area!"

"What did Jock say?"

"He called him an uneducated twat of a Teddy Boy and asked him why he'd asked such a barmy question and Billy said he's seen a film about Bonnie Prince Charlie and the Scots not only had moustaches and beards but they wore skirts as well."

107

"And Jock belted him, I'll bet?"

"No but he told him that when he got back from the galley that night he'd have with him his rolling pin covered in margarine."

"I'll bet that Billy just laughed at him, eh?"

"Yeah, behind his back he did but I noticed he went to bed wearing two pairs of underpants and his trousers."

The youths were still laughing when the elderly Somali who'd showed kindness to Daniel following the Chief Steward incident, appeared from below and went to the rail.

"Do you know him?" asked Daniel.

"Oh yes," replied the Deck Boy. "A decent old stick is Abu. He's been like a dad to me. Warned me about the problems when going ashore if I didn't look out like. Pro's, booze and the suchlike. But at any rate, I wasn't intending to rush into things. To take my time like."

Once more they were in agreement and the word 'ashore' brought them to the subject of possible destinations.

"Nobody's sure," said Martyn, "but Ianto says the officers will likely know by now. Perhaps the Third Mate will let on if you're so friendly like?"

"We're not exactly best mates," returned Daniel, "but if he's about when I'm cleaning tomorrow I'll ask him. As long as he lets me get a word in edgeways that is!"

"What sort of schooling have you had then, boyo?"

It was customary for an officer to vacate his cabin during its daily clean but the Third, seemingly untroubled by convention or difference in rank, appeared to enjoy staying around to chat with his daily visitor.

"Elementary school and no further education, eh? Well, there's plenty of time for you to make up for that if you so wish?"

On this occasion, in contrast to the previous day's meeting, the Third's manner began more stiffly but as he continued, any check on how he expressed himself quickly faded and he was in full flow again.

Unlike Daniel, he said he'd taken and passed the non-compulsory Eleven Plus examination which had led to him attending one of the best schools in Swansea. His praise for the particular school however, was not just for its high educational standard but oddly, for the 'situation' of the building itself. Hardly imposing structurally but in such an elevated position looking out over the town and Swansea Bay, that its pupils were inspired even before they'd opened their first text book, he said.

"A view that's inspired many a soul! A view that has a student looking *outward* from his very first day!" he enthused. "Of little importance, a school's situation some may scoff. But take them to the top of a mountain and see their faces light up as they look about them! The effect of an elevated school is similar in that it stimulates the pupil to look outward; to travel both mentally and physically if you follow, young man?"

"Er – yes, sir," began Daniel, wondering how he might interrupt this waffle and edge in the question of 'what was their destination?' "I, er – do know what you mean cos it so happens that my school was on top of a hill and the views did kind of make us look outward as you say. But – but, while it did make me want to travel, I honestly didn't know where I wanted to travel to and that, sir, was almost as frustrating as now, sir, not knowing our destination."

How cunning was that? He'd slipped in the question tidily but the Third wasn't the best of listeners and seemed completely unaware of the deviously-angled question.

"The phrase *outward looking*," he began again, "means simply that one so gifted sees more than what is immediately beneath his nose, thereby enriching himself with what may be on offer along life's path. And – and I don't mean just material things such as a nice house, a new car and so on. Material things are okay but never so rewarding as say, discovering the love of one's life unexpectedly in the most unusual of circumstances as did . . ."

The youth's vacant expression had been noted and the Third began an apologetic ramble which only served to further distance his listener.

"And yes, son, you might well be wondering why I, one who is fortunate enough to be gifted with forward vision and set to enjoy the benefits of being thus equipped; just why the blazes has my life amounted to little more than plying the oceans for something as mundane as monetary needs?"

Daniel's thoughts hadn't been remotely along those lines but if the officer noticed as much, he was still intent on continuing his self-pitying monologue, his tone and expression suggesting that something deeply pained him.

"It hasn't been all bad. Oh no! There were the good times before and after the war, so I'd be a liar to paint it all black. But what happens as the years roll by is that the boredom sets in. Yes – boredom and disenchantment with what once had so much appeal. *A life on the ocean wave* and all that sentimental tosh. Whoever penned that line wouldn't have had a clue as to what being cooped up in a tiny cabin such as this for over twenty years, a man's best years, his eager, anticipative, creative years is really like! The futility of it all! The waste of all that time leading to nowhere! You show me a seaman who knows where he's going, boyo and I'll show you a bloody mermaid!"

His voice was now pitched and he was gesticulating wildly as he repeated himself.

"You show me a seaman who knows where he's going, boyo and – and . . ."

He appeared to run out of steam as he sank back into his chair.

Out of context maybe but the Third was asking the question that Daniel had almost given up attempting to slip in.

"Where, – er – where are we going, sir?" he enquired, seizing the opportunity presented. "I, er – mean . . . on this trip like? Where are we bound for, sir?"

"Where are we bound? You're asking me where are we bound?"

The officer's voice was now low and trembling, his expression so miserable as he turned to point at the framed words above his bureau, that Daniel wished he'd never asked.

"He tells us, boyo. with those few words he tells us where we're all bound. *And death shall have no dominion.* He's telling us that we're all on a course leading to a place where all tormented souls can exist without fear of mortal pain and mortal termination. That's what he's telling us."

Another prolonged stay in the Third Mate's cabin (as reported by Billy) was once again the subject of much derision on Daniel's return to his accommodation and despite his reluctance to tell all that had been discussed, he finally gave in.

Nothing untoward, or as Billy queried *sexual* happened he told them much to their howls of disbelief.

"But he talks about things I can't understand a lot of the time and I feel, er – uncomfortable."

"What kind of things, sonny?" asked Reno mischievously. "What kind of things does he talk about?"

"I don't remember, er, most of it but – but he finished with saying something about us all being tormented souls and how we were heading for mortal termination. Sort of scary the way he came out with it, whatever it means?"

"'eadin' for mortal termination?" echoed Billy. "Did 'e let on if mortal termination's any-fuckin'-where near South America?" he ridiculed. "I told you 'e were a nutcase! What else did the loony 'ave to say?"

"Er – not a lot but one minute he's talking normal and the next he's almost crying," replied Daniel, bringing a stern warning from Jock.

"It'll nae be in your interest, laddie, considerin' your station aboard, to spread disrespectful gossip about your seniors! Any more o' it an' I'll be reportin' you to the Chief Steward!"

"That's right, Jock!" supported Reno. "Report the little bugger to the Chief Steward for disrep . . . disrect . . .er . . . for gossiping!"

Daniel did regret his unwilling disclosures. Even more so when returning to the Third's cabin the following day when the man showed no sign of his previous disturbed behaviour other than appearing anxious to explain himself while indicating the framed verse.

"You've heard of the man who wrote those words have you, boyo? Dylan Thomas, poet, playwright and broadcaster?"

"Er – I – I've heard of him I think, sir," replied Daniel, unsure of himself but after being caught out on the Bill Haley question, keen not to be christened ship's dunce.

"The most highly regarded Welsh poet of all time and you only *think* you've heard of him?" scolded the Third good-naturedly.

"Well, er – we must have been taught something about him because our headmaster was Welsh but we got more Shakespeare than anything else, him being sort of local like. Yes, he was definitely more inclined towards Shakespeare."

"And your inclinations, boyo, literature-wise? Anybody, anything ever got you thinking?"

Daniel's love of comics ranging from the *Dandy* and *Beano* to the *Film Fun* and *Eagle* came to mind but he sensed that the question pertained to more serious literature.

"Er – not anything that comes to mind," he answered eventually. "But I've always enjoyed a good read and, er – putting compositions together like. Not sure about poetry though. It never really did much for me and being made look daft when reciting in front of the class and suddenly forgetting the next verse like."

"That's a pity," tut-tutted the Third. "I'll warrant many a pupil has been persuaded against poetry because some inadequate teacher made a fool out of him in front of the class. We've not all got photographic memories have we? A teacher's real job is to get his pupil to look into what the poet is saying and how he says it. Now, if your teacher had gone about it like that and used the likes of Thomas in the process; he'd likely have won you over rather than put you off. I say, the likes of

Thomas, because the man was a revolutionary in written, artistic expression, a genius whose work has gained millions of admirers who, to this very day . . ."

Daniel's stifled yawn had been noted.

"I've done it again, eh, boyo? I've snared you in my web and am acting just like the teacher I've just criticized! We Welsh do have a tendency to rabbit on a bit though you'll likely have noticed since coming aboard," he joked apologetically. "So don't let me keep you if you've other duties to attend to."

"Oh no – I've finished unless the Steward finds me something else to do. I was only going back to me cabin and . . ."

"And my re-introducing you to the art of poetry? Has it done anything to undo the damage inflicted at school?"

"Oh, er – yes, sir, thank you," lied Daniel. "I've been quite interested in what you've been saying. Like you, er – say. It could have been made much more interesting if they'd tried like. There's got to be something in it if this poet chap you spoke about has got so many people liking it. Millions, you say? Just like Johnny Ray and Frank Sinatra; millions of fans like?"

"Similar in one respect I grant you," replied the officer thoughtfully. "My lady friend certainly admired him in that way. In the way that a fan follows passionately a singer or film star. I – I've not spoken to you about Heloise, my lady friend before have I, boyo? She fitted the term *fan* in that respect. Being a fan of his *is* tremendously important to her. She wanted so much to be part of the legend he became. In fact, in an indirect kind of way, she *was* part of the legend. Me too, once she'd woven me into her fanciful ways. Good at that, is Heloise. Casting spells over others in order to get their involvement. And without my involvement, which gave me much pleasure I must admit, without my involvement she'd never have got so near to him as she did. But I don't regret being instrumental in that. No! Not for one moment have I regretted helping her on those occasions which gave her so much joy at being so close to the legend. Not for one moment!"

The uncomfortable silence following this particular outburst only eased when Daniel conceived that he seemed actually to be talking to himself (as was often the case he began realize) thus excusing him of trying to respond to an oration mostly beyond his ability to comprehend.

"What I'm so poorly attempting to explain, young man," he continued as if suddenly aware of the youth's presence, "is that Heloise *did*, in a very minor way albeit, become part of the legend. Her involvement, mine too, entitled us to claim that of all the countless fans, it was she and I whom he couldn't help but be aware of!"

His eyes, burning so deeply into Daniel's, told that this obscure revelation would bring questions but delaying any, added, "He – he must have been aware! Just had to have been!"

"You, er . . .? You and your, er – lady friend met up with this poet chap did you, sir?" asked Daniel while really not wanting to be there but respectfully feigning interest.

"Get to meet him? Did we get to meet him you ask?"

The officer appeared to have retreated into himself again as he answered distantly, "Not – not exactly but – but that we were on the fringe of the legend is - is how best I can explain our involvement. But Heloise tended to claim much more than that, such was her imagination and need to be in the picture, so to speak."

Something he'd said seemed to prompt the Third to open and delve into a bureau drawer from which he produced a photograph.

"I can see that all this is hardly of interest to you, son," he sighed while inviting his visitor to look at the photo. "But my mention of Heloise's *need* to be in the picture becomes obviously apparent in this snap look you now. For here she is doing exactly that while walking in Laugharne in close proximity to the man himself. Our favourite photo this one and if you study it closely, you'll possibly note his, I think, resemblance to yourself; as a young man that is or maybe my memory is playing tricks on me? What's your opinion, son?" he added, thrusting the photo under Daniel's nose.

"He – he's getting on a bit," replied the youth, studying the snap which depicted a rather paunchy man who, by the frown on his heavily-jowled face wasn't pleased at being confronted by the camera. His tousled, curly hair and unkempt dress, baggy trousers, crumpled jacket and open-necked shirt reminded him of the farming types back home. Taken in a busy street, the photo showed that immediately behind and almost brushing the man's left shoulder, walked a strikingly attractive young brunette looking nervously into the camera.

"Very beautiful my Heloise, eh, boyo?" chuckled the officer as if reading his mind.

"Er – yes but – but the man? I – I wouldn't say that he . . ."

"Looks anything like you?" completed the other. "Well, as I said, it was his younger self that I was referring to but a few more years and a lot of boozing and you'll likely catch up with him I'm thinking," he smiled while searching through the drawer again. "You'll see what I mean," he announced producing a newspaper cutting with a head and shoulders inset whom the officer went on to say was the man in question but in his earlier years.

"Now do you see a likeness to yourself, son?" he asked irritably.

"Er, no – I – I can't say that I do," replied Daniel meekly. "It – it is quite faded though so it's very difficult to make out . . ."

"Of course it's faded!" retorted the Third. "Heloise was only in her early teens when she started collecting them for her album! Only in her early teens!" he repeated in an increasingly fretful tone. "It's bound to be faded!"

"Is – is that your lady friend, sir?" asked Daniel, still feigning interest to appease the officer as he pointed to the girl in the photograph. "Where – where is she now, sir? Back home in, er – Swansea?"

Suddenly preoccupied with his typewriter, the Third answered quietly, "I'll not know Heloise's whereabouts until our first port of call. Not until our first port of call."

Chapter 9

Shore Leave

"You are listening to Radio Demerara, British Guiana!"

The bouncing tone of the voice calling out from Jock's wireless made one feel that the announcer was about to burst into song. Beneath the fiercest sun that Daniel had yet experienced, the *Roundcape* traversed a mill-pond sea devoid of any sign that this day would be any different to the last ocean-locked nine.

"Looks like they're sending the navy to check us out, Dai. Leanin' towards Communism these days I hear tell!"

"Navy be buggered! Through these binoculars it's a bloody dredger. Shallow waters in these parts."

Daniel joined in the horizon search with enthusiasm. Even some of the more laid-back seamen were now craning their necks for that first glimpse of land, he noted: the name 'Georgetown' tumbling frequently from their lips.

Drrrrrrring! Drrrrrrring!

Seconds after the order from the bridge, the rhythmic thump of her engine which to Daniel's ears, had not missed a beat since Cardiff, began to slow. Next, the rattle of the anchor chain caused him to ask why stop now when they were still out of sight of land? Why sit there in this crippling heat with 'Georgetown, British Guiana', lying intriguingly just over the blooming horizon?

The Pilot, they told him. They'd stopped to await the Pilot. It was kids' play aiming the ship over thousands of miles of open ocean but the last bit was tricky. It would take local know-how for that. So out came the Pilot's launch: growing from a dot in the shimmering distance into a vessel which but for the shiny black faces beaming broad white smiles up at them, could well have been the craft that Brumpud had arrived on. Even the man who came aboard to guide them in was black. Fascinating stuff.

Coloured men with authority! No European officer wielding his cane as in the films. Not a white face among them.

Within minutes, the pulsating sound of the prop' told them they were underway again, following the trail of the homeward-bound launch across that sea of glass.

Suddenly, the horizon changed to what appeared to Daniel to be an endless row of palms growing out of the sea. But this was it, it seemed. This flat, unspectacular coastline was that of British Guiana. Part of the vast continent of South America.

But it was still very exciting! So much so that he momentarily forgot that his main hope was for a speedy about-turn and then home. He could see beaches now and they were entering the mouth of a large river; the Demerara, he was informed. A name that reminded him of the large-grained, sticky, brown sugar that his mother sometimes bought. They passed a rusting old dredger in midstream, her crew staring blankly up at them, the weariness of their hot and isolated task etched on their faces. A small Esso tanker flying the red ensign swept past them downstream; the *Roundcape's* Liverpool registration bringing acknowledgements from rail-hanging sailors. The ship brought Daniel's brother to mind. He was serving aboard Esso super tankers in the Persian Gulf. Watching the vessel slip elegantly by, he recalled his words.

'Fit to eat your dinner off, the decks of a super tanker. But don't get caught for one of those bloody tramps if you want any kind of comfort!'

Amidst the greenery on the distant banks, he now spotted the occasional building. And yes! After all of those days at sea, a bus! Well, a bus of sorts, brightly painted, hurtling along on what must be a road just above the river's edge. His thoughts on seeing the vehicle took him back to the bus ride in Cardiff which would have led to him avoiding so much hell had he not relented and caught another one back to the docks. Consequently, during those miserable hours of seasickness and persecution, he'd vowed that if given a choice again, in whatever the circumstances, he'd risk it and put the hell that was a sea life well and truly behind him.

Back to the more tolerable present. More vessels were coming downriver. A small coaster, her all-black crew busily securing the hatches before the open sea, followed by a 'three island' type freighter (three superstructures) very similar to the *Roundcape* but much lower in the water. Registered in Liberia, her crew appeared to be of mixed nationality. Daniel's counterpart aboard, a young oriental, gazed, dishcloth in hand, across at him from her pantry until a hot, foreign tongue from within caused him to scramble out of sight.

"You too!" yelled their own Chief Steward standing authoritatively at the pantry door.

"Grab a mop and bucket and get down below! We don't want any jumped-up customs official saying we British live like pigs!"

So a disgruntled Daniel arrived at his first port of call mop in hand in the dimly-lit confines of the ship's storeroom. His first glimpses of Georgetown were achieved by dashing up the ladder when the Steward wasn't about, taking in as much as he could while cursing the man for his bloody-mindedness. Eventually, he was summoned up to fetch over the midday meal, by which time they were anchored mid-river, opposite the port.

His first reaction to the scene before him was that the whole waterfront had been quaintly assembled as a setting for one of those classic Walt Disney real-life films in glorious Technicolor. The port itself was hardly bustling but on one wharf between the few ships tied up alongside, a market, teeming with a mass of colourfully-dressed patrons was in progress. The wooden, rickety warehouse buildings behind appeared to be held together by a haphazard assortment of company and advertising signs, dominated by a gigantic Coca-Cola hoarding. Through the gaps and to the sides of this ramshackle but picturesque waterfront, could be seen a town of both modern and period buildings rising out of lush, tropical vegetation.

"Why aren't we goin' alongside?" Billy asked Jock, while queuing at the galley.

"Dinnae fuckin' ask me!" retorted the Cook, snatching his containers. "Besides, seein' how keen the Mate was to know how you came by that swollen lip that last night in Cardiff, I'd reckon there's one Ted aboard who'll nae get to see what that port over yonder has to offer. That's unless," he added with a smirk, "you've mebbe charmed yourself into the old man's good books along the way?"

Before a fuming Billy could retaliate, Big Paddy shouted from the opposite serving hatch.

"There'll be no shore leave hereabouts for any man, so the Bo'sun tells. Says we're goin' eighty miles upriver to Mackenzie to take on bauxite."

'Bauxite'. The word spread like wildfire among the crew, their despondent looks eventually causing Daniel to ask Billy, "Bauxite? What's bauxite then?"

The Assistant Steward had only just discovered what bauxite was himself but typically he delivered his pessimistic reply with a voice of experience.

"It's the mineral ore they makes aluminium from. Looks like cement and feels like cement. It gets in your 'air, eyes, nostrils, in your grub, in your clobber, in your bed, behind your foreskin and then in every other fuckin' place you can think . . .! Oh Christ! My clobber! My fuckin' suit! It's been through the mill as it is but this will ruin it . . . unless . . .? Unless . . .? Compensation! I could claim compensation!"

"What compensation's that?" asked Daniel.

"Dirt money, you twat! Dirt money! The sea lawyers aft 'ave already got their teeth into it!" replied Billy smugly. "Fuckin' dirt money."

The Cabin Boy's excitement over the forthcoming journey up that Guianean river was somewhat dulled by the thought of all that dirt at the end of it. He was still in deep contemplation of what had been said when later that afternoon he approached the rail to empty the slops pail. The split second it took him to realize his mistake, was a split second too late. The white-uniformed customs officers aboard their sleek, white launch below had neither time or room to escape the deluge of pantry waste cascading down on them. The glimpsed horror and anger on their faces had him literally shaking with fright as he returned to the pantry to proceed with his chores in the pretence that *nothing*, absolutely *nothing* had occurred.

But something *had* happened and minutes later a cough at the pantry door announced the arrival of the Chief Steward to tell him so.

"Have you recently emptied your pail over the side, son?"

"Er – yes."

"Weather or lea side?"

"Er – there was no wind blowing."

"So you had a choice did you? And you chose to chuck it over a boat full of boarding customs officials?"

"Can't say that I noticed anybody," lied Daniel hopelessly.

"Well, they bloody-well noticed you, son and they're not too bloody-well happy about it!"

The Chief led him out on deck by his ears where he proceeded to lecture him on international relations.

"See that colony of our dwindling empire over there, son? Well, it's riddled with anti-British Commies and you, son, have done more to further their cause in the last five minutes than any inflammatory speech by their independence-obsessed Doctor bloody Jagan! Now, get hold of your mop and bucket and get down there on the double and put right the international incident that you've just bloody-well sparked off!"

After the ordeal of scrambling down the ladder to clean up the launch under the uncomfortable glare of its bespattered occupants, Daniel's return to his shared cabin was no escape from his humiliation. While Jock rained a torrent of abuse at him for his stupidity, Billy and Reno rolled about their bunks splitting their sides.

"Christ, Danny boy!" howled Billy. "Is it right that the Guianese army are lined up on the banks wavin' their fuckin' spears at us?"

"Laddie!" barked Jock. "You've embarrassed the whole fuckin' ship! Customs officials are like ambassadors boarding an' expect a dignified reception!"

"Not a chewed pork chop 'roun' the lug 'ole!" joined in the cabin comedian. "But I 'ear tell that one of 'em quite took to an empty Kellogg's cornflake box. Chucked 'is own cap in the river an' went back ashore a fuckin' general 'e did!"

"It's nae laughin' matter!" thundered Jock. "I've known guys finish up in clink for less! In fact, it wouldnae surprise me if they didnae compound the ship until there's a government level apology an' even mebbe demand that the man involved be handed over to the fuckin' authorities!"

Daniel later began to worry that maybe there was some truth in the Scot's words because it wasn't until the afternoon of the following day that the *Roundcape* finally up-anchored and began the journey upriver. From then on however, everyone's interest was held by the scenery about them as Georgetown slipped away; its shantytown suburbs reducing to the odd landing stage and riverside shacks. After about a mile the roar of a seaplane which earlier had been on the river not far from their anchorage, disturbed their preoccupation as it swept over them heading inland.

The only other means of transport into the interior, it was said by one of the older hands, there being no metalled roads or railways connecting the main habitations.

They were now passing small, uninhabited islands dense with vegetation similar to the thickening jungle now evident on the Demerara's banks. At intervals, this dense growth gave way to reveal small settlements where bright-eyed children at play would wave to them from the water's edge. Occasionally, a jeep or a truck could be seen bumping along behind the trees but the main transport route was undoubtedly the river, upon which numerous craft ranging from primitive to motorised, scurried or lingered beneath a merciless tropical sun.

By late afternoon, the river had narrowed and the stretches of jungle between crude habitation had become longer and more dense. Animal and bird life was now more plentiful than human, the antics of small monkeys in the treetops and a multitude of beautifully coloured birds provided deck-lounging seamen with splendid entertainment until profuse overhanging foliage finally blocked out the last rays of sunlight. Then, almost as if the setting sun had been a cue, the creatures of the forest began an overture which, from the odd croak and chirrup, erupted into a full scale orchestration of grunts, whistles and howls which was to continue right through until dawn.

The journey which normally, it was said, could be made in twelve hours, was to take double that time. Delayed loading of other vessels and consequently no berth available in Mackenzie, was the reason given for them dropping anchor for the night in what resembled to Daniel on turning out next morning, a huge lake; one of several such anchorages, he learned, where vessels could pass each other on the widening river or await a berth being vacated at their destination.

As was apparent by the water-borne market surrounding the *Roundcape* that morning, the local natives used these anchorages to sell their wares to the ship's crews, their cries of, "You buy from me, man! Freshest fruit on the river, man!" piercing the still, morning air. The ship now carried two extra souls, the Pilot and a policeman, the latter having boarded off Georgetown, as was apparently customary for large, foreign vessels plying the colony's rivers.

"To keep us buggers from raping and pillaging!" joked Ianto. "And I wouldn't mind taking my hat off to one of them little darlings look you," he added, pointing to one particular canoe crewed by two smiling young river maidens immediately below.

"Hello, sexy! What a lovely pair of melons!" and an abundance of wolf whistles didn't appear to trouble the grinning policeman as he sat on a hatch, sipping tea. The entertainment was short-lived however, the water-borne marketers not staying around once aware that the seamen had little money and none whatever in the local currency; the few that had anything, saving it for a drink in Mackenzie should the Master not sub out so early in the trip?

Very soon after they'd watched a ship low in the water pass by heading downriver, her decks and superstructure coated with this light grey, powdery substance called bauxite, they were off again on the last stage of their journey. Nearing Mackenzie, Daniel noticed that the general light-heartedness of the crew seemed to fade as rumours of a ban on subs, gathered strength.

"Take care the locals dinnae rob you, laddie," advised a suspiciously cordial Jock. "Stay close to your cabin mates an' we'll see you come to no harm."

"Jocks' right, Danny boy," sided Billy. "An' mind you don't get struck across the wrong bit of action, else your cock'll 'ave dropped off by the time we gets back to Georgetown," he added with his usual tact.

"I'm not going to get stuck across anything," insisted Daniel.

"Then you'll nae have any use for that odd quid or two you're still carryin' I'm thinkin, eh, laddie?"

The badgering succeeded only in persuading Daniel that it might be wise to go ashore with his 'cabin mates'. The 'getting stuck across' bit, he took to be just part of their endless teasing and was, therefore, quite shocked when the Chief Steward appeared at the pantry door and began throwing packets of contraceptives among the crew.

"Not for you, son," he mumbled to Daniel. "Save yourself for a nice young virgin back home."

Brumpud joined in the scramble and promptly adorned the galley entrance with a bunch of inflated condoms. It was also rumoured that the Second Mate had found one floating in his soup later that day but, coming from Billy, who openly disliked the man, Daniel guessed that it was more likely wishful thinking rather than some prank by the eccentric but not stupid, ship's Cook.

At midday, they finally slipped into the bauxite port of Mackenzie but it was a long, hot afternoon before Daniel's ten-days-long prayer to set foot on a static surface once again, was answered. At first, all they could see alongside were the huge mounds of bauxite and the machinery for loading it onto the ships. The town, they were told, was some ten minutes walk from the loading wharfs along a riverside path. The policeman manning the gate at the end of it eyed them curiously as they passed through. Brumpud sported a bright, floral shirt but wore the same filthy chef's hat and trousers that he'd worked in since boarding. Jock had on the same clothes as he'd worn ashore in Cardiff as did Billy, his brilliant-red Teddy Boy suit looking completely outlandish in this tropical setting. Almost as eye-catching was the immaculate Reno in his Steward's whites impressively decorated with gold buttons and black epaulettes. He and Daniel, who, at the last minute had thrown on his training school uniform, suffered from Billy such witticisms as, 'Christ! They'll be puttin' out the buntin' when they gets wind that the governor general an' 'is aide are in town! Get on your knees, you colonial riff-raff! 'er majesty's most senior of Senior Assistant Stewards an' 'is entourage is comin'!' causing the pompous Maltese to fume every step of the way.

Their first stop was a ship's general provisions store where all four chipped in from what little money the Skipper had begrudgingly handed over, to purchase a bottle of scotch whisky; the Chinese proprietor looking decidedly alarmed when Jock proceeded to guzzle from it on the spot and began meaningfully pointing towards the door with a gleaming meat cleaver. Led once again by the nonchalant Scot, the troupe resumed their trek into Mackenzie, passing the whisky around as they walked.

Most of the town's buildings were of wooden construction and raised on stilts. The rainy season apparently brought heavy flooding to the area necessitating the raised houses and shops plus a network of deep drainage ditches directed towards the river.

125

Daniel likened the place to a Wild West town but more scattered and seemingly without any main street. The bar where many of the *Roundcape's* crew had assembled, was simply a mid-town shack with a serving hatch, its patrons sitting around at tables on an adjacent area of concrete. Following a discussion with a girl behind the counter, a frowning Jock returned to their table with a bottle of 'jungle juice', the local rum. Although a British colony, it appeared that British currency was not generally acceptable and the *Roundcape's* crew were having to do a lot of bartering. Jock was highly indignant over this, especially as the Chinese storekeeper had accepted their money without comment yet this chit of a girl only took it by overcharging for the liquor. Fired by the already depleted whisky, he took a long swig at the rum and began ranting about the 'miserable illiterates who dared to call themselves citizens of the empire!'

The local populace it appeared, were two-thirds of African descent, the remainder being made up of Chinese and Indians (Amerindians). The Africans especially, eyed the seamen unfavourably and it may have been these baleful looks which brought on Reno's sudden stomach ache and his need to go back to the ship. Daniel too was beginning to feel uncomfortable but when he made some excuse to accompany the Assistant Steward, Jock wasn't having it.

"There's nothin' wrong wi' you that a wee drop o' this'll nae put right, laddie!" he insisted, topping up the Cabin Boy's glass. Daniel had supped very little of the throat-burning whisky but found the rum decidedly more palatable. However, in mind of the somewhat precarious riverside path back to the ship, he took his time over the rum and declined a further refill.

Minutes after Reno's departure, his seat was taken by the *Roundcape's* Apprentice Engineer, an amiable young Anglo-Indian known aboard as 'Izzy', who was already a little worse for drink. He, Jock and Billy got into a huddle and minutes later, Jock told Daniel and a very drowsy Brumpud to drink up as they were moving on to find a more lively venue.

After a short stroll around town, Jock and Izzy approached an insidious-looking character sitting astride a bike on a street corner. After a mumbled exchange, the man indicated for them to follow and began cycling slowly away. On the outskirts of town, they stopped at a small landing stage on a quieter stretch of the Demerara. There, they were introduced to a boatman who pointed to scattered lights on the river's far bank and told them he would do the round trip for three BG dollars. Jock accepted but told him that payment would only be forthcoming on the return journey. All present, including their guide and his bike climbed into the boat and after ten minutes rowing helped along by a tipsy rendering of *A Slow Boat To China* by a suddenly awake Brumpud, arrived safely on the opposite bank.

Music and the sound of female laughter rang out increasing Daniel's concern as to exactly where they might be taking him? The lights they'd observed earlier came from a group of raised shacks nearby. On reaching them, their guide climbed the wooden steps of the largest and best lit building which, judging from the noise echoing from within, was where the action was taking place, and went inside. Suddenly, to Daniel's dismay, out of the shack poured a laughing, whooping procession of women of all age and size.

"Nooooo!" he yelled as two of them flung their arms about him and began showering him with kisses.

Brumpud too seemed to have been taken by surprise but grabbing the pimp's bike he leaped into the saddle and began zigzagging around the shacks with a huge woman in hot pursuit.

"You like me, mon? You come my house, mon?"

Each visitor had at least three ladies begging to be their companion, demonstrating their charms with unrestrained fondling and whispered promises.

"Come wid me, young sailor boy! You never forget Sadie an' dat's a promise!"

Daniel struggled in vain to escape 'Sadie's' grip as a warm palm caressed his stomach through his unbuttoned shirt. Even Billy looked overwhelmed by so much attention.

"Alright! Alright, girls! Keep your cool 'til - 'til we gets inside!" he pleaded.

Brumpud reappeared at high speed out of the darkness ringing his bell. Sportingly, he stopped and allowed his exhausted pursuer to mount the crossbar and was off again. A scream and an "Oh bugger me!" and the crazy spectacle disappeared into one of the drainage ditches. Leaping in after them, the unamused pimp retrieved his bike leaving the comical pair rolling about in fits of laughter at the bottom of the cavity.

"Come on wi' you, laddie!" called out Jock as he ascended the shack stairway along with Billy and Izzy and several of the women.

"No. You come Sadie's house," insisted Daniel's newfound admirer, wrapping her arms firmly around him.

"I – I can't. Me – me mates want me up there," gulped Daniel, pulling himself free to climb after them.

Arriving at a small veranda, he gingerly pushed open the door and peered inside. To his relief, nothing improper was yet happening in that dimly-lit room which was half filled with a large bed upon which his three shipmates and most of the girls were sitting or lying as bottles of beer were being handed around. His bike propped up against a chest of drawers, the grumbling pimp was trying to free a sticking brake block with a table knife. A loud cheer greeted the youth and an attractive young black girl stepped forward to lead him to a chair. A gramophone was blasting out a song which had been very popular in Britain during his time at the training school.

"Down on the Caribbean that's not a dream you're seein' when you dance with the lady with a smiiiiiile!"[12] sang the man appropriately as a bottle of jungle juice was passed around. Another cheer rang out as a rather heavily-built girl slid off the bed and began swaying to the catchy rhythm.

"Gerrum-off!" went up the cry and in a trice she'd removed her blouse and bra to three hearty, *"Ooooooohs!"* Her back was

---

[12] Down In The Caribbean. Written by Mitchell Toruk 1953. Sung by various artists.

towards Daniel but Jock, noting his perplexed expression roared, "Show the laddie! Show the laddie! Show the laddie your tits!"

"Noooo!" protested the youth as the huge, pendulous breasts slapped warm and moist against his face.

"Give 'er a nibble, Danny boy!" guffawed Billy.

"Tink we got a virgin here, girls?" laughed the woman depositing herself on the embarrassed youth's lap. "Tink he's mebbe a little shy or perhaps it's somebody a little younger he's after?" chanted the woman, making room for another girl to sprawl on the already overburdened Cabin Boy. Meanwhile, Jock and Izzy had selected their partners, the Scot's curious choice being a middle-aged lady with horn-rimmed spectacles whom he was addressing as 'mother'. As they exited, Billy, looking suddenly dejected went to follow them out on his own.

"Where – where are you going?" asked a flustered Daniel, desperate not to be left to cope alone.

"She wants four dollars and I've only got ten bob left," replied Billy miserably, while pointing to the vexed-looking girl who only minutes ago had been in his arms.

"I know what!" he added with a smirk. "I can stay an' watch you with them two for a cheap thrill, that's if you don' mind like?"

"I – I'm not doing anything," replied Daniel struggling frantically to break free of his captors. "I – I'm not in the blooming mood."

"Tell 'em you're fuckin' broke an' they'll soon let go," remarked Billy petulantly. "'ow much dosh 'ave you got on you anyway?"

"Just a quid and enough cash to chip in for the boat ride back, that's all."

"Well, if you're not goin' to 'ave a dabble, you might just as well lend me that quid cos I'm really up for it if this bint'll get 'er knickers off for thirty bob!"

"Of course she will," interjected the pimp, still labouring with his damaged bike. "Thirty bob's worth more than four BG dollars," he said knowledgeably. "An' anyway, mon, even if she wore any knickers she'll get 'em off for one pound an' you can use de ten bob to settle up wid me for my bike here. Dis wheel's out of true since your fat friend had de accident just now. It's distorted, look for yourself, mon."

Surprised by both, the pimp's comprehension of local exchange rates and his sudden audacity, Billy's response took a little longer than usual.

"Ten . . . ten fuckin' bob to settle up with you?" he eventually shrieked. "It weren't me that buggered it up! Fuck you and your fuckin' bike!"

The pair squared up to each other and only the girl's intervention cooled the situation. A compromise it seemed, was better than having the place wrecked by two brawling men and no fee at all.

"Okay – okay," she sighed. "Give us what money you got, an' we'll pay for the bike later. Only ten minutes, mind, cos I've got better tings to do wid my time," she added, lying back on the bed and pulling her skirt up in a businesslike manner to prove that the pimp was indeed, a well-informed man.

"Rosie! For heaven's sake!" one of Daniel's captors seemed none too happy with this vulgar exhibition and, to the Cabin Boy's relief, sprang up and fled from the room. The other girl seemed to be about to follow her but instead rose and began coaxing him towards the bed.

"I – I'm not in the blooming mood!" he protested again, pulling himself free as she drunkenly collapsed alongside her uninhibited friend.

"Oh yeah!" whooped Billy. "A threesome! Just what I always wanted!" he yelled ecstatically.

"I – I'll leave you to it then," said Daniel, anxious not to be involved and making a beeline for the door.

"Hang on a mo', Danny boy! A favour for your old shipmate?"

Daniel paused, knowing full well what the 'favour' would be.

"If you're not 'avin' a dabble yourself, lend us that quid will you, mate?" pleaded Billy.

130

Reluctantly, Daniel handed over a pound note and dashed out onto the veranda where he collided with Jock's pistoning rump.

"Clumsy wee bastard!" roared the Scot lashing back at him with what was mercifully a bare foot but which, nevertheless drove the boy back into the hut where he landed with a resounding crash upon the pimp's bike.

"Changed your mind then 'ave you?" quipped Billy.

Daniel groaned and lay there for a few painful moments. Eventually, it occurred to him that he oughtn't be hanging around while Billy might want privacy but, glancing up, he saw that the two women were lying on the bed chuckling as their partner to be was painstakingly arranging his Teddy Boy suit upon a clothes hanger. Despite his painful fall, the absurd picture of the shirt-tailed youth finicking with his beloved clobber in such circumstances, brought a smile to the Cabin Boy's face.

"Fuck off!" snapped Billy.

Trying to keep a straight face, Daniel clambered to his feet and this time, with caution, made his exit.

"You come within an inch o' me again, laddie, an' I'll break your fuckin' neck!" Jock barked after him as he flew down the stairs.

Spanner in hand, the pimp was on his way back up. Pausing at the bottom, Daniel awaited the inevitable eruption which culminated in a loud scream as the unfortunate man came crashing back down.

"Are – are you alright, mate?" ventured Daniel.

Groaning and cursing, the pimp limped off into the darkness.

With little else to do, the Cabin Boy strolled over to the ditch where moonlight illuminated another comical situation, that of Brumpud and his large, jolly companion having made themselves comfortable, were chattering amicably over the inevitable bottle of rum.

"Wanna swig, Cabin Boy?" offered the Cook which Daniel declined then, after a brief whisper, the couple climbed out of the ditch and entered a hut not many yards distant. For five minutes or so, Daniel stood glaring at the building, despising the

Cook for having sunk to the same level as his depraved shipmates.

"Oooooooh! Bloody lovely! It's spiffin', my wench!"

Brumpud's sudden exclamation didn't have a sexual ring so a curious Daniel thought it okay to venture up the hut's stairway and peer inside.

"Bloody delicious, my wench! Better curry than I could produce at such short notice!"

Daniel was smiling again as he watched the old rascal tucking into a heaped plate of food, the broad smile on the woman's face showing delight at having found her partner's true appetite.

An hour later, all were aboard for the return crossing. As they pushed off, the women called out their goodbyes.

"See you, mother!" called out a for once happy Jock.

"Best I've ever had!" shouted an exuberant Izzy.

"Me too!" belched Brumpud loosening his belt while a glazed-eyed Billy grunted something incomprehensible and flopped to the bottom of the boat. Nearing the opposite bank, the oarsman stopped rowing and began mumbling to the pimp who was outraged more it seemed, by the damage to his bike than his manhandling by Jock.

"He want you pay now!" demanded the angry cyclist. "Pay for de boat now an' I'm wantin' sometin' for de repairs!" he added, thumping the bike's saddle.

"You'll get your cut frae the lassies," snarled Jock, handing the boatman a pound note.

The pimp simply scowled back in silence but his companion, after examining the note in the moonlight, thrust it back into the Scot's hand saying, "Foreign! I not take foreign! You give me three BG dollars!"

The boat rocked uncomfortably as Jock stood up to reason with the man.

"Look, Jimmy! This is a British pound! Worth a fuckin' sight more than three o' your BG dollars! Any bank'll change it for you!"

"Man, him not deal with bank!" intervened the pimp.

Jock pointed towards the lights of Mackenzie and growled, "The only fuckin' bank he need concern himself wi' at this particular moment in time is that river bank yonder!"

For a moment it seemed that the Scot's vehement personality had won the day but no sooner had the boatman took to his oars again, he swung the boat round and began rowing back across the river.

"Blimey!" exclaimed Brumpud. "I don't think I can manage any puddin'!"

Jock however, didn't find the matter humorous.

"Alright, Jimmy!" he threatened the pimp, grabbing his precious bike and lifting it above his head. "Tell your buddy to turn aroun' or else this goes to the bottom!"

In a flash, the pimp was up and reaching for his machine, everybody yelling as the boat began to list with the sudden movement. Intended or not, into the water went the bike together with its owner, plus Jock and Billy. Only the combined weight of the boatman and his remaining passengers clinging to the boat's lifting side, saving it from totally capsizing. Even before they were stable, Izzy was reaching out and hauling the unfortunates to safety and within minutes of completing the rescue operation a much subdued assembly, all but the pimp that is, who sobbed bitterly over the loss of his bike, were once again heading for Mackenzie.

On landing, the boatman miserably accepted the pound and vague promises of compensation for the bike were made.

"You can't miss 'er, mate," Billy assured the pimp when he demanded the name of their ship. "She's the *HMS Victory*, she's pink with green spots an' 'as ten stacks!"

Walking back to the docks, Daniel shuddered at what might have been his fate, a non-swimmer, had he gone into that river along with the others. The craziest night of his life he told himself following his bedraggled shipmates up the gangplank, wondering if they might be in trouble arriving back in such a state? But the night was by no means over yet it became apparent as he stepped aboard.

A throng of drunken seamen were assembled beneath the bridge walk from where the First Mate appeared to be challenging all-comers. Mr Purdoe, usually a reserved and well-spoken man, seemed to have forgotten his status and was suddenly the Cockney tough-guy.

"Let's be 'avin' yer then! Not a bugger among yer would last a minute wiv me!" he bragged, swaying unsteadily, his fists raised. "Come up 'ere and take a real man on!"

His captivated audience parted to allow someone through. It was Gozo. Muscular but one of the shortest men aboard, the expressionless AB climbed the bridge stairway as casually as if he was going for a spell at the wheel.

The unsteady Mate blinked with surprise at the man's determined approach but quickly gathered his wits and took a boxer-like stance.

"Here, sucker!" he rasped, sticking out and tapping his chin contemptuously. "Hit me right here!"

Gozo did exactly that. The *Roundcape's* First Officer appearing to lift a few inches before dropping out of sight behind the covered walkway like the much-punished baby in a Punch and Judy show. That entertainment over, the ship burst into song.

"Breeeead of heeeeeaven! Breeeead of heeeeeaven! Feeeeed me 'til I want no moooooore!"

The harmony petered out as attention was drawn to the Third Mate and the Fourth Engineer climbing unsteadily aboard.

"Fuckin' marvellous what a few tots'll do!" laughed Billy, still dripping wet from his ducking. "Turned the Mate into a would-be prize fighter an' them two into a couple of piss-'eads!"

"Show me the way to go hooooome," chorused the crew as Big Paddy helped Edgar up the last few feet of the gangplank.

The Skipper, now on the bridge walk with the Chief Steward tending the Mate glared down at the two boarders.

"Breeeead of heeeeeaven! Breeeead of heeeeeaven . . . !"

Throats lubricated by the so-called 'Jungle Juice' now being passed around, the jungle backwater was suddenly Cardiff Arms Park on big match day.

Daniel watched in amazement. Only the Chief Steward incident had marred an otherwise trouble-free trip to date and now, all hell was breaking out! The officers at least, he'd expected to retain some sense of dignity but it seemed that the only two people of rank still sober were the Skipper and curiously, the Chief Steward. Not wishing to be involved should things get out of hand, the Cabin Boy decided to slip away from the explosive scene and was about to enter the alleyway to his cabin, when a familiar voice called out to him.

"Not so quick, boyo! me an' old Dai here are in need of a strong coffee!"

The Third Mate and the Fourth Engineer were having a smoke on the rail.

"Er- sorry. It's much too late," replied Daniel apologetically. "The pantry'll be locked up and besides, the Chief Steward doesn't look any too happy!"

The Third drew on his cigarette and chuckled.

"Now he's a fine bugger to find fault with the likes of those enjoyin' a little drink, eh, Edgar? Could well have shot the boy here when he was on his bender I'm thinkin'. Might never have set eyes on that village home of his again this boy, Edgar. Did you know that, Dai? Boy here hails from a valley as green as Cwmdonkin Park over there!" gushed the tipsy officer pointing across the river to where a wilderness lay silhouetted against a moonlit sky.

"Dai here's a valley-man, in't that right, Dai?"

The old Engineer nodded and coughed a yes, then raised his eyes to meet Daniel's for the first time.

"Whereabouts are you from, boyo?" he asked quietly.

"Not so green and pleasant as yours is Edgar's valley these days," interrupted the Third, winking mischievously at Daniel. "Edgar's brook got sludged up years ago. An' even the birds cough 'emselves to sleep, eh, old timer? Even the birds cough 'emselves to sleep?"

"It was 'ome to me," replied Edgar soberly, his eyes still upon Daniel.

"Maybe," returned the Third still grinning, "but people thereabouts aren't quite exactly content these days. Slag heaps are so high, there's no sun can get in, in't that right, Dai?"

"Compares well with your neck of the woods if wanderin' the local park is the closest you get to Nature!"

Edgar's sarcasm obviously related to something personal between them that would have been better not touched on seeing how quickly the Third's smile vanished.

"That was hardly called for, Edgar," he countered sharply. "A tot too much and you show your true colours, eh? So much for troubles shared. If that's your attitude, mun, I suggest you unburden yourself to the likes of the Cabin Boy here in future!"

"Oh! Cabin Boy is he now?" retorted the Engineer, his derisory smile broadening. "Thought 'e was the bard of Swansea a couple of days back?"

"Now there's bloody gratitude for you! Put the first smile on your face since Cardiff and you're belittling me over a throw-away comment about the boy's likeness!"

"If you're so bothered about how the boy sees you," Edgar was going for the jugular now, "then I think it'd be fuckin' wise not to involve him in your fantasy world, else he'll likely become as cynical as you've made me!"

"Well! You thankless old hypocrite! I'll not let you into my confidence again, I'll be damned if I will! I'll be off to my bunk if you've got everything off your chest? And I'll thank you for not seeking my company again!" concluded the Third, staggering slightly as he turned to set off in the direction of his cabin.

An alleyway light caught the twinkle in the old Welshman's eyes as he watched him go before turning to address Daniel.

"Well, that's cleared the air some, eh, boyo?" he chuckled. "Can't say that he really deserved it but he's begun to get me a tad rattled and it had to come out."

Daniel had felt uncomfortable throughout the bizarre exchange and had only stayed on deck in the hope that his cabin mates had fallen into a drunken slumber by the time he stripped off to take to his own bunk. About to go, Edgar spoke again, his speech only faintly slurred considering how inebriated he'd appeared on boarding.

"Well acquainted with our Mr Williams are you, boyo?" he asked. "You clean for him so he tells me and you have these little chats from time to time."

"Er – yeah. He – he's been friendly to me since I came aboard but – but . . .?"

"But what, boyo? You find Mr Williams friendly but *strange* on occasions, is that what you're tryin' to say, is it?"

"Er – sort of. But – but nothing that worries me any."

"And don't let him worry you, boyo! Don't let him!"

"He, er – seemed a bit drunk."

"He's drunk all of the time is our Mr Williams. Drunk with a passion that's consuming the sad bugger if you get my drift?" mumbled Edgar appearing sympathetic.

Because of his introverted nature, the Fourth Engineer had been nicknamed 'Edgar the Silent' by Billy. But Edgar was definitely not living up to character at that particular moment as he continued to voice his thoughts about the *Roundcape's* Third Mate despite his listener's stifled yawns while struggling to appear interested.

"See here, boyo! I'll not tell you it's difficult to understand where the mun's coming from because my recent past has seen to that! But the more I see how a busted relationship has took over his very sanity and I'm not exaggeratin', believe you me! The more I'm inclined to see how I was on the same course as our mutual friend and the need to change tack to avoid being sunk without trace as he's about to be, mark my words. 'We'll help each other', he says. But while my problems are *real*, his are . . . how can I word it . . .? Look, son, have you ever heard of an illness called *'delusion'*? 'Out of touch with reality', in layman's terms . . ."

Daniel's frown told him that however described, such an illness was beyond him.

Comprehending this, Edgar began to relate the evening's happenings so as to illustrate his concern.

"We're having a quiet drink and he's suddenly suggesting we get hold of a boat and take to the bloody river like a couple of juvenile delinquents! Well now, Edgar Reece, I tell myself. Maybe things haven't been so rosy of late but that river's treacherous, so they have it and it'd take all the fuckin' rum in town to risk takin' to the oars with our Mr Williams, it would."

"Almost fell out of a boat meself tonight," said Daniel, yawning. "Some of the others got a soaking but I managed to cling on like."

"What the hell were you doing in a boat for Christ's sake, boyo?"

"Oh, er – we went to a sort of party with, er – ladies and drinks like. Is – is that where the Third wanted to go?"

The Engineer's reply began hesitantly, as if in disbelief of what he was attempting to explain.

"Well, er – yes . . . It – it was to have been a similar rendezvous he had in mind," he began quietly, turning to gaze over the moonlit river. "Ladies, or to be exact, *one lady* he was intending to meet up with until I talked him out of it or to be quite honest, made out that I was even too pissed to make it back to the ship, let alone take to the river; hence my drunken act on boarding."

Edgar fell silent, probably uneasy at continuing with something so absurd. Observing this, Daniel, quietly pleased at being in his confidence, felt he ought help by showing interest.

"Er, this lady he, er – wanted to meet like; is she, er – over here?"

"Oh yes," came the grinned reply after some thought. "In fact 'she's sitting pretty as a princess' in one of those bum-boats at the last anchorage downriver if you believe that that moon up there is made of cheese! I say 'yes' because if it makes him happy that this young lady prefers life on a jungle river to working as a dental receptionist in Swansea, then why should the likes of you and me tell him otherwise and that he's barking mad?"

"Oh, er . . .? He's like, kidding himself you mean?"

Daniel was feigning interest now, too tired to appreciate Edgar's rambled explanation.

"Phew, boyo! We're gettin' somewhere now! But if I were to go on and tell you that this 'pretty as a princess' of the river was apparently waiting for him in New York up until just a few days ago then you'd be justified in thinkin' me to be as confused as he is. But as to why I can't help but sympathize with him, if his delusions stem from what he's been through. I can only hark back to my own recent experience which pains me every day. Some men, you see, can go from woman to woman, while others idolize only one. But sayin' that, even those that flit about, when probed, will admit that there'll always be a certain female of their past who they'll go to sleep thinkin' about more than any other. There's a word for it, boyo but by the looks of you, you're not awake enough to take in my view on that particular human condition, so I'll bid you goodnight."

"Er – goodnight," echoed a relieved Daniel as Edgar departed, both eager to turn in.

The Welsh he'd learned somewhere, were a loquacious people and tonight the supposedly withdrawn Fourth Engineer hadn't let the race down, even comparing well with their talkative Third Officer. Edgar's reference to *certain* women however, was not completely lost to the youth, as later, he found difficulty in getting to sleep in the stifling hot cabin. Patsy Harding or Hilary? Or would there one night be another female on his mind keeping him awake into the early hours?

Edgar knew little about the Third's family, only meeting the man himself on joining the *Roundcape*; scant mention of them only part of some dialogue concerning the wonderful woman in his life. Should he have met his sister Megan, he'd have been much enlightened in regard as to his unhealthy obsession with that particular young lady, Megan's concern being such that she'd approached their family GP to discuss his odd behaviour; such as, in whatever the weather, his prolonged visits to the local park where he'd first met the young Heloise. But of greater concern, she stressed to the doctor, was that his demeanour of late tended be somewhat immature, so unlike the brother she knew.

This behaviour included him preferring to converse of late with young people rather than adults. An example of this being his friendship with a sixteen-year-old lad who did some gardening and decorating around their home (Ivor being no handyman and her seaman husband being mostly at sea) a friendship that gave Ivor a static target who'd no choice other than listen to his rambling. Rambling that was mostly about his absent girlfriend rather than general man-talk, making Megan feel guilty for having stopped entertaining being subjected to his diatribe, causing him to bother the more vulnerable, such as the affable young handyman.

Megan had had mixed feeling when her brother surprisingly informed her that after two years, he'd convinced the shipping pool doctor of his fitness to return to sea. Selfish relief that he'd not be permanently around to worry about, while uneasy for not having revealed her anxiety to the medical authority involved, as to how he'd appear to his contemporaries at sea and, more worrying, that he'd mentioned casually of his plan to meet Heloise while on his travels.

A meeting that Megan knew to be . . .

Chapter 10

Sinking Of The Geoligist

"Aaaaaaaah!"

The early morning scream announced bauxite casualty number one as the first grabful of powdered ore collided with the lip of number three hold before depositing its contents deep within the *Roundcape's* bowels.

"Christ all fuckin' mighty!" yelped Billy. "It's broken every fuckin ' bone in me foot!" he moaned, stooping to pick up the clothes iron dislodged from the cabin table by the sudden jolt.

"What you want to bother ironing your clobber for?" scolded Reno, annoyed at being shocked out of his slumber. "You think anybody will care a toss about saloon appearances with all this shit about?"

"Saloon appearance, my arse!" whined Billy. "Best part of me last pay off this suit cost me and to date it's been in the galley boiler, ripped off me back by a couple of whores an' dipped into the shitty Demerara with me still wearin' it!"

"If you dinnae stop wailing over that bastard suit o' yours, Billy, I'm gonna stick it on the galley fire an' throw you back in the fuckin' Demerara with that iron stuck up your Teddy Boy arse!" came the guttural threat from the bunk above Daniel.

Over the side came the same pair of hairy legs that the Cabin Boy had woken to every morning of the last two weeks.

"You'll be compensated wi' dirt money so leave it at that, you moanin' wee sod!"

The much aired 'dirt money' began to have meaning as Daniel battled to the pantry through swirling, choking clouds of bauxite.

"Keep that bloody door shut!" was the order of the day and as the sun rose over the barricaded ship, temperature and tempers contributed to a living hell. The galley, with its coal-burning range was an inferno, its occupants doubly unco-operative. The serving hatches were only flung open when the bauxite grab was landward scooping up another load. Then, out would come the food containers and the race back to the pantry before the arrival of the next spewing grabful was on.

"You're not comin' in here in that shitty state!" yelled Billy, grabbing the breakfasts from a dust-covered Cabin Boy at the door. "An' if any of that shit 'as got into these containers I'll kick you into the 'old along with the next fuckin' load!"

Despite closed doors, vents and ports the dust infiltration was as bad as promised. The catering staff's efforts to keep the bridge area clean was futile and by the afternoon rest period all were so weary that the bother of queuing for the single shower amidships resulted in all but first-comer Jock, tumbling, sweat-soaked and filthy on to their longed-for bunks. Sleep however, in the shared cabin's sweltering atmosphere was difficult, while out on deck, even if shade from the blazing sun could be found, shelter from the swirling bauxite was impossible.

When at last the rattling, squealing, dust-belching machinery finally ground to a halt, a party of grumbling sailors were summoned from aft to begin the laborious cleaning down operation; their grumbles becoming louder after being told they'd be doing the same thing in just a few days time. The holds, only partly full, were to be topped up in Trinidad: the Demerara being too shallow to give it navigable draught for fully loaded vessels. The moans over this revelation persisted but when the holds were finally covered and secure, a definite, if only temporary air of relief, could be sensed throughout the ship. Loading berths in Mackenzie were evidently in great demand, for within minutes of the sailors completing their task, the *Roundcape* had pulled out into mid-river and was turning about for the return journey.

"There's a spot of overtime to be had, son," the Chief Steward informed Daniel after the evening meal.

Overtime! Blooming overtime! The Chief was suddenly Mrs Bloom exclaiming her pride in Maurice's time and half on

Saturday morning. He recalled his scorn of her small-minded comment and how it had contributed to his decision on that fateful day; a decision that had resulted in him now being thousands of miles from home on this jungle river. Okay, hardly an adventure to rank him with the Scotts and Livingstones of this world but . . . oh yes! Last night! Last night had been something to brag about to his mates back home! His first brothel and the boat capsizing on the river. Yes! They'll be all ears and wanting to sign up and say goodbye to overtime and all that went with it. But, oh yes! Best not to mention that he'd heard a crew member (Billy White) asking Jock whether he thought it too early to ask the Chief Steward for a precautionary injection. No, best not to mention that.

It may have been the slowing of the ship's engines or even the distant rattle of the anchor chain that awakened Daniel in the early hours of the following morning. Whatever the cause, the sweltering heat of the cabin made further sleep impossible so, clad only in his underpants, he crept out of his quarters and made his way to the lifeboat deck above. One such uncomfortable night a day before Georgetown, he'd discovered this alternative from the stifling cabin, his only concern being discovered by the notorious Somali Petty Officer, Yussef Rashid, whose cabin, along with that of the ship's Chippy, was situated on that deck. For comfort and 'modesty' he'd brought with him two light blankets which he spread on the still-warm deck. Dropping down on the makeshift bed, he wrapped one blanket around him and closed his eyes.

Other than the irritation of flying insects, the boat deck was a great improvement to the perspiration-odoured quarters he'd just left. The night seemed even warmer than the previous one in Mackenzie but, reminding himself of both, the sudden drop of temperature to be expected around dawn and not least Martyn's experience in Petty Officer Rashid's cabin, he arranged the blanket for full coverage before re-settling himself.

Their moonlight-bathed anchorage he recognized as the spot where, two mornings before, he'd awakened to find the ship surrounded by a flotilla of trades folk voicing their wares. No sight or sound of humans now. Just the eerie sound of howls, screams and whistles echoing out of the shadowy wilderness on the distant banks. Voices caused him to uncover his eyes and look forward towards the bridge. A sailor, probably the Helmsman, came down from the wheelhouse and headed aft. Seconds later, the Third Mate and the Pilot appeared on the external bridge walk, chatted for a minute until the latter stretched out his arms yawning something about 'getting his head down' and stepped back inside the bridge. Concealed by a lifeboat, Daniel watched as the Third paced the bridge walk for a short while before eventually descending to the deck and positioning himself at a point on the rail overlooking the river's southern bank.

Yesterday had been so hectic that the youth had scarcely found time to fully reflect on the bizarre experience of visiting his first brothel and the ensuing river drama, let alone his later encounter with the intoxicated Deck Officer and his companion. Now, as he observed this puzzling character, the old Engineer's snide remarks about him came to mind.

What was the remark that had come across as childish in the extreme? That 'she was sitting pretty as a princess in one of them bum-boats downriver!'

Yes! This was the anchorage where he recalled seeing young women among the traders. Even by moonlight, he recognized a landing stage so fragile in appearance that just one more load placed upon it would surely cause it to collapse. Yes, this was the spot!

For quite some time, the boy gazed down at the officer seemingly at vigil at the rail until the glow of the man's fourth or fifth cigarette began to fade. He'd probably slept for two hours or more before suddenly coming to with the strange sensation that his covering was being slowly pulled off! For a few uncomfortable seconds, he kept his eyes closed, assuring himself that he was merely experiencing a recurring childhood dream. It was a light breeze playing on his back that finally convinced him otherwise. Simultaneously came the sound of a door being pulled to. He sat up and glared suspiciously towards Yussef Rashid's cabin. Could he have maybe . . .? Could the kinky little pervert have crept out and . . .?

It was getting light. A million birds heralded the dawn from the distant treetops. Too long on that hard, now cool, deck he was about to return to his quarters when something caught his eye on the deck below. The Third's accommodation must have been as unbearable as his own but had the officer spent all night down there leaning doggedly over the rail looking . . . ? Yes! Out there on the water! A small boat heading away from the ship: its sole occupant facing away from him but clearly . . .? Yes – even in this light, clearly female! 'As pretty as a princess . . .'? Had it not been for a fit of shivering that convinced him that he was well and truly awake; what he was seeing could quite easily have been a dream induced by old Edgar's words. But this was no dream he assured himself, following the girl's progress until suddenly, she rested her paddle, looked back at the ship and – and waved! Then she was off again and within minutes had vanished into the riverside shadows.

Daniel returned his attention to the Third and suddenly, what he'd observed began to make sense. No romantic tryst this. The basket of fruit in the Officer's arms suggested nothing more mysterious than an early morning purchase. The girl had probably spotted the lone figure at the rail and, having no competition at that early hour, paddled over to do business. Picking up his blankets the Cabin Boy reproached himself for allowing his imagination to run wild and seconds later, while descending the boat deck ladder, reproached himself again for having imagined that the two white circles he'd glimpsed in the blackness of Yussef Rashid's porthole were . . .? Were eyes?

An atlas contains certain place-names which fill the mind with warm and colourful images. The 'Caribbean', the sea they next traversed while making for the West Indian island of

145

Trinidad, fulfilled Daniel's expectations to the utmost. Tiny islands, some even smaller than the *Roundcape* herself, jutted out of a placid, transparent sea, like emeralds scattered about a silver tray. Passing by them, one wondered how, beneath such a sun, did they maintain the lush, green vegetation covering their slopes from sea to pinnacle, the only shade being provided by the larger fronds overhanging their briny-lapped perimeters where, when close enough, signs of habitation in the form of a moored yacht and a luxurious holiday chalet could frequently be glimpsed.

"Now you know where your ship-owners and shareholders take their fancy pieces for a dirty weekend, boyo," the grinning Ianto informed Daniel. "More than likely the man paying your pittance is shacked up on one of 'em," he chuckled.

"Long way to come from, er – Europe isn't it?" ventured Daniel.

"Don't kid yourself now. There'll more than likely be a seaplane at their beck and call if money counts for anything!" winked the big sailor. "Got to be prepared for a quick getaway in case his fancy piece's old mun comes looking see?"

Daniel's brief lift of spirits began reverting to thoughts of desertion on reaching the bauxite wharfs of Chaguaramas. After topping up, the *Roundcape* was to take her cargo to Canada, he was told. And then it would be back to Mackenzie for another load, that is unless her orders were changed en route. The news was as bad as it could be. The thought of more sickness and bullying once back on the wild Atlantic on an endless voyage, filled him with despair. He confided his fears and contemplated desertion to Martyn who, although none too happy himself, said he was going to stick it out at least until Canada. They were bound for the St Lawrence, he'd been told and due to that waterway's annual freeze-up, only so many trips could be made before Winter set in.

"And then where?" argued Daniel. "Half a dozen times round the world like me brother's first trip more than likely!"

"Tell you what, mun," offered the Deck Boy, "wait 'til Canada an' I'll likely come with you. Part of the British Empire is Canada see? Much easier to get home if you jump ship there I'd say."

"Trinidad's a part of the British Empire as well!" countered Daniel. "So if we're going to jump, might as well do it now I reckon."

Martyn was still not convinced but at least agreed to help study the layout of the port which disappointingly appeared to be even more isolated than had been Mackenzie, in respect at least, of there being no adjacent town. A few more discreet enquiries however, revealed that Port of Spain, Trinidad's capital where administrative buildings such as 'embassies' would be, was only a short taxi ride away. Things were looking up!

Jumping ship wasn't all that difficult they had gleaned from better informed crew members. Once out of the port one had to lie low until the ship had departed then present oneself to the appropriate embassy or consulate. There'd be red tape from the local authorities to get round but it was more or less inevitable that they'd eventually deport you back home. How to get out of the port then? A further study of their surroundings was required.

Behind the bauxite-ravaged loading area rose a steep, wooded hill. As the dock gates were manned and there was no shore leave permitted (events in Mackenzie had seen to that) Daniel decided that he would investigate the hill for another way out. Several of the crew had slipped away to swim off a beach not far from their berth and with the excuse of fancying a dip himself, he'd followed them ashore. Minutes later he had darted behind the mounds of bauxite and was struggling up the wooded incline. It was mid-afternoon and extremely hot. From the ship, his chosen route had appeared easy but, already sweating profusely as he encountered the vegetation, stings from insects and nettles, began to aggravate matters and suddenly it became very clear that 'jumping ship' was going to involve discomforts he'd hardly considered! Midway up the slope his fast-disappearing

147

enthusiasm collapsed entirely as he came upon a towering wire-mesh fence supported by concrete posts. *US NAVY. KEEP OUT* read the signs attached to this impenetrable barrier.

"Get your doggone arse away from here, boy!"

He froze as the threatening military guard approached from the other side of the wire, the fixed bayonet on his rifle glinting in the sunlight. The man's further utterances escaped him as he tore back down the incline, not stopping until safely back on the quay where, at the bottom of the gangplank, another angry face confronted him.

"Where the hell were you off to, son?" yelled the Skipper furiously.

"I – I was just taking a walk . . ."

"Never leave this ship without permission again, son, or you'll be in serious trouble! Do you hear me? Serious trouble!"

It transpired that the old man, still vexed over the Mackenzie commotion, had ordered the bathers back on board and found Daniel missing. Meanwhile someone on the bridge had followed the youth's movements up until his cutting off into the undergrowth and informed the fuming Captain Roberts. Being at the receiving end of his wrath greatly changed how Daniel viewed the *Roundcape's* Skipper. His gentle, somewhat 'feminine' manner could in no way be interpreted as weakness he fast learned about the man who, when he needed to be, was as tough as any other on board and only a fool would dare to cross.

"It'll have to be Canada then," a subdued Daniel agreed with Martyn. "We're bound to get shore leave up there so let's wait until then."

Chaguramas, they found, was adjacent to a US naval base which would have been extremely difficult to bypass so Canada it would have to be. There was no time to sulk over the matter because suddenly, every spare man was involved in cleaning down once again: on this occasion in such heat, visibly enjoying the task of hosing down the ship and themselves with cool, cleansing water; the officers turning a blind eye to the horseplay until an 'accidental' jet passed through a galley porthole removing Brumpud's hat and spectacles which resulted in anyone approaching that department for the next thirty minutes or so being attacked with buckets of galley slops.

The general uplift in mood aboard lasted only until the morning of the following day, the fourteenth of July. Tension became evident throughout the crew following an order from the bridge that reduced their passage to a crawl. His curiosity aroused by the sudden quiet about him, Daniel approached the one person whom he knew to be always ready with an answer.

"It's a ship that's gone down," muttered an unusually glum Billy. "A Harrison boat out of Liverpool. Went down in minutes. The poor sods didn't stand a chance."

Ominous whispers from those coming off watch rousing others with unprecedented haste confirmed his words together with a news bulletin on Jock's radio. The freighter *Geoligist*, had sunk after colliding with a bauxite carrier, the *Sun Princess*, north of Trinidad the previous night. Twenty lives lost off the *Geoligist*, the other ship suffering nothing worse than a dented bow. 'How, in such weather?' was the question asked around. The fully loaded *Sun Princess*, heading north, would have been as low in the water as themselves: a weighted, powerful projectile that had caused the ultimate damage with little to herself as the *Roundcape's* crew would later witness.

The sinking, it was eventually explained, had occurred too far away for the *Roundcape* to assist but she'd slowed should she be called on. Survivors had been picked up quite soon after the collision, Daniel learned, causing him to dwell on a question that went unanswered. Had her cabin boy been among them? He grieved quietly for this unknown youth and his shipmates, his anguished looks drawing unexpected attention from the Third Mate who, since his petulant exchange with old Edgar that night back in Mackenzie, had even distanced himself from his daily visitor.

"Looking a bit down in the dumps of late, boyo. Something's bothering you, eh?" was how he broke his silence as Daniel tidied for him a few days after the event.

"That ship . . .? The, er – *Geoligist*? I – I can't get over it sinking as easy as it did. They – they were all, er – seamen just like us weren't they? Just going about their business and – and . . ."

The officer's marked silence meant that he was either too preoccupied with his own reflection as he stared into his bureau mirror or that he was lost as how to reply. Having completed his chores, Daniel gathered his cleaning utensils and was making to leave when the officer spoke.

"The loss of the Harrison boat has got to you, eh, boyo? And you're not alone on board, including myself. Tragic, bloody tragic but chances are if you stay at sea you'll find that accidents as serious as that are few and far between and nowhere near as commonplace as serious road accidents ashore. Not that it lessens the tragedy of the *Geoligist's* sinking. I'll guess that nigh on everybody on board has said a little prayer for those lost souls look you. So try not to dwell on it. You'll live a long and healthy life I'm sure."

The Third's explanation so impressed Daniel that his friend Edgar's 'barking mad' accusation a new nights earlier could only have been groundless ridicule. A few moments later however, the youth wasn't so sure when the officer reacted dramatically to the youth's statement that it wasn't so much the fear of losing his own life that was troubling him but the terrible suddenness with which some of the *Geoligist's* crew lost theirs.

"Cabin Boy! I caught you one morning reading those words out loud!"

His tone was stern and tutor-like as he gestured towards the framed motto on his bureau mirror.

"And death shall have no dominion!"[13]

There was a slight tremble in his voice as he spoke, his eyes searching Daniel's like a teacher waiting for a reply.

"You haven't a bloody clue have you?" he said eventually, shaking his head as if giving up on his pupil. "Mind you," he continued in a softer manner, "there are those who *pretend* to

---

[13] The collected poems of Dylan Thomas. The new centenary edition.

interpret his words so as not to appear ignorant while their interpretations prove them to be just that. The so-called *educated* types are the worst at that. They'll take a stab at any answer hoping that their listener is more ignorant than himself if you follow my meaning?"

No, he didn't, was how the officer read Daniel's blank expression and accordingly seemed to drop the idea of explaining the motto and began an exchange more suited to his daily cleaner. He asked about his background and education and on learning that his entire schooling had been spent in a village primary school so elevated that it overlooked a panorama of Worcestershire extending thirty miles to the Malvern Hills on the county's western border beyond which, Daniel boasted, on a clear day one could even make out the Welsh mountains. This interested the Third enough to suddenly produce an atlas of the British Isles and turn to the appropriate page. Redditch he found but Daniel's home village and that of Crabbs Cross where he went to school were not mentioned. Neither was the elevation upon which the school stood causing the officer to comment, "No elevation given means elevation insignificant. But being able to see the Welsh mountains must have been inspiring," he added as if not to appear scornful of Daniel's boast. "A school with a pleasant physical outlook gives its pupils a good mental outlook, I have already told you, together with teachers who can also inspire of course. Teachers who encourage their pupils to seek the meaning of words such as these!"

The Third's morbid tone and expression had returned as he gestured once more at the framed motto, reminding Daniel of yesteryear's teachers who seemingly enjoyed torturing lesser informed beings.

"The, er . . . the Steward'll be wondering where I've got to so I'll be on my . . ."

"You *were* fearing for your own life, boyo! Just as I and most aboard were when meditating the awful loss of the *Geoligist*, it happening right under our noses as it did! *And death shall have no dominion!*"

The officer's voice was now mournful and slow as he recited the words once again.

"Your Welsh headmaster . . .? When he touched upon Mr Thomas's work? If he'd given you those words to decipher would you have been able to?"

Not if Janet Tyler had been distracting him with an impromptu knickers-down flash while crouching in the gangway in the pretence of retrieving a dropped pencil might have been the answer to curtail what was becoming too morbid a sermon. But the officer gave no sign of coming down from his pulpit giving Daniel time to think better than such flippancy and respectfully answer, "Er – no, sir. I – er, don't think that I could have."

"So I'll decipher them for you, boyo, so as you'll not utter them every day in ignorance while in this cabin."

"I – er, really ought get going, sir."

But the Third wasn't ready for him to leave and continued in that same oratorical manner.

"He was saying that *death* releases one from all mundane hardship, pain and boundaries! So not to fear it! So not to fear it!"

"Er – I'm off, sir. The Steward'll be going barmy if he can't find me."

Daniel was almost in the alleyway as he turned to find that the oration was no longer directed at him but to the framed words.

"Though they sink through the sea they shall rise again! Though they sink through the sea they shall rise again! Though they sink through the . . .!"[14]

The Third's solemn demeanour on that particular day was hardly typical of his behaviour throughout the following weeks, he becoming more loquacious, walked more briskly and smiled

---

[14] The collected poems of Dylan Thomas The New Centenary Edition

more often with each passing day almost until the day that he disappeared from the ship.

Much of that smiling was directed at Daniel who, though wary of such a complex man but always welcoming of friendly company aboard, eventually gave in and, though cautiously, resumed the unlikely liaison.

Although frank with each other on many matters, the Cabin Boy refrained from disclosing his wish to jump ship: the man was still an officer and would surely try to dissuade him or even report him. Or could his reluctance to voice the matter possibly mean that he, at last, was acclimatising to life at sea? Seasickness, a certain factor in his unhappiness, was definitely less severe: the ship, now low in the water with its tonnage of bauxite, instead of bucking and rolling over the waves, channelled her way through them, providing a steadier and consequently healthier passage for her long-suffering initiates.

And also of course, was the music: when occasionally Jock would permit it and on numerous others when he wasn't around to forbid it; Billy would play with the controls of the Cook's powerful wireless until it seemed it would vibrate off its shelf as it blasted out the new pulsating 'Rock' sound from a hundred and one American radio stations. For the more youthful aboard, Daniel not least, feeling so close to the origin of the Rock and Roll phenomenon was an exhilarating experience. The indistinct offerings transmitted by Radio Luxembourg had never sounded quite like this, the genuine Yankee-land rock that had Billy jiving crazily around the cabin with an imaginary guitar. Daniel too, while lacking the exhibitionist traits of his 'with it' cabin mate, became enraptured by the vibrant sounds being transmitted from the homeland of Abbot and Costello, Flash Gordon and President Dwight Eisenhower: explosive sounds which might well have been a late celebration to the end of the explosions of war but a decade ago.

Billy's repeated claims that this form of music was destined to change the face of entertainment was angrily disputed by Jock who would storm into the cabin and retune the receiver until the pompous air which heralded Britain's overseas broadcasting service or the 'slow slow, quick quick, slow' ballroom tempo of Victor Sylvester's orchestra came crackling through over the waves.

"Your Yankee blacks were belting out that fuckin' racket long before they even set foot on American soil, you ignorant wee twat o' a Teddy Boy! That's how *new* is your so-called Rock and Roll!" the Cook scornfully informed him.

"Strewth, Jock!" retaliated Billy, determined not to be browbeaten over the one subject he revelled in. "Your black musicians have been stuck with that crap called jazz for yonks which in my book's as unmusical as the fuckin' racket what comes out of a set of bagpipes!"

"You cheeky wee bastard you! Such wisecracks'll nae disguise your sheer pig-ignorance!" bellowed the Scot with the usual clenched fist. "I'll gi' your fuckin' Rock and Roll six months at the outside before it fizzles out! The proof's wi' your major Yankee stations who're still pluggin' your Sinatras and Comos!"

"Puttin' off the inevitable is what they're doin', Jock!" stormed back Billy. "James Dean, Bill 'aley an' the Teds are changin' the whole fuckin' scene! Your Sinatras an' Comos 'ave 'ad their day."

But Jock wasn't at all convinced.

"Listen here, you West Country wanker! The only change your fuckin' Rock and Roll has brought about is the breakdown in law and order caused by the likes o' you an' your delinquent tearaways tearin' the local dance halls an' cinemas apart an' coshin' old grannies for their last couple o' bob!"

"Bloody hell, Jock!" countered Billy. "You're a fine one to spout on about violence. I've 'eard you can get your throat cut in Glasgow just for askin' the time of day an' your clansmen 'ave been runnin' around stickin' their dirks up each other's kilts for yonks. Even the redcoats couldn't civilize you fuckin' lot!"

By the time the exchange was over, Daniel's fingernails were as short as they'd ever been and all that the argument proved was that Billy could run as fast as any clansman and that the refrigeration room on a merchant ship, even on a sweltering hot Atlantic day, was far from being the most comfortable of hiding places.

Arguments and any new topic of conversation, Daniel found, spread quickly throughout the ship and the music debate was soon taken up by her largely Welsh crew with the true passion of a singing nation.

Rock and Roll could hardly be considered 'music' which anybody who's attended the annual National Eisteddfod couldn't possibly refute, was the general opinion. Youthful Martyn however, stood alone in opposing the view of his countrymen, sharing Daniel's liking for the new trend, an agreement which led the pair to broach the subject with their old friend, the knowledgeable Abu Shalaan.

Stroking his large beard, Abu gave some thought to their confusion then, in his usual cordial manner, said, "Boys, what is music to your ears may not be music to mine but there are always sounds which will captivate us all. Come, let us put it to the test," he added, leading them to the stern rail and pointing down to the spuming turbulence created by the *Roundcape's* huge propeller.

"Listen awhile, boys," he indicated while finding an ear to cup amongst his profuse gray hair. "The commotion down there. Is it pleasurable or discordant to your ears?"

"Er – kind of exciting I reckon," replied Daniel.

Martyn agreed.

"Then to all three of us it is music," concluded Abu, patting their heads like a fond old uncle.

While both youths praised Abu's wisdom, the Deck Boy's opinion was that old age brings wisdom to all men. But Daniel wasn't so sure.

"Not *all* men," he countered. "The Fourth Engineer is getting on in years and at times he seems to be lost and confused. I feel sorry for him. Let's call on him and you'll see what I mean."

[15]Minutes after leaving Abu, the couple's knock on Edgar's cabin door was answered by a gruff invitation to enter.

"We'll try and get his thoughts about the music," whispered Martyn. "Just as an excuse for visiting like."

Daniel had agreed while concerned about Edgar having given him little more than a nod since their intimate conversation that night in Mackenzie and thought it unlikely that he would engage in any type of discussion. But Edgar, livened by rum, not only engaged in the music debate with them but went on to personal revelations so farcical that they boys found themselves struggling to keep from laughing.

He described Rock and Roll as 'the devil's music' and backed the Welsh opinion aboard that it ought be banned and scolded Martyn for abandoning his heritage for such a racket.

"The music that resounds from our Welsh valleys is God's own music!" he enthused. "I met my wife by joining such a choir," he told the pair. "She'd the voice of an angel and beautiful to boot and I thanked music for bringing us together," he added mistily.

He was sitting on his bunk still clad in his oily engine-room garb and a bottle of rum in his lap when they entered.

"Like a drop, boys?" he offered, his visitors declining with, "No but thanks all same."

"All the more for me then," he grinned wickedly, taking a long guzzle from the bottle. "Now then. My thoughts on music? Well, as I said, your Rock and Roll's not my style but I'm not averse to so-called popular music such as that of our very own Donald Peers if you've ever heard of him, boys? He used to charm British housewives and such with his weekly half-hour show on the BBC . . ."

"Yeah, er . . . *By A Babbling Brook* was his signature tune," contributed Daniel. "Me mom and sister used to make us all be quiet while they sat around our radiogram to listen to him."

---

[15] Donald Peers 10th July 1908 - 9th August 1973. Heart-throb Welsh Crooner. 'Cavalier of song' radio show 1950s. TV show 1960s

"You've got him, boyo," smiled Edgar. "My missus used to be the same and send me to my shed to have him to herself. But I'd got my own wireless installed in my hideaway and listened in myself. A golden voice with charm and sincerity was how my missus summed him up. So popular he was that a Barry Island woman got so taken away with her favourite crooner that she extended her wireless lead to listen to him in the bath. Together with him in their own babbling brook, it was joked. But electrocution caused her hair to stand up like the bristles of a bass broom, somebody said. But to me it was insensitive gossip. Insensitive gossip in my opinion."

Grinning as he spoke, Edgar revealed an innate sense of humour but, while guessing as much, the boys refrained from laughing lest they'd guessed wrong! And the old Engineer wasn't finished yet as, with rum still in hand, he prostrated himself, boots and all, on top of the freshly-changed linen to continue his outpouring.

"Put Donald Peers on a bloody pedestal did my missus! That is until Crusty Lightfoot came into the picture. And even my own soddin' brother was in on the fact of our baker, sly old Crusty, in my absence was giving her a daily delivery instead of the usual Monday, Wednesday and Friday, would you believe it? A loaf a day instead of . . ."

A sharp snore signalled that Edgar was gone to the world and that the boys could make a stealthy exit. On deck, they found themselves for once clutching the rail with mirth rather than misery. Both were later to express guilt for having found the old man's tale of woe hilarious but at that moment in time his lament provided them with a welcome tonic. Even the news later that day that engine trouble had reduced the ship's speed by half didn't completely dishearten them. As long as they were moving, at whatever speed, each day brought Canada, the venue for their long-deliberated plan, that little bit closer.

The *Roundcape's* Master however, anticipated Canada with anguish. Their reduced speed brought home to him his earlier misgivings over their Chief Engineer's competence. Not a hint of trouble from the man until their suddenly reduced headway. Now, the prospect of expensive and time-consuming repairs in Canada despite the old fool's assurance of self-repair at anchor, were fast becoming a disturbing reality. Not helping his mood were the sudden dense mists now being encountered while crossing the busy North American, European shipping lanes in a vessel too long overdue at the breaker's yard to justify fitting radar. His crew at least, since Mackenzie, appeared more committed. The Chief Steward, once off the bottle was as good a caterer as could be wished for. The Mate too, after embarrassing himself on that unfortunate night on the Demerara, had returned to his dedicated self and if overlooking their eccentric Cook's shabby appearance and a couple of culinary mishaps, his cooking was generally acceptable.

The Third Mate too, whose service he'd been made aware of at his time of signing had been broken for some two years, had become less withdrawn and was going about his duties in an irreproachable, if sometimes, over-genial manner. A puzzling character the Third. Slept little and didn't appear the worse for it according to the Mate. Either walking the decks or tapping away on his portable typewriter it's said. Unusually chummy with the Cabin Boy too. Can only hope he'll influence the lad into not going walkabouts as in Chaguramas. The lad was definitely up to something that day and appears to have taken the Deck Boy into his confidence of late. Must keep an eye on the pair of them.

Booooooooooom! Booooooooooom!

After two days and nights of almost constant blasts, Daniel gave up staring about him to see if there really was anything out there in that positively endless mist and began doing what all other off-duty crew did at such times and curled up on his bunk with a Mickey Spillane.

One incident though, was scary enough to bring many scurrying onto the decks. On that extra-murky evening a siren, many times louder than their own, started booming from somewhere out in the gloom, their Skipper's strained expression while perambulating the decks and bridge as they boomed their way for'ard, causing many alarm but it was his shrill commands to their Helmsman that had Daniel and other novices quaking in their boots as they stared into the solid grey wall ahead. The next ear-splitting blasts seemed to crash down from somewhere above them, the *Roundcape's* reply pitifully inadequate!"

"There she goes!" shouted someone as a huge, dark shape loomed suddenly out of the mist off their starboard bow.

"Like a fucking sponge we are with the holds full of bauxite," somebody had said following the *Geoligist* sinking. "The *Sun Princess* would've gone to the bottom in minutes if she'd taken the broadside!"

These pessimistic words came flashing through Daniel's mind as the towering liner bore down on them!

"They have it all tied up by radio, young fella," promised Big Paddy appearing at his side seconds before the liner, an impressive sight with row upon row of lit portholes twinkling through the haze, slipped safely across their path to vanish as quickly as she'd appeared into the murk.

"'er officer's would've been too busy shagging the passengers to put on earphones for our fuckin' benefit!" was Billy's reaction to Daniel's praise of modern-day navigation. "They'd not 'ave 'ad a clue that we were anywhere around!" he prattled on. "Strewth! If I know anything about bloody liners they'd 'ave been so carried away by orgasmic pleasure, they'd 'ave sliced us in 'alf an' not known it!"

"Orgasmic! Now there's word I've never heard you use before, Billy," commented a recumbent Jock. "It wouldnae be any coincidence that your attempt to speak better English has only come about since you've been decoratin' the old man's quarters these last few evenin's? It's got me wonderin' what other kind o' lessons he's mebbe given you, Billy!"

"It's about time he improved on his usual filthy language," muttered Reno pausing from letter-writing. "And what do you know about navigation, Billy, if this is your first deep-sea trip?"

Daniel was all ears at the revelation which was conspicuously brushed aside by the Assistant Steward.

"What was that about me 'avin' lessons from the old man, Jock?" he asked quietly.

"That's your business an' forget I ever brought it up, ducky," the Scot replied. "Now what's all this about this bein' your first deep-sea trip.?"

"I'll tell you all this much for nothin'," retorted Billy. "This trip's been more like a cruise on fuckin' daddy's yacht compared to my experiences on coasters! Now you'll back me up on that won't you, Jock? You've 'ad a spell on coasters so tell old spaghetti chops Reno 'ere about the roughest ride you've ever had apart from that old bint in Mackenzie last week!"

"Any more o' your lip an' you'll be the roughest fuckin' ride I've ever had!" came the growled reply.

"Point taken me old acker, Jock. Just ribbin' but serious like, what I were sayin' about that liner just now. They'd most likely not 'ave seen us would they?"

The Assistant Cook shifted in his bunk to meet Daniel's eyes with hard, cold stare.

"For once, Billy," he began, his eyes darting between the Bristolian and Daniel, "for once you're nae speakin' total bullshit. Some o' the worst seas I've ever encountered have been off our own shores. But I'll stress this point for you an' the Cabin Boy to digest. Never forget how cunnin' an' merciless any sea can be regardless o' its situation or appearance. Believe you both what Jock McLaughlin is tellin' you this day the bell at Lloyds had tolled for many a ship lost in seas far less disturbed than we've encountered up to now. Take the *Geoligist* for instance. A collision in perfect conditions! But what brought those ships to collide in such weather is a mystery that only the sea can answer! Och aye! They'll insist on the human element for insurance purposes just as they would have if that fuckin' liner had sent us to the bottom!"

"Like I said!" cut in Billy. "They never even see us did they?"

"Mebbe they did or mebbe they didnae or mebbe we were just jammy! Near misses happen all the time an' never made public!"

Jock was now sitting up and plainly enjoying his lecture.

"In the maritime world, a wee tub like this is fuckin' insignificant but if by some strange fluke we'd sent that liner to the bottom, it'd be a different story, believe you me. The sinkin' o' a passenger liner makes headlines the world over when we'd be lucky to rate a couple o' lines 'neath an Osbert Lancaster cartoon in your fuckin' *Daily Express* an' if they'd just put a penny on a pint o' beer they might just stretch to a couple o' lines 'neath Rupert the fuckin' Bear! Strewth! Marilyn Monroe's bare arse is of far greater interest to your average reader than the loss o' a measly freighter like ours! It's a fact that folk dinnae want to know or begin to appreciate the dangers we face every God-forsaken day!"

"Is that why the Fourth Engineer sleeps with his boots on?"

Daniel's sudden impulse to cheer things up was just as suddenly regretted as Jock pounced.

"Laddie!" he roared. "Mebbe up to now it's been as Billy says, a cruise on daddy's yacht an' for the time bein' your guts are nae stuck in your fuckin' throat. But, laddie, before you take over as wit o' the ship, I want you to know that there's talk aboard o' weather brewin' south as bad as it can be and just in time for us hittin' the Caribbean smack on time for our return trip. So just remember this, you wee bastard, that when you're washed overboard into the wildest o' shark-inhabited seas an' screamin' for a lifebelt to be thrown down, it'll be that great chunk o' fat that's still hangin' in yonder galley that'll come your way! By fuck it will!"

"It's about time somebody took the cheeky young bugger in hand," chimed in Reno.

"But – but what, er – was that all about. . .? About . . .?"

"About the weather brewin' you mean?" completed Jock.

"Er – no . . ." returned the Maltese. "What Billy was on about, orgasmic pleasure? What – what's orgasmic pleasure?"

"For fuck's sake!" Jock was really losing it now. "It was Billy's feeble attempt at takin' the piss out o' his seniors in the merchant service as is his habit! Officers, like 'em or loathe 'em, deserve their subordinate's respect an' I assure you that any

161

sexual contact between passengers an' crew is out o' the question. The crew o' that liner that nearly rammed us'll be nae different to us in anticipatin' port to get their ends away except that New York or whichever Yankee port they're makin' for'll be a damn sight more expensive than the few fuckin' dollars we paid back in Mackenzie! New York especially is . . ."

"Mr Williams, the Third Mate had a lady friend in New York," interjected Daniel, thinking he'd something of interest to contribute. "But – but his mate, the Fourth Engineer says 'that if the moon's made of cheese' she's moved to Guiana," he added, while instantly knowing that his interjection had been a waste of breath.

"What the fuck're you witterin' on about, laddie? An' dinnae even begin tryin' to explain yourself afore you've sprinted up to the pantry for my cocoa!"

"Er – I – I'll explain when I get back," replied the Cabin Boy.

"Nobody's explained to me what orgasmic pleasure is," whined Reno into his pillow.

Chapter 11

Meeting In The Park

On the day following the liner incident, Daniel was introduced to Heloise. Prior to this formal introduction however, while going about his chores in the Third Mate's cabin, he'd taken the liberty of acquainting himself with the very attractive young brunette whose photographs, eight in all, had suddenly adorned the officer's bureau.

One photo was the one previously shown to him by the Third while suggesting his, Daniel's, likeness to the said poet (refuted by the youth) walking alongside the girl. Studying the other photos, it was three head and shoulder portraits which most captivated Daniel. Eyes hinting at oriental but larger and mischievously expressive with long, dark lashes and gleaming black hair that fell, perfectly groomed, to frame the most beautiful face that Daniel was convinced he'd ever seen.

"Green," he guessed to be the colour of those eyes seemingly following his own as he dusted around the black and white snaps which, after much scrutiny satisfied him that hers was a natural beauty free from any artificial enhancement. Certainly no lipstick. Oh no. Those generous, even over-full, lips, slightly parted with her smile were temptingly asking to be kissed.

Of the remaining four photos, three had been taken with a bandstand in the background in what looked to be a park. Two of them portrayed her in Summer frocks and smiling the most skittish of smiles, while another had her seated on the bandstand steps in tennis whites showing as much of her shapely, long legs as did the final snap which depicted her posing seductively on a beach wearing the skimpiest of bikinis.

Her age? Assuming that she was the girl who, according to the Fourth Engineer the Third was losing his mind over, then she was older than her looks or the officer was guilty of 'cradle snatching' was Daniel's opinion, arrived at by an undoubted touch of jealousy. His fixation with the pictures intensified on discovering that the girl's bikini in the beach snap was an 'afterthought'. Someone, probably for modesty's sake, had painstakingly used a white substance to touch up what must have been a 'nude' photograph.

It was the Third himself who, bursting into his cabin unexpectedly and not showing any objection to his photos being perused, revealed the girl's identity and age. He picked one up and kissed it.

"She'll be twenty-two next month and I'll be looking for a present and card in Canada!" he announced jauntily.

His sudden willingness to discuss his lady friend wasn't that surprising considering the conspicuous display of her photos but Daniel, not wanting to appear too interested, simply answered, "Oh – I – er, see."

"Come on then, boyo! Don't shy away from asking her name, where she comes from and why she's gracing my cabin?"

"I – I'm just being careful since you nearly bit my head off the last time I asked about her," replied Daniel, taking advantage of the other's high spirits.

"When was that then? I can't recall discussing Heloise with you?"

"It was when you showed me that picture there," replied the youth, indicating the photo depicting her alongside the non-too-happy poet.

"Oh yes, I remember, sorry about that but I wasn't up to discuss personal matters just then. Things were complicated then see but I'm glad to say that things are more favourable now. Definitely more favourable so ask away."

Still wary but feeling more at ease, Daniel asked, "The girl in the photos – er – she's your lady friend is she, sir? Your girlfriend like?"

"Fiancée's more apt, boyo! Heloise is my fiancée!"

"Yes, sir. I – I thought she was the girl you'd mentioned before, Heloise. She's very, very nice, sir."

"Oh yes, she's a looker right enough. Every man's dream is Heloise, wouldn't you agree?"

"Yes, sir. She's, er – very pretty."

"You were bloody-well drooling over her when I came in so why don't you come out with it that she's the most beautiful female you've ever clapped eyes on!"

"I – er, didn't want to appear too forward by saying anything like. But – but she's . . ."

"What are you hesitating over, boyo? Why the guilty look? You've not been feeling a bit randy while ogling my gorgeous fiancée, have you?"

"No! Of course I haven't! I was just having a look at . . ."

"Something's puzzling you, eh, Cabin Boy? Come on, what's puzzling you?"

"Nothing. I – I'm just embarrassed about what you said just now, er – about me looking at the photos, that's all. I – I only gave them a quick, er – glance."

"I'll take your word for it then," grinned the officer, "but something's definitely got you puzzled but then there's a lot aboard puzzling over me so don't let it worry you because it'll all be explained shortly. It'll all be explained."

❖ ❖ ❖ ❖ ❖ ❖ ❖ ❖

The Third Mate, when his off-duty periods coincided with his cleaner's visits, seemed to relish talking about his association with the girl in the photos (probably because no-one else would listen) and, while uncomfortable, Daniel simply listened.

The girl Heloise hadn't been the Third's first love. He'd married in his early twenties and divorced in his early thirties, was as much as he revealed about his marriage other than if perhaps there had been children, things might have worked out differently. His home ashore was now with his married sister in Swansea, the mother of a girl aged ten and a boy of eight whom he spoiled as if they'd been his own. The company of his niece and nephew helped fill the void in his homecomings following the break-up of his marriage and he'd become a substitute father while their own, also a seaman, was absent. It was on a visit to the local park with the children in the Summer of '52 when he'd first met Heloise, his recollection of which he found so pleasurable, it became the subject of one of his diary-like letters. Daniel came across the strangely-headed account still in the officer's typewriter and later, on finding what must have been an unsatisfactory first typing of the letter in his waste bin, took it out and concealed it on his person.

Third Officer Ivor Williams,
Somewhere off the east coast of America
19th July 1955

Hearts meet in Cwmdonkin Park

I recall first seeing you while shading beneath a tree and watching Flo' and Davy doing what kids do when let loose in a park. It was as if you'd materialized out of thin air to sit on the bandstand steps at about ten yards distant and facing me. It's said that lovers never forget the details of their first meeting and especially if they're meeting the love of their life.

I distinctly remember my pulse beginning to race and my temperature rising as if I'd just downed a large whisky! Warm day, pleasant surroundings and your Adam, first sighting Eve but I doubt that Adam was so immediately smitten! Smitten, mesmerized, are the only words meaningful enough to describe my feelings at that moment. And then, I'm rebuking myself because of being old enough to be your father and it wasn't right to sit gawping lest I appear scary. So I try everything from counting the clouds, which didn't take long on such a day, to helping young Florence make daisy chains. But still my eyes kept returning to this raven-haired beauty until you were on to me and tugging at the hem of your skirt and then it's the usual 'I don't exist any more' and you're looking in any direction but mine. I'd become part of the tree I was sheltering beneath and was accepting that it was just another instance of a man admiring the unobtainable, when fate would intervene and young Davy came tearing out of the bandstand to collide with the object of my admiration who, having just begun to stand, became entangled with my young nephew, a situation which required help and apologies from my good self, a move that brought you into my arms and into my life.

"Thank you," you smiled while helping me to pick up Davy with me oblivious to my arm being still around your waist. "I think he's okay," you said followed by, "and I am too," a hint to be released I guess, which I reluctantly did. And that was the moment our eyes met searchingly with me thinking 'green as the sea before a storm, those eyes' and you seeming to be aware of my thoughts (fancying you) in plain English because your blush told me so and I'm hoping that you'd not find me over-familiar and walk away. But you didn't and we sat down together on the bandstand steps and used the children's antics as a talking point followed by me asking, do you live round here to which you responded by jumping to your feet and throwing back your long, black hair to perform a pirouette with the grace of a practiced ballerina, arms spread wide as if embracing Cwmdonkin and the spread of Swansea.

"Oh yes!" you enthused. "Oh yes! This sea town is most definitely my town!" On your feet and making such a theatrical gesture was your polite way of saying goodbye thought I, downheartedly. But no! To my delight, you rejoined me on the steps and pointed seawards.

"And you? You belong out there, am I right?"

"How do you know that?" I was bound to ask.

"Your gait," you answered cheekily then chuckled cutely before continuing your explanation. "I noticed your gait before sitting down over there and you have that slightly unbalanced walk that sailors have."

"Well, you're spot on, young lady," replied I, a little embarrassed. "I wasn't aware of it."

And then you told me how envious you were of my working and living on the sea and I responded by telling you that life at sea wasn't always that rosy with day after day of nothingness between ports which led on to me asking, had you ever travelled, holidays or otherwise?

"Well, yes," you replied, "but not travel as you know it, abroad that is. But my father used to rent a tiny, rundown cottage every year in the English Midlands and but for missing the sea, I loved it. Oh no, going abroad was only in my dreams, a repetitive dream of being on some tropical river in a kind of small boat and I've got a lover, sweetheart, you know, who is well-elusive and . . ."

I wanted to know more about the lover in your dream but some distant thought stopped you continuing so I didn't push it and our conversation went back to the kids' play and much to my pleasure you stayed with us 'til late afternoon as I recall and the rest is history.

Yes, darling. I've relived those first hours countless times and to anyone reading this memory of it might find it mundane and wonder why we found it so wondrous an occasion. And, darling, we'd have to explain the magic of its venue. The magic of Cwmdonkin Park plus love.

Yours Ivor x

On overhearing the Bo'sun complain to the Chief Steward that someone had been in his store and opened a tin of white paint made Daniel chuckle. The Third was indeed something of a mystery and the letter he'd read in private, while not of real interest to a seventeen-year-old, did contribute to that mystery. The girl Heloise though did interest him and the more the Third talked about her his interest grew, even attempting to scratch away the paint on the bottom half of her bikini; but a sense of guilt and concerned about damaging the photo, he gave up before a single pubic hair had been revealed. His interest in Heloise did wane a little when the Third began to bore him with his and hers admiration for the earlier spoken-about Welsh poet. To him, this made them 'highbrow' and much removed from the poorly educated such as he. Heloise apparently, was the keener fan while he quite happily helped finance her to attend many of his performances.

To explain her admiration the Third described it as being hardly different to the thousands of fans who queue for hours to see the Donald Peers and Johnny Rays of the entertainment world. No, he wasn't a singer but Heloise and hundreds of other, mainly female, followers were taken by his eloquent stage delivery, his deep, Welsh, quavering voice stirring many hearts and minds. The poet, raised but streets away from the Third's and Heloise's homes, was popular not only in Britain but had a strong fan base in the college campus's of the United States where his young audiences would later recall him as being the forerunner of the Brit rock-star invasion to come. Yes, the Third happily accepted his girlfriend's near obsession with the man which led to her many visits to the park next to his childhood home where he'd played and later written fondly of. Cwmdonkin Park, the place of their first meeting as described in the Third's letter, the letter secretly read by his daily cleaner.

Maybe the lack of reading material aboard was Daniel's excuse for quickly perusing the letter before throwing it overboard. His only interest in the Third's affairs, he would admit, was sexual in regard to the young woman whose not-so-young beau was very fortunate to have in his life, mused the youth, his jealousy motivated by his belief that the young belonged with the young. Also, her interest in this poet chap was open to suspicion but when talked about, the Third simply dismissed it, insisting that it was the norm with modern young folk to admire, even adore, those unobtainable stars of stage and screen.

What the officer was saying reminded Daniel of his own fascination with the voice of Christine Archer, teenage daughter of farmer Dan Archer of the popular evening radio serial *The Archers* who'd touched on something in his waking adolescence, even causing him a wasted cycle ride to the village of Hanbury to ask if she was ever there when outside recording took place; so strong was his desire to see if her face matched her alluring voice. So yes, then. If a voice alone could have such an effect, Heloise's attraction to this poet was likely the norm as the Third had said. Yes, he was likely right so . . .? So what? Enough of this absurd distraction from his and Martyn's plan for Canada! Because only this morning he'd overheard Ianto say that even at their present speed, they'd reach the St Lawrence in just a couple of days! The 'St Lawrence'. Gateway to the land of the maple leaf!

Any fool knows that!

Chapter 12

Canada

Via river, ocean and sea, Daniel's brook now followed a broad, snaking, mountain-fringed waterway called the River Saguenay. Sometime the previous night, the Pilot taken aboard on the St Lawrence had guided them into this picturesque river which would take them to the bauxite smelting plants of Port Alfred.

The jungle-encroached Demerara had appeared mystically exotic whereas the lofty, scenic beauty of this Canadian river was, literally, breathtaking. Two days earlier, a squall off Nova Scotia had managed to shift the now-weighted *Roundcape* enough to rekindle Daniel's thoughts of jumping ship. Now, if but temporarily, he found himself experiencing the most contented phase of his sea venture to date.

"Oh – Rose Marieeee – I love yooooou . . .!"[16]

The current hit recording of an American named Slim Whitman rang out melodiously from every cabin radio.

"Oh – Rose Marieeee – I love yooooou . . .!" joined in a choir of rich Welsh voices, causing Daniel to scan the conifer-shrouded slopes for the inevitable mountie. Desolate. Not even a lone grizzly bear to be seen on those majestic heights which, when close enough, enhanced the crew's vocal efforts with rolling echoes. But, as on the tropical Demerara, man, it appeared, wasn't far away as the first of several minute habitations, glistening white in the July sunshine, was sighted nestling in a distant cove.

How were they reached, Daniel wondered? Those remote waterside communes, each dominated by a cross-tipped spire, luminous against a dark mountain backcloth. No river craft here of any abundance as on the Demerara.

---

[16] Rose Marie sung by Slim Whitman. 11 weeks at No.1 in the UK charts 1955.

Roads, it was explained, wending their way through passes undetectable from the river. This, after all, was Canada. As highly a mechanised country as any on Earth. A 'Chevrolet' in every driveway would take these pious come Sunday French Canadians through the mountains to their churches, shops and bars.

French? They were *French* Canadians? Yes, they were in Quebec, Martyn had been informed

"Jumping here, language and all that, could be troublesome," he said. "Ianto says that the only English these Canadian Froggies know is, 'Take your lust-ridden eyes off my daughter, you bastard Limey seamen' and what's more, they'll throw you in the clink for just one verse of *God save our Queen!*"

Excuses! Excuses! If Martyn was getting the jitters then why the hell didn't he come straight out with it and confess that he'd changed his mind about jumping? French maybe. But Canada, like a good third of that school atlas was 'pink'. From the Great Lakes right up to the Yukon, it was 'pink' which meant it was part of the British Empire and there'd be officials who'd welcome ill-treated young English seamen too immature to have ever gone to sea and who now wanted to go home. So if Martyn wasn't up for it, no problem! He's jump alone. Yes, he'd jump alone.

The ship approaching them downstream was conspicuous, firstly for her colour, a very deep green from waterline to rail and secondly, for the dent in her bow. Nothing unusual about dents in ship's hulls. The *Roundcape* herself bore the scars of a few berthing collisions. But her name? *Sun Princess*, surely . . .?

Yes, Daniel had it confirmed. She was the bauxite carrier involved in the sinking of the *Geoligist*. Hours behind them following the collision, she'd since overtaken the *Roundcape* (the latter's engine a much-discussed topic aboard) discharged her cargo and was now probably heading back for another one.

"Did you expect her to be wearin' a wreath around her fuckin' stack or somethin', you morbid wee sod you?" scoffed Jock on detecting the Cabin Boy's awe.

No, you sarcastic bastard, he wanted to tell him. It was just how small was the damage she'd sustained compared with what she'd inflicted on the *Geoligist*, God rest those of her crew lost. But he resisted admitting his feelings to the Second Cook because he knew only too well 'how fuckin' tough was the lot of a seafarer' and that he, Daniel, was too fuckin' soft to have ever gone to sea which in turn might provoke him into revealing to the bullying fucker that, once on Canadian soil, he'd be putting thousands of miles between himself and the loathsome arsehole who'd done more to engender his out-of-character swearing than any other fucker aboard!

The heat of the Canadian Summer was as tiring as that experienced in the Caribbean, the deserting Cabin Boy discovered while climbing another hill out of another port. His discomfort was made worse by having donned as much of his clothing he dared without drawing attention to himself as he made good his departure. Mercifully, on this occasion, there were no pestering insects, prickly undergrowth or a bayonet-wielding sentry to hamper his progress. Only the odd car coming up the hill gave him cause for concern lest it be carrying someone from the ship intent on stopping the absconder. Nobody had taken interest as he'd walked through the docks but on encountering the small township outside, he'd felt conspicuous under the gaze of its residents whose penchant, it seemed, was lazing about on front verandas watching the world go by. He paused for awhile on reaching the crest of the hill to survey the road descending on the other side to where it disappeared into the distance. Decision time? The notices prominently displayed at the dock entrance warned of imprisonment for illegal immigrants but those same notices had included the word 'deportation' and 'deportation' had figured in his plan. He must get to the next township inland away from the port then a few days in a cell followed by a flight home. England, here I come!

So why then did he seem to be rooted to the spot, gazing down on the berthed ship he'd planned so long to escape from? The Saguenay appeared to have expanded into a huge lake upon the shore of which stood Port Alfred and its smelting plants. A short distance away from him on the hill stood a large, metal-framed cross which, after dark, he had noticed while at anchor off the port, was imposingly illuminated. A symbol close to the hearts of these French-speaking Canadians he guessed, recalling their journey upriver. Was it perhaps their way of giving thanks for living in such a beautiful country, he wondered, taking in the panoramic splendour before him?

At anchor on the blue expanse of Lake Ha-Ha below, the vessels awaiting a berth could well have been the toy boats he'd played with on the static parts of his boyhood brook. No indication from up here as to the abominable conditions existing on ships such as his. The Engineers slaving away on those 'critical' repairs below were really suffering. Old Edgar, dripping with oil and sweat seemed near to collapse every time he came up for a break. What a thankless job they had. To go to sea and be stuck down below in those dreadful conditions seemed as pointless as had been his own, similar experience in the factory. Sadly, despite its picturesque surroundings, Port Alfred had an industrial air about it. No trappers and lumberjacks evident there. Most of those locals he'd seen lying about on their verandas were probably dreading clocking on at that sprawling smelting plant down there.

The town's nightlife though surpassed anything he'd experienced back home he'd decided after strolling around in yesterday's last few hours of sunshine, this vibrant new Rock and Roll sound pulsating from every café and bar, well patronized by groups of French Canadian dollies scantily dressed in the evening heat. Other than the odd smile, he regretted not having made any contact with any of these girls.

While their chattering away to each other in French served to heighten their sexual charm, the fact that they might not speak English together with his inexperience in chatting up the opposite sex had put him off trying to socialize and the evening was to have a completely different finish which resulted in much teasing on his return aboard.

"You went 'ome with this Canadian bloke without blinkin' a fuckin' eyelid?" Billy had ridiculed. "Don't you know that every port is crawlin' with perverts waitin' to pounce on cunts like you?"

But the young, English-speaking Canadian whom he'd got talking to in a bar and who'd taken him to his apartment block to meet a neighbour, a young woman from Nottingham who was in Quebec to marry her Canadian Air Force boyfriend had been genuinely friendly and had even driven him back to the docks after a pleasant hour with a fellow Midlander who'd plied him with imported Herefordshire cider, happy to talk and get news about home.

Jock's intervention in the barracking had weighed heavily in the decision that had resulted in him being where he was at that present moment, after he'd refused to believe that he'd not been involved in some kind of orgy.

"I've a good mind to drag you into yon shower an' scrub your cock wi' Dettol in case you infect any o' us!" had been one more of the bully's threats helping to make up Daniel's mind.

The sound of a car crawling up the hill towards him interrupted this unpleasant recall. He recognized it as being a local taxi and, alarmingly, he recognized the front seat passenger too! Was the Third Mate looking for him? The taxi pulled up beside him and the frowning officer beckoned for him to get into the back seat. His decision had been made for him and, accepting it, climbed into the cab, the Third remaining unusually quiet all of the way back to the ship. His silence fortunately extended to those that mattered aboard because no-one in authority ever approached Daniel in respect of the matter and things remained quiet until he eventually heard on the grapevine that somebody aft had voiced concern for him which had been passed on to the officer who was thought least likely to see the Cabin Boy in trouble and who could also get shore leave without attracting questions. That same officer's powerful binoculars had picked him up where the road was visible from the ship, he guessed. But this and exactly how his venture had been foiled would never be openly revealed to him but while many aboard continued to be critical of the strange Mr Williams, Daniel wasn't one of them.

While Captain Roberts was oblivious to the escapade involving his catering staff's most junior member, the most senior of the department, on that very same day, was once again inebriated as a man can be while still on his feet. Even this ability however, as the Captain followed his Chief Steward's ungainly progress up the gangplank, appeared no longer practicable after Mr Bond had knelt to pick up the dropped package which, at a guess, contained the replacement china tea service that five hours ago he'd gone ashore to purchase.

This disturbing sight spoiled for the *Roundcape's* Master what otherwise had been turning out to be a cautiously optimistic day. Over tea in his accommodation he'd just informed the company agent of the successful repairs carried out by their own Engineers when the sound of laughter caused him to glance out of an aft-facing porthole from where he'd earlier that day watched powerful extraction ducts complete the discharge of their mineral ore cargo: an efficient and clean operation which would rule out any claim for 'dirt money' and an early departure from the port.

So why the hell did alcoholic Mr Bond, now on his hands and knees and proceeding along the deck towards the bridge, have to cast his great, fat shadow over things? The agent must not see this embarrassing sight!

"The toilet, Mr Richards? Of course, that door over there."

That should keep him occupied until the old piss-head has reached his cabin. Where is he now? He – he's back on his feet and staring into that open hold! Where – where's your tea service, Albert . . .? Oh no! He – he's lurching towards the bridge and looking up this way! *Nooooo*, you drunken old fool! I've subbed you once and you're not coming up here in that state! Go below to the bond store and play with your bloody guns! Go and play with your bloody guns!

His desertion foiled, Daniel was back on board in time to witness the Chief's unseemly return from shopping and found the spectacle as hilarious as the next man. On discovering what his boss had been shopping for then lost had him recall his first mishap aboard, making the present spectacle less funny. Another, whose laughter ended abruptly was Brumpud who became so dizzy with mirth that he collapsed onto the galley range in mistake for his stool. His retribution for delighting in another's misfortune was furthered in that the butt of his mirth, in his intoxication, just happened to mislay his medical cupboard key, consequenting in the Cook being deprived of any proper treatment for his badly burned backside until the key reappeared two days out of Port Alfred.

'You'll be bored stiff between ports but once berthed expect anything!' had been another of his brother's prophecies to prove true and further substantiated later that day by Martyn's account of Ianto's antics ashore.

"He's so pissed that he just walks into a shop and takes anything he fancies does Ianto! He's got watches and cameras and the last thing I saw him nick was one of those fantastic lumber jackets that everybody's after. Reckons he even had a free shag last night by climbing out of the window while the girl was showering. He said that she'd enjoyed it more than he had so why pay?"

It was then Daniel's turn to raise Martyn's eyebrows with his account of the Chief Steward caper.

"What! You actually saw him on his hands and knees going up the stairs to the old man's cabin and the old man was hitting him with a broom?"

"Yeah. After he'd stumbled and lost his parcel in the hold, he kept falling over cos his trousers were 'round his ankles. So he went onto the bridge on his hands and knees and almost tripped up the agent as they met on the stairs and that's when the Skipper started whacking him with the broom! I saw it all when I was told to collect the Skipper's tea things!"

"Christ, mun! What happened next?"

"Oh, I didn't stay around much longer cos Brumpud came tearing up the stairs with his arse on fire and knocked the tray out of me hands."

"His arse on fire? Brumpud had his arse on fire?"

"Well, not exactly in flames like. But his trousers were definitely smouldering. Sat on the galley range and set fire to himself, so they say. And he was on his way upstairs for treatment cos the Chief Steward was too pissed to know what he was doing."

"Bloody hell! Did the Skipper give him any treatment?"

"Oh, he gave him treatment alright! He started whacking him with the broom as well!"

"I'll bet they both get logged won't they?"

"That's what I asked Jock but he was too busy treating Brumpud with this great poultice to answer."

"So Jock's got access to medication has he?"

"I don't know. All he did was grin and told me to tell Reno to cross Yorkshire pudding off this evening's menu."

At dawn the next day, a still furious Captain Roberts was threatened with a heavy fine if he failed to vacate his berth immediately. That half of the *Roundcape's* crew were still unofficially ashore was obviously of no interest to the harbour authority and it was a very irate Skipper who took his vessel out to anchorage on Lake Ha-Ha that morning, his temper rising from irate to sheer fury by the time the sun had begun to sink and there was still no sign of the absentees.

As the tension spread amongst the officers and the size of the predicted loggings grew, Daniel found himself listening to what terrible punishments would have been inflicted on such irresponsible seamen of yesteryear. His interest in such maritime history quickly faded however, when rumours of a desertion because of conditions aboard, began to circulate. If this proved true, it was said, they could well be at anchor on this lake for months awaiting a replacement crew. And then her owners would likely send her tramping to recoup their loss until her bottom fell out!

Bitterly regretting his own return aboard, Daniel reacted more quickly than most to the eventual cry that announced the revellers' return, his eyes filling with tears as the launch, rolling with the antics of those boozy, singing Welshmen drew closer.

"Sospan faaach – yn berwi ar y taaaaaan . . .!" they sang with unrestrained gusto, etching the occasion on many a memory.

Enhancing that memory was the brilliant splash of colour emerging with the launch out of the hazy distance.

"That's the bloody jacket he's nicked look you!" laughed Martyn, pointing to where the resplendent form of Ianto swayed precariously on the launch's fo'c'sle.

"Looks like most of 'em have got one now!"

"Every Evans, Edwards and Jones by the looks!" agreed the chuckling Bo'sun appearing behind them. "Most colourful bunch of seagoin' lumberjacks I ever set eyes on. And I can only hope the Steward's found his key to the medicine cupboard!"

"Why's that then?" asked Martyn.

"Cos, boyo," replied the Bo'sun, tapping his pipe empty on the rail, "I'll wager there's not a healthy chopper left between 'em!"

Chapter 13

Hurricane Connie

Mindful of his punishment at Jock's hands for 'whistling up the wind', sea superstitions, Daniel now knew, were not voiced to be made fun of. Therefore, he refrained even to smile when Hassan, the greaser's Mess Boy told he and Martyn that some of his elders were quaking in their boots at the sight of a spectacular red sunset five days out of Port Alfred.

Sheer hysteria he thought but, nevertheless, the impressive sight of that glowing red orb setting the heavens ablaze and turning the sea into an ocean of blood was enough to have the Cabin Boy join the many others at the rail taking in the spectacle and on spotting the Third Mate, seemingly in deep contemplation of the same, approached the officer and repeated what Hassan had said.

The Third's reaction was, as usual, anything but straight to the point and only after a rambled speech which inevitably got round to Heloise and how enraptured she would have been by such a sunset, did he even begin to accept that a question had been posed.

"You're wanting an explanation as to their concern, eh, boyo? Well, it's an *unusual* but not entirely *unique* sunset as anybody who's spent a few years at sea will tell you and them aft enjoy scaring each other witless over the silliest things. Their imaginations loosen their bowels quicker than the Cook's hottest curry, believe you me," he chuckled. "Takes only one of 'em to get a fixation over something and the whole daft lot have to follow suit. And today it's this sunset that's disturbing them, eh?"

Shading his eyes to look skywards he added, in a less jocular tone, "Well, in this instance, boyo, in these waters . . . maybe they *do* have something to be concerned about."

"Er – what over?" asked Daniel. "Why should they be concerned?"

"Well now, Daniel, the old timers in that village home of yours, one glance at the evening sky and they'll know what they'll be at in their gardens next day, am I right?"

"Er – yes . . . but at sea? What does a sky like this mean at sea?"

But the officer left him in suspense as to what the phenomenon might indicate as if he'd suddenly been given a cue to enquire about Daniel's rural upbringing and, as usual, the youth felt he'd no option other than to go along with it.

The pattern of this particular conversation differed from their previous chats inasmuch as the officer became so fascinated by Daniel's account of his boyhood in the countryside that he, for once, almost gave him free rein to continue without interruption. He did interrupt though, on sensing Daniel's reticence to be more specific when talking about the reclusive, unconventional Bloom family and, after having his curiosity aroused by a brief mention of this quaint rural family and the tumbledown, isolated cottage, the Third's interest grew.

"Bloom? Their name was Bloom? They couldn't have had a more fitting name, eh, boyo?"

Perhaps, Daniel mused. His story might have sounded more credible if he'd given the Blooms a fictitious name. but the 'Blooms' were the 'Blooms' and if the name was a fabrication as was being suggested then so could be the fanciful name 'Heloise', he hinted. But the Third was flying too high to be baited.

"And that was your innocent perception, eh? Living so remote with no gas or electric or running water and yet you still thought they'd got it made! I like it, boyo! I like it!"

His enthusiasm seemed a little over the top considering that he came from Wales, much of which consisted of small, isolated communities, mused Daniel as the officer enquired on about his and the Bloom family and, significantly, their respective teenage daughters.

"Both fair of face with long, black hair and shapely figures like my own beautiful Heloise, eh?" he enthused, convincing the youth that the sexual aspect of rusticity was very much at the heart of his intrigue and that's what he wanted to hear about.

"Er – yes. Dinah, that's Maurice's sister like. She looked a little bit similar to the photos you've shown me of . . "

"Shapley young limbs, peach-like skin and looks a man would die for, eh, Daniel?"

"Yeah . . . she – she was smashing looking with lovely skin and . . . and when she smiled she'd make you feel kind of . . ."

"She'd make you feel weak at the knees and gave you a warm, glowing sensation where your mother said you oughtn't, am I right?"

"Well, er – yeah, she did make you feel sort of . . ."

"Randy!" completed the other. "And why shouldn't she, looking like that? Her back-to-basics upbringing would've had much to do with such perfection! That water-well you spoke of in the garden for instance? Good for the skin and a lot to do with that pearly smile of hers, the everyday use of well-water I'll be bound! Your 'oppo's sexy sister was likely the most striking beauty in the village I shouldn't wonder?"

"Er, yeah . . . she was kind of a looker alright. But – but me own sister was made carnival queen a couple of times while Maurice's sister only made lady-in-waiting," stated Daniel proudly. "And our water came from a tap at the sink!" he added with a grin.

The Third's 'I give up' expression suggested that he'd just heard something verging on stupidity and that he was considering a suitable reply.

"Look now, son," he began eventually, in a much subdued tone. "If one day you get around to telling your grandkids about those Blooms of yours, tell 'em about the tumbledown cottage and its withered old orchard. Tell 'em about this superhuman chum of yours. His long-limbed, rosy-cheeked sister and her pearly-white smile. But *don't* look you, go ruining the tale with a stupid remark such as 'your sister was prettier because your house happened to be connected to the bloody water main'!"

"Er – sorry," offered Daniel sheepishly. "Just – just my little joke like."

"That's alright, my young comedian," smiled the other, ruffling his hair and increasing his discomfort. "Heloise blushes like that" he chuckled.

"I – I'm not blushing. It's the blooming sun. it's making everything red. The sky, the sea and everything. What's it a sign of anyway?"

The Third's narrowed eyes were suddenly two flashing red rubies as he looked skywards.

"A bloody hurricane I'd say, boyo," he answered gravely. "A bloody hurricane."

The 'tail lash' of hurricane Connie hit the *Roundcape* at around six a.m the following morning . . . despite her navigator's claim that they were well clear of the hurricane's full wrath, the weather encountered was, according to older hands aboard, some of the worst they'd experienced.

It was the clatter of loose doors and furniture that stirred Daniel from his slumber. Next, loud creaks and groans from the very bulkheads together with the tumultuous sound of the sea, wind and rain, convinced him that no-one would be expected to turn out on such a morning! His pulse racing, he became aware of Jock's legs dangling from above and in the far, upper bunk Billy's cigarette glowed ominously in the darkness. Somebody, it must be Reno, was stumbling and cursing his way about the cabin.

"Where – where's the lifejackets?" cried the Maltese flicking on the light. "On lifeboat drill where'd they say we'd get our lifejackets for God's sake?"

Daniel's heart began to pump faster and he wished that he was at home collecting the still-warm morning eggs from his father's hens. Jock too, had eggs on his mind.

"Lifejackets, my arse! She's nae even reached forty-five degrees yet! Perfect conditions for fryin' eggs! They'll move aroun' the pan wi'out me layin' a hand on it this mornin'!"

Suddenly, all was bedlam as a tremendous roll to starboard pitched Billy out of his bunk.

"That's the quickest I've seen you get out o' your pit since boardin'!" guffawed Jock. His legs were suddenly replaced by his smirking face. "While you're down there," he addressed the groaning Billy, "would you mind askin' our Cabin Boy if he fancies a nice, greasy slice o' fried bread wi' his breakfast this mornin'?"

His laughter continued at the sight of a dazed Billy attempting to stand, his extinguished cigarette stuck to his bottom lip.

"This tiiiime!" yelled the Scot as Daniel's bunk seemed to drop from beneath him.

Swaaaaaaak!

The bulkheads shuddered as an angry sea tested them and suddenly they were rolling again!

"This tiiiiime! She'll nae come back this *tiiiiime!"*

He had to be right! The great, hairy bully had to be right! She couldn't possibly come back this time! Empty ships can only roll until their heavy superstructure can no longer defy gravity? Another violent shudder followed by the groaning of stressed metal somewhere below and then they were coming back at such a speed that the opposite roll would surely be impossible to . . .?

"This tiiiiime! She'll nae come back this *tiiiiime!"*

And she wouldn't! She couldn't! Billy and Reno had been thrown together in the middle of the cabin and were clutching each other in fearful anticipation of her definitely not coming back from such a roll!

"Is it's dancin' you pair o' nancy boys are in the mood for this mornin'? Let's see if Victor Sylvester's up an' about wi' his orchestra!"

Jock's raucous commentary ceased momentarily as he fiddled with the controls of his powerful receiver.

"The next time I catch you fuckin' about wi' this radio, Billy, I'm gonna . . .!"

"On-ly youuuuu – can make this chaaaange in meeeee . . ."[17]

The harmonious sound of The Platters rang out as the *Roundcape* shuddered her way back from yet another impossible tangent. Any sense of normality brought about the music was quickly dispelled as an oilskin-clad sailor burst into the cabin carrying four lifejackets.

"Not to panic, boys, just a precautionary measure look you," he said with an un-assuring grimace.

"Not to blooming-well panic! But just slip one of these on in case you find yourself floundering about in the storm-raged Atlantic! That's what the man was really saying as casually as his mother advising him to wear a mac when the rain threatened!"

"Strewth, laddie! Dinnae just gawp at it! Put the bastard thing on or didnae they teach you fuck-all at that poncy trainin' school?"

Oh yeah! They'd taught him how to go about saving himself right enough! But it had hardly been considered as important as laying cutlery and folding a napkin! And if there'd been just the slightest suggestion of him having to don a lifejacket because ships didn't always stay afloat, then his going to sea would have been considered as too blooming-well risky, you sarcastic bugger you!

The port and starboard companionways being intermittently awash, access for'ard was by way of the boat deck with the help of a hurriedly-rigged safety line. Having to turn out at all surprised Daniel. But nothing it seemed, not even a hurricane could interrupt the daily routine aboard a British Merchantman.

Battling his way for'ard in a wind that, without the strung line to hang on to, would surely have lifted him into space; it seemed totally absurd that the purpose of his mission was to perform simple pantry chores. Even when he dared look up from his precarious path, he could only imagine the true nature of the sea

---

[17] 'Only You', American group The Platters, released Mercury Records, May 1955.

on this, the blackest of mornings. Out of this blackness screamed a relentless fury intent on punishing all in its path! Decibels higher than this unholy blast came the eerie howl of the wind around the *Roundcape's* tall funnel which, during one, long, terrifying roll, he thought was toppling upon him, almost causing him to let go of the line.

After descending the fixed ladder from over the galley roof and following the line to the pantry door, he was dismayed to find it bolted from within. No sooner had he let go of the line to make for an alleyway door, he was enveloped by a huge wave which propelled him back across the deck to collide painfully but mercifully, with the port rail!

"It's still raining is it, son?"

The Chief Steward's unsympathetic reception of the half-drowned youth was typical of the man's reaction to any happening aboard however dramatic. That Daniel was sure he'd broken some ribs through colliding with the rail was of little matter to the Chief who'd barely recovered from his own misadventure and consequential broom battering at the hands of the Skipper. Had he noticed any smoke coming out of the galley stack when he'd passed, was of far greater importance than Daniel's close call! The old man was waiting for his breakfast kipper which meant that seconds later, Daniel was back outside and hammering on the bolted galley door pleading to be let in!

Dawn beginning to penetrate the tempestuous skies, he was now able to witness, in awe, the spectacular effect being wreaked on the ocean by Connie, this angry, tail-lashing hurricane Connie. Frantically he repeatedly banged on the galley door with his food containers.

"Who the fuck is that?"

"It's Daniel! Let me in for Christ's sake!"

"Fuck off, you . . .!"

The howling wind drowned the rest of Jock's dismissal.

"Let me in! It's bucketin' down and the sea's . . .!"

The youth froze as an angry green mountain rose within feet of him until its white crest seemed to merge with the swirling black clouds.

"Let me in! I'm gonna be drowned!"

His pleas unanswered, he steeled himself face on against the door to await the inevitable. Feeling nothing more than the pelting rain, peeped over his shoulder. No mountain, no sea and suddenly so uncannily quiet as he gazed skyward through the port rail.

"Hold tight! Watch out for this *bastaaaaard!*"

More yells followed by the clatter of pots and pans echoed from within the galley. A tremendous shudder seemed to run the whole length of the ship, her port side banking away to reveal a vast chasm large enough to consume a hundred *Roundcape*s then suddenly she was plunging sideways like a runaway toboggan into that aqueous valley, the heights of which were already beginning to curl and ensnare so easy a prey!

"Let me *iiiiiiin!*"

"Yeah! I'll open the door for the mouthy wee bastard! I'll teach the cunt not to go to the weather . . .!"

The thunderous roar of falling water cancelled out Jock's threat as he threw back the door bolt. Later, Daniel was to complain as to how anybody could distinguish between weather and leaside in such conditions! He'd chosen what had appeared the safest entry at that time and the ensuing disaster was brought about by Jock himself for not opening up on his first knocking. He'd been two steps back from the door and about to flee when the Cook had thrown open the door hoping to flatten him against the adjacent bulkhead which, as it turned out, was about the most ill-timed act of temper ever performed by the fiery Scot.

The tremendous hiss from theCooking range was Daniel's initial fright during his ocean-propelled entry into the galley. That the range fire had been extinguished was hardly as worrying as the sight of Brumpud and his scar-faced assistant floundering about in swirling, waist-high water amidst a flotilla of pots and pans, sausages, kippers and eggs and an armada of the previous evening's freshly-baked loaves.

"These things happen at sea. I hope the cat's okay," was the Chief Steward's cool response on being informed about the latest calamity. "I'm sure I saw him heading for the galley just before the storm broke."

Tiggy, to the Chief's relief was found asleep in the saloon but the man's laid-back manner quickly vanished on this occasion when informed that the whole crew's sustenance for the day would consist of warmed-up snacks on a makeshift stove in the pantry.

As the day progressed, the worsening weather resulted in many other shipboard functions not running as normal. These conditions climaxed mid-afternoon when the order was given for all unauthorized crew to keep off the decks. They were 'running for it' which meant, said an increasingly tense Billy, 'that they were heading in any direction that would keep them afloat'! In the same, pessimistic tone, he went on to inform Daniel 'that they'd been at half speed ever since the codged-up engine had deteriorated before even clear of the St Lawrence, and if it packed up completely, they'd be in the fuckin' lifeboats before tea'?

By this time, languid with seasickness, Daniel, despite having to keep his lifejacket on was as grateful as any man for the chance to sprawl on his bunk. But, even as the ship continued to pitch and roll excessively even along this 'safer course', Jock's constant shouts of *"This tiiiiiime!"* and "One more like that and she'll break her back!" along with morbid chat about death, had the youth wondering if his present resting place might be his last?

They most likely would have sunk hours ago, his cabin mates informed him, had the *Roundcape* been a 'Sam boat', one of the hurriedly-built 'welded' ships thrown together in the USA during the last war? Folded up, did those Sam boats in conditions far less severe than those they were presently experiencing. Their ship, fortunately, was a 'riveted' ship. Every last plate riveted together and as Jock took pleasure in telling his 'shipmate of the day' would last for at least another two, maybe even three hours before the order to abandon her was given!

So this was it then? Only seventeen years old, just beginning to 'live' life and, according to his gloomy shipmates, almost over. They'd hardly remember him back home.

"Oh, that Daniel Brazier? Lost at sea, eh? Didn't even know he'd gone to sea. Didn't seem the type. The only interest he'd shown in water was messing about in that blessed brook with Mrs Bloom's lad."

He'd never really made his mark in the village. His milk-top achievement at the age of seven had only been brought to notice by a measly two inches of a column secreted in an inside page of the local newspaper. Maurice had at least made a splash on the sports page when the school team had won the district cup and that had been much more recent than his tin-foil war effort.

Even his private detective caper had gone virtually unnoticed. A *'private eye kit that will give you a personal law enforcement status in your community'* the *Eagle* comic advertisement had read. *'Disguise and arm yourself and become a local celebrity by uncovering the criminals in your midst!'* But the large, ginger moustache wouldn't stay on and after he'd flashed his toy gun and badge of authority at the greengrocer for allowing his horse to foul a public highway, he'd told him to fetch a shovel and spread it around his dad's celery. Only the handcuffs had proved useful on arresting Eileen Bracewell, a regular visitor from Kent. But then she'd been an only too willing captive at age fourteen and always eager to show that she'd not only got hair under her arms but somewhere private if he cared to have a peek while he, at age eleven, was embarrassingly lacking, her demands to see prompting her early release as much as she'd objected. Oh, where were girls like Eileen when he'd reached fifteen and began to get those urges while the girls only wanted to take the piss because of his spreading acne rather than give free displays?

It was quite likely that her embarrassing him, plus Dennis Skinner's dad reporting him to his parents for handcuffing the six-year-old to the greengrocer's cart only causing him to lose a bit of skin off his knees, that caused him to jack in the detective lark and concentrate more fully on his and Maurice's pact. Their occupation and knowledge of the brook had undoubtedly provided a more worthwhile pastime and, certainly for a while, the draping of those empty condom packets around the bridge arches at both ends had seemed to have had some effect in keeping the opposite sex (other than Eileen Bracewell) away from their sanctuary.

Not that in retrospect Maurice had proved to be the sworn lifetime companion as agreed in the pact and now, his moving to Coventry would probably mean that he'd not even get to hear about his demise. He'd just keep working that lathe in complete ignorance of the fate of his once best mate. Even Patsy Harding, preparing to marry, wouldn't give him more than a passing thought. Bet she'd never been a willing prisoner daring lads to peek at her pubic hair? Too blooming-well stuck up for that! That little Cardiff redhead would have been the type though. She was the kind of girl he was beginning to like because they didn't leave it up to the bloke to do all of the running. Pity he'd wasted that golden opportunity back there. Could have at least had that *experience* before his time came.

With the exception maybe of Reno, biting his pillow in fear over there, his cabin mates, he knew, were experienced. The Maltese, Jock said, was just a mouther who never really got down to things. But then Jock hardly had a good word for anybody and that old woman back in Mackenzie had had him scratching himself since the Caribbean, Billy said. No, there was only one character aboard who'd experienced sex in a way he truly envied if his revelations could be believed. They'd become even more explicit of late, the Third Mate's revelations and even if she'd turned him slightly bonkers flitting about the globe as she'd supposedly been doing; his time spent with the gorgeous Heloise would make any red-blooded male envious.

Smack in the middle of a vast Welsh beach called Pendine Sands were one could drive on to the sands and park up in a remote spot, was where they'd first made love then and many times after, was his salacious recollection. He'd no need to elaborate about those occasions. Just looking at those photos of the vivacious Heloise while cleaning the Third's cabin every day was enough to stir Daniel into having lustful thoughts. He'd take her to that beach via a small town called Laugharne where they'd enjoy a few drinks in a local pub, he said, his anticipation when jollying up in that hostelry was increased by the attention her beauty drew from the locals while he alone, revelled in the thought that the girl, so admired, who'd shortly be cart-wheeling in the nude or lying in his arms on sun-kissed sands, was both mentally and physically his. Well, 'mentally' in most respects he'd sometimes intimate in that mysterious way of his; then fail to further explain as he'd gone on to chuckle about how she'd mischievously expose her thighs while climbing back into the car or how she'd sometimes start peeling her clothes off before they'd even parked up on that beach.

Yes, he'd really had a ball had the Third. Small wonder he paces the decks at night. Who wouldn't, being apart from a stunner like her? Give a certain Cabin Boy the experience of loving then losing a girl like Heloise and he too would go bonkers enough to take to a boat on the Demerara so as to find her. Just to have that experience though! And he would! They'd ride out of this blooming hurricane and on the very next quay there'd be a hundred and one similar, sexy-eyed Heloises waiting with outstretched arms . . .!

"An' what will our Mr Weather-side's last thoughts be when she finally breaks her back an' spews him out into the drink?" the crab-infected occupant of the bunk above peering evilly down at him was keen to know.

"I – er . . . I've got a feeling we're going to be alright."

"Alright, eh? Did you hear that, lads? Mr Weather-side over here reckons we're gonna be alright!"

Grateful for any distraction, Billy and Reno grinned to appear interested.

"Mr Weather-side's a *believer* I take it?" pursued the Cook. "Somebody up there'll take us away frae this hurricane to safer waters. Is what you believe, eh, Mr Weather-side?"

"Er – yeah . . . I do," replied Daniel unconvincingly.

"You believe in fuckin' miracles do you then, laddie? Brought up on the Bible were you?"

"No. To be honest, I've never owned one."

"This is unbelievable, lads! Mr Weather-side here has never owned a Bible yet he *knows* we're gonna make it! So what I'd like you to explain, Mr Weather-side, if you've never owned a Bible just *where* did you get such fervent beliefs? Out o' a fuckin' Rupert Bear annual I shouldnae wonder?"

"Well," began Daniel, after obligatory chuckles at Jock's wit, "he always manages to get home doesn't he?"

"Who? Who always manages to get home?"

"Rupert. Rupert Bear. Whatever scrapes he gets into he always manages to get home in time for his tea."

"You wouldnae be takin' the piss would you, laddie?"

"Of course not, Jock. You've had your say so I'm having mine. We can't meet our Maker today, you in particular."

"I've warned you about takin' the piss, laddie! Now, tell me an' the lads just why we, meself in particular'll not be passin' through the pearly gates today? Out wi' it, an' nae more o' your lip!"

Something told Daniel to be cautious but he wasn't backing down this time.

"Cos the Chief Steward's got other ideas," he said quietly.

"Christ almighty! I hadnae given a thought about the Chief bein' in control o' our fuckin' destinies! How the fuck did Mr Weather-side come to such a conclusion? Has the drunken old slob sobered up enough to climb the main-mast an' order the sea to calm down? Is that what you're tellin' us, laddie?!"

"Er – not exactly."

"Out wi' it then! We're hangin' on to Mr Weather-side Rupert Bear's every last word as to how the old piss-head has got our destinies sewn up!"

"Cos when I left the pantry," Daniel replied in as strong a voice as he could summon, "he told me to tell you that there's an inch of blue sky to the west and as soon as it's big enough to make a pair of trousers out of; to get off your fat arse and light the galley fire."

Jock's fury compared well with that of the hurricane Connie but, thankfully on this occasion, his favourite shipmate only suffered verbally while the hurricane, it was reported on US radio, caused widespread damage and claimed at least forty lives.

With the seas still extremely rough but now more navigable, why then the sudden change of course from southerly to westerly was the question being asked aboard? The suggested dash for safer waters before another hurricane was Daniel's worry as he watched huge rollers crashing over the ship's bows from the saloon's for'ard portholes and then alarm as he observed another freighter battling the mountainous seas about a mile ahead of them on the same course, drop out of sight for a full minute! His relief at her reappearance was short-lived and such was his concern that she had vanished completely, panicked him into announcing the fact to the Chief Steward!

"Don't worry son," reassured the big man in his nonchalant manner. "Her cabin boy has likely lost sight of us as well. But with her headway, he'll step ashore in Yankee-land long before you do."

Yankee-land! They were making for Yankee-land! The surprising but uplifting news turned conversation from morose to Marilyn Monroe and Knickerbocker beer! Even the black clouds began to disperse and make way for the sun. They'd made it! They'd escaped the Connie and were now heading for repairs in the good old USA! There were good times ahead! *Whoopeeeee!*

Elation though, was not typical throughout the ship. Three faces remained as gloomy as the weather they'd out-ridden. The burdened expressions of the Skipper and Chief Engineer required little explanation. But the Third Mate's woeful countenance, Daniel eventually realized, while related to their changed destination, was neither technically or financially connected to maritime matters.

Having little desire to be involved in the officer's sudden depression, Daniel thought it best to avoid him, preferring to listen to the light-hearted banter concerning their next port of call and the sight of Billy grooming his much ravaged suit in preparation for shore leave was an obvious choice.

"You'll nae be walkin' ashore with me wearin' that!" baited Jock. "The Yanks are witch huntin' for Commies these days and the mere sign o' some twat tarted up in Soviet red'll have them alertin' the fuckin' White House afore you're even clear o' the dock gates!"

"Jock's right about Communists," backed Reno before Billy could protest. "I hear they screen everybody for political reasons these days. One wrong word and they'll not let you ashore, the American authorities. Very sensitive about politics these days I'm told."

"And the clap!"

All eyes were back on Billy.

"Very strict about the clap they are, so I was told by this Taff sailor this mornin'. 'e says they've got two screenin' receptions. One for revealin' your politics an' if you get through that, the second is for revealin' what you might 'ave picked up on the Demerara?"

"Small chance o' you gettin' through either reception, eh, Billy?" teased Jock but not with his usual confidence while scratching his groin.

"Billy boy'll pass through both receptions an' wearin' 'is clobber!" declared the Bristolian positively. "This sailor aft's been tellin' me as to 'ow the Yankee entry officials operate. 'e says 'e was only stopped once an' that was in Philadelphia in the second reception."

"Because of infection?" asked Reno. "He had a venereal disease did he?"

"Naah, you dusky twat! It were 'is political beliefs they stopped 'im for!"

"But you distinctly said they stopped him in the *second* reception! The *clap* reception!" erupted the Maltese.

"Yeah, they did! An' 'e was as clean as a monk in solitary!" retorted Billy. "But once 'e'd dropped 'is pants it were the 'ammer an' sickle tattooed on 'is arse that stopped 'im goin' ashore; so this Taff sailor tells me at any rate."

"Rubbish! Which sailor filled your head with such rubbish?" spat Reno.

"The same sailor who gave me the disinfectant powder to give Jock," came the tongue-in-cheek reply.

On a bright August morning, some minutes after sighting the Virginian coast, a helicopter bearing US military markings swooped low over the *Roundcape*, circled her twice then, as if satisfied with Ianto's bawled, "Morning Dwight! No Commies aboard! Just a shower of sex-starved Taffs and a cat with a sore arse!" soared off back landwards like a huge, silver bee droning its way home in the morning sunshine.

"Just a last minute check that'll have been, boyo!" the jovial Cardiffian informed Daniel while grinning at Brumpud. "They'll have studied us with every device from sub' to radar! Even know what colour socks the old Cook 'ere's wearin'. In't that right me old shipmate?"

"Not this mornin' they won't, our kid," replied Brumpud, turning from the range to stoop and expose bare ankles. "They'm in the wash. Can't go ashore in Yankee-land wearin' stinky socks, can yow?"

The light-hearted anticipation aboard as they entered Chesapeake Bay, the long, Virginian waterway in the mouth of which stood Newport News, the port where they would undergo engine repairs and, it was rumoured, maybe take on a cargo of special type coal for Europe; a rumour which, despite a few adverse comments from men whose homes were in the

Welsh mining valleys, created further high spirits aboard at the possibility of being home and paid off within weeks.

As the American Pilot guided the old freighter to her berth, Martyn came amidships to take in the scenery with Daniel and his cabin mates. Both Deck and Cabin Boy were visibly excited at the thought of stepping ashore in the homeland of their film idols and those 'groovy' musicians who were currently making the Earth vibrate on its axis. Billy too, was happily voicing his thoughts but Jock quickly stamped on wasted praise for 'celluloid one-minute wonders' while a *real* man with the name of Campbell had won the admiration of the United States and beyond by becoming the fastest man afloat only weeks ago! And now, he went on to say bitterly, that they aboard the *Roundcape* were having to bear the shame of visiting the States on a crippled ship ten years overdue for the fucking knacker's yard, visually parading to the Yanks the state of a fading empire!

Such comments, it was observed, did little to dispel the eager anticipation of shore leave. The news therefore, on tying up, that there'd be no shore leave for any man that first evening was ill-received, Daniel included, who, on completing his chores, killed time by watching traffic streaming across the St James river on a bridge so finely constructed could only have been spun across that broad waterway by a giant spider!

"A remarkable example of Yankee Engineering, eh, Daniel?"

Something in the Third's approach suggested that his comment was but an opener with which to break his recent marked silence.

"I – I'll say," acknowledged the youth uneasily but began to relax a little as the officer went on to enquire as to what were his first impressions of the States, giving the Cabin Boy another opportunity to voice the magic he'd felt since they'd passed the Chesapeake lightship. It wasn't long though, before he sensed that his listener hardly shared his enthusiasm and that his brief comments were more out of courtesy than interest and only when he ventured to enquire as to might there be any truth in the rumour about them taking on coal and heading home, did the officer suddenly and angrily reveal his true thoughts.

"What's the bloody matter with you, boyo? One minute you're over the moon at being in the States and God knows why cos it's hardly paradise in my book and next you're asking is it coal and home?"

Stunned by his outburst, Daniel returned his gaze to the endless lights crossing the bridge in the falling darkness.

"Sorry, Daniel," the officer eventually sighed. "Unforgiveable, venting one's feelings on the ship's Cabin Boy. But if it hadn't been you, it would have been some other poor bugger see?"

"That's alright. I'm getting used to bollockings," murmured the other.

"Listen to me for a minute will you, Daniel?"

The Third's tone was now deadly serious.

"What I said about it would've been some other bugger? Well, it was a lie because I came out here to see you especially. To ask a favour, would you believe, considering the way I thundered off at you!"

"Er – what kind of favour?" asked Daniel, his eyes still fixed on the bridge.

"Just something I'd appreciate you holding on to until you get back to Blighty."

"The last time somebody asked me to hold on to something, I got lumbered with a blooming cat!" smiled the youth attempting to hide his embarrassment for having been singled out to perform this 'favour'.

"Do you think you could find your way to Swansea, boyo? It's only a short train ride from Cardiff. I'll make it worth your while."

"Er – I suppose I could but, er – why don't you ask somebody aboard who lives more local? There's many who live down that way."

"Because in all honesty see, there's no other aboard I could trust."

"Old Edgar . . .? Surely he'll help you out?"

"Yes, of course old Edgar would Daniel. Of course he would but . . .?"

The Third was suddenly clutching his arm, the peak of his cap nudging his head as he hissed into his ear.

"Promise to breathe not a word of this, boyo, but there's good likelihood if it's coal and home, myself and the Fourth Engineer'll not be sailing with you."

"Oh – I, er – see," began Daniel as casually as he was able. "Just, er – hand it over, whatever it is. I'll do me best to . . ."

"Thanks Daniel, thanks!" gushed the officer squeezing his arm affectionately. "I'm keeping my fingers crossed that it won't be necessary but if it's coal and home there's a small package I'd like you to deliver when you get back. Twenty quid for your trouble. How does a month's pay sound to you now?"

"Twenty quid! Surely you'd be better off posting it wouldn't you? Er . . .? I – I wouldn't be smuggling anything would I?"

"Smuggling? Heavens no! Of course you wouldn't be smuggling, boyo! There's no great mystery about this package. Let me explain."

The package, he said, would consist of a build up of retained correspondence to his lady friend which he wanted delivered by hand to his sister's home in Swansea. Nothing fishy about that but, after being told that he wanted the package delivered to his sister because of being unsure of the whereabouts of Heloise at that time, Daniel began to have doubts as to the wisdom of his agreeing to do this 'favour'.

His growing doubt regards doing favours for the Third was put to Edgar, the Fourth Engineer who'd spotted the youth in conversation with the man and had waylaid him while returning to his cabin.

"So he reckons I'm going along with him does he now?" he cackled, his craggy face twisted into a toothless grin. "Best man is what he'll be wanting me along for I'll wager. A wedding on the Demerara and me dressed up as a clown at the daft bugger's side I shouldn't wonder?"

Edgar had simply tolerated his friend's eccentric behaviour pretending to go along with his fantasies as a distraction from his own domestic problems.

"A few bevies too many and I was almost up there with him at times!" he chuckled. "And what red-blooded male wouldn't relish the idea of paddling around with some dusky beauty under a tropical sun?" he joked on. "But dreamin's one thing and reality's another, I tried to convince him back in Mackenzie! But he'd have none of it! She's back there waiting for him on the Demerara is his obsession! And there's no convincing the sorry sod otherwise look you!"

A quiet word with the Skipper had of course crossed Edgar's mind.

"But you see, boyo, this is his first ship for two years and if the pool doc' signs him fit to sail then I'll not be party to him losing his ticket which means his livelihood. Then no way will I be a party to that! No way!"

Edgar's outburst stopped just short of him revealing how truly 'unbalanced' he now thought his 'friend' to be. Such revelations however were not for the ears of his adolescent listener that night. Revelations so fairytale that even he, Edgar, had enjoyed a much-needed chuckle over their content but always returning to how serious was the condition, a psychosis involving a person being out of touch with reality he'd once read about and if such an illness was behind their Third Mate's bizarre behaviour, what experiences had triggered it? Should Edgar have known more than the little he'd gleaned, he'd likely have dismissed it as melodramatic fiction?

The courtship of Ivor and Heloise had been problematic from the very beginning. Not least of these problems was that at the time of their first meeting in the park, Heloise had been promised to another. Not an arranged coupling as such but while her mother was Welsh, her father was of Mediterranean descent long settled in Britain and very pleased that while holidaying in the country of his origin with his daughter, she'd met the son of an old family friend: a meeting that until Heloise's fated stroll in Cwmdonkin Park, had shown much promise.

The not-so-young or wealthy Merchant Navy officer had been rejected strongly by Heloise's father and, after one difficult visit to her home, the park in the Uplands district of Swansea would always be the favourite meeting place of Ivor and his rebellious sweetheart. Their love would not be thwarted by family pressure she bravely decided. Their future lay together. They were a couple in every sense . . .? Every sense but one it was eventually conceived by Ivor who, on comprehending the nature of Heloise's 'other love' rather than be jealous of, participated fully in it. That 'other love' was not of Mediterranean origin.

Cwmdonkin Park was at the heart of Heloise's 'other love' which their union had in fact benefited from, they told those who'd never quite appreciated her obsession with the park and the man whose fame was linked therein and who subsequently wrote poems about his memories and enchantment with the place. That man was the esteemed poet from Swansea. The poet Dylan Thomas.

Convinced that he'd found the woman of his life, Ivor Williams earnestly began to plan their future together. First, he'd win over her parents by proving to them that not only was he an honourable man but a man of substance and accordingly he'd keep his fairly lucrative seagoing job until they'd enough savings to start buying and furnish a home of their own. This was step one of their plan, a goal to pursue which would have him traversing the globe with the minimum of breaks for the next two years.

'Absence makes the heart grow fonder' and this was certainly their experience, their reunions in the park more joyous each time. But in the second year his absences became more prolonged, their reunions less frequent and, consequently, Heloise less happy. Her relationship with her parents still not cordial, she turned to Ivor's sister Megan for solace who unhesitatingly gave it, being much concerned by her future sister-in-law's growing depression which led to a serious discussion with her brother on his return from an extra long period at sea.

"She's far from herself," Megan told him. "She's unusually quiet and withdrawn. You ought come ashore, get a job and stay with us 'til you can afford that blessed house. Give the girl something to live for while enjoying your presence. Her only interest these days is hanging about that park, sometimes with the kids but more often on her own. The park and the poet is more her topic than you these days. That is on the odd occasion when she's in a talking mood look you? Think hard about what I've told you, Ivor. Think hard."

Much concerned, Ivor did think hard and the idea he arrived at would include lifting Heloise's spirits by financing a trip he knew she dreamed about but now rarely mentioned because of their current financial priorities. To personally witness the adoration of the poet's new American fans was the dream she'd unselfishly put aside but which now Ivor would make happen. He'd go back to sea for the last time in order to fulfil a contract and earn a promised bonus while, in the meantime, Heloise would travel to the States where her idol was currently receiving great acclaim. The trip would be an early wedding gift from her husband-to-be. The cost, if Heloise's health and spirits should benefit, as was evident from the very moment she learned about it, mattered little. Her elation led to an impromptu party to celebrate the trip during which a slightly tipsy Megan became amusingly philosophical calling it 'a fitting climax to adolescent dreams before the more mundane but joyous experience of marriage and babies' which brought a flush of embarrassment to Heloise's cheeks.

It was all settled then. She would take the excursion of a lifetime and her return, mid-November '53 would almost coincide with his return from Durban with the ring that would seal their future together. The venue for this, the most significant of reunions, just had to be the park! Heloise's exact return date was established, his being approximately days later. He would phone on berthing and whatever the weather or time of day, she'd be waiting in the park! At the bandstand in Cwmdonkin Park! But something had gone terribly wrong! And when the news of the poet's untimely death in New York was announced as they rounded the Cape homewards, he'd had this premonition! That she'd not be there! That she'd not be waiting for him in the park!

His premonition proved correct but he couldn't give up on her eventually making it. She'd simply been delayed so he would wait. He'd wait for her to turn up at the appointed place. A vigil that had him walking the park every day following his return right through until the first bitterly cold days of '54 and still no Heloise?

Nothing but the sound of a freezing sea wind blasting those hillside trees and that of his laboured breath as he traipsed the sloping, winding paths along which she'd once skipped and laughed childishly, teasing him to pursue while making the capture so easy . . .

But even before they'd coaxed him, cold and weary, from that place he'd conceived the reason for her non-return. That while 'he' whose words had immortalized his park could not return; then neither could she! That while her promise to return had been sincere; if he was physically lost to the park for all time then so was she. This was the only reason acceptable to him for her breaking that promise and thinking that the spell of Cwmdonkin would be broken for him too, she would slip away to another life expecting him to find and join her . . .

That night at berth in Newport News, Edgar imparted little of what he knew to Daniel because other than his immaturity the lad had a distant look in his eyes that suggested he'd other things on his mind like possibly his rumoured wish to jump ship? No, such adult matters, even if they'd not sounded so far-fetched, would be of little interest to him now or at any time which is why the Engineer was surprised when he referred to something personal about the Third's 'story' which suggested that he, Edgar, had not been alone in suffering the officer's repeated lament.

"Did, er – Mr Williams's lady friend really vanish in New York do you know?" he asked.

Edgar was as wise as he regards that tale, he replied. But there were a couple of things that he *was* quite positive about, he added. Firstly, she most certainly wasn't paddling about the Demerara in a canoe and secondly, he was definitely not quitting the *Roundcape* with the nutter to go and find her!

"How, er – does he reckon you'd get there? To the Demerara if you did quit like?"

"He's not filled you in how he'd get there, eh, boyo?"

Edgar's scornful smirk suggested that the answer was as outrageous as the rest.

"He's not told you then, eh? About the other bauxite carrier at berth here undergoing repairs before heading back to Mackenzie? Undermanned through ill health he's heard from our Sparks. So up he comes with the proposition that if we're taking on coal for home, where he assumes neither of us are particularly keen on going, then wouldn't it be in both our interests to try our luck with her like?"

That he'd consider it was how Edgar had left the matter simply to be left in peace and had been avoiding the man since.

"Would it be possible like," asked Daniel, "to, er – leave the *Roundcape* to join this other bauxite carrier?"

"No possibility whatsoever!" replied the old Welshman, his blood-flecked eyes narrow with mischief. "Our Sparks tell me she cleared her berth for Guiana this very morning! This very morning!"

Chapter 14

Ralph

On stepping ashore in the land of his film heroes, Daniel's mental high was such that but for meeting Ralph, the Third Mate business would have been as far from his mind as the last pile of washing up.

Ralph was one of a group of young American soldiers who befriended the *Roundcape's* catering staff on their first night ashore. Drinking with and being driven around the locality in the company of these fun-loving and genuinely friendly characters, proved to be the making of their stay in Newport News. Even the not-so-young Brumpud whooped and yelled as they sped around town in huge, powerful cars as the guests of the happy-go-lucky soldiers who seemed taken with their new British friends; a friendship that would never have been, as Billy put it, 'had they not been literally blown into port by a raging Atlantic hurricane'!

The real truth behind their stay in the port was that there'd been no alternative to their seeking costly repairs in the US which also meant as short a stay as possible and that the enjoyable get-togethers would soon be over.

On the last evening of their stay, the soldiers took them to a seemingly endless wooden jetty called the 'Baltimore Wharf'. The mood, despite it being their farewell session was as lively as ever as they boozed and chatted on subjects ranging from politics to sport and even Daniel's confession about his childhood worship of Abbot and Costello brought no hint of cynicism from the Americans who even commented that if there'd been time, they'd have driven the breadth of the country to Hollywood in the chance of giving him a glimpse of the comical duo and were heartily pleased to learn about the effect they'd had on cinemagoers in post-war UK.

Jock, predictably, steered conversation around to Donald Campbell's recent record-breaking triumph back home which brought much praise for the new World Water Speed Champion and the brilliantly Engineered *Bluebird* which led to a host of British and American achievements from literature to war until someone produced a harmonica and very soon the quiet Virginian night erupted with *Yankee Doodle Dandy, Land of Hope and Glory, I Belong to Glasgow*, and, oddly, a pitiful wailing of *We'll Gather Lilacs*, from a contentedly inebriated Brumpud.

On the ride back Ralph, who'd revealed himself to be a keen student of literature, showed great interest on learning that Daniel's home was but a short bus ride away from Shakespeare's birthplace. Embarrassed to discover that the American was considerably more conversant with the Bard's work than himself, Daniel gradually extended the discussion to more recent British literary figures only to find that the other far surpassed his own limited knowledge and only after Dickens, Kingsley, Carroll and Stevenson were exhausted and a name more recently familiar to him was mentioned, did the Cabin Boy, while not in a *literary* sense, feel he had something worthwhile to contribute.

By the time the merrymakers had tumbled from the car at the dock entrance, Ralph's curiosity was at fever pitch.

"An' you mean this guy . . .? This Third Mate character actually still writes an' pens poems about this young dame who . . .? This girlfriend of his who goes missin' after trailin' all the way over to New York jes' to go to those final recitals one of which I myself had the great pleasure to attend! Christ, man! We could have brushed shoulders jes' before she vanished if what you're sayin' is . . .? No, man! You're not the type to go shootin' off bullshit for the hell of it! You're not the goddam type! Let's go over it again an' see if you're seein' what I'm seein' . . .?"

At three o'clock in the morning, the only thing Daniel wanted to see was his bunk and besides, he couldn't help thinking that Ralph was over-dramatising the matter and respectfully told him so. But Ralph wasn't having it and was already beginning his own investigation into Heloise's disappearance. Maybe people did get knocked off every ten minutes in New York but in most cases there'd be a corpse to prove it and as this case was not even two years old, there would surely still be clues as to what had become of her?

Even when Daniel quoted the opinion of a close friend of the Third's aboard, that she'd likely gone off with somebody else; Ralph's wild conjecturing continued and when Jock announced minutes later that he'd attempt to sneak the soldiers on board for a last drink, Ralph was as keen as any man.

But there was no chance, Daniel insisted to his enthralled friend, of his meeting the character who'd so grabbed his imagination. The Third was surely in his bunk by now and besides, as an officer he'd be duty-bound to report unofficial boarders.

While Commies and seamen of suspected poor health were said to be unwelcome in the US, the defection of a group of her own nationals, soldiers to boot, would have been no difficult feat because within minutes of Jock's suggestion, they'd bluffed their way past a sleepy gate official and the final celebration aboard the *Roundcape* was underway. Celebration though, was far from Ralph's mind and soon after boarding he'd taken a very weary Daniel to one side to pursue the Third Mate business.

"Look, buddy," he began, "if I can't meet the man or any other on board to substantiate what you've told me, what should I believe? In fact, if you can't produce a single thread of evidence, I might just be inclined to think that the whole goddam story is bullshit after all!"

Stirred by the accusation, Daniel produced the poem salvaged from the Third's waste bin and took Ralph outside to the quiet of the alleyway to read it.

"Look, mate," he said tiredly, "I'm not bullshitting but this is all I've got and I reckon it's about the park where he says he met the girl. Make what you want out of it?"

"An' – an' he wrote this . . .? This Third Mate guy wrote this you say?"

Ralph was suddenly Sherlock Holmes, armed with a vital piece of evidence!

"Wow!" he gasped. "It's about *her* isn't it, goddam it? A kind of incidental history in the makin' an' you jes' kind of stumbled across it in complete ignorance aboard this old ship of yours? *Wow!"*

"Well, I fished it out of his waste bin if that's what you . . ."

But Ralph, engrossed in the poem again, wasn't listening.

"Yeah! He's talkin' about never bein' able to walk in the park with her again! *'Ne'er to trace with arms entwined, the hunchback's route immortal from the poet's mind'.* He's talkin' about Thomas's *Hunchback in the Park* an' never bein' able to walk again with her along the hunchback's route . . .! It's pure magic, man! It's pure magic!"

Enraptured by the poem, Ralph jotted down a copy of it which he tucked carefully away in his wallet. Was there anything more he pleaded? No, there wasn't but give him an address and he'd forward anything else thrown away by the officer, agreed Daniel, the other's enthusiasm making him wonder if maybe he had stumbled on something significant?

"Okay! Okay! Mebbe last year I was into Mark Twain an' the year before that Dickens or was it Tolstoy?" admitted the American apologetically. "But this year . . .! Well, it just happened to be the late Welsh genius an' along comes you with this crazy tale which, yeah . . . I'll admit when I wake tomorrow I'd have said was complete bullshit but for this!"

He tapped the pocket that held his wallet.

"This, man, is pure magic!"

Exchanging thumbs-up with Ralph as he descended the gangplank with his buddies, Daniel experienced a fleeting pang of regret for having held back other parts of the story. But, on reflection, to have told the young soldier that in one mind the missing Welsh girl was thought to be alive and well and selling her wares from a canoe on the Demerara might well have revived the 'bullshit' insinuation and finally convinced him that he had, after all, been talking to a young English ignoramus. Well, that's what the Cabin Boy had deduced from his expression when he'd let slip about having been virtually

207

ignorant as to the poet's existence until one certain officer had made it his business to remedy such unforgiveable 'ignorance'!

Should Daniel have been foolhardy enough to rouse the Third at that late hour, he'd likely have found, for the oddest of reasons, the man in one of his better moods. Earlier that day, Captain Roberts had found a letter balanced on the door handle of his accommodation. Anonymous, it informed him that his Third Mate, of all people, was planning to jump ship, possibly that very evening. The Skipper immediately called on his First Mate, Mr Purdoe and requested him to follow the Third ashore at a distance and to detain him if what he'd been informed about, looked possible. Happy to oblige, Mr Purdoe followed the suspect deserter across town to the port's main bus terminal where he entered a ticket office and engaged with a sales person. After about ten minutes he left the office and appeared to be heading back to the docks. Once out of sight, the First Mate slipped into the office to ask a few questions. The bemused clerk told him that the Brit customer had enquired as to an overland journey to British Guiana of all places! "So I advised the guy that our services would only get him to the Mexican border and that his best option would be to fly, but I wasn't familiar how to go about it, us bein' a bus company only," chuckled the clerk. "Then without so much as a thanks, the guy is lookin' as fogged up as your Stan Laurel, an' then tries to get outa that door with the clumsiness of your Charlie Chaplin! But I couldn't let it end there, an' while he messed with that door, I jes' had to ask him why? Why British Guiana? An' he's suddenly some kinda Shakespearean actor an' yells, 'Because my good man, on the tropical Demerara awaits love! Such love that when the story's told, those hearing it will find themselves driven to seek what I have found on that enchanted river!'

"Well, his words went something like that," chuckled on the bemused clerk. "An' I jes' wished him the best of luck but assured him that enchanted river or not, he still wouldn't be getting' bussed down there!"

On reboarding later that evening, the Third's despondency quickly faded on learning that the rumour of 'coal and home', had been just that. A rumour.

Chapter 15

Jungle Juice And Sara

Three days later, the *Roundcape* left Newport News, her holds as empty as when she'd arrived and bound once again for British Guiana.

The unofficial reason given was another cargo of bauxite before her bottom fell out which, within a few hours seemed imminent, as once again they were being tossed and pounded by yet another hurricane. The hurricane Diane.

Again, their navigators insisted that they were only experiencing the hurricane's extremities; a statement as absurd to Daniel as the talk from aft prophesying doom: talk that soon escalated to mutterings of concern from every quarter about the weather's severity and even reducing Jock's raucous commentary to more ominous groans and curses towards the climax of every impossible roll.

And yet still she held her own! Even when her Helmsman's efforts seemed pointless and the tangents were so near to horizontal that the tall funnel appeared to be skimming the waves; still she would shudder her way back to meet what next the ocean chose to throw at her as if challenging every furious encounter!

At the start of this tempest, when the catering staff were ordered to await a lull before making a dash to their accommodation, Daniel swore that he even saw fear in Tiggy's eyes, causing him a moment of guilt for having brought the animal on board. Minutes later, any sympathy vanished on observing how the cat was unconcerned enough to chase after a dislodged cruet set and then proceed to devour morsels from an overturned waste bin. How beneficial at such times, a limited intelligence and thereby no fear of the shifting decks which in fact, made life more interesting for the playful ship's cat.

Curiously, Tiggy wasn't alone aboard to be uncaring about the dreadful weather. While others spewed and cursed, the Third Mate's smug attitude was little less than infuriating. Why that annoying smile when other countenances showed the strain of wondering if she could possibly return from this roll, or his hearty laughter at mishaps in the saloon which simply were not funny?

Easily answered, recalling Edgar's words. The sorry loon was returning to his princess. His princess on the river.

Undoubtedly, 'if the *Roundcape* hadnae been a 'riveted' ship' the Third's expression would have been as grim as any others aboard on arrival in Neptune's Kingdom. But, thanks to her Clydeside builders and, Daniel suspected, despite his earlier scepticism, a degree of 'know how' on the part of her navigators, she neither folded up or turned turtle and on arrival at the place where the Demerara's muddy red water merges with the vitreous blue Atlantic, she looked as inviolable an old sea warrior as her Cabin Boy now knew her to be.

At anchor off Georgetown, Jock's radio told them that the hurricane Diane, which had ravaged mainly the north eastern states of the USA had claimed 191 lives, injured 7000 and caused 1600 million dollars worth of damage. The bulletin, while confirming that they'd always been moving away from the hurricane also convinced them that they'd had a lucky escape; a thought that did much to revive Daniel's desertion ideas as he watched a crowded river ferry slip across their bows heading for the port's ramshackle waterfront.

"Georgetown, capital of Her Majesty's only territory on the continent of South America, boyo," said the Third appearing at his side. "Fancy going ashore do you?"

"Er –yes. Why can't we?"

"Because, boyo," replied the officer gesturing towards the bridge, "him upstairs knows only too well he'd not get most of 'em back 'til we came back downriver. It's hardly a teetotal crew we have now is it?" he chuckled.

The understatement of the trip, mused Daniel having noted that the Third himself had been even more lively since purchasing four bottles of rum from river traders on dropping anchor.

"If you fancy a noggin, boyo, be in the Fourth Engineer's cabin when he comes off watch this afternoon. A little celebration's called for you see?" he added with a grin that suggested all would be revealed later.

Sighs of relief accompanied the sound of the anchor being hauled from the bed of that motionless river some hours later. Even the slight breeze produced by the ship's movement was welcome on an afternoon so hot that the prankster Brumpud cracked open and fried an egg on the deck and then devoured the shrivelled result.

It was mid-afternoon and an hour upriver when the storm broke. Daniel had just made it back amidships after a chat with an unwell Martyn when the first huge drops began to fall from a suddenly black sky. He'd all but forgotten his invitation for a noggin until the Third called out to him from Edgar's cabin where he accepted rum and from an aft-facing porthole watched the torrential downpour fall hissing and steaming on 'cooking hot' metalwork.

Unlike the blinding hurricane rain of a few days ago this inland deluge was very welcome, not least by the huge Somali fireman who emerged from below to strip naked on the immediate hold.

"Come and take a gander at this 'well-blessed bugger', Edgar!" beckoned the Third to his rum-guzzling companion. Edgar hauled himself off his bunk and nudged Daniel aside.

"Christ, boyo!" he exclaimed. "You could do a lot of damage with that, eh?" he chuckled, the youth becoming suddenly and embarrassingly aware of what he was being urged to look at and happily moved aside for the Third to take his place.

"Look! Look you now, Edgar...!"

The officer almost choked on his last swallow of rum.

"It's growin' bigger by the minute I'll swear it....!"

Edgar's only reaction was a grinned wink at Daniel as he made for the door muttering, "I'm away aft to see a mate. I'll have a tot or two with you later, Ivor."

"You – you'll give some thought to what's been discussed will you, Dai?" blurted the Third hurrying to catch the other's arm as he left.

"Let's have something to think on with then!" chuckled Edgar giving Daniel another wink as he snatched the Third's bottle and took one last swallow before exiting.

"Why I try to help that man Heaven only knows," sighed the officer after him. "Come on then, boyo, looks as if it's eased off a bit out there. Let's see if it's cleared the air, eh ?"

They stepped on deck just as the sun broke through to cast a sheen on the saturated vegetation along the Demerara's banks and when the Third spoke again there was lit cigarette between his fingers and his eyes were seeing something a world away from that tropical river.

"Have you, Daniel," he began distantly, "have you yet, in your young life, slipped your hands around the waist of a beautiful woman, looked into her eyes and discovered that you wanted for nothing?"

"Er – not yet except for just a couple of, er . . ." Daniel began falteringly, "but if there's anything that takes me fancy in Mackenzie this time, I might ask to see a bit more of her," he added, his cheek surprising even himself after a couple of warming rums.

But the Third wasn't troubled by his cheek. Wasn't even listening.

"Heloise was as beautiful to me clothed as she was naked," he said quietly while drawing long on his cigarette. "But being naked on a remote beach or quiet cove came as easy to her as to our Somali friend just now. A warm sun on her back and she'd as much use for clothes as those natives out there," he smiled, nodding towards the thickening jungle.

"They don't go naked these days surely?" grinned Daniel, keen to steer the other away from his favourite subject. "I thought the missionaries made 'em cover up?"

"Look now," the Third was indicating landwards again, "this is the continent of South America and just a few hundred miles over there's the biggest wilderness on Earth where going naked's as natural now as when Adam and Eve were around! Heaven help them if somebody thought it in their interest to open a Montague Burton's and Dorothy Perkins! Cover their genitals and they might be silly enough to fit outboard motors to their canoes and head for the world of capstan lathes and atomic bombs! Those bloody missionaries have a lot to answer for, boyo. Having the gall to lecture them that after thousands of years of going their own, carefree way with not so much as a fig leaf to draw attention to where attention was never drawn; that they were *indecent* in their innocence! Progress now? Progress is fitting for some but by no means for all! Your Bloom family's a good example of what I'm driving at. No telly, washing machine or vacuum cleaner to be bought and maintained. No petrol-guzzling car just to join the zombie horde on an annual trek to the coast where they'd likely get arrested if so much as a nipple became exposed when struggling to keep *decent* while donning their swimwear. What a tragedy, boyo, your Blooms having to fall in with the rest just because Mrs Bloom developed this penchant for tapped water when all they really needed to do was take off their clothes and live happily ever after in their paradise on Earth."

"We tried to get Maurice to strip off with the rest of the gang but he was always a bit shy," offered Daniel with an enthusiasm prompted more by the rum than the officer's rhetoric. "In the Summer we'd take off our clothes and pretend to be wild natives defending our territory along the brook. Scared old Mrs Bennet half to death when we ran through her smallholding starkers one day we did. So shocked she was that she staggered backwards and fell onto her big sow which went wild. Didn't go near her place again in the altogether in case she told our parents. But as I said, Maurice was always the shy one in that respect."

"And the rest of you had no such inhibitions, eh, Daniel?"

"Well, er . . . if near the houses there was the cotton-supported dock leaf to sort of cover the front where it mattered like. We, er – were never too bothered about our backsides being on show to each other like."

"You'd need a giant of a dock leaf around your backsides if some aboard this ship had been your playmates I'm thinking, boyo," chuckled the officer, "but Heloise would have loved your anecdote and then most likely have enjoyed telling you about her own lack of inhibition when relaxing in the altogether."

Such candour and the theme of the following discourse had been arrived at as the rum-stimulated Third went on to enthuse about his times with the lovely Heloise.

They'd spend hours naked together, he romanced, on that huge Carmarthenshire beach called Pendine Sands as if they were the last two people on Earth.

The beach, so vast that it was once used by Malcolm Campbell, the late father of Donald Campbell presently attempting water speed records in the US, for racing his legendary *Bluebird* car back in the 1920s and 30s. These days the only cars on those endless sands were driven by such as Ivor and Heloise for the simple bliss of isolation. Other users were rarely less than half a mile away from wherever they'd chosen to park and even disregarding his warnings of possible voyeurists with binoculars, Heloise delighted in teasing him by performing cartwheels around the car and even go dashing into the sea wearing nothing more than a sun hat.

"Daniel, boyo, if your Bloom family failed to recognize their paradise on Earth, Heloise and I were positive we'd found ours!" declared the officer, celebrating the memory with a long swallow of rum from the bottle he still held, the effects of which were to lead to even more explicit revelations.

Heloise had begun nude sunbathing in her teens. Prostrated herself unclothed on almost every beach and secluded spot on the Gower Peninsula was her boast. Rhossili was her favourite place, a remote point on the peninsular where it was said her poet idol used to sit in thought as poets do. She'd spoken of her disappointment at never seeing the man out there but if they had actually met, she'd joked, it could have been a tad embarrassing for both of them; a statement that had Ivor mischievously hinting of her probable regret that such a meeting had not occurred and how unfortunate for the poet to have missed out on such a vision, to which she'd replied with a painful jab to his ribs, chuckled on the Third with yet another long swig at the rum.

"Do you get naked beauties roamin' your neck of the woods?" he asked Daniel, still grinning.

Without the rum loosening his tongue, Daniel would have thought better than to hark back to Maurice's tale of the naked girl in their field and instantly regretted it as the officer responded.

"That's some tall story, boyo!" he laughed. "How long did it take you to make that one up?"

"Well – he did, honestly. She – she was tailing me and just vanished," Daniel attempted to explain.

But while the Third enjoyed spinning yarns he was, it seemed, quite sceptical of others doing the same.

"Well, you want me to believe stories that some people think daft!" the rum helped him to snap back.

"Cool it, son!" grinned back the other. "Look now: your story about your Blooms, the family that got by on just well-water and the odd apple I like, but embellishing it with naked young women vanishing into thin air as you have, could be thought a tad fairytale you know?"

"I, er – suppose so," agreed Daniel reluctantly, while tempted to counter with the tale of another 'vanishing young lady'.

"Hope you two buggers have left a drop for me!" quipped the returning Edgar.

"Of course we have, me old shipmate, and it's so bloody strong it's got our Cabin Boy here weaving the most unbelievable tales," replied the Third to Daniel's embarrassment.

"Now it's your turn to tell us a yarn, Edgar. Come on with you. Give him the one about the sea-widow and the randy old baker."

Edgar's expression told that he wasn't too happy with his friend's request.

"No! You've got a far better one than that," he replied angrily. "You get and tell him the one about the fucking runaway bride that I've been subjected to since Cardiff! Small wonder the boy's took to weaving tales if he's had to put up with the same, poor bugger! Small wonder!"

"Now that was uncalled for, Edgar!" gasped the Third, obviously too drunk to comprehend that it was his remark that had sparked things off. "Runaway bride did I hear? What did you mean by that?"

"Since you see fit to make fun of my personal matters, I'll make it bloody-well clear what I mean!" snapped back Edgar, determined to have his say. "What's clear to me is that you've been *dumped*. Well and truly *dumped*. Dumped is the modern-day word for our situation which I'm beginning to accept but your fucking pride'll not let you do likewise. The fact is that your precious darling's somewhere with a bun in her oven courtesy of her first choice! That's what I fucking-well mean, Ivor!"

Surprisingly evident to Daniel as he witnessed the eruption, was that in drink, mature, educated men were capable of immature slandering so that perhaps he wasn't too immature after all?

The Third, while obviously stunned by his friend's hurtful remarks, failed to further challenge them and left for his cabin where three hours later, Daniel found him as drunk as a man could be.

"Er – Billy said you wanted to see me, sir?" he asked.

"Ah yesh, Daniel. Come – come in an' 'ave a lasht tot with Ivor an' an' time's come for thash favour, re-remember?"

"Er – I – I remember, sir. The favour you asked me to, er – do," replied the Cabin Boy on eventually interpreting the officer's slurred speech.

He'd found him sprawled on his bunk clutching a bottle of rum to this chest and his struggle to sit up revealed that he wasn't just vocally impaired but managed to take a sheet of typed paper out of a bunk-side drawer and handed it to his visitor.

"Yoursh – yoursh poem, boyo, an' – an' the parsh . . . parcel's inna locker see. I – Ivor's goin' for a walk inna park look you. Ivor's goin' for a walk inna park."

"Oh, er – the, er – poem, sir," Daniel began hesitantly. "An' – and the parcel's in the locker, sir? Er – what parcel is, er – that, sir?"

But the Third, struggling to stay conscious, appeared not to have taken in the question.

"An' – an' Ivor's goin' for a walk inna park," he continued. "Ivor's goin' for a . . . walk inna park do ya hear"

"Yes, er – sir. Which – which park is that, sir?"

"Which f-f fuckin' park? You know which fuckin' park, you daf' bugger Daniel! Cwmdonk . . . Cwm . . . Cwmdonkin Park! Ivor's goin' for a walk in Cwmdonkin Park!"

The Third, appearing exhausted by getting the words out, lay back and closed his eyes.

"Are – are you okay, sir!"

With no answer forthcoming, Daniel placed the typewritten poem on a bedside shelf and quietly departed.

Within an hour of stealing out of the Third Mate's cabin, Daniel was looking down into the lovely face of . . . Heloise?

She'd paddled alongside when they'd stopped briefly at a point where the river broadened enough to allow the passage of downstream traffic and, within minutes, her charm rather than her wares had drawn a group of admirers to the rail. He recognized her immediately. Even in the poor light, her beauty was evident. That same sculptured face framed perfectly by thick, raven hair falling wide across her back right down to the tiniest of waists. Those same smiling, enticing eyes and that

218

same, full, heart-shaped mouth promising to be as sweet as any of the succulent fruit she had to offer.

"Christ, Dai! Those legs must go right up to her armpits!" sighed an AB as her slit skirt fell open as she turned to reach for tossed coins: the reason for her popularity with the seamen evident by their wolf whistles as she unhurriedly covered her exposed thighs, her eyes meeting Daniel's mischievously on detecting his spellbound gaze.

"You want buy? You want buy from me, sailor boy?" she cried, her lilting English not unlike the southern Welsh accent he'd listened to every day of the last few weeks: a thought that convinced him that she truly was the girl central to the Third's hallucinations and who soon lost interest in one dumb Cabin Boy, a rejection that turned to near jealousy on later hearing about the telling request she'd given a rail-hanging sailor.

"I've been putting it off too bloody long now! I'm going in for my Third Mate's ticket the minute we get back to Blighty!" declared the comedian from aft. Those still lingering at the rail awaited Ianto's punch line.

"That sexy young bint with the 'shag me please' eyes has a preference for officers would you believe? Asked for the Third Mate specifically she did! Special business she'd arranged with him so she says! 'Won't you do special business with me?' I ask her. 'Oh no,' she replies, 'I do special business with Third Officer Mr Williams only.' And then to top it she asks can she come aboard to do this special business with Mr Williams. Mark my word, boys! I'm putting in for my Third Mate's ticket the minute we get back to Blighty! The minute we get back to Blighty!"

If, as the river girl had said, she'd made some kind of arrangement (special business) with their Third Mate why, wondered Daniel, when they were back on the Demerara had the officer drank himself incapable of doing whatever that special business involved? All rather odd but his brothers had forewarned him that sea life could throw up some odd people and odd situations but 'to go with the flow' was the advice given. Yes – that's all he could do. Not to worry and 'go with the flow'.

Chapter 16

Where's Edgar?

An industrial outpost carved out of a wilderness, the jungle port of Mackenzie bustled beneath a punishing sun. The roar and clatter of mechanical monsters feeding bauxite into the moored ships rang out incessantly. A light breeze wafting suddenly off the river, while otherwise welcome, only served to hinder the loading operators as the powdery mineral ore rose in choking, blinding clouds.

In the sealed, oven-like confinement of the *Roundcape's* accommodation, many of her crew eased their discomfort by supping cheap rum until such time as they could open doors and ports and once again breathe clean, fresh air. Others, in defiance of the 'no shore leave' order tacked to the head of the gangplank, had slipped ashore to pass time away in more bearable conditions.

In common with most of the Somali crew, Petty Officer Yussef Rashid observed ship's orders without question. And indeed why should he risk losing his status when his simple pleasures could be pursued aboard? A good stock of liquor in his single accommodation where he could indulge out of sight of his abstaining brethren aft. Deserted decks where, hidden by the billowing dust, he was able to glimpse and sigh his appreciation for young males in their prime, attired to suit the sweltering heat: an appreciation which, kindled by several whiskies, had led to his presence in the starboard companionway amidships where, through one particular porthole . . .

"And what the fuck are you feastin' your evil eyes on, you sneakin' little perv?"

Yussef spun in shock to face his accuser.

"I – I look for Cook" he lied.

"You look for Cook with your fuckin' flies undone!" yelled back Fourth Engineer Edgar Reece, his leathery face distorted in contempt. "You look for boy! You look for sexy young boy!"

"No – no . . .! I – I speak the truth!" pleaded the Somali, hardly audible above the roar of machinery feeding the ship.

"Need fuckin' castratin' the lot of you!" raged Edgar. "Performin' bullock-naked in rainstorms an' snoopin' through portholes at boys arses! Used to be kept in your place in the old days an' now look at you! Cabin as good as mine an' the run of the fuckin' ship to vent your perversions! No! Don't bother to button yourself up cos I'm goin' to drag you by your balls up to the old man an' get you lodged back aft with the rest of your cronies before we're out of this port! You see if I fuckin'-well don't!"

Yussef cowered under the Engineer's tirade. He'd surprised him by boarding through clouds of dust and while obviously the worse for drink and hardly capable of manhandling him up to the Skipper's quarters; should he go mouthing his accusations about the ship, then his envied position aboard was indeed threatened! Threatened simply because the stupid old man had risked boarding at such a dangerous time and even now as he stood screaming his threats at the side of an open hold, seemed completely unaware of the next bucket of ore hurtling routinely, but blindly towards him through the murk . . .!

Yussef's reaction was little more than a stifled gasp as the speeding bucket's leading edge dropped and collided with Edgar's neck, freezing a last uttered curse on his lips before in the same horrifying seconds depositing both man and ore deep within the *Roundcape's* bowels. As the horrified Somali stared in disbelief at the few spots of blood on the hold's rim, the discharged bucket rose back out of the ship, its flying residue obliterating all evidence of the calamity dealt. Pausing only to glance anxiously towards the thick cloud of bauxite veiling the operator's cab, the accident's only witness slipped furtively away.

With so many of the crew flouting orders on their second berthing in Mackenzie, the Fourth Engineer's prolonged absence ashore attracted little comment other than such jokes as him not even being sober enough to manage the gangplank, let alone the engine room ladders when he did make it back. His 'chum' Mr Williams however, whose continued drinking spree aboard had caused the Skipper to confine him 'out of sight' in his cabin, was greatly disturbed by Edgar's non-appearance.

"Silly old bastard's gone off on 'is tod!" he repeatedly informed Daniel between swallows of rum from the one bottle he'd managed to conceal from the Skipper and Mate. Sent to his cabin with black coffee by the Chief Steward, the youth interrupted his drunken babble by telling him that on the previous afternoon, the river girl had come alongside and asked for him. This information seemed to shock him speechless until he began blaming Daniel for not waking him at the time.

"You – yoush – should 'ave come an' an' tole me!" he complained. "Why did – didn't you fuckin' wake – wake me an' an' tell me she . . .!"

His rant petered out and he had suddenly twigged something pleasurable.

"She – she – she is 'ere, eh! 'eloise – is 'ere! 'eloise is inna park along with Edgar! All've us together, 'eliose, the 'unchback an' an' me, see boyo?"

The insane grin that spread across his face as he pictured some get-together in the park made him chuckle: a chuckle which, by the time Daniel had arrived back in the pantry, had risen to a hysterical guffaw that resounded throughout the lower bridge accommodation.

On turning out the next morning, the sight of the holds being sealed told Daniel that a kind of normality was returning to the ship. The troubled look on the Chief Steward's usually expressionless face however had him suspecting that things were far from normal as he greeted him at the pantry door.

"Skipper wants to see you in his quarters right away, son," he mumbled solemnly.

Climbing the inner bridge stairs, the youth's pulse quickened as he pondered the reason for his first audience with the Captain since his Chaguaramus reprimand.

Hardly seven a.m. but the ship's Master was pouring himself a scotch as the Cabin Boy made a nervous entry into his luxurious, by *Roundcape* standards, quarters. Sipping whisky and snatching at the cigarette dangling effeminately between long, slender fingers, the Captain began explaining the reason for his summons.

It had been brought to his attention, he said, that he, Daniel, had a good relationship with a ship's officer, namely their Third Mate Mr Williams. Off-duty liaisons between ship's officers and ordinary crew were not generally encouraged in the service, he pointed out. But, and disregarding the opinions of others aboard, he'd decided not to interfere with the association. Now though, something quite serious had occurred and he wondered if he might be able to help him?

"To begin with son, your relationship with Mr Williams? Just how intimate were you?"

It may have been how the Skipper's long eyelashes fluttered as he mentioned the word *intimate* that brought the hint of a smile to Daniel's face but on detecting it, the man stiffened, his voice becoming sharper.

"This is a very grave matter, son! Now please tell me what exactly was the nature of your conversations with Mr Williams? What could you have possibly had in common?"

We, er . . .we used to talk about all kinds of things . . . er – sir."

"Like what, son? For instance, did he ever mention to you the possibility of him leaving this ship?"

"Er – sometimes, sir. But – but I never really took him serious like."

"I'll be straight with you, son! I've been told that you went aft last night and told the Deck Boy that Mr Williams was very drunk and that, during the last few weeks, you've been receiving written messages from him so, with such confidence in you son,

224

did Mr Williams, especially yesterday, infer that he might be going ashore to look for our Fourth Engineer, Mr Evans or maybe that he was just leaving the ship?"

"Er – as I say . . . I – I didn't take him too seriously, sir. About him going ashore that is."

"Well, it would appear that he has, son."

"Oh, er . . . they've both gone have they?"

"Yes, son. And that's why you are here. Now what exactly did Mr Williams say about his going ashore? What did he say was his reason?"

"Er – he was very drunk but he said something about, er . . ."

"Something about what, son? Out with it now!"

"Something about going for a walk in the, er . . . in the park, sir."

"A walk in the bloody park, son?"

The Skipper's voice had risen to almost a scream.

"Now, son! We've enough bloody comedians aboard without you adding to . . .!"

A timely knock on the door saved Daniel from embarrassing himself further as the Chief Mate and a uniformed policeman made their entry.

"I'm sorry, Captain but dere's nothing new to report I'm afraid," the policeman was saying as Daniel was motioned to leave. "Your Mr Williams was last seen by the ferryman at aroun' midnight last night an' in respect of your Engineer Mr Reece; de last person to see him says he was walkin' unsteady towards de ship yesterday evenin'."

An hour after leaving their Mackenzie berth, Daniel was summoned once more to the Skipper's quarters and to bring along anything written by their Third Mate but, having declined what he'd been offered yesterday by the inebriated officer, took along all he had which was the poem enthused over by the soldier Ralph back in Newport News.

"But this is some kind of poem, son!" exploded Captain Roberts. "It doesn't mean a bloody thing to me! Does it mean anything to you?"

"No," Daniel lied, recalling the previous day's frustration and how that frustration would be multiplied if he'd tried to explain that only he and the Third knew about a ubiquitous brook that meandered about the Earth taking one to childhood haunts and even a mysterious park where the man in question was quite likely at that very moment busily searching for a woman of his past. No, he couldn't possibly explain that.

Despite wanting to distance himself from the Skipper's investigation, the Cabin Boy was as intrigued as any man regards the missing officers. Furthermore, Ianto's patter about the river girl having asked for the Third by name added to that intrigue; so if only to prove that the big comedian might somehow be aware of the ludicrous connection between the pair, if she came alongside on the journey back downriver, he'd make a point of having a word with the girl and prove what could only be ridicule on Ianto's behalf.

Unfortunately on this occasion, there was no sign of the young Guianese beauty and by the time they'd arrived in the Trinidadian port of Chaguramus to top up with bauxite, the happenings on the Demerara were overtaken by the sudden loss of his good friend Martyn who was rushed ashore with acute appendicitis.

As with the Third, the Deck Boy's sudden departure occurred at night giving Daniel no chance to say goodbye and wish him luck. Not that Martyn was entirely luckless he brooded. A few days of discomfort and then probably a plane would whisk him home: a thought which did much to revive his own plans to desert in order to avoid experiencing another of those terrible hurricanes which were once again the main topic of conversation aboard.

An opportunity was spotted that same afternoon as he relaxed with the crew on a beach adjacent to the loading wharfs. The guarded fence he'd encountered during their last visit was obviously impenetrable but noting that the barrier continued onto the beach, where it ended some some twenty yards into the sea, was clearly the way he should go.

After the terrible conditions on board, the water was as enticing as that sun-kissed Trinidadian beach rolling away into the distance. Some of the crew were sitting astride or hanging onto huge lengths of timber found floating in the sea and selecting one for himself, the scheming youth joined in with the fun.

A non-swimmer, he found that shoving the timber forward and then hanging on to it was great sport especially when caught up in the lazy rollers a short way out. It was also, he realized, a way of getting around the end of the fence should the water be too deep to walk at that point. Slowly, he moved away from the others towards his goal. Moments later he began to panic! So engrossed, it suddenly occurred to him that he'd forgotten to toss his getaway clothes over the fence before taking to the sea and on trying to manoeuvre the timber in order to return to the beach, he discovered, to his horror, that he was out of depth and was being carried by the outgoing tide! Time after time he reached with his toes to where only minutes ago there'd been sand! The absurd notion of reaching the bottom, hold his breath and walk ashore flashed through his mind. Dare he let go of his support and make an underwater dash or do all doomed persons think crazily? The seabed must be only inches away or was it now even further? He began clawing frantically at the sodden timber to get a more secure hold of the only thing between him and certain drowning but in doing so momentarily lost his grip as a mischievous wave swept over him. His fingernails once more embedded in the wood, he looked back to where his shipmates had been enjoying themselves a shout away. Not a living soul! He was alone and drifting out to sea!

"Heeeeeeelp!"

Someone would hear him! They couldn't be far away so soon! If he could only get astride the timber as he'd seen others doing? Attempting to do so caused him to lose hold completely and the feeling of helplessness as the water closed over his head convinced him that it was all over, but the sea was still playful and chose to throw him back up again and miraculously reunite

227

him with the timber to which he clung, summoning up energy until, with one last desperate effort he managed to throw one leg over and gradually clamp himself to his bronco of the ocean!

In shocked amazement that one of the least agile pupils ever to grace the Crabbs Cross school sportsfield could have pulled off such a feat, he rested a minute and pondered his next move. He must paddle! Keeping a tight hold with his legs, he must paddle with his hands as he'd seen the others doing earlier! But the others were all swimmers and falling off had been part of the fun so he'd have to paddle with just one hand which only achieved a circular movement which in turn achieved nothing more than all round surveillance!

"Heeeeeeelp!"

Could he hear or see him, that person on the beach gesturing wildly seawards but not directly at him? Yes, he could, thank God and was shouting something back that sounded like . . . *shaaaaaaark!* Billy White was trying to warn him that any moment now that there'd be razor-sharp teeth slicing through his legs if he couldn't get them out of the water and try doubly hard to cling face down to that slippery surface which, in such a swell, was an exercise impossible to maintain for more than a few seconds until . . .!

"Heeeeeeelp!"

But Billy was no longer in sight and had probably gone back to the ship for help which would be too late because something was cutting the surface some twenty feet away and heading directly for him!

"Heeeeeeelp!"

To stay put or to launch himself into the sea were his only options in that moment of terror! That he'd chosen the latter and desperately hoped he'd find the bottom and actually walk ashore by holding his breath was his later, stupid guess as to what happened. Billy (the shark) had only been a few strokes away at the time, said that it had been the sea that had parted the hysterical Cabin Boy from his only means of support, having observed a large freak wave literally flipping the timber high into the air before descending to complete the job with a blow on the head that knocked the gormless twat unconscious and consequently in more serious need of rescue.

His account, which kept many laughing for weeks ahead, was exaggerated on every telling. The shark (there were some sighted) becoming a Great White and the distance he'd swam after being alerted by his screams, rising from a quarter of a mile to at least three quarters in shark-infested waters.

The Cabin Boy's own versions of the event were hopeless attempts to cover his own stupidity and in truth felt no justification in challenging Billy's self-congratulatory story or his derision when knowing full well that had it not been for one Bristolian Teddy Boy, his planned departure from the ship that day would likely have been very different to the one envisaged.

AND DEATH SHALL HAVE NO DOMINION.
Daniel rubbed the sleep from his eyes and re-read the familiar words: celestial words but this was no celestial place. This was the Third's cabin and he was in the Third's bed!

Next, he became aware of the throbbing pain in his head then, miserably, he began to recollect why? But the Third's cabin? Oh yes. The officer had gone for a stroll in the park along with old Edgar and his cabin, being handy to the Chief Steward and his medicine chest, the obvious choice while the 'ship's hospital' was crammed full with the Bo'sun's tack. That they'd brought an 'unconscious' man back on board because he'd 'feigned' a similar condition before, was Daniel's sorry conclusion. Already depleted by three crew, he recalled somebody saying he'd be okay and that engine hammering away below meant that hospitalization on Trinidad had likely not even been considered. The bastards!

His petulant decision therefore to make the most of his 'invalidity' didn't fool Billy who, indignant at being ordered to wait on him, was determined to expose the malingerer.

"You're playin' on it, you skivin' little fucker!" he accused, while serving him his tea. "I'd 'ave left you to the fuckin' sharks if I'd known this is 'ow you'd pay me back! It fuckin'-well serves you right that Reno's got permission to give you a thorough bed bath!" he'd ranted on, making Daniel question the wisdom of continuing his masquerade? But continue he did (the threatened bed bath not materializing) for three days and three nights determined to spite those who'd chosen to risk his health and denying him the opportunity to join up with his pal Martyn. And besides, should the weather turn nasty again, hadn't he always obtained the greatest relief in the horizontal position?

Inevitably, with time on his hands in that particular cabin, his thoughts turned to its departed occupant and equally, the beautiful young woman who, in some obscure way, was linked to that departure, one picture of whom was still conspicuously displayed attached to the bureau mirror. The other snaps he could only assume the Third had taken with him but just this remaining photo of her in tennis whites with that same park bandstand in the background, was tantalizing enough to arouse in him the most erotic of thoughts.

Had she been aware, he wondered, that the photo had been taken while her knees were raised and slightly apart in that conspicuously revealing manner? And had she perhaps unfastened the buttons of her blouse in the heat of the day or was she trying to make the onlooker guess as to whether or not she was wearing a bra and wonder if just one more button would reveal most of those full, young breasts? And did that smile, that oh so enticing a smile, suggest that whoever was behind the lens was very welcome to come over and . . . ?

On the afternoon of the third day, he peeled off the sticky tape securing the tormenting photograph to the mirror and took Heloise to bed. He recalled the officer teasing him that he'd fallen for his girl by just perusing her photos: an assumption, the Cabin Boy mused, that hadn't been far from the truth! He now also clearly understood the Third's own admittance of *lust* at first sight for this exquisite, young female whose striking looks even on just one photo were, he swore, responsible for the rise in his temperature that convinced the Chief Steward into prolonging the term of his recovery.

In the course of those dreamed hours of intimacy with the lovely Heloise, the girl in the park became to Daniel as she had to her estranged beau, the innocent young girl plying her wares upon the Demerara which was hardly surprising he later concluded on rationalizing his fevered thoughts: because while Heloise was just a girl in a photograph, the girl in the boat was as real as himself. Furthermore, in enhancing his lascivious dreams, it proved better to forget the complications surrounding the Third's girlfriend and to base his yearnings on a female who, except in the hallucinations of that same ship's officer was, and the thought made him happy, yet nobody's sweetheart.

In the heat of his dreams though, there was no such rationalization. Just a fevered longing to hold this desirable young woman. To run his fingers through that gleaming black hair: to tilt her lovely face slowly towards his own until their lips fused moistly and sensually together while his free hand explored those secret parts of a woman so long denied to him but now being yielded so readily in anticipation of his gentle but total invasion.

Having savoured every delectable detail of Heloise in tennis attire, he eventually tumbled from his bed in the hope that he'd maybe been wrong in assuming that the Third had taken the bulk of the photographs. Confirming the widely-held view aboard that the officer would eventually turn up and probably be flown to rejoin the ship in Canada, his remaining belongings had been stowed away in his locker and drawers to await that event. Only the top drawer in his bureau was locked and, after a fruitless search elsewhere, Daniel unhappily reasoned that if the photos were in the cabin, that's where they'd be?

Throughout the search, he'd been uncomfortably aware of the trouble he'd be in if caught looking through another's belongings and especially those of an officer. Consequently, such was his haste, he was back between the sheets before he'd

231

fully digested what he'd seen during his last quick check of the locker. Clothes hung neatly for once (probably by the Chief Steward) along with his covered typewriter and footwear on the floor and, placed upon a pile of woollens on the top shelf, a small package. A small, brown paper package?

Hardly able to contain his curiosity but fearful of interruption, he waited until after Billy had delivered his evening meal before returning to the locker and taking down the package. That it might contain what he'd been requested to deliver helped lessen any guilt he felt about prying. Delivery though, wouldn't have been possible. No address and too poorly wrapped for safe transit, he noted before opening it. On doing so he guessed instantly that the sheaf of typewritten paper was the build-up of correspondence that the Third wanted delivered, each letter secured separately by a paperclip. On top of the sheaf was a typed poem which he also guessed to be the one he'd declined on that boozy day on the Demerara.

The poem, while embarrassing in that an officer had written it for someone as lowly ranked as himself was, he thought, a nice gesture. The subject of verse had come about when the youth had enquired in regard to the Third's many discarded attempts which his daily cleaner had to dispose of. The officer had discovered him perusing one and, thinking him interested, began conversing on the subject. Some verses were easy to compose, some painstaking, he said, but a good mental exercise and on getting it right, very satisfying. As a way of passing time he put to Daniel, why not have a go himself?

"But – er, what should I write about?" he responded doubtfully. "I've never been much good at . . ."

"Something you enjoy or have simply experienced and want to remark about," cut in the other. "Such as your brook. It seems to have meant something to you in childhood: pleasantly memorable, yes? As is my park. Cwmdonkin Park is especially a place full of pleasant memories I hold. The place where I first met and held my sweet Heloise. Where we . . . er – yes, your brook should be your subject. Don't worry, I'll be kind." His school entry on that subject was Daniel's first thought, but on recalling that other efforts had been rated above it, wrote anew. This attempt however, so poor, he cringed on handing it over. But the Third was kind as promised, saying, "Not bad for a beginner. Do you mind if I improve it and include thoughts of my own?"

His promised improvement hadn't been seen since Daniel had declined it from the much intoxicated officer just hours prior to his going absent from the ship. Now, with a tingling curiosity, he began reading the poem for any changes made to his original and noted that there were and had much enhanced it. Also, while his had borne no title, this version did.

The Brook to Cwmdonkin

Sprung midst landlocked hills,
Winter gush Summer trickle,
through valleys verdant and fertile,
snaking 'round hills and hummocks,
some topped with leafy crowns,
babbling 'neath whispering willows,
stooped to ask on misty morns,
where to, Daniel's brook?

Rain made, to travel forever,
to parts beauteous and bleak,
to places too distant for children,
whose mothers at dusk will seek.
Via lakes and hurrying rivers,
down to ports a'bustle with craft,
the child is safe in Cwmdonkin,
mother home of Daniel's brook.

Flow on, lithe travelling water,
hasten on ubiquitous brook,

233

to the warmth of a mother's bosom,
no child has its mother forsook.
Journey's end she'll embrace true companions,
at a place where unions are made,
Cwmdonkin is haunted with memories,
the kind of which never do fade.

On reading the poem a second time, a tear escaped Daniel's eye and then, on glancing through the typewritten pages, becoming embarrassingly aware of their personal content, felt shame for his prying. With this shame came a sense of loss because whatever could be said about the Third Mate those improved verses and his general manner towards him, told the youth that he'd lost a sincere friend. And how was he now repaying that friendship? By snooping through his personal belongings. By seducing in mind the woman he adored and was now about to intrude on personal letters intended only for her. Embarrassed, both by his cheap curiosity and sudden compassion, he reassembled the package and returned it to the locker.

On the afternoon of the fifth day in the Third's cabin his prolonged recuperation came to an abrupt end. While mentioning in a letter home their unscheduled visit to the United States, he recalled his promise to Ralph, the young soldier he'd met there. The poem! He'd promised Ralph that he'd send anything else that turned up in regard to the Third's writings. And the poem, being a joint effort of his and the Third's, surely gave him the right to do whatever he thought fit and with the officer's absence plus him gaining an American friend to impress those back home with . . . His mind was made up, he took out the package again and after quickly jotting down the verses was returning it to the locker when Billy breezed in!

"Gotcha! You scivin' fucker! Out of your bunk an' nosin' where you've no right to be nosin' to boot!" he spat contemptuously.

"I – I've just come back from the lav!" lied Daniel unconvincingly.

"An' this'll be bum fodder I suppose?" echoed Billy, wrenching the package from the Cabin Boy's grasp and tearing it open.

"Give it back! It – it's private! We – we'll both be in trouble!" pleaded the younger as Billy tore out of the cabin visibly delighted on glancing back to see the 'invalid' wearing just his underpants in hot pursuit.

Two laps round the bridge were followed by a mad sprint aft, the Assistant Steward clearly revelling in having exposed the true state of Daniel's health to half the ship's crew.

Despite it being afternoon siesta for those not on duty, the commotion attracted a considerable audience and when the youths began to circuit the poop mess room, the chase halted abruptly as the couple ploughed into a group of emerging seamen. Thoroughly enjoying the ensuing scuffle the crowd parted to allow the pair much of the stern deck to continue their rough and tumble. So engrossed was Daniel in retrieving the Third's paperwork it was some time before he associated the whistles and bawdy remarks with his brief attire which led to Ianto later joking that the rapt expressions on the faces of the Somali onlookers suggested the sight of Daniel's scantily clad rump would keep them busy in their pits for weeks to come!

The sudden wilt in the Cabin Boy's struggle had Billy up on his feet and throwing all manner of abuse in order to prolong the fun but Daniel, suddenly acutely aware of the situation he'd been drawn into, backed slowly away.

"Thought you wanted these then?" taunted Billy, holding the papers aloft.

"For God's sake!" howled Daniel. "They're the Third's private letters! We'll be in real trouble if they get damaged!"

"Bleedin' well 'ave 'em then you whinin' twat!" retorted Billy, hurling his prize into the air where, to his own surprise and Daniel's horror, the papers were immediately picked up and dispersed in all directions by a playful Atlantic breeze.

Aghast at the sight of the Third's written work fluttering about like a swarm of butterflies, it was seconds before Daniel gathered his wits and launched himself at the last few sheets drifting towards the stern rail. Unfortunately, his vain attempt was thwarted by an AB who stole up behind him and yanked down his underwear and by the time he'd made himself decent, even with the help of his old Somali friend Abu, only seven of the Third's typewritten sheets were back in his possession. With laughter ringing in his ears, he dashed to the rail just in time to see the bulk of the sheaf merging with the *Roundcape's* milky wake.

"Aa-hem!"

It took another loud cough before he lifted his disbelieving eyes and turned to meet those of the Chief Steward standing immediately behind him.

"Before you go for another frolic with the sharks, son," thundered the Chief tugging at his 'ex-patient's' underwear, "there's a mountain of dirty pots and pans cluttering the pantry!"

Two days on, five more crumpled typewritten sheets appeared on the Cabin Boy's bunk. He cared little about who may have deposited them there but after reading just one, still legible sheet, he regretted even more the loss of the rest? The loss of the Third's letters to the girl he'd met in Cwmdonkin Park.

It was an experience Lise, that I have relived a thousand and one times, if only to bask in the warmth of that moment, the moment of you, touching my arm and instinctively knowing that the woman of my life was at my side once again. Turning to see your radiant smile had me rebuking myself for having begun to doubt your turning up at any other venue than our beloved park. A small consolation for my impatience was that Royston always pulls a good pint (I'd downed three pints in the hour you were overdue) but little did I know then how one

hour of petulant impatience would eventually become months and years of waiting and wondering and with only the prop of strong Welsh bitter to sustain me! But yes, my darling, your adorable face at the moment is imprinted in my mind and I recall embarrassing the two of us in my clumsy eagerness to embrace you (or might my almost losing my balance have been due to Royston's bitter too?) And what a spectacle I made of us both with a passionate kiss so drawn out that Royston threatened us with a soda siphon! Such cavorting could give the Antelope a bad name, he joked, but I've long suspected there's been a touch of envy since I introduced him to my Cwmdonkin Rose. He's untypically quiet whenever I broach the idea of holding your return celebration at his place. But wherever we hold it, darling, what a party that will be! If one kiss caused such a stir we'll likely be banned from every blessed pub in the district!

Heloise, my sweet, I've paused from my writing simply to indulge myself in the memory of that kiss! If only – if only I could press my lips on your soft, exquisite mouth at this very moment! Do you remember my helping you to your feet on that first day in the park? Our eyes met and yes! In the same moment as you uttering your first words to me, I wanted to cup your lovely face and kiss you! Yes – I know I've told you that so many times and you have answered that if I had kissed you at that moment that you'd have probably run away screaming that some pervert was loose in the park! But, my darling and I don't care if I've also told you this many times before; that in those last conscious seconds before I sleep or during those cursedly wakeful hours when I hear your voice on the wind, it's your kiss that I most yearn for: to feel your soft, moist lips against my own.

Another reflective pause, my sweet and I can hear your teasing reply accusing me of being an immature romantic! To which I reply without hesitation that if the fruit of immaturity is a lifetime of your kisses then I pray to God for an eternal adolescence!

'A lifetime of your kisses'. An over-sentimental statement maybe but please interpret lifetime as meaning all of our times together condensed into one, glorious Summer of love which sadly ended too abruptly: a thought which, until recently, I had been blaming myself for letting you slip out of my life as easily as you slipped into it. 'Until recently' that is, because if we were destined to meet in his park then surely whatever force controls one's destiny must have had some hand in the remarkable coincidence of my first ship in two years having orders to visit one certain river where . . .

Finding none of the salvaged pages consecutive was hardly as frustrating to Daniel as the loss of the remainder until reasoning that should the officer re-board as rumoured, he'd simply deny any knowledge of the package and that it was highly unlikely that Billy or any other who might have been aware of what had been scattered to the wind would tell on him. This much about a ship's crew he did know and he also soon knew that exposed malingerers could expect no mercy because the Chief Steward very quickly re-introduced him to certain chores which, by the time the *Roundcape* was once again steaming up the mountain-fringed River Saguenay, had transformed her inner bulkheads amidships from the shade of Brumpud's burnt custard to a gleaming hygienic white.

Chapter 17

The Big One

It was surprising, they said, that old Edgar's body hadn't been discovered during the unloading at Port Alfred. The huge suction duct in number three hold had given signs of being intermittently blocked throughout the operation.

"The old wretch has been in an' out o' that duct like a ferret after rabbits," Jock callously remarked on hearing the old Engineer's corpse was not only badly mutilated, but headless.

To Captain Roberts, the grisly find, which came but a few hours out of Port Alfred during the recovery of a fallen hatch timber, was the climaxing disaster of the trip. He saw little purpose in adding to their troubles by facing a delaying enquiry should they turn back and accordingly ordered those involved in the find to say nothing until the river Pilot had disembarked.

On the evening of the following day some one hundred miles off Nova Scotia, the remains of 'Edgar the Silent', weighted and wrapped in a piece of tarpaulin were, after a brief ceremony, committed to the deep.

From the time he witnessed what appeared to be nothing more than a bundle of rags being hauled up from below up until a good couple of days after the ceremony on the rail, Daniel remained in shock. The gruesome discovery had occurred just as he was getting over the unfortunate chain of events at the Caribbean end of the shuttle and sea life was beginning to look up a little.

The atmosphere of Port Alfred had done much to lift his depression. The vibrant new music which was elating enough just echoing out of Jock's wireless seemed to reverberate out of every open window of the a sun-kissed port on the shore of Lake Ha-Ha. Or were his raised spirits more to do with the fact of him beginning to come out of his shell? Instead of creeping around with the thought of how best to jump ship, blinding him to all that was about him, he was now having a beer or two and had even summoned up the courage to wink at one of those sexy, French-speaking cuties. Things were definitely improving.

Even the usually officious Chief Steward had the hint of a smile on his face when he at last made it aboard with his wife's new china tea service in one piece.

"It's not such a bad life after all is it, son?" Daniel was sure he'd heard him murmur as they steamed away from the lakeside port, its impressive hilltop cross peeping out of a thin, morning mist.

The Fourth Engineer's body lay in the cabin which served as ship's hospital and Bo'sun's store until it was despatched to the ocean bed. Daniel vowed that he would never again, whatever the circumstances, step inside that cabin, the thought of what it had housed haunting him for weeks to come. It was this terrible haunting which caused him to seek assurance from the only man aboard who he knew would answer compassionately and without derision: the Somali greaser, Abu Shalaan.

"You do not grieve alone, my son," he told him in his usual paternal manner after Daniel had spoken out about the complacency aboard regards Edgar's demise. "Many men hide their feelings lest they should appear to fear what is coming to us all in time and that such fear may make them 'lesser' men in the eyes of their brothers."

"Yes but the Second Cook is saying things like, if they find Edgar's head he'll stuff an apple in his mouth and display it on the Sunday lunch table!" protested Daniel. "That's downright blooming wicked I reckon!"

"Scriptures tell that a man was once displayed on a wooden cross and that man forgave those responsible for the pain and humiliation of exhibiting him so," replied Abu with a warm smile. "Doing and saying cruel things would appear easy to some men, my son, while forgiving they would find most difficult."

As was quite often the case, Abu's answer puzzled Daniel while his tone suggested it to be wise.

"I – er, didn't know that Muslims read about Jesus and that?"

Abu gestured towards the sea and answered simply, "Reading is my pastime, son."

"Why do you do it? Why do you just drift around the world reading?" Daniel asked. "What I mean like, is you hardly ever go ashore like the others do you?"

"I've no need to go ashore, my son," replied Abu. "Some people crave physical pleasures while others such as myself get pleasure from mental stimulation. I am as much addicted to mental stimulation as another may be to alcohol. Maybe I'm missing out but I think not when I observe what goes on around me."

"I don't think you're missing out," said Daniel. "I mean, you always look happy to me."

"Thank you for that," replied Abu. "Now tell me, what is it that costs nothing and is worth nothing until you give it away?"

"Er – I've no idea."

"A smile, my son, a smile."

There was not a hint of a smile on Jock's face when, later that day, he entered their cabin to find Billy playing with the controls of his radio.

"Radio Memphis! I just had Radio Memphis!" he cried out to Daniel, too busy to have seen the Cook.

"I'll gi' you fuckin' Radio Memphis you prat! That fuckin' trash'll do its valves in! I'll nae tell you again! Leave my radio alone!" barked Jock with the usual clenched fist.

Since Newport News, Billy had been obsessed with tuning in to hear the 'new' music from US radio stations after one of the group of soldiers who'd entertained them there had enthused to him about one new performer he'd seen while home on leave in Memphis. This handsome and talented young guy had a voice like no other, played aggressive guitar and his gymnastics around the stage had the mostly young chick audience in a screaming frenzy, he'd raved. Bill Haley was old hat and would soon be blown away by this dynamic newcomer whom he called *'the big one'*, the *'real big one'*, information that Billy had already gleaned from US radio stations and now tried to impress Jock with.

"The only *big one* you'll be gettin' is my *big boot* up your arse if you dinnae leave my set alone!" he threatened. "An' considerin' we've only recently despatched old Edgar, that fuckin' racket is downright disrespectful!"

"That's what I was about tell him," moaned Reno from his bunk. "And some people like to nap in the afternoon. What's all this arguing about anyway?"

"It's about the fuckin' *big one* if that means anythin' to you!" spat Jock. "This pair o' Sassenach dimwits are searchin' for another plastic god to replace their Bill Haley who's nae longer worthy o' their prayers! Your young generation change their gods willy-nilly an' if it cannae sing it's o' fuck-all use. Such as your Pope an' the like aren't worth a toss cos they cannae play a guitar and prance aroun' the stage like some nancy-boy. Orators such as your Churchill and Hitler wouldnae get a look in cos they never took singin' lessons, that's what it's comin' to. If somebody had crept up on your balcony orating Mussolini an' stuck a pitch fork up his arse he'd have been number one in the charts next day! Whatever your political views, those wi' mere oratorical skills cannae be leaders is the opinion o' your young folk these days!"

"Or . . . orator . . . er – what's it mean, Jock?" enquired Reno.

"For fuck's sake you . . .! Oratorical is the power of speech!" bellowed the Cook getting on his pulpit. "One who can sway the masses by speech alone. You'll all have listened to somebody or other, mebbe on the radio or stage who's got you hangin' on to every word he utters, somebody like your Churchill or . . ."

"Or like the poet chap that the Third used to go on about," interrupted Daniel spontaneously. "He – he used to get the crowd hanging on to everything he said so the, er – Third told me. He'd got this great booming voice that even got the Yanks calling out for more. So the, er – Third . . ."

"So the fuckin' Third told you," mimicked Jock, hardly pleased with Daniel's offering. "Laddie, the Third, wherever he

242

is now, hangin' frae some tree wi' the birds peckin' his eyes out I shouldnae wonder! Your precious Third didnae live in the same world as us it's been noted an' any such rubbish he's passed on to gullible prats like yourself aren't worth repeatin' is my advice to you! Do you get me?"

"I – I was only saying about this poet chap that the, er – Third's lady friend admired, had this orat . . . oratorical, er – thing you were on about. She used to follow him everywhere just to listen to his foghorn of a voice. Even followed him to America, the Third has it. As I said, the Yanks couldn't get enough of him so the Third told . . ."

"Laddie! I'll nae tell you again!" cut in an exasperated Jock for a second time. "The Third was in a league o' his own aboard an' the only two unaware o' it were you an the pantry cat! So shut it, I'm warnin' you! Fuckin'-well shut it!"

"There's talk aft that 'is jumpin' ship might 'ave been something' to do with old Edgar finishin' up in number three 'old," sprang Billy. "What do you think, Jock?"

"I wouldnae have said the Third was the barmy sort who commits murder," replied the Scot grimly. "But who knows what a man is capable of when he loses it like that nutter surely did."

"That's blooming daft talk!" protested Daniel. "They – they used to be good mates until . . ."

"*Shut it, laddie! I said fuckin' shut it!*"

Chapter 18

A Walk In The Park

Abu's reluctance to condemn outright Jock's intolerance to everything and everyone frustrated Daniel.

"In every group of men or women there'll be one who 'upsets the applecart' I think is the saying," was how the elderly Somali began to explain. "In about every situation from shipboard life, factory life or even government, people will want to disagree and even go to war over disagreement," he continued pensively. "So your question is bigger than you think when you take in that many wars in recorded history were often sparked off by one disagreement which only proves that the people of this Earth are still in their infancy but one day, son, we will hopefully grow up and regret the centuries of war along the path to maturity. But, son, by then you and I will be long gone. As for today, I cannot help or interfere with your problem but will promise that if things get dire, I will help you." Abu would keep his promise.

On the night of Abu's prophesy, a sky ablaze with stars provided the perfect setting for such a speech and he tried to better explain himself. The world hostilities he'd spoken of, he said, proved that man was at the beginning of himself and ought learn with each other and take care of their planet home before future developments in science ruin the only home they have.

"Are there any others like us out there do you think?" asked Daniel pointing skyward. "And if there are do you think we'll ever get to meet them?"

"My son," replied Abu, "the answer is numerical. The sheer magnitude of the heavens can be compared with every grain of sand on Earth which makes the idea of our planet being the only one with life nonsensical. But as to us ever meeting whatever form of life is out there, the answer is no because we'd have to travel outside of our solar system which is impossible for humans because distance makes it so. That, son, is why it is crucial that we take care of each other and planet Earth, our adjacent planets being unable to sustain life as we know it which leaves us with just infinity."

"Er – what exactly is infinity?" was Daniel's pointless question.

"Nothing son," smiled Abu, "because virtually everything known has a beginning and an end, while infinity has neither and nothing in between."

While Daniel always felt comfortable with fatherly Abu, such 'wise' explanations often seemed far removed from the question posed causing the youth, as on this occasion, to approach the matter from another direction.

"Er – I'm not quite with you," he began, "but I came to see you because you seem to know what makes people what they are and so much has happened since I came aboard that I just can't get my head round, like the Cook's wicked talk and your own fellow countrymen's weird superstitions which make everybody else uncomfortable like. I mean, are they barmy or do they just enjoy giving everybody the shits?"

Smiling and typically unruffled by Daniel's blunt query, Abu replied, "My son, while I hide away in my book, many others on board seek release from boredom by inventing gossip intended to agitate or even, as has been your recent experience, to disturb with satanic statements albeit for no better reason than to ease themselves through another monotonous day at sea. It's as simple as that and I apologize for elaborating my answer but I would ask you not to dwell on ultra mundane things that I have spoken about and perhaps confused you with. And more importantly, my son," he concluded, laying a hand on the youth's shoulder, "do not overlook today while reminiscing yesterday or contemplating tomorrow because today could be the best day of your life and one day you may regret maturity and wish that time had stood still."

*'If the fruit of immaturity is a lifetime of your kisses,
then I pray to God for an eternal adolescence.'*

While easing his own boredom by re-reading the Third's salvaged writings, it occurred to Daniel that the similarity between the officer's romantic statement and Abu's words about regretting maturity was reason enough to go aft for another conversation with the friendly old greaser. He found him on the stern rail with the greaser's Mess Boy Hassan, an amiable youth with whom, since Martyn's departure, he'd become quite chummy. On presenting Abu with the typewritten sheet its personal nature appeared to disturb him and he politely refused to read what was intended for another. His stance though, didn't stop Daniel broaching the subject of the absent officer and a discussion developed which led to quite interesting revelations concerning the man.

The occasion of this particular conversation coincided with their taking on the Demerara Pilot for the third time. Abu listened attentively to Daniel's concerns and by the time they'd reached their Georgetown mooring the Somali (a yawning Hassan had long since gone below) all of Daniel's worries, from the loss of the Third's written work to the discovery of Edgar's corpse, had been aired before the *Roundcape's* anchor had rattled its way back down to the bed of the muddy Demerara.

Considering his reticence to criticise individuals Abu's comments surprised the youth. He advised him to tactfully avoid further intimacy with the Third should he re-board because, he said cautiously, the man's rumoured mental state would appear to have some foundation.

"But I know him better than anybody aboard!" protested Daniel! "And except for when he's had a drop too much to drink he's always seemed okay to me!"

"I sincerely hope I'm wrong," declared Abu, "but please understand that I'm not given to speaking about such things lightly."

His reluctance to spread gossip became more evident when he asked for Daniel's discretion should he enlighten him further. He also insisted that once having disclosed what he knew, he wished not to talk on the matter again; a wish that had the Cabin Boy extra curious when, minutes later, he led him to the Somali's quarters telling him that there was someone he would like him to meet: someone who had previously sailed with their Third Mate and had a good recollection of the events of that sailing.

In the cabin they entered Hassan lay on a bunk thumbing through an old *Picture Post* magazine. On an opposite bunk sprawled an elderly fireman known to Daniel as Shukri, Abu's most constant companion. Unlike Abu, Shukri rarely spoke to anyone outside his immediate circle but his broad, almost toothless smile, as on that occasion, portrayed his irenic nature. The ensuing conversation between the two elderly men began, it seemed out of politeness, in English but very soon lapsed into excited bursts of Arabic. As they continued, Hassan grinned across at Daniel, apparently finding his presence in their accommodation amusing. The visitor though, in keeping with the serious tone of the discussion awaited an interpretation with a straight face.

When the exchange finally ended, Abu turned to him saying, "Shukri, my friend here, has sailed with Third Officer Mr Williams three times. The last time he says was about two years ago aboard the *MV Michsteve* running between Cardiff and South Africa. He recalls the officer becoming very sick up here," Abu continued, tapping his forehead, "and drinking so heavily that their Master saw fit to lock him up for his own safety until home. This account, my son, Shukri has spoken about before and I was reminded of it by something you touched upon in our chats about the officer once mentioning to you about his receiving bad news while . . ."

"About receiving bad news while on the South African trip!" completed Daniel. "He spoke about being upset on hearing that this poet chap had died in America while his lady friend was over there to see him. It – it all seems to fit doesn't it?"

Toying with his whiskers, Abu studied him for a moment, then said warmly, "My son, your young friend Hassan over there will accept as fact the contents of his magazine because he believes he's reading a factual compilation. You also, in your innocence readily believe what you are told especially when the teller would seem to have nothing to gain from mistruths or inaccuracies, am I correct?"

"Er – yes but . . .? Oh – the Third's been sort of spinning me a yarn has he? Is that what you're saying?"

"Sort of, yes," smiled Abu, "but not intentionally as I see it and I'll help you understand."

"Understand what?" asked Daniel. "Look, I know that he waffles on a bit and to be honest I'm not always listening but his tale about this famous poet dying in New York while his lady friend was over there to see him on stage sticks with me cos while telling me he suddenly went ghastly white and looked as if he was gonna drop down dead himself. But – but what he told me was true wasn't it? That's what happened didn't it or – or . . .?"

"Not quite, my son, because my friend Shukri here," gestured Abu, "my friend Shukri recalls well the reason for the officer's irrational behaviour at that time and with all respect it does not quite tally with your account or to be fair the account which you have been led to believe."

"Oh – er . . . what – what's he have to say about it then?"

"He says, my son, that the news received by Mr Williams was indeed the news of a death but not, he assures me, the death of an illustrious Welsh poet in New York."

"Who – whose was it then?"

"The death of Third Officer Mr Williams's lady friend, my son," replied Abu softly, "so my friend Shukri positively recalls."

"Why is it that your lot seem to look to old Abu when that creepy little pervert Yussef is your real gaffer?" Daniel asked Hassan on meeting him in the galley queue the following morning.

"Because Abu knows everything and Yussef knows nothing," replied Hassan simply.

"Not *everything*!" disputed the Cabin Boy. "That business about the Third for instance. I reckon Abu's a bit confused about that."

"Abu knows everything," repeated Hassan. "He even knows that Yussef saw old Engineer fall into the hold before everybody else know," he added mysteriously.

"I wasn't talking about old . . . Eh . . .? What's that you said? Yussef saw old Edgar fall into the blooming hold?"

"You speak yesterday with Abu about somebody die . . . I – I think you speak about old Engineer and . . ." Hassan began to falter on realizing his blunder.

"You mean that that little creep Yussef saw old Edgar fall into that hold and never breathed a word about it?" gasped Daniel.

"He – he just speak with Abu about it and Abu promise not to tell in case . . .!"

"In case they think that he pushed him in!" blurted the Cabin Boy. "He more than likely did! They never got on, them two!"

"Please say nothing about what I say!" pleaded the Mess Boy. "They think I am sleeping when Yussef tell Abu! Please say nothing! It was an accident!"

For the sake of his Somali friends, Daniel kept quiet about what had been accidently disclosed to him. But then his mind on that occasion of sailing the Guianean river was filled with more pleasant thoughts; lascivious thoughts intensified by the heady aromas wafting over the ship as they skirted banks spilling over with an abundance of rich, tropical growth. The thoughts of a young adult male in the pink of health. Romantic thoughts; sexual thoughts. Thoughts about a beautiful young woman. Thoughts about Heloise . . .?

Yes, he had accepted a few tots of the jungle juice suddenly much evident aboard after Georgetown and the Guianean humidity always had caused his temperature to rise. But Heloise . . .? Oh no. Heloise was dead so it wouldn't be her eyes he'd soon be amorously gazing down into depending of course on their stopping at the particular anchorage usually graced by that sexually enrapturing, intoxicatingly beautiful river princess *whoever she was . . .?*

A cold shower did nothing to calm his yearning, in fact his nudity only served to heighten his expectations and very soon he was back at the rail, his eyes trained permanently for'ard in dogged anticipation of what lay around the next bend.

Lunch was being served when at last slowing orders rang out from the bridge. Darting out from the pantry he was thrilled to recognize their whereabouts as being the anchorage frequented by Heloise's double. Ahead of them and surrounded by a flotilla of traders lay another bauxite carrier. Even before they were stationary the larger part of the flotilla having obviously exhausted demand for their wares, were speedily making for the newcomer. As they converged on the *Roundcape*, Daniel anxiously scanned every boat, his interest mainly on the singly-manned canoes, three of which headed the procession.

Disappointed at not seeing her among the first arrivals, he despondently looked back towards the other ship. Within seconds, his heart was beating so rapidly that he wondered if perhaps he'd stood too long beneath that equatorial sun? Moving into the shade of a companionway, he refocused on one of the two small craft still attending the other vessel. Of course, he chuckled to himself with relief on positively identifying her. Her popularity with the seamen was such that business always improved whenever she threatened to leave.

The thirty minutes that passed before she paddled over the *Roundcape* gave Daniel time to complete his chores and be free to study her at will. He was convinced as she came alongside that it was *his* eyes she met first with that enchanting smile.

"Ye' – yeah!" he stammered in answer to her sales cry. "I – I'll buy from you!"

She reached for his lowered basket and awaited his choice.

"What a lovely pair!" came the inevitable chorus from the rail as the swell of an unfettered breast was glimpsed as she reached out.

"I'm okay for bananas, my darling!" called out a freshly-showered sailor lifting his towel and draping his penis over the rail. "But I'll give you this for a bite of them cherries look you!" he quipped to the howled delight of his shipmates.

A bellow from the bridge ended the girl's embarrassment and stopped a fuming Cabin Boy from making a fool of himself. She wasn't exactly too shocked by such bawdiness though he had to conclude on noting that the buttons of her cleavage remained unfastened. This however, was all she was prepared to reveal it seemed, judging by how quickly she tugged at the hem of her grubby white frock when only so much as a tantalizing brown knee popped into view. The *real* Heloise, he mused, recalling what the Third had told him and by the evidence of her photos, had been far less coy.

"A woman's behaviour towards the man she loves is far removed from that on public display," was how he'd excused his sweetheart's *style* in *personal* photographs; an excuse that gave Daniel erotic thoughts because of something approaching wanton in her expression while posing for the camera: a certain look that appealed to him in the snaps as it did now while studying the smiling beauty below. There was no avoiding it. From playground giggles to factory pornography and now upon this tropical river: *sex* was everywhere! Even female compositions in the flow of his boyhood brook may have been subconsciously affected by that pleasantly inescapable driving force: a force as ubiquitous as that very brook. No place, no one, was untouched by it. Even the demure young woman down there in the canoe might be 'getting her fair share' as Billy would crudely phrase it. Their eyes met again as he hauled up the basket. Was she as innocent as her smile suggested? Was her likeness to Heloise only physical or had she . . .? Might she . . .?

When at last the crowd began to disperse, he called to the girl while lowering his basket again. Inside was the photo of Heloise

251

in tennis whites which he'd kept since his 'convalescence' in the Third's cabin.

Her initial reaction was one of confusion but as she studied the snap and listened curiously to Daniel's, "Same you! Girl same you!" she smiled radiantly and nodded her understanding.

"But this girl very beautiful! I not so beautiful as she!" she exclaimed bashfully. "She is your lover?"

"Oh – er . . . no." Daniel hadn't expected such a direct question. "She – she's someone's lady friend aboard. Well . . . he *was* aboard until, er – recently," he replied, completely taken by her simple charm.

"Er – listen a minute, I – I've got something to ask you," he continued, feeling ridiculous even before his question was out. "Do you . . .? Do you remember selling fruit to an officer on this ship one night some weeks ago?"

Pointing to the ship's name on her bows it suddenly occurred to him that because she spoke intelligible English, he was expecting her to be able to read it.

"As – as I say, it was some weeks ago," he repeated weakly.

Her blank stare only added to his discomfort until suddenly, after a thorough scrutiny of the ship, her eyes widened with interest. She paddled towards the bows to check out the ship's name then turned to race back.

"Officer man!" she called out excitedly. "You speak with officer man to come see me now!"

"I – I just said, he's not on board. Why, er . . .? Why do you want to see him?"

She chuckled cutely, her head slightly bowed but her eyes still meeting his as if embarrassed about something.

"Officer man says he likes me fine! He give me dis!" she cried, stooping to produce a small, oblong tin from beneath her seat. Opening it, she lifted out, with obvious pride, a small heart-shaped pendant on a delicate chain.

"You tink is beautiful, man? I give officer fruit in exchange. Good, eh? He say next time he come he give me ring to match but I tink he forget me, eh, man?"

"Er – no," replied Daniel awkwardly. "He – he didn't forget you and there's a chance he might re-board in Mackenzie, so look out for us when we come back downriver."

"I tink he forget me," she repeated, her smile fading momentarily. "He even forget my name when he stop by in de police boat. He call me some other name so I tink he mix me up wid somebody else. Dat's not my name I tell him. Why you call me . . .?"

"Heloise?" blurted Daniel. "Did he called you Heloise?"

He glanced furtively about him on suddenly becoming aware of how bizarre this exchange would sound to an eavesdropper.

"Someting like dat," she chuckled back, her pearly smile returning. "Oh yeah! He call me Lise! De officer call me Lise!"

Her answer had Daniel struggling for words.

"As – as I said, he could be rejoining us in Mackenzie. So – so I'll tell him you'll be waiting."

"Yes, man! Tell him Sara is waitin' for de ring he promise!" she called out happily, while replacing the photo into the basket.

Moments later she had manoeuvred her canoe away from the ship and was paddling landwards. He watched her go, her shrill laughter ringing in his ears.

"Yeah . . .! I'll tell him Helo . . . er – Sara? I – I'll tell him . . . But – but what was that you said? Something about a police boat? He stopped by in a police boat . . .?"

❖ ❖ ❖ ❖ ❖ ❖ ❖ ❖

On arrival at Mackenzie, Daniel returned aft to confide his strange conversation with the river girl to Abu. The Somali at first reminded him of his expressed desire to talk no more on the subject but on detecting his excitement he allowed him to continue.

"Okay, I agree with you that the Third's a little odd," concluded the youth, "but I can honestly say that only in drink did he seem really strange to me and he's hardly alone aboard in that respect is he?"

With his usual smile Abu replied, "My son, I have spent my time at sea puzzling why so many men render themselves temporarily insane? I have seen them go ashore in the most idyllic places only to see the inside of a bar. Surely, I ask myself, the world is beautiful enough without the need for such stimulants? Or could it be that my stubbornness to at least sample these dubious pleasures mean that I have missed out on something? Perhaps I shouldn't have resisted because after all it has always been my philosophy that life is an adventurous voyage along which only by encountering the storms do we fully appreciate the calm seas ahead."

Abu had cleverly avoided the matter put to him as politely as he could, Daniel irritably suspected. Just talking about the Third wouldn't do him any harm whereas he, Daniel, would be held responsible for the items missing from the officer's cabin; a charge which in all probability he would now face if the river girl's innocent chatter meant that the officer was being detained until the return of his ship? About to reiterate his concern, he was stopped from doing so by the arrival of Shukri with more news about the very man.

"Third Officer Williams," he began before lapsing into his native tongue for a hushed chat with Abu who listened intently before relaying the news to Daniel.

The Third, he said, had been detained by the Mackenzie police some days after leaving the ship as an illegal immigrant and subsequently been put on a boat to be dealt with in Georgetown. On the journey downriver however, he'd escaped custody by jumping ashore and had vanished in the jungle and had not been seen or heard of since.

"At least, my son," comforted Abu, "your dilemma regards meeting up with him again has been resolved for the time being."

"I – I wasn't all that bothered," lied Daniel. "Haven't they got any idea at all as to where he might be?"

The old Somali gripped the rail and replied quietly, "It would seem, my son, that our Mr Williams has gone where he indicated to you he had in mind to go."

"Where – where's that then?"

"He mentioned something about going for a walk in the park did he not?" replied Abu, gazing across the water to the infinite wall of green.

Chapter 19

Horrific Discovery

During their passage from Canada, an offensive stench had developed amidships and shortly before Mackenzie on opening up number three hold in preparation for loading, it became obvious that the source of the smell lay within. On investigation, it was discovered that a fractured sewage pipe had been leaking into a bulkhead recess clogged with rotting corn from a previous cargo. It was during the removal of this rancid substance that the horrific discovery was made.

Daniel first became aware that something important was happening when the Skipper and First Mate took a shortcut through the pantry to join an agitated Bo'sun at the side of the hold. Next on the scene was the Chief Steward who, after a brief exchange with the Master, hurried into the pantry, lifted the storeroom hatch and went below. Moments later he reappeared carrying a small cardboard box which he handed to the Bo'sun who promptly tossed it into the hold. Minutes later, it was hauled back up on a rope and placed gently onto the deck as if it contained a primed bomb. The atmosphere was electric; all eyes on the Bo'sun and the box but instead of opening it as the onlookers were willing him to do, the Bo'sun, looking decidedly uneasy, stood back and began to fill his pipe

Hesitantly, the Skipper and Mate stooped together, the latter cautiously doing what the Bo'sun was reluctant to do. The Mate had his back towards Daniel so it was the Captain's face he studied during the climax of this strange performance. In a flash, his lightly-tanned complexion had turned to a deathly grey and his eyes were so tightly closed that he seemed to be in great pain. It was Big Paddy who caught him as he reeled back into the crowd while the Mate, looking equally fragile, slumped down onto the edge of the hatch.

It was Brumpud who then ambled out of the transfixed throng, closed and picked up the box and at the heels of the Chief Steward carried it into the makeshift ship's hospital.

"Oh shit!" gasped an AB. "Thought he was goin' to put it on show in the galley for a mo'."

"What – what is it?" asked the Cabin Boy in the same awful moment as conceiving the answer himself.

If, by not handing over a body to the Canadian authorities because of possible costly delays; then why, when the missing part of that body turned up, should they declare it to the Guianese seemed the logic behind that part being ignominiously secreted away together with the Bo'sun's tack in the all-purpose cabin.

Anxious to avoid further confrontation with the Guianese officialdom, Captain Roberts was highly relieved to hear that the river policeman on board had been fast asleep throughout the incident and that the Pilot had been too preoccupied navigating a difficult stretch of river to have been aware of anything unusual happening.

"And after all," a suddenly pious Jock pointed out in support of the Skipper's action, "it'd have been hardly fair on the old bastard to dump the bulk o' his carcass in the north Atlantic then lay his head to rest in some jungle clearin' an ocean an' more away. Might just as well display it on the saloon table!" was the follow-up remark that collapsed his sentiment.

As obnoxious was Billy's comment about Edgar being reunited with his other half on the run back to Canada.

"At least the Chippy ought be able to sort out enough timber to despatch the poor sod proper this time," was how the Bristolian laughed off his own unease.

"Now *that*, Billy," groaned Jock, on catching Daniel's disapproving expression, "was the most despicable crack o' the trip to date! An' judgin' by the baleful looks you're gettin' frae our Cabin Boy here, he'll readily agree wi' me, am I nae right, Daniel?"

"He's had some real bad luck has old Edgar," said Daniel to no-one in particular. "His missus left him just as he was about to retire then this happens. So how you can joke about it beats me. I used to talk to him and he wouldn't have hurt a fly. The only bloke he'd got it in for was this baker chap and quite rightly so I think!"

"Weren't it more the case the baker 'ad it in for 'im?" quipped Billy typically.

"Very fond of music was old Edgar," continued Daniel, ignoring him. "He loved soft ballads and suchlike. Very keen on Donald Peers he was, so he told me and Martyn . . ."

"Och Aye! That'll explain it, lads!" announced Jock, dramatically. "Just now outside yon paint store come fuckin' morgue. I was just passin' an' there was this mournful renderin' o' *Babblin' Brook* comin' frae wi'-in! Nigh on shite meself I did! Nigh on shite meself!"

"Enough! Enough! I have heard enough!" erupted Reno who, until then, had been literally dumbstruck by the horrific discovery. "For once I agree with the boy! Such joking is evil and I think it unbelievable that we keep this . . . this thing on board for one day more let alone 'til Canada or thereabouts! The Muslims aft will not stand for it! They will mutiny I'm sure!"

"Christ almighty!" goaded Jock. "Mutiny is it? Much more o' that kind of talk, Reno an' the Master'll likely incarcerate you in the fuckin' ship's hospital along wi' the object o' your torment! An' come to think o' it," he added in an ominously less humourous tone, "when the Skipper gets round to doin' the Christian thing by old Edgar, you, as senior Assistant Steward'll have to go in there an' carry out the preparations afore the final ceremony."

"What – what preparations are you talking about, Jock?" ventured Reno, looking puzzled.

"Layin' him out o' course! I distinctly heard the Steward tell he'd nae the guts to lay out the old bastard a second time. So who'd you think old fat guts'll be lookin' to do the honours, eh?"

"Don't talk rubbish, Jock! There is nothing to be laid out!" shrieked the Maltese. "Whoever heard of a head being laid out? This is crazy talk!"

"Dinnae you come the *crazy* bit wi' me, Reno, else I'll be layin' *you* out an' quick about it!" retorted Jock. "Accordin' to Brumpud just now," he grated on, "nae only was that maggot-infested head in need o' a wash an' shave . . . aye, it's a well-known fact that facial hair grows after death an' even after decapitation an' the Skipper's hardly likely to take him into the local barbers in Mackenzie if that's what you're hopin'. An' there's his eyes to be closed an' as the Cook told me, the man's eyes were burnin' into his own every step o' the way into yon ship's hospital! Every step o' the way so Brumpud tells me!"

"Reno – I – I'll get Edgar's glasses if – if . . ." began Billy, so cracked up with mirth he could hardly get his words out. "He – he'd not look so scary if 'e was wearin' . . ."

"I'll nae warn you again, Billy! This is nae laughin' matter an' you'll be laughin' on the other side o' your face if Reno here chickens out o' doin' his duty an' it falls to the next in rank to do the washin' an' shavin' an close the poor old bastard's peepers!"

Reno's screams of protest as he dashed out of the cabin demonstrated clearly that the pre-ceremonial duties were not for him. While disgusted, Daniel wasn't so naive as to be taken in by such insensitive nonsense but it at least put Jock in a good mood until, that is, he discovered that all shore leave in Mackenzie had been cancelled.

"That bastard o' a Skipper cannae do it!" he roared, feeding his wrath with gulps of jungle juice.

But the Skipper *could* and he *had* as the notice strung across the head of the gangplank proved. Not that a mere notice would stop them, mused Daniel and found himself correct within an hour of docking, noting that as soon as the rum-induced fire in their bellies began licking at their brains, in ones and twos, by all routes safe or otherwise, they hopped it. And the old man was hardly blameless, for prior to whatever prompted his last minute ban, he'd paid out subs in local currency taken on while off

Georgetown for that very purpose (Daniel, working below, had been missed out) and if they'd got money to blue it was an odds-on certainty that those rum-primed seamen would up and blue it! An odds-on certainty!

Evening time and alone in the sweathole of a cabin that had been his home for the last few calamitous months, he finally vented his feelings. Why he cried was not even clear to himself. A measure of sorrow for people now departed maybe? But in truth he knew that his tears were more out of self-pity and self-reproach for having been stupid enough to cross that gangplank from normality to nightmare. Small wonder he brooded, that seamen became alcoholics, insane, or both. The pretence of being the equal of his brothers had proved farcical. Especially the elder who, even while stricken with polio, had become a 'card' in that Cornish hospital: always insisting that he'd soon be returning to sea as soon as if he was anything like fit. How would he have tackled such a situation left alone aboard with only thirty-five Canadian cents to his name? He'd have said bollocks to the Skipper and followed the others ashore and had fun! He'd have got up off his arse and chanced the old man's wrath even with just thirty-five Canadian cents . . .! Thirty-five Canadian cents? What fun could he possibly have with just thirty-five Canadian cents?

Misery fully restored, he showered and returned to his bunk. He could go aft for a chat with Abu or Hassan but just wasn't in the mood and he might get lumbered with Reno out on deck along with the others who'd chosen not to defy orders. Nothing left to read either. Boredom on the run back from Canada had exhausted the few books aboard. Nothing! Well, that was except for . . . and it was extremely unlikely that he'd ever meet the man again. Not a trace of him other than Sara's odd mention of him being seen on some police boat. Hardly his cup of tea but those salvaged pages which now had risen to twenty or so, deposited on his bunk by someone who'd probably found them scattered about the decks, would help to pass time. Pointless handing them over to his seniors or returning them to where he'd found them. And of course, even if he had an address, the fact was as he now knew; there was no recipient.

. . . and the reason, my beautiful Gower Pearl, why I didn't object when you suggested Laugharne was because, my sometimes gullible sweetheart, getting a drink in that neck of the woods is decidedly easier than trying to get one in places as remote as Oxwich and Rhossili! Yes – scheming old Ivor had his way once again, my sweet Lise and you actually thought I was compromising on our destination while Laugharne (Browns Hotel) was my preference all along. And why not? Especially recalling our last trip there which you hardly stopped talking about for the rest of my leave! Like a starry-eyed adolescent you were. Giggling and swooning and oh! those delightful blushes when I teased you about your behaviour. They were well worth the painful jabs to my ribs you punished me with. Well worth them!

So where were we? Ah yes – somewhere along the road out of Laugharne (and I never did tell Owen about the makeshift exhaust repair after I'd lost concentration on that bend.) Those shapely knees of yours could have been the death of us! Such a distraction! Regards the exhaust though. Serves Owen right for overcharging a mate! That clapped-out Morris wasn't worth one shilling a day, never mind ten!

What a day though, eh, Lise? A wonderful, unforgettable day! Days such as those are the blooms on the tree of life, eh, Lise? And such perfect weather. 'So unlikely a prelude to the October winds' was your apt description of a September day to crown all September days if you recall? I

261

certainly do because you sighed those words only moments before the exhaust came adrift for the second time one mile before Pendine!

Pendine. Yes, it was always inevitable that after Laugharne and Browns that our mood would take us to Pendine. And on that particular day it could well have been Libya except for the odd palm that is. Sun-kissed and scarcely a breath of wind on those infinite sands haunted by mirages. But we never did get bowled over by one of those phantom racers did we, Lise? Not that we'd have known what hit us, eh, my insatiable beach nymph? Ouch! I think you've broken a rib this time, my sweet. A glutton for punishment is your Ivor!

Talking about punishment our Cabin Boy received a nasty pasting from the Assistant Cook yesterday. (No, Lise, I'm not trying to pad out my letter with trivial incidents aboard but you'll understand my mentioning this when you read on.) This young English lad had his first lesson in shipboard manners it seems. He appears inoffensive to me so how he upset the Cook will be interesting to learn. Not that I'm yet fully acquainted with the lad other than the odd word while he tidies for me. But it's his appearance that's prompted this mention and if I remind you of the head and shoulders portrait by Augustus John? Well – others would say that a thatch of shapeless, curly hair and churlish looks is about all he has in common with DT and of course they'd be right because while not wishing to be cruel to one in the throes of adolescence, the lad, according to a Steward *he shares with, would climb to the crow's nest for eggs if told to! Oh well; such trivial observations at least give me something to impart to you other than another recount of one of our memorable outings (how ever many recounts, I still get pleasure in doing so) which happily returns this poignant anecdote to Pendine. Yes, I'm ahead of myself again because in truth I never could wait to spread our rug on those sands in anticipation of what I'll get another dig in the ribs for should I dare to graphically describe those memories which help little with my current insomnia. So wind back time perhaps three hours before arriving at that beach and I've just pinched your bottom as you so indecorously reach into the back seat of the car for your handbag to prepare for your siren-like entry into Browns public bar. Ouch! Well, it's your own fault, you provocatively beautiful woman you! Your contrived lack of modesty on occasions makes Jane of the Daily Mirror a nun in comparison!*

But I'm not complaining, my sweet Lise, because your act I know is designed to fill our relationship with fun which can only lead me to that one aspect of our union which at first I found not easy to deal with until eventually conceiving that my accepting your other passion only fuelled what we already had: an acceptance that led me into joining you in something that I'm uncomfortable with to this day!

'Poet-spotting' is the phrase we whispered only to each other lest we be exposed to ridicule. But while I 'panted for Pendine', ouch! Should our reconnaissance suggest it worthwhile? After refreshment in Browns, poet-spotting we would go!

And did not the limited success of that game confirm the wisdom of keeping it to ourselves? And while we derived much pleasure from our being in places frequented by him or at best where he'd hopefully be, just being there with you was reward enough for me and of course, is why I chose not to discourage you by perhaps saying what I was often tempted to say as to how futile was the pursuit of a shadow!

An equally toiled-over thought on seeing your disappointment, perhaps outside the boathouse or by his quaint excuse for a studio was one of being thankful for you having at least attended those few recitals and also the occasion which oddly appeared to thrill you the most when our patience with the cameras in the vicinity of Browns was rewarded with what you called your 'scoop', the result of which I hasten to add has taken pride of place on my bureau since Cardiff.

The wonder of you, Lise, is that whatever the outcome of our time in Laugharne and Pendine Sands, our next objective (the thought of which made even more enticing by refreshment in Browns) your attention would refocus totally on that venue and just about every male in the pub would be dumbstruck with envy as they watched me stroll out of that place with 'the loveliest thing in creation' on my arm. Our exits I'm sure, couldn't have been better staged on a Hollywood film set and I was always so grateful that the old Morris didn't break down before we were clear of the town because my lying beneath a jacked-up car or you having to remove a stocking to substitute a broken fan belt would hardly have been in keeping with the theatrical appearance of those occasions!

Stockings? Oh no, not on the Pendine outings! If my memory serves me well there'd usually be only one other garment beneath those sexy little frocks which you were so often in a hurry to discard as we sang (and backfired) our way down to our favourite beach; a memory which I still warm to now on recalling that the little material those scanties consisted of wouldn't have been enough to make a

264

*standard size handkerchief as I would tease, ouch!
And I recall that you did your share of 'teasing' in
Browns Hotel, my sweet rascal; and I still get
embarrassed at the thought of my own naivety for
remarking as to what poor shots were Browns
patrons that they should be constantly on their
hands and knees retrieving rebounded darts from
around our table! Hardly surprising them crying
into their beer when we drank up to leave! 'Pendine
here we come!' you would cry while I added to their
frustration by patting your pert bottom on the way
out.*

*Oh dear, my sweet! on glancing over my last few
lines it would seem that I've subconsciously allowed
myself to drift from romanticism to salacious so to
make amends I'll offer you this little poem inspired
by those precious days.*

*To infinite Pendine, in bliss we'd ride,
Cwmdonkin's sweet rose at my side.
Through lanes of Autumn-touched trees,
I and the girl with the sun-kissed knees.*

*Windows down, wind-blown tresses,
asking glances through breeze-teared eyes.
Random braking, impulsive kisses,
'neath cloudless blue, Carmarthen skies.*

While the Third's poetry was of vague interest to Daniel, the
preceding, more explicit account of his times with Heloise, he
found a more worthwhile read and so was mildly disappointed to
find the sequential pages missing. He did though, on thumbing
through the remainder, find another reference to himself which,
while not as uncomfortably clear as Billy's 'crow's nest'
uncalled-for fabrication, suspiciously as derogatory. The
messages containing the reference were largely melancholic

recollections which, to Daniel, suggested that the officer was confidently writing to someone very much alive, while to someone perhaps more perceptive, underlying sentiment in his correspondence revealed maybe 'a glimmer of doubt'?

. . . How to say this and not hurt your feelings, dear Lise, isn't going to be easy. But lately I'm suffering bouts of depression for having made your New York trip possible, not least because my doing so could mean that we'll never walk hand in hand in the park again. Is it my fate to pursue every head of long, black hair only to find that the face that turns in the crowd or in some quiet street is not the face that took my breath away on that first unforgettable day in Cwmdonkin Park. Also there are times, my sweet love, when I wish that we'd chosen somewhere other than the park to say goodbye because it's nearly always there that when I'm on hand, that young Davy and Flo want me to take them to play for an hour or so. Oh yes, they still like me to scare them with my fiendish version of the hunchback. Unkind to the man really who apparently was a nice old gent who suffered from children's taunts, so DT's poem construes. And yes, the bandstand is still central to our games and I still recall our ideas for that neglected structure should our plans for bricks and mortar not materialize. How we'd fill in the sides and keep ourselves warm on Winter nights with an all-purpose central stove. And its name 'Cwmdonkin Cottage' was the one agreed on during those hazy, childlike days we spent there. Yes, our envisaged home came to mind only yesterday while idly chatting to my cleaning lad whom I recently coaxed out of his seventeen-year-old shell. Oddly, he described the very home we'd hoped to find (the factual one) his being the once home of a chum back

in the English Midlands which, from its rose-covered trellis around its front door to its remote situation was virtually identical to our much-discussed dream home. In truth though, his chum's home was a dilapidated near-ruin which, as I took in his description, became alike to the holiday cottage your family rented (same part of the country I think) and loved throughout your childhood. Dilapidated was my unspoken thought from the old photo you'd kept because of pleasant memories despite it not being connected to elec', gas and water (just a water well I recall) the very necessities that his chum's mother craved and why they eventually evacuated their cottage home; a move that our Cabin Boy says lost him his best mate which upset him. 'Blooming-well stupid' were his words. No, no, my sweet Lise; it's not my practice to sit around jawing with a person of lower intellect but you'd be surprised how long periods at sea can affect your choice of with whom to converse and while you might find the lad obtuse, once accepting his immature delivery and flat English accent, his tale about his chum's family the 'Blooms' (bucolic enough?) has, I'd go so far as to say, a simple charm about it.

The cottage not connected, as I mentioned, to any services and unpopular with the trades people because of its midfield situation, resembles our envisaged abode (don't we both love remote places?) the lad, seeing it as we would, perfect and because Mr and Mrs Bloom always appeared happy, he read this as contentment. Even their smiling teenage daughter, despite emerging from this ramshackle building on weekend evenings looking like a glamorous fashion model seemed to fit in, he says, which I'll confess gave me the passing thought that maybe the long hours he'd spent there with his *chum weren't totally devoted to boys playing! But no, once he'd opened up about how long and strong had been his friendship with the Bloom's son; apart from his brief mention of a female apparition being seen around the property and him wondering if this might be linked to Mrs Bloom's sudden desire to leave; it would seem that girls were simply not part of the equation.*

Not that at present he's devoid of any interest in females (I must tell you this) because I recently discovered him scrutinising your photos intently and such was his embarrassment I had to assure him that admiring the most beautiful woman ever to come out of Wales wasn't exactly a crime!

Oh, my darling, writing this has my thoughts drifting back to that Welsh beauty and so I'll conclude while I'm in this uplifted mood which has also been aided by us having at last ridden out of that atrocious hurricane weather. Also and not least, my darling, of great benefit to my mood was a dream I had last night: a dream of a joyful reunion at the place we're now heading for. The place where the jungle stoops low over dark water: the monsoon-muddied water of the tropical Demerara.

Chapter 20

Dancing In The Jungle

'Obtuse'. One word would lead Daniel to the culmination of his troubles. His vanity-motivated search for a dictionary proved fruitless because Apprentice Engineer Izzy, the only person aboard he knew to possess one, could not be found and his cabin locked. In the alleyway leading back to his quarters, the engine room door swung open and out lurched Chief Donkeyman Yussef Rashid looking the worse for drink.

"You no go ashore with others, boy?" he rasped, his large, bulging eyes fixed insidiously on the youth.

"No blooming money!" retorted Daniel, attempting to shove past.

"You want drink, boy?" hissed Yussef, thrusting a hip flask under his nose.

"Oh – er . . . okay, just a drop," replied the youth, accepting it hesitantly.

"You come my cabin while I change clothes and then you come ashore with Yussef okay? Plenty more drink my cabin, you come."

Martyn's chuckled description of a black totem pole came to mind as Daniel considered the offer.

"I – I'll come ashore with you if you'll lend me a few BG dollars but I'll wait for you out on deck," he replied, taking a long swallow from the flask.

Jungle juice; he found it quite palatable and instantly warming.

"Good, eh? You drink plenty more, eh?"

Taking advantage of the Donkeyman's sudden, if suspicious, generosity, he supped the rum as if it was lemonade, the Somali's evil grin becoming less worrying, the long, bony fingers clutching his arm almost friendly.

"Yeah, as I said. I'll come ashore with you but I'll wait out on deck."

Minutes later, after a furtive dash down the gangplank, the unlikely couple were making their way along the riverside path towards beckoning Mackenzie. Initially, for the sake of being indulged with rum, Daniel tolerated the arm around his shoulders but when his companion's thick, wet lips began slobbering around his neck he quickly tore himself away cursing the man.

"An' this soddin' thing's empty!" he screamed, throwing the flask at a suddenly cringing Yussef. "Gemme some more else I'm pissin' off back to the ship!"

His anger gave him a sense of power as he watched the Somali scuttle into the first bar in town to do his bidding. He'd give 'em 'shit of the ship'! From here on the Cabin Boy would be someone to reckon with aboard, he congratulated himself, revelling in his newly-found confidence. Things were going to plan. He'd get merry at the expense of this perverted little bugger then slip away and join his shipmates.

The melodious sound of a steel drum band rang out ahead. Squatting down outside the bar the tinkling, rhythmic sound and the evening warmth completed his sudden contentment.

"Come on! Come on!" he bawled as Yussef returned with a bottle of rum and two glasses. "More! More!" he demanded after tipping back the first glass in one greedy swallow.

By the time they'd moved away from the bar the bottle was three parts empty and he was still demanding more.

"Give me! Give me!" he bellowed, plucking the bottle from Yussef who craftily smirked his encouragement.

"Doncha worry, Yusshef!" he laughed, drunkenly. "I'll leave a drop fer you doncha worry!"

Walking towards the music, two bright-eyed black infants staring out at the from beneath one of the raised shanty houses began laughing as Daniel broke into a jig.

"Come on, my pervy little shipmate!" he sang out to Yussef. "We're off ter the bloomin' ball!"

The steel band was playing in a roped-off open space where townsfolk and many of the *Roundcape's* absconders were letting off steam. Yussef paused at the entrance: his penchant for Western style entertainment did not include dancing it appeared.

"Well, pay fer my admission at leasht!" demanded Daniel, keen to join the party.

The scheming Somali was not to be rid of so easily and after a long swallow of rum which almost emptied the bottle, entered the compound with his tipsy young protégé.

"Steady dere, boy!" shouted the Guianese admitting them as Daniel lurched against his table. "Is dis boy okay, mon?" he snapped at Yussef. "He looks good an' drunk to me! Drunk whiteys ain't welcome here, mon!"

"I – I look out for him," replied Yussef uncomfortably. "I see he make no trouble."

"I'll nosh make any trouble, mate," gabbled Daniel. "Ole Yusshef 'ere'll look out fer me same as I 'ave ter look out fer ole Yusshef an' keep me arse ter the rail!"

The gatekeeper looked bemused as he continued.

"One bloke aboard fergot an' an' when 'e turned ter see old Yussef doin' up 'is flies, Yusshef says to 'im, 'It's only the rolla the ship, mate' an' the bloke said, 'Rolla the ship be blowed! Felt more like a rolla lino ter me!'"

While clearly unamused by Daniel's rendition of the most repeated joke aboard, Yussef paid the admission and gestured to the comedian to get moving.

"Don't tink I'm not watchin', boy," warned the Guianese. "You get too drunk an' I'll be chuckin' you out!"

But he'd come ashore to do exactly that, Daniel grinned insolently back. He'd been an observer of this 'temporary state of insanity' as Abu called it, for much too long. From the first sip of Yussef's rum 'temporary insanity' had been his objective and when he re-boarded he'd make a point of telling his old friend just what he'd been missing through all his years of abstinence. In the meantime though, he was going to enjoy finding out what *he'd* missed! Every swinging minute of it!

Amidst the colourful dancing throng, Billy, in full Ted splendour was jiving with a strikingly attractive local girl and not far away Brumpud, as equally conspicuous in his galley togs, hat and all, was attempting to modern waltz with a large woman who appeared remarkably similar to the woman with whom he'd socialized on their first visit to this jungle port. The Cook's footwork was being cheered on by several of the *Roundcape's* crew assembled at the makeshift bar.

"Hard to port! Steady as she goes! Watch her stern, mun!" Ianto was yelling as Daniel joined them.

"Hellooo, cabin boy! Brought along your own dancing partner, eh?" he teased, grinning towards the trailing Yussef.

"Carn ger-rid-ov 'im," muttered the Cabin Boy, drunkenly.

Ianto's grin broadened.

"You're bloody-well pissed, Cabin Boy! Eh, lads! Our Cabin Boy's pissed look you! Three sheets to the wind 'e his!"

"I – I've 'ad-a-drop-a-rum. I'm awright," Daniel assured him puffing out his chest.

"Nothin' wrong whatsoever, Cabin Boy! Good to see you enjoyin' yourself! Now, what can I get you?"

"Jungle juish. I'll 'ave a jungle juish. Polished off Yusshe'sh bottle an' ish wen' down-a treat. Gerrim one an' all."

"Comin' up, me old shipmate! Two large rums if you please, bartender!"

"Breeead of heeaven! Breead of heeeeeaven! Feeed me 'til I want no moooore . . .!"

What had begun as scarcely audible harmonizing suddenly swelled to a boom of voices which brought disapproving looks from band members and patrons alike.

"We'll keeeep a welcoooome in the hillsiiiide! We'll keep a welcooome in the vaaaales . . .!"

Daniel knew this one! Had not their Welsh headmaster invited him to give a solo deliverance in assembly after overhearing him blast it out in a toilet cubicle? The embarrassment of his not being able to reach the highest note on the occasion would not frustrate tonight's performance considering how his audience had already been stunned by the young tenor's enrapturing perfectly-pitched golden tones ringing out and . . .!

Well yes, that top note was still problematic and a bucket of ice-cold water for his trouble proved only that the Guianese were definitely not so welcoming at their jungle jigs as were the Welsh to their hills and vales and the official who'd thrown the water was now verbally endorsing that fact.

"De band leader would appreciate de music to be left to dem employed specifically for dat purpose!"

"The band leader can get stuffed, mun!"

Ianto's reply served as a cue for singing to recommence with the steel band seconds behind in fierce competition.

"Eh, Danny boy?" Billy had left the arena hand in hand with his winsome partner. "Take my bint for a whirl while I 'as a piss and a pint 'll you?"

Daniel's protest about being soaked to the skin was cut short as the smiling, dark beauty was thrust up against him.

"Might even let you keep 'er if that big-titted darlin' over there keeps flashin' 'er pearlies at me!" laughed Billy, making for the toilet. "First Ted to hit South America an' they all want a fuckin' piece!" he boasted. "Bleedin'-well spoiled for choice I am!"

"I – I carn – dance . . .! I – I've never . . .!"

But the girl was intent on being taken for that whirl and within seconds had dragged Daniel into the action.

"Okay, jus' a slow one," she purred, clasping him with both hands around the waist and leaning back so far that her nipples threatened to pop out of her low-cut blouse.

"I tink Vicky's gotten herself a virgin!" she chuckled on detecting his embarrassment then increasing it by sliding a warm knee between his legs and then leaning forward to kiss him full on the lips causing him to spontaneously enter his first sexual embrace while thanking God for inhibition-removing rum.

"Dat's more like it," she whispered. "Hold me tight, sailor boy. Hold Vicky tight."

273

Yes, he would hold her tight because it was fast becoming apparent to him that there were other senses rum could remove and the sense of balance was definitely one of them! Fortunately though, there was a remedy for this he discovered on pausing for another glass of the cure-all jungle juice and then the night was his again as the band exploded into a calypso come rock and roll number perfect for the most capable of dancers ever to perform on Guianean soil.

"Move it, white boy! Move it!" encouraged the sexy, black vision spiralling away from him to demonstrate her own party piece.

And the white boy moved! His stage illuminated by the fullest of moons decorously impaled in distant treetops, he moved! Instinctively, his nimble feet following the rhythm with the graceful perfection of Fred Astaire; his pliant frame moving in faultless co-ordination with the pulsating beat; an exhibition so breathtaking that his fellow dancers were moving aside to look on in awe. Only a black boy in white skin could put them to shame at doing what came so naturally to them, they were thinking as he accepted his whirling partner back into his arms with such perfect timing that they gasped in unison.

"Look ooooout!"

Self-absorbed, the night's star attractions had thought they'd the stage to themselves until the obese duo of Brumpud and his partner, after pulling off the spin turn of the evening, then bore down and effected a collision with them so comically spectacular that it was said afterward, created almost as much laughter as had the ship's Cabin Boy's impromptu performance.

"Gerr – 'er off me!" Daniel gasped eventually.

But Brumpud's large partner was too winded herself to stand unaided and only when the less-than-happy gatekeeper and two burly companions arrived on the scene, were the huge pair lifted off him.

"I warn you 'bout no trouble, boy!" barked the gatekeeper. "Now get out, all of you! We don't allow fightin' hereabouts!"

"Fightin'? Dis was an accident, mon!" protested the Cook's partner. "If it's fightin' you're wantin' try dis fer starters!" she screamed, slapping the man's face as he went to take hold of her arm.

"Leggo of my lady!" yelled Brumpud as the gatekeeper's aides took hold of an arm each and began propelling her towards the exit. For a man whose momentum was a standing joke aboard, the Cook's immediate action was unbelievable as he jumped up, chased after his lady and brought her escorts' heads together with a resounding crack which brought boos from the happy but now suddenly hostile crowd. The reason for Brumpud's out of character violence it appeared to the few crew members capable of taking the incident in, was the thumping his partner had received during her attempted eviction and such was his indignation at her treatment, he'd even flattened the gatekeeper before other officials arrived to subdue him.

His manhandling was short-lived however, the Guianese becoming distracted by another melee breaking out by the band stage. In seconds, the whole arena was bedlam. Ianto appeared bowling a colourfully painted oil drum pursued by band members whose anger was being compounded by others from the *Roundcape* taking up Ianto's game. Drums flew in every direction, each one being chased by a happily intoxicated seaman intent on creating havoc. Daniel, scarcely on his feet, was sent sprawling again by a group of screaming women rushing to avoid being bowled over. Attempting to rise after this tumble, he became acutely aware of his own inebriation. His feet, so nimble moments ago, were now leaden; his balance as distorted as on his first days at sea. But such minor inconveniences mattered little. Having almost no control over one's limbs and continually tumbling over was just another aspect of the pantomime happening about him. A scene as outrageously comical as anything dreamed up for Abbott and Costello.

Old Abu, bless him, should really have indulged himself in this 'temporary insanity' game. The Third's philosophy had to be right. Laughter was easily the best of our senses he maintained. Food, he said, could lead to digestive and weight problems. Exercise painful and sometimes crippling while sex, much overrated and often unsatisfactory, not to mention more diseases than you had fingers and toes. And alcohol; alcohol was great for a time but hangovers and future illness, penalties not worth the few hours of mental relaxation obtained. But laughter was free and rather than having a mental and physical downside, could lift your spirits for hours, even days, and help lift those around you like a worthwhile infection. Okay, this present fun owed something to alcohol but when he'd got back on his feet he'd take it easy and just keep laughing!

Some minutes had passed since he'd made the resolve to stand up but the rum's effect was such that not only was he failing to do so but also that he was feeling no pain as the gatekeeper who'd come across the instigator of the night's fiasco, was kicking him to death! And still he laughed! Well, up until one boot sent a bolt of pain through his groin area which appeared to equally upset his earlier dancing partner because this stiletto-heeled darling was suddenly there and kicking away at the gatekeeper whose yells suggested him not having partaken in the local elixir.

The night, it seemed, had turned in his favour again with the girl wading in like that to protect his vital parts for whatever she'd in mind? So, must keep this magical night alive! Must not let things slip away just because he'd got the little problem of staying upright. The evening was young, as romantic novels tell you (not those that Jock reads) and the night of his life could be climaxed with him sharing his bunk with the nubile young beauty now helping him along the path back to that bunk was his hazy contemplation only seconds before vomiting over the object of his lust.

From then on 'downhill' would aptly describe events, the first of which was his 'Cinderella' being replaced by Yussef who'd shadowed them (out of concern for the intoxicated youth) and had the girl not proceeded to exhibit herself by removing her skirt and blouse to cleanse in the nearby water, an act so alluring that Daniel, peeved at the prospect of she being replaced by the insidious Yussef, began a clumsy attack on the lesser inebriated Somali who retaliated with a flurry of body jabs followed by a stunning jaw punch which sent the youth staggering back into the darkness and then turn to flee from further punishment. Yussef was only seconds behind his quarry, when it suddenly dropped out of sight. Aware of what trouble he'd be in for brawling with the ship's Cabin Boy, hesitated, then resumed walking back to the *Roundcape*.

In common with his boyhood brook, the water level of Mackenzie's drainage ditches alternated with the weather and while relieved not to have fallen in water or even the river, the stinking black ooze in which Daniel now found himself was hardly the place he'd so eagerly anticipated retiring to on that night of nights.

To seek revenge with the man who'd thwarted his first carnal indulgence and try to reclaim the girl he'd been about to indulge with was his intent had he been sober and agile enough even to climb the frustratingly slippery ditch banks, and by the time he'd waded and stumbled his way through the quagmire to a section of the channel shallow enough to extricate himself, he was back under the lights of town and beginning to give the night up as lost. About to tackle the incline, a familiar voice made him pause.

"The troublesome wee fucker's for the high jump this time alright!" Jock was telling his companions seated outside the bar where Daniel and Yussef had begun their evening. "He contrived that collision wi' Brumpud an' sparked off the whole fuckin' rumpus," he growled, unaware that the person he was accusing lay but feet away.

"An' Izzy 'ere says 'e's been scrappin' with Yussef on 'is way back to the ship!" contributed Billy. "Cursin' an' swearin' at 'im an' callin' 'im a murderin' bastard for 'avin' pushed the Fourth into that fuckin' 'old, in't that right, Izzy?"

"Along those lines," confirmed Izzy. "but the lad was pissed out of his mind and ran off just as I arrived like."

"Never thought the Cabin Boy 'ad it in 'im, mon," intervened someone with a thick Geordie accent whom Daniel recognized as their Chippy.

"A bomb waitin' to explode, that wee fucker!" Jock assured him. "An' if the Cook's nae out of yon slammer afore we cast off I'm gonna take hold o' him an' ram my biggest rollin' pin up where the sun dinnae shine, fuck me I will! Spent too much time in the company o' that loon the Third is my opinion. He should've tagged along wi' the cunt when he jumped I'm thinkin'. Is there any word frae the local constabulary as to his whereabouts, Izzy?"

"Nothing more than what we know about him jumping ashore off that police boat taking him to Georgetown," replied the Apprentice Engineer. "Can't help but think that his taking off like that's got more to do with old Edgar finishing up in that hold than any nonsense about the Donkeyman. They'd fallen out over something so the Chief Engineer has it."

Talk about murder an' mystery," chuckled the Carpenter. "Likely we'll be in the papers back 'ome, eh, lads?"

Daniel had heard enough! Accusing the Third of murder was as absurd as blaming the earlier disturbance on himself! Unable to restrain himself any longer, he crawled up the bank and rose to confront them.

"Bollocks!" he screamed. "A load of bloomin' bollocks!"

The art of instant verbalism had never been one of his strong points while their stunned looks suggested that his entrance had been dramatic enough without his announcing it!

Or might it be possible that due to him being caked from head to toe with mud, his identity wasn't immediately apparent? Any lack of recognition however, was over as quickly as the ridicule began.

"Who the . . .? It, it's Al Jolson 'imslef I'll swear it!" began Billy's torment. "Come on then, Al, give us a song! You've proved that you can dance so let's 'ear if you can bloody-well sing as well!" he teased.

Jock though, was not amused telling Billy to 'shut it'!

"You, laddie!" he began slowly, while rising to his feet to address the mud-covered figure standing unflinchingly before him. "You, laddie, are up to your neck in trouble tonight an' I wouldnae want to be in your fuckin' shoes for all the whisky in Scotland!"

"Looks like 'e's been up to 'is neck in summat else, Jock!" laughed Billy, unable to contain his wit.

"I said *shut it*, Billy! Dinnae lead the fucker into thinkin' that gettin' Brumpud thrown into the slammer an' scrappin' wi' petty officers is some kind o' joke! Now, we either hand him over to the authorities for causin' a civil disturbance or take him back on board for the Skipper to deal wi'. Which shall it be, laddie?"

"Bollocks!"

While jungle juice converted one's natural timidity to steadfast defiance, words with which to express such defiance were frustratingly blocked in the same anaesthetising process.

Only one word but Jock was anxious not to hear it again as he advanced towards this upstart of a Cabin Boy.

"Bollocks!"

As when he'd stood his ground for 'whistling up the wind' Jock replied similarly to that occasion with a bunch of fives which sent Daniel sprawling for the umpteenth time that night.

"That's enough, Jock!"

Izzy's concern went unheeded and before the youth was back on his feet the Cook had got him in a headlock and was ramming a bottle of rum down his throat.

"If it's more Dutch courage you're after, laddie, then get some o' this in your belly!" he snarled while force-feeding him rum. "Have this one on me, you troublesome wee bastard! Drown in the lovely stuff! Fuckin' drown!"

The forced consumption continued despite his victim's retching and Izzy's protests and the bottle had been drained before he was finally released.

On his knees, Daniel continued to retch violently, rum spewing from his mouth and nostrils but was still not ready to capitulate. Grabbing the empty bottle at his feet, he rose and shattered its neck on the edge of a table. Armed but lacking in expertise as how to use such a weapon, his clumsy thrust was quickly foiled by Jock grabbing his wrist and redirecting the jagged glass towards the face of his inadequate assailant.

While Jock's strength and temper could have resulted in a nasty disfigurement at that moment, something caused him to check the thrust and Daniel escaped with just a cut above his top lip but which alarmed Izzy into bravely coming between them and insisting that he would accompany the youth back on board before he really got hurt.

Too inebriated by now to appreciate that any mercy had been shown to him, Daniel was still vaguely capable of realizing that however much he might deny being the instigator of happenings that night, others were seeing things differently and his retaliation against the Cook certainly wouldn't have helped matters. Heading back to the ship along with Izzy and the Carpenter, a decision therefore, was arrived at. Hasty maybe but in such a situation and bolstered with alcohol, a decision quite easily put into action. Going for a pee in the bushes had them completely fooled and just feeling so clever about it seemed to sober himself up enough to break into a jog.

"Where the bloody hell are you off to?" Izzy yelled after him.

"I'm going for a walk in the park!" he replied but only to himself lest they detect his route which was already being hindered by trees, bushes and even the occasional person. A ship's siren told him that the river was to his left making any other direction okay. Only scattered lighting now which, while part of his plan, had him stumbling into the infuriating but fortunately shallow enough to negotiate ditches crossing the town. Very few buildings now. Just the odd dimly-lit shack and not a soul in sight and then suddenly it was there! Towering in front of him, the great wall of the jungle! A few more yards, a few more seconds and he could well be chatting away in Cwmdonkin Park with the one person who'd understand his predicament and look after him. And even if such contact not be made, he'd hide away until the ship had gone, then surrender to the authorities who'd eventually have to deport him.

"I'm on my way, Mr Williams! There's lots to tell you and some of it not very nice. Like what they did with old Edgar's . . . stuck it in an Ovaltine carton and stored it away with the Bo'sun's tack they did. You'll not be too pleased about such disrespect for your old mate, eh, Mr Williams? And that insensitive bastard Jock was wicked enough to joke about old Edgar not being too pleased about it either! It's such insensitive remarks as that drove me into trying to murder him just now and that's why I'll have to lie low awhile out here in the park if that's alright with you? Which reminds me, Mr Williams, I've met Heloise and I've got to agree with you, she's a blooming stunner! I understand now why your thinking you'd lost her, affected you as it did. And I'm very happy for you that she has turned up and I couldn't care a fig about you suffering from some illness as old Abu tried to explain. If I lost somebody as lovely as Heloise, it wouldn't bother me if I deluded myself that she'd arrived back in a spaceship, never mind in a canoe on some tropical river as long as I thought that she was back!

Mr Williams, sir, you might be wondering how, in my hurry to meet up with you again, I've found time to idly contemplate like this? Well, sir, the fact is that I failed to negotiate the last ditch and after many attempts to climb out of the blooming thing, I'm resting up awhile until I've got some strength back. In the meantime, sir, dreaming about your Heloise (incidentally, she now calls herself Sara) is a very nice way of passing the time. Yes, as you guessed, your reminiscing about the gorgeous young lady in your bureau photos, did have quite an effect on me. Thoughts of you and she running around naked on that beach at Pendine kept me awake many a night I have to admit. Jealous? Oh yes, I was jealous alright! And now that I have seen her in the flesh, I wish even more that it had been me cavorting with your sweet Heloise on those sunny days by the sea. You'll note, sir, that I say *your* sweet Heloise so as not to make you feel uncomfortable about my joining you both, should I perhaps have an ulterior motive for seeking your company? No, sir, rest assured that my motive is purely to be in the company of someone I both respect and admire and to see you and she together again as has so long been your dream.

The word 'together' (I'm treading on eggshells here) might lead you to think that I might be alluding to a 'togetherness' of the carnal sort but should there be little privacy in the park and you wish to copulate naked with nature as you used to, then any observation of mine will not be for personal gratification but simply to study techniques so as not to embarrass myself when my turn arrives. By saying *my turn* please do not interpret that as meaning that I have ideas of taking over when you are spent, sir. Nothing is further from my mind, Heloise's and my relationship will be as platonic as that of hers and that poet chap and should she come on to me, I'll simply turn her down. Oh – and I must remember to ask you what *obtuse* means?

It could well be, Mr Williams, that you of course will want total privacy for those intimate moments in which case I'll make myself scarce while you're, er – doing it: because being spied on is something I've found irksome myself these last few weeks with Yussef's big nose pressed against our porthole. And, oh yes! I tried to murder him as well tonight but I'm hardly proving to be one of the Crippens or Christies of this world so you and Heloise have nothing to worry about on that score.

The galley incident? No, I still strongly deny attempting to drown the Cooks that day and I'm sure that nearly everybody on board sympathized that it was nigh on impossible to differentiate between lea and weatherside in such weather. Another point in my favour I can hear you saying, sir and please believe me when I say that while I look forward to meeting you again, should you be suspicious of any lustful digression contained in this letter in my head, please rest assured, sir, you read me wrong.

But I'll admit, sir, that it was likely my anticipation of joining you both in your tropical paradise that prompted this, er – erotic dream last night. (I'm told that jungle juice can induce the most vivid and nonsensical dreams.) Well, this one had me searching for you in the park and guess where I found you? Yes, in your bandstand and you'll find this quite funny because I find it built within the branches of a tree with you and Heloise not only living as Tarzan and Jane but dressed in the same jungle-style attire as that movie twosome.

You haul me up on a vine, very happy to see me because you say you're usually a threesome but your pet monkey has gone missing; an inference I find disquieting but with Jane (Heloise) showing so much leg and virtually topless all but a garland, I pretend to overlook it for fear of being ejected from such a promising situation until, that is, your mischievous young lady points out that monkeys look pathetic dressed like humans and insists that I play the part naturally.

A compromise is thankfully reached and very soon you and I are swinging through the treetops wearing brief loincloths but minus the compulsory underwear allocated to jungle kings in keeping with young U Certificate audiences.

Yes, Mr Williams, jungle juice inspired dreams are truly nonsensical but so real as for me to have been on the lookout for Yussef, a character whom no self-respecting Tarzan would want lurking beneath his flight path. I can picture the devious little pervert now, secreted away in the undergrowth, perspiring with lust as the king of the apes, his loincloth in disarray, goes sailing through the canopy unaware that his passage is being studied . . . ? Er – by his *passage*, Mr Williams, I'm sure that you'll not think I'm stooping to Billy White-type innuendos and understand that I was referring to Tarzan's *motion* through the canopy; his *forward* passage and not to his, er . . . well, you already know that I'm not given to such vulgarity and will open your arms in welcome in the knowledge that your sweet, innocent Heloise will not be subjected to the like.

Oh yes, my dream. And what better way of making you confident about receiving me into your love nest than to describe how impeccable was my behaviour in that dream such as when you hauled me aloft to be greeted by Heloise, her thighs parted and pert breasts on show and yet my reaction to such an appealing confrontation was casual and brotherly with not a hint of impropriety which I maintained even when later, her long, nimble fingers lingered while adjusting the hem of my loincloth, her eyes, smiling roguishly into my own as if daring me to react which, of course, I didn't, she being yours and me being the perfect gentleman that I am.

There are just a couple more things I'd like to be open about before joining you in paradise, sir. Firstly, I'd like to be honest with you about my thoughts as I encountered Heloise in my dream. About my fixation with those long, brown legs and perfectly sculptured young breasts as I arrived in your tree house. The way she made me feel as her dark *brown* eyes searched mine just as they had at the time of our first meeting on the river. You'll note, sir, that

I emphasize *brown* whereas you led me to believe that your Heloise was white of skin and that her eyes were deep green like the sea before a storm. Okay, she's been long enough beneath the Guianean sun to have become as brown as a native I expect you to explain. And I accept that deep green and dark brown might look similar in a certain light and I'm in no way suggesting as have others, that you have become confused and that you may even be writing letters to someone who no longer exists. No, Mr Williams, sir, you know that I simply do not have the guile with which to have arrived at such a preposterous conclusion. But, sir, I do wish to be frank about another matter that I must broach with your understanding self which concerns, er – your letters, sir.

The letters I came across in your cabin which you'd intended to entrust to me. Correspondence which I took the liberty of browsing through and would have found quite interesting if only as complete as when you had written them. What I'm trying to say, sir, is that the odd page appears to be missing. Well – quite a lot of pages actually and I'll explain as best I can when we meet up again. In the meantime, sir, I've got visitors. Two Guianese gentlemen are in the ditch with me and are going through my pockets . . .?"

"Nuttin' but a few foreign coins on him, mon!"

"Look out! Somebody's comin'!"

"Alright, ma bonnie lad! Geordie Thomson's got ya! Geordie Thomson's got ya!"

"We jus' happen along an' find him lyin' here talkin' to himself, mon! Looks like e's good an' drunk, eh?"

"He's that alright! Away with ya, ma bonnie lad! Away with ya!"

Our reunion in paradise will have to be postponed a while, Mr Williams, sir; because our Chippy offered to take me back to the ship, not realizing that I'm merely dabbling in 'temporary insanity', an offer I now regret accepting with the Skipper barking his head off outside this quayside shed they've locked me up in because I can't resist throwing punches at everything that moves.

"I want the name of every man absent! I'll have 'em blacklisted in every pool in the kingdom!"

"We've secured the lad in this shed over here, sir. For his own safety like."

"Open it up, Thomson! Let's get him on board!"

Our reunion, sir? I think I've no alternative other than to make it happen as soon as I've extricated myself from this net I'm being hoisted aboard in because even in fiction Robert Louis Stevenson knew his readers not gullible enough to believe that cabin boy Jim Hawkins would have punched his Skipper bang on the end of his nose which is what I've just done and which I'm sure will hardly benefit my seagoing career!

"Ouch! The bugger's bit me! The little bugger's bit me!"

"Just keep him in that net, Thomson! Bo'sun! Get the Steward to open up your store and to send someone below for a straitjacket!"

"There's not much room in there, sir. Took on more paint in Canada. And then there's you know what, sir! I, er – don't think the Steward ever got round to transferring it to his cold store. Thought it unhealthy like."

"Ah, there are you, Albert! There's enough of us to hold him down while you get that jacket on! Get his clothes off as well if you can. Embarrass 'em into calming down I say. Even a drunk's not so tough minus his pants."

I think, Mr Williams, sir, that the situation in which I now find myself, secured in a straitjacket and pinned down by half of the crew, is bound to delay our get-together. Strangely though, as dire as my predicament is, my immediate concern, being totally in the buff, is that Yussef might be attracted by the commotion and come along to feast his evil eyes. But of even greater concern is the thought of something not yet transferred to the cold store from where they're about to install me for the night. How is it, Mr Williams, that Jungle Juice gives the courage to take on the whole crew and yet fails to overcome the terror of being locked away with something that the Chief Steward considers unhealthy to have in his cold store?

"Nooooooo! Not – not with Edgar's . . .! *Noooooo!"*

"It's registered, sir! He knows who, er – what he'll be sharin' with!"

Bloody-nosed Captain Roberts cared little about who or what the drunken Cabin Boy shared with and determined to avoid another fatality on his ship, ordered the youth to be trussed up and locked away until sober.

"Nooooooo!"

"Yeeeeeeah!" taunted Jock and co, arriving back to learn about how Daniel's night ashore had climaxed with him being incarcerated in the all-purpose cabin along with the object of his torment.

"There's me, the Donkeyman an' then if that wasnae enough, he clobbers the fuckin' Skipper! His first ship an' his last, that's for sure."

Jock's night was made and he wasn't quite finished when he found that the key had been left in the door enabling him to look in.

"If old Edgar's nae too bristly will you gi' the old fucker a goodnight kiss frae me, laddie?" he taunted, laughing raucously at his own wicked gibes.

The torment continued until a shout from above sent them chuckling to their bunks leaving a prostrate Daniel, his arms pinioned about him, still protesting wildly and kicking out at everything in reach until pain reminded him that his shoes had been removed together with his clothes. Time after time, he attempted to rise from his makeshift bedding, his maniacal efforts achieving only frustration and more pain as he fell back among the shipboard tackle concealed in the darkness. Fortunately, his head had contacted with something less hard, less sharp then the paint tins rolling and clattering about him. He wriggled away from this object but curiosity caused him to turn full circle to probe it with his feet. Definitely not metal or rounded but square and cardboard and ominously weighted. A small box?

A small cardboard . . .

Chapter 21

Flight From Murder?

His second attempt to murder Yussef had succeeded. Well, that's how those who judged him would see it, while the truth was that he'd not intended to kill the Donkeyman at either time.

But would they believe him when he explained how he'd simply pushed the Somali who'd then trodden on a paint tin, lost his balance and cracked his head on the bulkhead? And describing how Yussef had taken advantage of his predicament by slipping into the tackle store in order to fondle him while he was restrained and out cold would sound laughable when they learned about his violent evening ashore.

"You bastard!" he'd screamed on becoming aware of probing fingers and laboured breath. "You filthy little bastard!"

Panicking, Yussef had stifled his cries with a sweaty palm, lying that he'd come to apologize for any misunderstanding while ashore. Was there anything he could get for him? A glass of water and a couple of aspirins maybe? He wanted to help him.

"Yeah. There-ish summat you can do," he'd replied to his grovelling visitor. Get him out of the blooming straitjacket and he might even accompany him to his cabin and patch up their differences with a drink, was how he'd tricked the Somali into releasing him, an ordeal throughout which he'd had to contain his temper as bony fingers lingered unnecessarily on naked flesh.

"You speak with nobody that I help you," Yussef had begged and to which he'd muttered agreement until the last strap had been loosened.

"Okay, you come my cabin now," were the Somali's last words on helping him to his feet, to which he'd replied with a torrent of abuse culminating with that fatal push as the Donkeyman had tried to calm him.

He'd expected him to get up and retaliate or to at least groan but he'd just lay there, a shaft of light from the porthole illuminating his large, staring eyes which he ought close and perhaps, like in the films, check for a pulse but he'd loathed physical contact with the man while alive and now, in death, was even more repulsive.

No, he'd not intended to kill Yussef, just to punish him for taking liberties with somebody who was one hundred per cent male. He'd had another visitor. Big Paddy. Being the genial soul that he was, had looked in to tell him he wasn't the only one in the wars that night. It was coming back . . .? About how Billy White had boarded so drunk that he'd not made the gangplank and had fallen into the river and they'd found him yelling his head off, clinging to the screw which was fortunately still out of the water awaiting loading. And then Paddy had gone on to joke about Billy's main concern as usual being for his precious suit which he'd hung up to dry in the galley. All very amusing but what he so desperately wanted the Irishman to do was to release him or at least remove the thing that so terrified him, the latter which he did, enabling him to at last relax and eventually fall asleep until disturbed by a much less welcome visitor, the outcome of which was now greatly troubling him.

He was at least free of the jacket and, finding the door still unlocked, he could perhaps seek out old Abu who'd advise him what he ought do? But then others astern might give him away and Abu would most likely advise him to risk going to the Skipper and explain the accident rather than jump ship in such a place. Accident? Oh no, everything was stacked against him and hadn't he just read in one of Ianto's newspapers from home that they'd just hung a young woman named Ruth Ellis in London for murdering her lover in very doubtful circumstances. So what chance did he have when the night's events were disclosed in an English court, that is of course if they waited until home to hand him over? It might be that they were legally bound to hand him over to the Guianese and then what? There was no alternative other than to jump. Slip ashore, lie low for a few days and then wander into some police station pretending he'd lost his memory or even better, his mentality as well! They'd hardly put to death an insane young seaman who didn't even know his own name. Perfect! Must get things moving right away!

Emerging cautiously to a deserted, moonlit deck, he became conscious of his lack of clothing. Even the best laid plans would be difficult to put into practice while nude! Ah, the galley straight ahead where Big Paddy had said Billy had hung his suit and only inaccessible when one was desperate to gain entry in hurricanes! Making for its starboard entrance, the rum badly affected his balance but he managed to stay upright and battle on. Inside the galley however, with the minimum of light penetrating its grimy portholes, the going was difficult causing him to grope about until he came across the suit hanging on a makeshift line next to the range. Taking it down, he found the skin-tight drainpipe trousers impossible to pull on: one soaking too many and they'd probably not even fit the narrow-hipped Billy. Frustrated, he tossed them aside and tried on the long Edwardian jacket which, while also a tight fit, sufficed inasmuch when buttoned, provided the necessary cover he'd need to proceed ashore. But must rest awhile because his head was spinning. Yes, must rest to conserve his energy for ashore . . .

Ashore? In his haste to reach the galley, that they were no longer alongside the loading wharfs had almost passed unnoticed. Stepping back out on deck, the moon, casting its glow over a large expanse of water told him that they were once again at anchor at a point where the river widened. Even worse, they were midstream and midstream offered no chance! The hatches being covered could only mean that they'd loaded and then proceeded to this anchorage while he'd been out cold. At least twenty-four hours must have passed with him oblivious to everything going on. Well, not quite everything. His visitors were proof of that, especially his last one; the thought of whom sent him to the port and then starboard rail, desperate as to how he might expedite his plan.

"Officer mon? He join you in Mackenzie?"

The voice startled him. Defeated and about to go and knock up the Chief Steward, he turned back to the starboard rail and looked down on her.

"Officer mon? He join you in Mackenzie?" she asked again, her canoe so close alongside, he'd not seen her before.

"Er – no . . . he – he's not on board," he stuttered to the girl of the Third's hallucinations. "How, how long have you been waiting?"

"Since ship come. Mebbe two hours I tink," she replied forlornly while preparing to paddle away. "I go home now. Sara go home."

"No! Wait!"

He mustn't let her go! His prayer had been answered in so unlikely a way! Her turning up like this, as surreal as the events preceding it!

"No officer mon, no business for Sara. I go home."

Her paddle was in the water. "Why officer mon make promise an' den forget?"

"He – he didn't forget! I – I have something to tell you! The Third . . . Officer man . . . he's ashore, looking for you! You – you take me ashore and we'll find him!"

Looking both puzzled and curious, she paddled back alongside and appeared to be waiting for him.

"Some – some rope! Hang on while I get some rope to lower meself! There's always a length in the fo'c'sle. Wait for me!"

"Okay, mon," came the reply which meant all of his immediate problems were over! Returning with the rope, he attached one end to the rail, climbed over and began his descent.

"Stay where you are!"

As if just lowering himself wasn't precarious enough, she'd pushed herself away from the ship with her paddle and was averting her eyes from her would-be passenger!

"Come back!" he pleaded, in the same awful moment as conceiving that her embarrassment was to do with his dress! An embarrassment which, with him fast losing the strength just to hang on and certainly not having enough to go back up, would have seen him in that river had not the current miraculously brought the canoe back alongside, enabling him to slide the last few feet and land on a cushion of soft, squelching, Demerara fruit.

"Hell' – hello," he greeted the river princess with as much decorum as a man whose bare backside was embedded in a mire of ripe, tropical fruit could summon. Her glare dropped to the wares he was seated on, causing him to adjust the jacket's hem and throw one leg over the other in a feminine manner that did nothing for his embarrassment but seemed to satisfy her.

"Okay den, sailor boy?"

She was frowning but nevertheless extraordinarily beautiful.

"What's dis about officer mon go ashore lookin' for me? I don't believe you."

"Take – take me with you and we'll, er – look for him. He, er – told me he was going ashore to look for you and – and I know where he is."

He was squirming both physically and mentally now but had to gain her confidence. Yes, he'd told a half truth about knowing the officer's whereabouts but once ashore he'd simply point to the jungle and make a dash for it before she could ask exactly where in thousands of square miles? Lifting himself slightly, he removed a cluster of prickly-skinned fruits and tossed them overboard.

"How much you pay me for de trip an' for de ruined fruit?" she asked.

"I – I'll sort something out when we get ashore," he lied. "But – but we'd best be off before somebody finds out I'm missing."

"Dis better not be some kinda trick," she warned sullenly. "An remember, Sara's not some easy lady from Mackenzie, Sara's a virgin an' she's gonna keep that way."

Not according to the Third, you aren't, was the passing thought that jolted Daniel into thinking how truly absurd was his situation.

'Every man's dream to sail a tropical river in the company of a beautiful woman' had been old Edgar's sentiment with which he couldn't help but agree. So why now, when he was actually living that experience, was he beginning to have doubts? Surely going ashore was his best option? Lie low for a while as planned and then hey-presto, deportation! And in the meantime, commonsense telling him that there wasn't any real connection between the *Roundcape's* Third Mate and this young beauty; some kind of liaison might develop between them and the idyllic dream could bloom. In fact, she'd already lost that hostile look and seemed to be studying her passenger more curiously, even sexually because, while adjusting his posture so as not to offend her innocence, there'd definitely been a hint of a grin on that lovely face; and now, as the side-to-side motion of her paddling rucked up her skirt, virgin or not, something in her expression was surely daring him to look and appreciate those glistening brown thighs?

"What you lookin' at, sailor boy? Sara tinks you'm gettin' ideas!"

Playing hard to get but her legs remained teasingly apart as if he didn't know her little game. Edgar had been right. A tropical river, a boat and a lovely young female to make real the perfect fantasy . . .

"Hope you got plenty of dollars, sailor boy?"

No, Sara! A full moon is shining down on this most perfect of settings where two young people are about to enjoy the first true romantic encounter of their lives and you are saying . . .

"Sara's wantin' five dollars now!"

Her tone was acid again, her legs closed and his doubts rekindled.

"Empty dem pockets!"

But dem pockets were pretending pockets because, for the perfect slimline fit, Billy's drape had been cut that way.

"I, er – haven't got any money and, er – it doesn't matter cos I've decided I'm going back to the ship and take my chances."

His sudden decision had little to do with having no money but the embarrassing thought of going ashore, perhaps to be greeted by her relatives and friends and him wearing no trousers was as daunting as facing up to things back on board!

"Oh, it's back to the ship is it, sailor boy? You tink Sara's some kinda free ferry for dimwit sailors wid no trousers, eh?"

The idyllic dream was fast fading, the river princess turning into some kind of water-borne witch whom he must somehow appease.

"I –I've got money back on board. I – I can pay you if you take me back. We're only halfway."

"Den you can swim back!" she snapped, taking her paddle out of the water. "An' if you'm not payin' dat's what you'll have to do!" she added, grabbing the canoe's sides and rocking it violently.

"I – I can't swim!" he yelped as the motion increased.

"Den go an' learn!" she screamed in the same instant as he rose to launch himself towards her to stop the madness!

"Fuck off!" were the river princess's parting words as he lost his balance and plunged into the river along with most of her wares.

In retrospect, only his frantic thrashing about kept him buoyant long enough to reach and take hold of the small upright jutting from the canoe's stern and she, having recommenced paddling, was only moments away from the riverbank when something caused her to turn and discover that he was still with her and hanging on for dear life. His life though was apparently of little concern to her as she made him let go by chopping at his fingers with the paddle, the canoe's momentum leaving him quickly behind and devoid of any form of support. All hope gone but not quite! Because, as the muddy brown water closed over his head, he recalled being at the mercy of the sea off Chaguramus when he'd conceived the notion of reaching the bottom and walking ashore! With a full intake of air, he sank to the riverbed praying desperately to survive! Any hope of a miracle though quickly vanished as his feet sank into deep, clinging mud, his frantic efforts to free them clouding the already murky water and reducing visibility to nil. Stretching himself upright, his lungs about to burst, his prayers were answered as his head emerged from shoulder-high water and he was once again breathing the sweet, fresh air of life!

Chapter 22

Hurricane Janet

One day out of Chaguramas, his ship's holds full to capacity, Captain Roberts hoped for a trouble-free passage back to Canada, then twice back to Mackenzie for profit-making cargoes before the St Lawrence froze over for the Winter. Unfortunate events aboard had depleted his crew by four, a deficit that caused problems that he'd have to live with. The Chief Donkeyman with a bandaged head but now back to his duties, was rumoured to have knowledge concerning the unfortunate demise of their Fourth Engineer but while denying this when interviewed, did speak about the incident leading to the hospitalization of their Cabin Boy in Trinidad. He'd stated that on hearing the inebriated youth's screams while trussed up for his safety in the Bo'sun's paint store, had entered to see if he could be of assistance and on entering, the boy, free of restraint had attacked him for the second time that night. He said that he'd caught him off guard and pushed him over causing his head to strike the bulkhead and recalled little else until discovered by the Bo'sun next morning. As to who'd freed the youth, and it could have been the Donkeyman himself, remained a mystery and the Cabin Boy had been found unconscious in the galley, probably due to Demerara alcohol which had led to the deaths of many a seaman over the years, and such was his condition en route to Chaguramas, fearing another demise aboard, had been hospitalized there. Exactly what had occurred that night was still not clear but the Donkeyman's involvement in both it and the demise of their Fourth Engineer, would be investigated at a later date. In the meantime a more immediate concern had been dramatically delivered by their Sparks with a report of the weather ahead.

"Another hurricane, sir!" he announced, near panic in his voice. "And we're directly in its path! Hurricane code name Janet, sir!"

"What a load of pathetic crap!" moaned Billy, handing the last of the salvaged Third's letters to his cabin mate in the bunk below. Reno, unable to relax in his siesta, grunted and let them fall to the floor.

Billy, he sensed, had turned to the letters in order to take his mind off the panic aboard, which only minutes before, he'd helped spread. The awesome darkness cloaking ship and ocean ten hours out of Chaguramas was nothing else but 'the end of the fuckin' world!' was how his for once glum understudy had relayed the disquieting opinion of the Somalis aft.

"I – I tell you it is nonsense, Billy! Children's *nonsense!*"

Reno's rebuke was answered by the eerie howl of a gathering wind.

"It – it's just a storm building, that's all," he added to reassure himself.

"There's storms and there's storms, me old acker," replied Billy, "an' it's as black as a Zulu's bongos out there if you dare take a look! Summat's not right cos Jock's wireless 'as never packed up before an' our Sparks is 'avin' problems accordin' to the Mate. Summat's up that's for sure."

"Scaremongering, Billy! That's what you are doing, scaremongering I tell you!" retorted the Maltese in a tone that conveyed his growing unease.

Reno's unease was now shared by most aboard, not least by the ship's Master who'd stayed on a course that he and the Mate had calculated ought see them avoid the weather's extremes. Now, as atmospherics played havoc with their instruments of navigation, the direction of their headway was uncertain and when mountainous seas began crashing over the decks of the heavily-laden freighter, a new direction was ordered that had them 'running for it'. Any relief however was short-lived as the raging wind and pounding seas vented their fury in an ever-changing pattern denying any safe headway.

"To port, man! Hard to port!"

"She's not answering, sir! She's not answering!"

As if playing with her Helmsman, the *Roundcape* 'answered' with a suddenness that spun the wheel from Ianto's grasp and sent Master and Mate reeling across the bridge.

"Hold her steady, man! Keep her . . .!"

The Skipper's cries were lost as a thunderous mass of water drove over her bows to meet her bridge with an impact that together with a violent roll to starboard, sent bodies crashing painfully into bulkheads and fixtures throughout the ship. In the same tumultuous seconds, all lights aboard flickered then died completely as her engine and generator shuddered to a standstill, groans and curses ringing out in the darkness followed by warning screams as the unrelenting sea boomed in over submerged rails, crashing and splintering sounds telling of grave damage inflicted.

"Starboard lifeboats, sir!" came the Mate's cry. "Free of their davits!"

Amidships, beneath the boat deck, talk was equally fearful.

"What the fuck were that racket, Jock?" gasped Billy.

"Yeah! What you think it was, Jock?" echoed a pillow-clinging Reno. "An' why no lights, eh?"

"If you pair are so fuckin' keen to know what's goin' on get yourselves out there an' find out what's goin' on, if you dare?" Jock was deadly serious having just survived a perilous dash from the pantry.

"It's the bloody lifeboats!"

The strained tones of Izzy springing out of the darkness answered their question.

"What's left of them are hanging over the side! I can see them from my porthole!"

"An' – an' what's happened below?" whimpered Reno. "Why's the engine stopped an' why's there no lights?"

"I dunno!" called out the departing Apprentice. "But I've just been summoned below to assist!"

"It's a long way back up them fuckin' stairs," muttered Jock ominously as the ship groaned and trembled its way up the side of another shifting valley to be tossed like a toy from where its heights collided with an angry black sky.

"One more like that an' she'll break her back!" yelled Jock.

"O Mother in Heaven!" gasped Reno as they rose again then banked to port with an unprecedented suddenness.

"She'll nae come *baaaack!*" screamed Jock in the same instant as the lights flickered back on and his wireless crackled. "She'll nae come *baaaack!*"

The *Roundcape* defied his prediction by returning from the roll as urgently as she'd entered it, the sea accepting the challenge by propelling their huge tonnage once more to the heights of an aqueous hell where all was momentarily hesitant as Jock's powerful receiver burst into life and a rich, bouncing American voice was singing to Mama and the world that everything was alright.

"*That's alright, Mama! That's alright for youuu! That's alright Mama, just any way . . .*"[18]

---

[18] That's All Right written and recorded by Author Crudlup Sept 1946. Recorded and released by Elvis Presley July 1954.

Chapter 23

Visiting Ffokcuf

Dawn was breaking as he finished his wade and pulled himself onto the riverbank. He'd been lucky, the river being shallow where he'd *fallen* out of the canoe but any good feelings at being alive were quickly dispelled as he looked out at the *Roundcape* at anchor and reflected on his predicament, a predicament likely made worse by his leaving her. The hot-tempered girl and her boat had vanished, ruling out any possibility of an immediate return to the ship. But for the sounds of the jungle, he was alone and in a desperate situation and clueless as to what his next move ought be? He remained in that spot for two hours or more before biting insects prompted him to start walking downstream along the riverbank until suddenly he'd left vegetation and was treading sand.

A beach? He'd not expected a beach and a large one at that, stretching out into the distance, its sands golden beneath a sun now high in the sky. He walked on for a few minutes into those vast, seemingly empty sands until something caught his eye. Yes! About half a mile ahead a small, dark object, which as he drew closer changed from a blur into a car. Closer still and he could even make out that the car was a black, two-door Morris Eight of pre-war manufacture. Nearing the car, he shaded his eyes from the bright sunlight reflecting off its windows and made out that someone was standing beside it and looking towards him. A few more yards and that someone was a young woman; a naked young woman. She waved to him then, perhaps out of modesty, dropped to lie face down on a rug alongside the car.

"Enjoy your dip?" she asked, turning her head to grin up at the newcomer.

"I – blooming-well didn't!" he frowned back at her. "Why – why did you do it? I could have blooming-well drowned!"

"I knew it was shallow and you being dressed like that, I thought I'd best cool you off before you got any ideas," she chuckled back. "And that's a big pair," she added, studying him teasingly, causing him to redden but on reaching down, found that thankfully, Billy's long drape kept him respectable.

"Your knees I'm talking about!" she laughed. "I was admiring your knees especially the left one. It's really quite cute or haven't you noticed, you silly boy!"

"I – I've never really, er – noticed any diff . . ." Daniel began, replying to her stupidity.

"Not getting *too* well acquainted I hope, you pair?" intruded the Third, appearing from behind the car. "And what on Earth made you come ashore in that silly clobber, Daniel?"

Startled by his sudden appearance, the youth stared disbelievingly at the officer and girl in turn.

"Don't look so shocked, Daniel!" The Third was still smiling as he spoke. "You of all people aboard shouldn't be shocked at what you're seeing considering that you were in my confidence as to my intentions. We've been waiting for you, Heloise and I, ever since she dumped you overboard. I've told you many a time how childish she can be on occasions, have I not? Have I not?" he repeated.

"Er – yes, I – I suppose you have at . . ." began Daniel vacantly. "But – but, she – she's *Heloise* are you saying, sir?"

"Of course she's Heloise, you silly young bugger! Who else could she be?"

"Well, er . . . it – it was Sara who I came ashore with, I – I'm sure of . . ."

Daniel wasn't making sense seeing how the Third was tut-tutting and looking perplexed. His smile returned as he looked down to address his naked girlfriend.

"Turn over, Lise. Perhaps seeing your full beauty will jog his memory. You were longing to see my Heloise's *full* beauty, eh, Daniel? Her photos, remember?"

"I, er . . . I only gave them a casual look while I was dusting," lied the embarrassed Cabin Boy, looking anywhere other than Heloise as she rose to her knees.

"And the scratch marks on the bottom half of her bikini?"

The officer had caught him out! He'd known all along that that particular photo had been tampered with!

"I – I . . . don't know what you're talking about, sir!" he continued to lie, unconvincingly. "You know I'd never touch anything private like!"

"Up with you, Lise! Show Daniel what he so desperately wanted to see while he sweated over simple images of you! Come on, my sweet! show him!"

Heloise stood up then took a bottom-swaying stroll over to the car and turned to pose full frontal, one hand caressing a wing-mounted headlight.

"A fine specimen, eh, boyo? She's perfect wouldn't you agree?"

"Er – yeah," murmured the youth uncomfortably, his eyes darting back and forth from car to girl, the latter embarrassingly and increasingly holding his attention the longer until becoming aware of being studied himself, causing him with difficulty to direct his gaze on the car alone which brought a chuckle from the girl and "I think he's seen enough, Ivor."

"As perfect as any model you've seen, eh, Daniel?"

The Third had played into his hands as long as he kept his eyes focused on the car which wasn't easy.

"Er – yes, sir. What year is it?"

"*She* you mean, boyo! Have some respect! *It* indeed! What year you ask? Well, nineteen-thirty-four was the year that the world was blessed with her arrival. Am I correct, Heloise, my sweet?"

"Yes, Ivor and he's making me uncomfortable staring at you-know-where!"

"He does appear transfixed. Have you never seen one before, Daniel?"

"Well, not one of that year but Mr Horton at number seventeen had a thirty-nine model I think it was but it didn't half burn some oil. Smoked like hell on cold mornings, once he'd got it started that is."

"We wouldn't have got our lines crossed by any chance would we, boyo?"

"I – er, don't think so, sir. And by the way, this model's almost identical to the Ford Popular that me dad had. He reckons that Morris copied it then came up with a much-improved version with the headlights buried in the wings and concealing the spare wheel in the boot. Streamlined it from front to back they did, sir. Er – does this one take much starting, sir?"

It was the Third's turn to look transfixed.

"Take much starting you ask?" he began eventually. "No, she's hardly ever a problem starting and even if she's a tad fickle, a little tickle of her carburettor and she's away . . . Are you sure we've not got our lines crossed, Daniel?"

"Have you two mechanics quite done?" yawned a frustrated Heloise, back prostrate on the rug, her legs slightly apart. "Ask him if he wants a go Ivor? Let's see where his true interest lies?"

"Do you want a go, Daniel?"

"Er – I'd like to but I've only ever ridden a motorbike and I haven't even got a provisional licence for a car."

"Yes, boyo. We have got our lines crossed. I think you were more turned on by Heloise's photos than her in the flesh."

"I'm not so sure about that by the way he's been eyeing me," chuckled Heloise, jumping to her feet to go cart-wheeling around the car, completing two circuits then stopping to confront him, hands on hips, daring him to look.

"Er – would you take me back to the ship?" he asked quietly. "I – I'll pay you once I'm aboard."

"What ship?" she asked teasingly, pointing towards the river. "I see no ship."

He turned to discover that she was right. The *Roundcape* was out of sight or must have moved on. But then he'd walked quite some distance since coming ashore . . . ?

"That settles it then, young man!" beamed the Third. "Don't worry though cos even I had second thoughts immediately after jumping ship. And after all those promises to do just that, there was I doubting the wisdom of what I'd so long planned which, as you'll recall, I confided in you over; that is until I found Heloise waiting for me as promised. Then I knew there was no going back and to crown it all, you've joined us! Our unhappy young Cabin Boy has joined us and welcome he is too! Very welcome!"

"I – I suppose I've got no option," replied the very welcome Cabin Boy. "Seeing it looks as if I've been left behind."

"Don't look so down in the mouth about it, Daniel, cos in time you'll really get to like this place and then you'll not want to leave as Heloise and I surely don't," reasoned the officer then added mysteriously. "But sadly, the truth is that it's not really your time right now and one day you'll have to follow your brook back home where you truly belong. But make up your mind to linger awhile and enjoy the excursion of a lifetime."

"Where – where exactly is this place?" ventured Daniel.

"This place . . .?

The Third hesitated with his answer then said, "This place, Daniel, is where all three of us can take refuge from our mundane problems. This place is the answer to where your brook would lead. Not in the midst of some inhospitable ocean but a place where you'd rather it led which you'll discover if you do as I suggest and linger awhile."

"Ivor, darling?"

Heloise sounded impatient and was now seated in the car's front passenger seat.

"It's opening time in town or are you going to stand around all day trying to convince that obtuse young Cabin Boy?"

Obtuse! That word again! And her haughty manner was fast causing Daniel to go off the darling Heloise even though it was partly her sexual appeal that was prompting him to stay around: an appeal hardly lessened by her having slipped on a white cotton frock which had the effect of making her visually even more erotic as she swung her shapely legs out of the car to reveal that she wore nothing beneath it!

"I'll have a nap along the way, Ivor!" she called out while uncaringly exposing her bottom as she leaned to tip the front seat to clamber onto the back one.

"It looks as if you're warming to this place already, Daniel!" grinned the Third, having noted the youth's fixed gape. "Are you coming along or not?"

"I – I've got a problem, sir. She – she said something about a town and I, er – seem to be having a, er – a recurring dream that has me in public wearing nothing but a short shirt and Billy's jacket is just as exposing if, er – I'm not careful, sir," answered Daniel, his embarrassment not helped by Heloise's cheeky grin from the back of the car.

"Easily remedied, young man," replied Mr Williams. "Put the blessed thing on back to front look you. It's well long enough to cover what matters."

Not without difficulty, Daniel did as advised while the Third fastened a couple of buttons at the small of his back. Little wonder that the Third was an officer, being able to come up with such a brilliant answer to the problem.

"That'll do lovely, boyo!" he congratulated himself, giving Daniel's backside a friendly pat. "But don't get bending to scrub the bloody pantry floor if Yussef's about," he chuckled, giving him another pat.

Yussef was on the youth's mind when, minutes later, the Third at the wheel, they were racing along the seemingly endless sands. The unfortunate incident with the Donkeyman was reason enough not to return to the ship, he'd decided. An accident that could well have him charged with murder, his earlier attacks on Yussef, Jock and the Skipper all counting against him. This option, as surreal as it had begun, had to be better than re-boarding even if that was still possible? Far wiser biding his time here if only until the *Roundcape* had loaded and departed from Chaguramas, to where they could still despatch him to be locked up on board again until handed over to the appropriate authorities. Yes, far better to lie low here where he'd already turned down sex with an appealing young woman on a beach under a tropical sun. Every man's dream (that is other than Yussef) which he'd likely get offered again, if those tantalising smiles she kept giving him meant what he thought? After all, he was much nearer her age than was the Third and as much as he liked the officer, if she came on to him, a friendship could be patched up as soon as her present beau accepted he was out of the picture. So just let it happen and everything the Third had reminisced about happening to him during those heady days on Pendine Sands, would be his for the taking. He could even further ingratiate himself by pretending to be a fan of her poet idol. Not to lay it on too thick though in case she asked him to recite something out of his repertoire . . . ? No, perhaps not. Just keep his hair combed and return those sexy smiles and oh yes! Remember not to bend over in her presence while wearing this embarrassing back to front jacket.

The Demerara had become the sea, Daniel noted, waking up in the front passenger seat as the Morris traversed the long, flat beach. If the *Roundcape*, that dot of a ship out there was well on her way to Chaguramas without him, he mused?

"Still no qualms about staying, young man?" enquired the Third, seemingly aware of his new passenger's thoughts.

"Er – no, sir. I'm okay, really."

As if to reassure him about his decision, the officer opened up again about 'this paradise on Earth' and how, after Heloise and he had so fortunately been reunited, she'd expressed having no desire whatsoever to return to Wales and so they'd decided to stay put and recreate the haunts of their past in the much preferable climate of Guiana. The vast beach upon which they now rode wasn't unlike the sands of Pendine, Carmarthenshire, renowned for being Sir Malcolm Campbell's (father of Donald Campbell) choice to test and prove his *Bluebird* racing car and where he and Heloise had spent many happy hours in complete isolation, as is the wont of true lovers.

Even the town they were now making for, he said, was a miniature replica of their favourite haunt on the Welsh coast and was inhabited mostly by Welsh seamen who, like himself, had seen the potential of jumping ship in such a scenic and tranquil place.

Why Welshmen, Daniel was curious to know? But as usual, the Third monopolized the talking and only quietened a little when Heloise in the back showed signs of waking.

"She needs her beauty sleep, does that one," he remarked with a telling wink, "but when she wakes there's nobody livelier and if you were a tad embarrassed by her antics just now you wait 'til you see her in full form! The liveliest of live sparks is Heloise! You wait now!"

Thirty minutes must have passed before the beach ran out and the Third had changed down to negotiate a metalled incline, lined by the familiar palms and greenery.

"Did that faster than Sir Malcolm!" he joked as stilted wooden homesteads amongst the vegetation suggested they were back in civilization.

"Here we are then, boyo!" he announced minutes later, pointing to a roadside sign which read *FFOKCUF. TWINNED WITH INFINITY.*

"Ffokcuf? Is that a Welsh name, sir?" enquired an increasingly curious Daniel.

"I know that many Welsh place names begin with identical letters but they're usually the letter L, like in Llangollen near to where me dad used to take us on holiday. Welsh is it, sir?"

"In this instance, Daniel, no. It's not Welsh but its arrangement was inspired by a Welshman: in fact that very famous Welshman whom I brought to your attention whose admirers were engrossed in deciphering the every last word of a genius whose sense of humour had those eggheads toiling over maps to find a town he'd used as the location for one of his famous works, only to be red-faced on being told that he'd simply reversed a rude word, possibly to create the confusion it did."

"Ah yes!" chuckled Daniel, catching on. "A sort of conundrum, eh? Ffokcuf backwards! I get it! But why twinned with infinity? You can't twin something with nothing? You'd not get any exchange visitors or . . ."

"Precisely, Daniel. And if we did get prying visitors, they'd hardly feel welcome if they interpreted the town's name as quickly as you did, eh? And by the way; how come you're so informed about infinity?"

"Oh, old Abu was well up on infinity. He told me that infinity's problematic inasmuch as it's difficult for the mind to rationalize because everything else has a beginning and an end. He says that it's only because our minds are conditioned to . . ."

"And the *end* of our journey's coming up," interrupted the Third, as he steered the Morris into the main street of a small town very similar in appearance to Mackenzie.

"What did Heloise say?" asked Daniel, turning to see that the girl was still fast asleep. "I, er – thought she said something about me being severely dehydrated?"

"You're hearing things," yawned Heloise coming to. "Where are we, Ivor?"

"Well, somebody spoke to me. I distinctly heard a woman say . . .!"

"Just pulling up outside Browns, my sweet," cut in the Third, the youth's voices of no matter.

Browns Hotel read the crudely painted sign adorning the wooden shack on stilts, suspiciously similar to the Mackenzie brothel they'd visited weeks before.

"Er – why have we stopped here?" asked an alarmed Cabin Boy.

"For refreshment and entertainment! What else?" replied Mr Williams, already out of the car and assisting his lady friend to follow.

"And a little more decorum this time, eh, my sweet?"

The Third's trifling concern about entering the building hardly matched that of Daniel.

"I - I'm not going in there!" he prostested. "There's hanky-panky happening on a big double bed and me mom says I'm not to get involved with…!"

"Hanky-panky did you say? *Browns* is an establishment of the highest repute! Hanky-panky indeed!"

Despite the Third's indignation, Daniel would not budge from the car while anxiously studying the building and street.

"What's got into you, boyo? And what are you looking for?"

"A pimp! A pimp on a bike! Well, er – he could be walking if he's not, er . . . if he's not fished his Raleigh out of the river. A nice bike it was. Four gears it had if me memory serves me, er – right."

The officer and his lady companion weren't in the slightest bit interested in how many gears had the pimp's bike and not waiting to find out how well Daniel's memory served him, proceeded to drag him from the car in order to introduce him to the highly reputed Browns Hotel.

"Make sure he don't struggle free from dat drip nurse!" another voice was insisting as they bundled him up the outside stairs leading to the *WELCOME* illuminated entrance of Browns Hotel.

"I think I ought go and find him to apologize for his bike going into the river!" was Daniel's last desperate ploy to get out of the situation as they shoved him through the curtained doorway.

'Never question or doubt an officer's wisdom' the training school had drummed into him was his reflection on entering the typically British pub lounge bar with its typically British patrons sitting quietly with their gin and tonics and half beers.

"What will you both have?" asked the Third, his manner in keeping with the room's aura, as he led them to a table.

"Whisky on the rocks, darling," replied Heloise, now seated and wearing the look of an attractive woman under scrutiny.

"A pint of cider, please, sir," answered a considerably more relaxed Daniel joining her at the table.

"No cider or *pints* of anything," the Third informed him in his newly-acquired plummy voice. "Only halves of ale or shorts."

"Er – half of, er – ale then," replied the youth, furtively checking out the other customers, six of whom were middle-aged to elderly white males seated around an adjacent table. Two similar characters stood at the bar while a third was sitting next to a radiogram sorting through some records. Other than the odd glance towards Heloise these other customers, after pausing briefly when the trio had entered, resumed chatting among themselves.

"They – they're not Welsh then are they?" Daniel broached the Third on his return with the drinks. "I – thought you'd said they were mostly Welsh seamen who'd settled hereabouts?"

"Does a Welshman have to have a bloody leek protruding from each nostril to confirm his origin?" retorted the Third, momentarily losing his new accent. "What on Earth makes you think they're not Welsh, Daniel?"

"Well, er – me dad used to say that when strangers entered a room full of Welsh folk, they'd all start speaking in their own lingo. That's what me dad says at any rate."

"Might your dad ever have conceived that those Welsh folk were likely to have been speaking Welsh before he or any other insecure *English* man had arrived among them?" countered the officer. "And incidentally, hadn't you noticed how accepting these gentlemen were of you, dressed so improperly? Think on that one awhile, young man!"

The initial shock of being propelled into the room had made Daniel oblivious to his temporary attire until this mention. Heloise's simple white frock and the Third's tropical whites conformed well with their surroundings; but a brilliant red, leopard skin trimmed, back-to-front Edwardian drape, minus trousers, would look bizarrely out of place anywhere! Could some of those glances have been directed at him? Even grins, he was surely beginning to detect? To stay seated was a must!

Appear nonchalant, even without trousers. To stay as cool as Heloise with no underwear, a rising hem and lapping up the growing attention!

"Heloise, my sweet! Decorum remember?"

The Third too, had noticed her careless display and tut-tutted his disapproval.

Attention though, was suddenly switched to one of the men at the bar who'd moved over to the radiogram and was twiddling its receiver controls, annoying the character sorting records who'd been about to play one.

"You've a bloody cheek, mun!" he protested.

"You know very well we always listen to *The Archers* at six-forty-five, weekday evenings!" argued the other as the radio serial's signature tune came through at high volume.

The agreed 'yeahs' from others caused the irate music lover to give in while quiet descended on the room as 'the everyday story of country folk' commenced.

"I, er – didn't know Welsh folk listened to *The Archers*?" whispered Daniel. "I told you didn't I, that I'd sometimes go actor-spotting in Hanbury which was said to be the setting for Ambridge? But – but I somehow always thought that it was only listened to in England."

"This'll be the Welsh version, boyo," explained the Third quietly. "It's dialogue's in Welsh and is about life on a Snowdonian sheep farm. Much more interesting, eh, Lise?"

"What – what's more interesting?"

Heloise hadn't been paying attention, so her beau had to repeat himself but wasn't happy with her answer.

"We used to tune into the English version at home and as a matter of fact, we used to find it quite entertaining," she replied positively.

"The BBC's come up with a good storyline according to Ianto's newspapers from home," contributed Daniel, at ease with the subject. "They had to apparently cos they're dead anxious that they'll lose millions of listeners when commercial TV starts up this Autumn. So they've come up with a really gripping storyline which has the popular Grace Fairbrother character dashing into a barn inferno to save her favourite horse named Midnight. But it's too late and she and the horse die, is what Ianto's paper guesses, while the BBC has got listeners on tenterhooks in order to keep them listening."

"Similar storyline in the Welsh version," offered the Third. "Only the girl goes in to rescue her pet lamb."

"The same sad ending though was it, Ivor?" asked Heloise.

"Not quite," grinned Ivor. "The scriptwriter's decided on the girl's lover saving her at the very last minute and everybody celebrated over a slap-up feast of roast lamb."

"Ivor! You're having us on!" scolded Heloise. "Welsh version indeed!" But Ivor continued with his tease.

"Well, somebody's got to cheer the place up, my sweet. Even you don't appear quite so enthusiastic as earlier in the car. Ah! You're missing the fun of checking the tables for thrown away gems of literature I'm thinking? That's how Heloise here used to pass her time away, Daniel. It was her habit to examine every scrap of screwed up paper in the original Browns bar where her perfectionist poet used to sit jotting down lines over a pint, so it was alleged. Sentimental value as well as maybe worth a bob or two if you'd come across anything, eh, Lise?"

"I suppose so," came the sighed reply.

"So she never found any, er – literary gem?" Daniel asked the smirking officer.

"Well – no but she once did come across a written note which she swore was in his handwriting. But not anything of literary value to her disappointment.."

"What was it?"

"If I remember correctly it read *'half a pound of sausages, a cabbage, twenty Woodbines and a box of Swan'*," he replied, his laughter causing him to choke on his beer.

"Ivor! You're asking for a jab to the ribs!" warned Heloise as *The Archers* signature tune signalled the end of another episode and gave a cue to the disgruntled gent holding the records to slap one onto the turntable.

"Hooray! Now who's for dancing?" she cried, regaining attention by leaping to her feet, skirts flying high as she began spinning around the room.

"Heloise!"

It was the Third's turn to reprimand as her lack of underwear was appreciated with 'oohs' and gasps.

"Well, aren't you dancing?" she asked loudly, pausing in front of her embarrassed companion as Tennessee Ernie Ford's deep, guttural tones begged, *'Give me your wooooooord! Our love will neeeeeever diiiiiie . . .!'*

"No!" he replied emphatically, her invitation quickly taken up by one of the seated gents who, despite looking the most elderly of the group, began agilely waltzing her around the floor while others threw themselves prostrate in anticipation of every revealing spin. The tempo not fast enough for such a lively performer was suddenly raised with *Cherry Pink and Apple Blossom White*[19] and then she was doing a solo which, as the Third's frantic protests indicated, was about to peak.

"No cartwheels, Lise! No cartwheels! There's not enough room!"

But the lounge bar had ample room for such an abandoned performance much to the delight of her fixated, applauding audience as her cartwheels gathered momentum.

"Now I see it, now I don't! Now I see it, now I don't!" chanted her besotted octogenarian partner, lumbering along in her wake and who suddenly, unable to contain his ardour, launched himself onto the object of his lust so clumsily that both fell heavily on top of the radiogram, collapsing it into a jumble of exploding valves and matchwood.

With the final explosion, a grimfaced Third left his chair to help the night's star performer to her feet, his efforts not helped by her aged admirer's reluctance to let go of his prize. Her

---

[19] Cherry Pink and Apple Blossom White written by Jacques Larue 1950. English lyrics Mack David.
Give Me Your Word written by George Wyle and Irving Taylor. Tennessee Ernie Ford's version 1954.

release finally achieved, the officer coughed and then addressed the now hushed room.

"Gentleman of Browns," he began, looking and sounding extremely embarrassed. "How – how do I apologize for such unseemly behaviour? How can I begin to explain why, the lady who you have seen in my company of late, could choose to act so foolishly and with such irreverence in this building of all buildings, which many of us consider to be Ffokcuf's temple to his memory? What would *he* have made of such disgraceful goings on doesn't bear thinking about? To shatter the solemnity of a place where solemnity must have been a crucial element when creating works such as the literary world had never before . . ."

"Nonsense!" interrupted Heloise's elderly admirer, still seated amidst the wrecked radiogram. "He'd get his solemnity after leaving here in his shed on the way down to the boathouse! This place was for having a pint, a fag and a laugh! Solemnity be buggered! He'd likely have enjoyed tonight as much as the next mun! Probably more so if the truth were known. He was hardly the dark, humourless soul the literary establishment portrayed him to be! Far from it when you see how he'd slip in puzzling phrases or titles so as to bait the too-serious reader into racking his too-serious mind for an interpretation anything but as intended. He was having *fun* with 'em; that's how I saw . . ."

"Like getting them puzzled over a rude phrase written backwards!" interjected Daniel; the general 'yeahs' and nods of agreement with the speaker making him feel at ease enough to continue but was stopped in his tracks.

"Shush, Daniel!"

The Third wasn't quite so at ease, that is until the now smiling customers began shaking his hand with assurances such as, "The old boy's right you know. A pint, a fag and a joke was his way in Browns."

So, nothing to worry about then, that is until Daniel looked up and saw that the barman had suddenly got an assistant. An assistant immaculately dressed in the saloon whites of a Merchant Navy Table Steward!

"Billy! Billy White!" Daniel's blurted recognition alerted the Third to turn and study the newcomer.

"What's this then, young White?" he asked. "A kind of moonlighting is it?"

Coming from behind the bar, Billy, cloth in hand, strolled over and began casually wiping down their table.

"No, sir," he began dismally, "just a change of situation and I was enjoying it until just now. You've heard the bad news I take it?" he asked, glancing towards the shattered radiogram.

"Oh, you're missing your music, eh? We'll pay for a replacement as soon as . . ." began the Third.

"Noo! *The* bad news!" reiterated Billy. "On the fuckin' radio!"

"Something's happened to the ship? Is that what you're saying, White?"

"Well, the hurricane Janet were no joke, sir. That's partly why I'm here. You two were lucky not to 'ave been on board," he continued, his eyes meeting Daniel's for the first time.

"Is – is the cat alright?" asked the Cabin Boy.

Billy's face confirmed his 'stupid' tag on board, as he turned back to the officer.

"It's the bad news on the radio just now is what I'm referring to, sir. You've not 'eard?"

"Oh, Grace Fairbrother and her horse you mean, White? That's just fiction. Nothing to get disturbed about."

"I'm referrin' to James Dean, sir! You've obviously not 'eard then?"

"The up-and-coming American film star? What about this young James Dean, White?"

"'e's dead, sir." Billy appeared unusually morose. "Believe me sir, September the thirtieth 1955 'll be a grey anniversary for yonks to come, I'm thinkin'. Stone dead 'e is! Crashed 'is Porsche just hours ago did James Dean! A legend in 'is own time an' 'is time is over, is what they're sayin' on the wireless.

316

Yes sir, September the thirtieth'll not be forgotten for yonks, I'm thinkin'."

"Oh, I'm, er – sorry," sympathised the Third awkwardly. "Not that I'm too familiar with his rise to fame other than he's developed into some kind of cult figure? Er – your customers here . . .? Their somewhat depressed attitude when we arrived? Surely it couldn't have been related to the tragic demise of someone they'd likely know little about?"

"Cult figure, yes, sir," replied Billy, "but only to us young and, as you say, these old 'uns wouldn't 'ave been too familiar with James Dean. Donald Peers is more their cup of tea. They wouldn't miss 'is weekly 'alf hour for all the tea in China. No, sir. It wasn't anythin' to do with the American cult figure that's given 'em the miseries of late. They've all been sittin' around mopin' since Grace Fairbrother an' 'er poxy 'orse got incinerated in that fuckin' barn the other night!"

"Me mother and sister used to be crazy about Donald Peers," chipped in Daniel. "Every Tuesday night I think it was and they'd be glued to the wireless and nobody was allowed to even move! We had a radiogram, the same as that one, er – over there and they'd sit around it on the cold lino, swooning away at his mournful voice and even the cat would get something thrown at it for just one mew. Me dad used to let them get on with it and go out to his shed and start repairing shoes or something. Not that he was anti-Welsh. In fact he used to take us camping in North Wales every Summer and me uncle used to say that we were originally from Wales, on my dad's side that is."

(Embroider the Welsh affinity and Heloise would be even more attracted to him.)

"Oh yes, even our next door neighbours were Welsh and we really got on with them: not to mention our Welsh headmaster who used to get me reciting poems (this will grab her) reciting poems in front of the school and used to ask me where our family was from and me dad used to supply him with cut-price eggs; a bit on the small side maybe but he never seemed to notice their size when I delivered them, it being part of my job as

317

well as mucking out and mixing the mash for a tanner a week which I . . ."

(Heloise wasn't even looking in his direction and whole pubful weren't exactly . . .? Best get back to the Welsh theme.)

"As I was saying, everything stopped for Donald Peers' weekly warble; talk about fixated . . ."

"*Brazier!*"

The Third only addressed Daniel by his surname if he was miffed about something!

"*Brazier!*" he bellowed again. "There's bloody hurricanes out there causing havoc on ocean and land! An' and, dead film stars and famous radio characters are being grieved over by millions and I'm worrying about how I'm going to pay for a new radiogram and you are informing us at such a calamitous time that you used to feed and muck out your dad's chickens for six bloody pence a week!"

"Er – and a bit more if I delivered the eggs around the . . ."

The Third was either stunned into silence or Billy got in there before him.

"Don't go thinkin' I've not noticed you're wearin' my best drape, Daniel!" snapped the Steward. "What's the fuckin' idea?"

And Daniel had thought it perhaps too dark in Browns for him to spot it.

"I – I'd nothing to wear to come ashore in, an – and it's only the jacket. The – the trousers were too blooming tight around the waist."

"No trousers?" teased Billy, sounding much his usual self. "Daniel's got no trousers on! Daniel's got no trousers on!" he sang out, causing Daniel to revisit that particular nightmare.

"Let's 'ave a look then!"

Billy was almost upon him, intent on further embarrassment but the Cabin Boy was a split second too fast and was on his feet making for the door which fortunately was open, allowing him to escape, shouts ringing in his ears.

Outside, he kept running until sure he wasn't being pursued. Of course! Billy being on duty was likely why he'd not followed him out of the building. He was temporarily safe but out on the now darkened street, unsure of where he should go?

"Lordy! He's almost out of his bed again, jes' as if he's tryin' to get away from someting! An' dat blessed drip's come out again wid his rollin' aroun' like somebody possessed! Better reconnect him before de Sister come lookin'!"

Somebody had spoken nearby again but there wasn't a soul about . . .? Except for a girl . . .? A girl standing with a bicycle some three buildings away?

He began walking towards her and she turned to look in his direction and even in that poorly-lit street, she was . . .? No doubt now; she was . . . she was Hilary!

But how could she have possibly . . .? Why even question as to how she'd got here considering all the bizarre happenings since coming ashore? He waved and was about to call out her name when, seemingly alarmed, she mounted her bike, pedalling off at speed and disappearing into what he discovered, after trotting on, was a narrow, unlit alleyway. Not a sign of her as he gingerly ventured into the opening but the glow of cigarettes in the gloom just ahead told him he'd got company but not as welcoming as he'd hoped!

"We've waited a long fuckin' time to meet up once again, sailor boy!"

The accent was Welsh, the speaker, Gareth. Hilary's fight-hungry cousin was approaching him, bicycle chain at the ready! Others joined him, growling the same threats as that night in Tiger Bay! No Hilary to save his skin this time and before he'd even time to plead, the chain slashing into his left cheek signalled the others to jump in with fists and boots unmercifully.

"Okay, lads! Let up! Let up I say!"

His saviour, a white figure brilliantly illuminated by the moonlight could well have been his guardian angel. Guardian angel or not, Billy White (aptly surnamed) an authoritative figure in his saloon whites, had saved him again! He must have obtained permission to come after him and the Cardiff Ted's had been momentarily distracted from their thuggery by his 'uniformed' appearance. Not waiting to see if they'd been totally fooled, Billy yanked their victim to his feet and hastily bundled him away before the muttering Teds gathered their wits to relaunch themselves.

"Jock was fuckin' right about you!" groaned Billy, once out on the street and sure they weren't being followed. "A disaster waitin' to 'appen you are, Daniel!"

Daniel, so grateful for his intervention, said nothing, that is until Billy revealed his reason for pursuing him.

"But – but it's all I'm wearing, Billy!" he protested when asked to hand over the jacket. "You wouldn't leave me walking about in the noddy, would you?"

"Oh, alright," relented the other. "We'll wait 'til we're back on board. I'm going back behind the bar now and the Third said for you to wait outside by the car so as you don't get borin' everybody with your borin' life with the your dad's poultry."

Happy not to return to the madness of Browns, the Cabin Boy, keeping an eye open for the gang, stayed around the Morris until the Third emerged with Heloise minutes after time had been called in the hotel.

"Is, er – Billy not coming?" enquired Daniel. "He, er – said something about going back on board?"

"Billy? Billy White you mean?" the Third looked puzzled by his question. "I've not seen our Assistant Steward since coming ashore. How much have you had to drink tonight, Daniel? And if it's not the drink that's affecting you," he chuckled, "there's a place down in Georgetown for seamen who imagine things look you."

The officer's mood much improved, it was best to leave it like that was Daniel's resolve as they motored out of Ffokcuf and back to the sands of Pendine. Yes, to leave it like that was best . . .? Even though, sir, you spoke to Billy yourself and –

320

and, do you remember that little redhead who waved me goodbye on the quay back in Cardiff . . .?

Chapter 24

Petulant Augustus John?

"Should you ever find yourself in the vicinity of Cwmdonkin Park," the *Roundcape's* Third Mate once enthused to a first-tripper Cabin Boy, "the experience, if only to listen to the sea wind in the treetops, would be both inspiring and memorable."

It would be twenty-three years later when his listener, while holidaying on the scenic Gower Peninsula, took up his recommendation and visited that haunted park in the Upland district of Swansea.

Inspiring indeed: because, as he lingered on those wooded slopes and gazed out over the spread of Swansea and its magnificent bay, well beyond the picturesque Mumbles headland to where the minute silhouette of a ship sank over the horizon into infinity; the story that owed much to that park and to happenings on board a ship out of Cardiff years earlier, was already being composed.

Memorable? Obsessively memorable! Because for most of his life thereafter, the author, often in neglect of mundane responsibility, would write and rewrite, if only for the pleasure of recollecting and embroidering the story of that park and the journey that led to it.

And as an old Somali seaman once preached, "Life is a voyage. Master the storms and always there'll be calm seas ahead." So, in pursuit of a calm sea, the author resumes his obsession and heads back to the park where, it has been said, *everything began.*

Considering that his arms were constricted by the back to front jacket and that he'd never driven a car before; Daniel could only congratulate himself for having mastered the Morris after being 'seconded' to take over the wheel. His 'romantically'

preoccupied rear seat passengers were certainly not complaining, even though the odd glance into the rear-view mirror did bring about the occasional need to sharply correct his steering. But motoring along an empty beach at sunrise was a piece of cake whatever the distraction until, that is, another distraction in the form of a ship at anchor some half-mile out to sea, began to resemble . . .? Began to resemble the . . . *Roundcape*?

"I, er – I've, er – just spotted something, sir."

"I *knew* he'd been nosing into that bloody mirror!" complained Heloise.

"I hope you haven't been, boyo? Just concentrate on your driving look you?"

"I, er – am, sir. But – but I've spotted something of, er – interest, sir. Something that you might not have noticed."

"I've seen every last inch of her so keep your eyes ahead!"

"Oh no, sir! I – I'm talking about . . ."

"That her legs go on forever? Well, I'm not complaining so why should you? Or do I detect an unhealthy interest in my sweet Lise, young man?"

"No, sir! I might just be seeing things again but I've refocused several times on her shape and from stem to stern, she's looking very much like . . ."

"I knew the little bugger had been getting an eyeful!" spat Heloise, adjusting her dress.

". . . she's looking very much like the *Roundcape*, sir," completed Daniel.

"It is that," agreed the Third with less enthusiasm. "Pull up, Daniel, so we can get a proper look."

Finding how to stop the Morris was another lesson learned by trial and error but was eventually achieved and all three alighted to survey the ship at anchor.

Yes, it was undoubtedly the *Roundcape* and at this distance, anyone on her decks would have been visible.

"They couldn't all be sleeping off last night's session?" joked the Third curiously. "In fact she looks deserted to me and there's only one way to find out. Is that your boat over there, Lise?"

Having stopped in the vicinity of Heloise's beached canoe was another of those strange coincidences and in Daniel's thoughts, not a happy one having suddenly no wish at all to re-board the ship looking as foreboding out there as on that first day back in Cardiff.

The Third too, appeared to be having sudden doubts saying, "We'll just row out so far and if we see any sign of life whatsoever we'll forget the idea?"

Why they were even going at all was still puzzling Daniel as minutes later the trio, Heloise paddling, slowly approached the ship?

"I – I can hear singing! Singing on board, sir!"

"Keep your voice down, Daniel! And ease off for a minute, Lise!"

That minute had fully passed when the Third spoke again to ridicule Daniel.

"You're hearing things now as well as seeing things, young man! Get a grip will you?"

"I – I could have sworn I heard the crew singing!" protested the youth. "You know? That – that, er – *Men of Harlech* that they used to belt out at full . . .? Listen. They're at it again! Can't you hear them?"

Men of Harlech suddenly became "*Sospan Faaaach – yn berwi ar y taaaaaaan . . .!*" but he being the only one to hear it was disregarded while paddling continued until minutes later, they were alongside and contemplating how safe was the rope ladder suspended from deck to waterline?

"Best you get up there first, Daniel, before the National Eisteddfod call it a day," suggested the Third, nervously cupping an ear.

"Why me? I – I'm not much good at climbing up . . .!"

"Up you go, boyo. It's not ladies first in this case. Heloise can go second for protection as it were."

Daniel's protests were ignored, the Third pushing him towards the dangling ladder. Halfway up the ghostly choir erupted again with *"We'll keep a welcome in the hillsiiide[20] . . .!"* accompanied by a thunderous blast from the ship's siren.

"I – I – I'm not going up there. . .!"

Daniel's attempt to clamber back down was thwarted by the officer's use of a paddle to prod his backside.

"Ouch! That was blooming-well cold!" The youth's discomfort getting a shrill chuckle from the girl below causing him to adopt a sideways-on ascent if only for his dignity.

Sniggers escaping the following pair, told Daniel that they were in league but on reaching the deck, his embarrassment was quickly replaced by nervous anticipation as Donald Peers' *By a Babbling Brook* came ringing out from the direction of his old cabin . . .!

"Where the bloody heck is that coming from?"

The Third, now aboard and helping his lady to follow, was now hearing it too.

"It, er – it could be Jock's wireless?" offered Daniel. "But – but there's no sign of anybody on the decks nor on the bridge as far as I can make out. Where – where do you think they all are, sir?"

But the Third wasn't listening, having moved quickly to the open porthole of Daniel's once cabin.

"Not a soul!" he called out. "But it's Jock's wireless right enough!"

His eyes met Daniel's in mutual concern while Heloise, her first time on board an ocean going vessel, began skipping about the decks to investigate.

"Every blessed door is locked!" was her frustrated report on returning to her fellow boarders now seated on tarpaulin-sealed number three hold.

"What's that box, Ivor?"

Ivor and Daniel turned to look at the small cardboard box on the hold just a few feet behind them.

"Was that there when we boarded, Daniel?" asked the Third.

---

[20] We'll Keep a Welcome in the Hillside written around 1940 by Mai Jones, Lyn Joshua, and James Harper

Daniel, too shocked to reply, simply sat staring at the box: a box suspiciously like the one used to . ..?

His acute discomfort obviously hadn't registered with the girl who leaped onto the hatch to take a closer look.

"It's sealed with loads of adhesive tape!" she called out and then began investigating it by probing the mysterious box with a bare foot.

"Give it a *real* bloody kick, Lise!" chuckled the Third, also oblivious to Daniel's frozen look of horror and was suddenly up and dashing across the hatch to do what barefooted Heloise was reluctant to do!

"Noooooo!"

But Daniel's plea was of no avail as the officer booted the box so hard that it rose high into the air before dropping onto the galley roof.

"That – that box . . .!" The youth was at last finding words to voice his horror. "It – it's what they kept Edgar's . . .!"

"Climb up and get it down will you, Daniel?" cut in the Third, proud of his kicking ability and more keen to have another go than learn about the box's use after being emptied of a popular bedtime drink.

"Get it down I asked you, Dan . . . ?"

Boooooooooooom!

The officer's request was suddenly cut short by an almighty blast from the *Roundcape's* siren which seemed to vibrate every last section of her superstructure!

"What the . . .?"

The Third's interest in football was over as quickly as it had begun.

"The – the bridge . . .! Somebody must be on the bridge! See anything when you were up there just now, Lise?"

"No," she replied.

As grimy as the bridge windows were, she was positive that there had been no sign of life up there in the wheelhouse.

Unconvinced, the Third led them for'ard into the bows where they took up different vantage points, "to look for any movement up there," he muttered gravely.

"Come here, both of you! Can you make out somebody at the wheel?"

A cloud, slipping across the sun obscured whom or what he was indicating but not before he'd glimpsed that face immediately above the wheel staring for'ard, transfixed, motionless, even – even lifeless?

"Oh my God!"

Why the Third was suddenly calling out the Lord's name in vain became frighteningly clear to Daniel as the sun returned to illuminate the face above them.

"It's – it's . . .!"

He'd no need to say his old shipmate's name because that particular bridge window, having been mysteriously cleaned, revealed that it was definitely Edgar up there!

"You devilish old bugger you!" yelled the Third dancing about and gesticulating wildly in order to get Edgar's attention.

That he failed was no surprise to Daniel knowing what he did. But the Third of course was ignorant of what befell their Fourth Engineer prior to himself leaving the ship in Mackenzie, and was definitely in no mood for such morbidity. And to tell him that Edgar, as he suspected, was *on* the wheel rather than *at* the wheel, would surely be a tad deflating at that precise moment!

"Why's the old bugger not answering?"

The officer's quietening tone hinted that even he was beginning to suspect that all was not as it should be.

"He was hardly the ship's laugh-a-minute comedian aboard but being reunited with his number one shipmate deserves at least an effort of a smile, eh, boyo?"

"Er – yes, sir . . . but – but there's something I've been meaning to tell you since I came ashore and – and now, if you'll listen just a . . ."

"Out with it then, Daniel! Out with it!"

All three were now seated on the hatch, the Third and Heloise awaiting Daniel's explanation.

"Have – have you noticed something, er – odd about Mr Reece up there, sir?" he began falteringly.

"Yes – yes, he's just done three somersaults while singing 'we'll keep a fucking welcome in the fucking hillside'!" came the sarcastic reply.

"And he's just pulled out his tongue at me!" was Heloise's attempt to top her beau's wit.

"His – er . . . shoulders, sir? Mr Reece's shoulders? Have – haven't you noticed, sir?"

"His shoulders . . .? One on each side as is usual to the homo sapiens species or are you seeing something out of the ordinary about Mr Reece's shoulders, Daniel?"

"Er – yes, sir."

"What?"

"He hasn't got any, sir."

Shading his eyes, the Third refocused on the bridge windows.

"You've better eyesight than me, Daniel, cos I'm finding it difficult to agree with you," he replied eventually. "But have you ever heard of an artist named Augustus John[21], highly acclaimed for his portrait painting?"

"Er – no, sir."

"Well, you will at least, through Heloise and myself, be familiar with possibly the most famous celebrity to sit for him? A poet who was also a friend of his and whom *some* allege once was a rival in love?"

"Who was that then?"

Boooooooooom!

The *Roundcape's* siren overwhelmed the officer's reply just as Daniel conceived the answer for himself.

". . . and this head and shoulders likeness of him as a young man," continued the Third, "depicted him perfectly except for one aspect of his physique in that he over-emphasised his

---

[21] Augustus John. Welsh painter. Acclaimed for his portraits including that of his friend, Dylan Thomas.

somewhat sloping shoulders; an exaggeration those same *some* suggest, could well have been the artist being petulant through his brush to demonstrate that the poet wasn't exactly a Welsh Charles Atlas, particularly in the shoulder department."

"I can't help but agree with those same *some*, Ivor," said Heloise positively.

"I've always considered that 'shoulderless' painting quite insulting. What's exactly your opinion, darling?"

Giving himself a Stan Laurel type head scratch, the Third replied as unpredictably as ever.

"The petulance of a rival in love is a theory one can hardly ignore, my sweet. But a more practical explanation has been aired suggesting that the artist simply ran out of blue paint."

"He ran out of . . .? Oh, Ivor! You stupid, stupid man!" shrieked Heloise. "Did you hear him, Daniel? Ran out of blue paint indeed! Did you hear him, Daniel?"

"Er – yes. But why didn't he use another colour?"

Booooooooooom!

Another siren blast saved Daniel from being labelled stupid himself and then Victor Sylvester's orchestra playing a foxtrot sent the trio back towards the youth's old cabin just in time to see the porthole close.

"Methinks somebody's having a little game with us," muttered the Third peering within. "Can't see anybody but the set's lit up and those stations aren't changing by themselves. I wonder now . . .? Nip for'ard again, Daniel and see if it isn't that old rogue Edgar dashing back and forth for a laugh."

"He – er, wouldn't be able to, sir. It – it's not physically possible."

"Not *physically* possible, Daniel? You'll be telling us next that as well as shoulderless, he's bloody-well legless into the bargain. Legless . . .! Oh yes, that was a night to remember back in Mackenzie when the old bugger was well and truly legless! I can see him now trying to . . .!"

But Daniel was now out of earshot and on his way for'ard to prove that it couldn't possibly be Edgar prowling back and forth in jest. Minutes later however, he returned to where they were seated on number three hold to reluctantly admit that the Fourth Engineer was no longer visible at the wheel.

"So I wonder where the old prankster is lurking now?" mused the Third.

"He – he could, er – be in there."

There was a tremble in Daniel's voice matching the horror in his eyes as he pointed to the box placed once again centre-hatch behind the couple who looked as concerned as himself on turning to view it.

A quiet moment passed before Mr Williams returned his attention to Daniel.

"It was on the galley roof surely? It – it couldn't possibly be *you* having a little joke with us, eh, young man?"

"Er – no, sir."

"Then please correct my suspicions that you might be intimating that Edgar – Mr Reece somehow, while we were absorbed in conversation relating to the possible motives of the painter Augustus John, managed to sneak out of the wheelhouse, entered your old cabin to entertain us with Victor Sylvester at full volume, then climbed onto the galley roof to retrieve a box just large enough to hold a football, placed it on the hatch and secreted himself inside it?"

At times, some questions require so much deliberation, that it's perhaps better to pretend that they'd never been asked.

"Er – I think it's going to be one of those lovely sunsets again," offered Daniel while two vacant stares told him that they weren't going to be sidetracked quite so easily but one more try might just . .?

"Er – I'm trying to think of two colours mixed which, if Augustus John had had to hand would have give a semblance of blue as near as damn it if he was so intent on using that particular colour if you, er – see what I'm . .?"

No, it wasn't going to work but – but that porthole in the adjacent galley swinging open was certainly distracting them.

"I see the laddie's still as connivin' as ever when he's tryin' to wriggle out o' self-made tight corners," yawned Jock, clearly visible through the opening. "I hoped never to set eyes on him again an' wi' luck, wouldnae have done had the Skipper nae got wind o' his whereabouts an' sent me after him. Hang on to him a mo', Mr Williams, sir, while I pour this tea I've brewed for you."

Moments later the Cook joined them on the hatch with the promised tea and a plate of biscuits.

"It – it was you then, McLaughlin? The siren, the music and goings-on since we boarded?" Mr Williams wanted to know but Jock said nothing for a few minutes as he sipped his tea and stared landwards.

"That Janet was some bastard o' a hurricane," were his first words after draining his mug. "I'll admit to shittin' meself through that one."

"But – but you came through it, McLaughlin and headed back to Guiana I take it?" enquired the Third, hardly in awe at the Cook's sudden appearance.

"Aye, we did just that, sir, an' we're presently waitin' on the company for a passage home."

"Where – where exactly is your accommodation? One would have thought that it would have been Georgetown?" the Third was beginning to appear uncomfortable with Jock's sombre, detached manner. "Is – is it, er – nearby, McLaughlin?"

"It's over yonder," replied the Scot, nodding in the direction of his stare. "In yonder park."

"A park? The company's put you up in a park? Anything to save a penny that blessed company!"

The Third appeared genuinely sympathetic while still troubled.

"There – there must be some kind of shelter in this park? You can't possibly be exposed to the elements in such a clime?"

"The Skipper's bagged the only shelter available an' is lookin' decidedly comfortable in that converted bandstand, sure enough."

Jock's last statement silenced the Third as he turned a worried face towards Heloise who appeared to be sharing his concern.

"Bandstand? A converted bandstand did you say?" they asked the Cook in unison.

"Aye, that's what I said right enough," he replied, appearing to sense their concern. "You wouldnae know o' such a place by any chance would you?"

Now visibly troubled, the couple went into a whispered discussion before the Third returned to Jock, saying, "Yes, we are very well acquainted with the park over, er – yonder and – and when you return there, we'd like you to politely put a question to the Skipper concerning his new accommodation."

"Aye, an' what exactly do you want to ask the Skipper?"

"Well, er – please inform him in the nicest possible way that regrettably, he, er – is squatting in what is our accommodation and would he, er – kindly move out into something that's maybe not quite befitting his rank but, in the circumstances, the best Heloise and I can offer."

"An' what's this 'not quite befittin'' accommodation you'll be offerin' the Skipper pray?" Jock questioned, his omitted *sir* increasingly ominous.

"A . . . er – mint condition, two-door Morris Eight with unblemished paintwork, imitation leather upholstery, uses little oil and has four as-new tyres, the spare still useable and very low mileage for the year."

Stroking his chin in thought, Jock asked, "Air con' an' a well sprung rear seat for a romp, this Morris?"

"The, er – sliding roof has unfortunately been permanently sealed but the window mechanism's fully operational so as to retain warmth or provide a good through draught as and when required, and the rear seat is very comfy indeed!"

The Third's more confident tone suggested that his offer was reasonable but it had never been wise to underestimate Jock who then asked, "An' a cocktail bar? Is this model fitted wi' the optional cocktail bar an' a double bed big enough for the Master's nocturnal pursuits?"

332

"Nocturnal pursuits . . . ?"

"Aye. The Skipper's fond o' entertainin' in yonder bandstand wi' its king-size bed an' all the trappin's that some idiot left for the takin'. Eh, you're nae tellin' me that he'll be denied his sexual indulgences in your *mint condition* Morris?"

"He'll manage to get a leg over quite comfortably on the back seat cos I've seen Mr Williams and his lady friend using it for that, er - purpose," offered Daniel, keen to help the deal along if only to see the back of Jock.

But his intrusion was as unwelcome as ever noting the hostile glares brought about by his comment and the Third's confidence was noticeably waning with or without Daniel's help as he half-heartedly advised the Cook as to there being no need for tax and insurance in a tropical wilderness.

"That, wi'out the shadow of a fuckin' doubt'll seal the deal!" smirked Jock, "an' I can even see the Skipper overlookin' a treadless spare tyre in his eagerness to swop his comfy abode for a clapped-out Morris Eight, that's for sure!"

But an arrangement would be arrived at once back ashore, Mr Williams assured him.

Yes, ashore, because that's where they were all off to right now he informed them as group leader! And an arrangement would indeed be arrived at!

About to disembark, another distraction in the form of a mewing Tiggy, appearing quite healthy and large, emerged from the galley.

"You – you've been feeding him!" sang out a delighted Daniel. "I thought you detested him, Jock?" he added, scooping the cat up as the Cook answered in form.

"Wi' the freezer empty an' a Chinese delicacy on hand that only needed fattenin' up . . ."

"We – we're taking him along I hope?" pleaded the Cabin Boy.

Protests about four people being too many as it was for such a small vessel were voiced but there was no physical intervention as they began to leave, the cat held firmly under Daniel's arm, he and Heloise leading the way down the rope ladder while being instructed by the Third to seat themselves centrally in the canoe and to take up the paddles. This accomplished, the Third followed and seated himself cox-swain-like aft, while Jock balanced things up by settling himself for'ard to face the couple about to commence paddling, his widening eyes embarrassing Daniel into snapping his legs shut while Heloise crossed hers in a ladylike manner, her eyes meeting Jock's in feigned modesty. The Cook smiled back then turned to Daniel, shaking his head in ridicule.

"I'd be desperate to hide somethin' that small meself, laddie," he growled. "An' how you're gonna explain yourself to the old man is gonna be worth listenin' to, that's for sure? But there'll be nae need for you to plead insanity cos when he sees the garb you've been wanderin' about in ashore, he'll have you back in that straitjacket afore you've even opened your fuckin' gob !"

The Third's shouted, "Get paddling!" helped Daniel ignore him as he turned to synchronise with fellow paddler, Heloise.

"On my God!" followed up the officer. "What about Edgar? We can't leave him!"

"The company'll nae be happy wi'out somebody lookin' after one o' its vessels, cargo an' all!"

Jock's reasoning appeared to satisfy the Third who gazed back wistfully at the ship as thunder and lightning began to explode from the black sky suddenly forming above it.

"This hurricane weather's full of surprises," he muttered, all joining his rapt attention to the eerie spectacle of the *Roundcape* in the murk, now only made visible by huge bolts of lightning discharging out of the blackness.

Boooooooooom!

"That'll be Edgar sayin' goodbye," muttered the Scot to his ill at ease companions.

"Sospan Faaaach – yn berwi ar y taaaaaaa . . .!"
Boooooooooom!

The ghostly choir was overwhelmed by another siren blast accompanied by deafening claps of thunder, the rain-bloated clouds simultaneously releasing so heavy a downpour that Tiggy leaped from Daniel's lap to seek refuge beneath his seat then immediately scrambled back as the canoe began rapidly filling with water.

"Get baling!" shouted the Third.

"What fuckin' wiiii'?" Jock yelled back, convincing Daniel that the sea would surely claim him this time unless . . .? They'd almost reached the beach now, so the water's depth might just be . . .? He stopped paddling and with difficulty because of the canoe's unpredictable motion, slid one leg over the side into . . .?

"Dis boy'll be in a cot for sure if Sister gets to know he's put his foot in de cleaner's bucket when he's *supposedly* comatosed! Or mebbe wid her impatience, she'll pour de blessed bucket over him to bring him roun' before de doc's expectin', eh, Masie?"

"Not if Doctor Jessop gets wind of it, cos Nurse Furber's guessin' dat he's keepin' de boy under on purpose so long as de shippin' company's insurer's don't be gettin' suspicious, an' she's even whisperin' dat she saw de doc' injectin' him wid someting on her shift dis mornin'."

Chapter 25

Exits New York

Yet another ordeal with water survived and as soon as he'd released his foot from this blooming bucket, he'd rejoin the others waiting for him on the beach.

"What kept you, Daniel?"

The Third looked much happier than ten minutes ago as he sat awaiting him, a comforting arm around Heloise.

"This blooming bucket, sir! I'll need a hand getting it off my foot!"

"What bucket?"

"This, er . . .? I, er – must have shook it off without knowing," was his excuse as he joined them, bucket free.

The expected tease didn't come, the subject having moved with the Third declaring the short-lived storm having been nothing less than phenomenal.

"An April shower compared wi' the fuckin' Janet!" came Jock's scornful reply.

"But you wouldnae 'ave known anythin' about the Janet while sunnin' yourself on some beach the likes o' this'n, eh, Mr Williams?"

Mr Williams dismissed the sarcasm by referring to something more pertinent.

"This park, McLaughlin? If it's the one I think it is then we'd best be on our way well before dark."

His words came just as Daniel spotted the Morris some five minutes walk away. He then looked towards the water where the dispersing storm clouds should surely have brought the *Roundcape* back into . . .?

"She – she's gone, Mr Williams! The ship's gone, sir!"

"So she bloody-well has by God! What do you make of that, McLaughlin? The ship . . .?

"Aye. That'll be Edgar receivin' company orders no doubt. Did you nae see smoke comin' frae the stack while aboard?"

Jock's explanation was too readily accepted, Daniel mused, as he picked up the cat and hurried after the others making for the car. The usually reliable Morris was refusing to start as he arrived.

"Er – Mr Horton, a neighbour of ours, his Morris Eight didn't like the damp and after that blooming storm, you'd best use the cranking handle else you'll drain the battery," he told them reaching for the handle which he'd earlier noticed beneath the passenger seat. Begrudgingly, Jock snatched it from him and began cranking while the Third played with the choke until the engine spluttered into life sending clouds of thick smoke pouring from the car's exhaust.

"Best let it idle for a while," further advised Daniel, "to let it dry out like."

"Fuckin' little know-all," muttered Jock. "As if I didnae know anythin' about cars."

Minutes later with the Third at the wheel, Jock at his side, Daniel, Heloise and the cat in the rear, the car was heading for 'Cwmdonkin Park'.

'Cwmdonkin Park' because according to Jock's description, gushed the Third, the park where Captain Roberts awaited them was undoubtedly the very park where he and Heloise had first met and found love. Love that had bloomed in so idyllic a sanctuary that they called it 'their own' and where, should they ever be parted, the place where they would strive to be reunited?

For once relaxed and congratulating himself for being instrumental in getting the car started, Daniel decided against disturbing the calm by airing his doubts about this being the said park if only because of its geographical location. No, if commonsense wasn't asked for, why offer it especially now that his interest was now more taken by the thick jungle encroaching the winding track they'd followed since leaving the beach. Impenetrable growth such as that on the Demerara's banks where colourful birds sang and small monkeys played and chattered. Better observation of this fascinating wildlife came during their many stops to top up the car's overheating radiator at the many fordable streams crossing their path. Not that other thoughts weren't crossing Daniel's mind such as the recent bucket incident when those other voices were definitely concerned about his welfare. Voices with accents similar to that of the Guianese and not unlike that of the West Indian immigrants currently arriving to work in parts of the English Midlands. He'd been tempted to respond to them but their apparently mundane existence promised nothing as eventful as his experiences since coming ashore which, even while including moments of concern, he'd come through them unscathed and most certainly were worthy of relating to those back home as they listened in gobsmacked awe. Experiences which likely wouldn't continue should he make that effort to respond to the voices rather than travel on to this mysterious park.

"The Skipper'll be delighted to meet up wi' his favourite shipmate again," was the sneering remark from Jock that helped dampen his growing optimism as they pulled up at a stream much wider and faster flowing than those previously crossed.

"It looks much too deep," groaned the Third, "and we know this old jalopy's not fond of the damp. It might be that we'll have to continue on foot."

"How, er – deep might it be?" asked Daniel, looking uncomfortable. "I – I can't swim," he added as all alighted from the car.

"Nae fuckin' matter, laddie. The Skipper said 'dead or alive'," rasped Jock, his attention suddenly being taken by Heloise slipping out of her frock and entering the water, the garment held above her head.

"It's lovely!" she cried. "So cooling!"

Midstream, the water was up to her neck, then everything was uncaringly on show again as she emerged on the far side and turned to face her fellow travellers.

"Put your frock on for Heaven's sake, Lise!"

The Third's frantic plea for modesty was laughed at as she struck a pose that begged for attention and succeeded.

"That girl will be the death of me!" gasped the Third racing into the water and struggling across until reaching her only to be made fun of as she began skittishly avoiding his attempts to cover up what was meant for his eyes only.

"You're not fit, old Ivor!" she teased as he finally collapsed at the side of the track. "Come on then, you two!" she called out to the pair on the other side still taken with her antics. Daniel was edging towards the water as she called out again.

"You'll make it, Daniel!" she assured him. "Take off that silly jacket and carry it likewise!"

"I – I'm not gonna take it . . ." he began to protest as the Cook propelled him into the water from behind.

"You stole it an' you couldnae care a fuck about carin' for Billy's prize possession!" he yelled.

His criticism escaped the youth as he battled through the torrent until he was alongside the tut-tutting girl.

"You would have found the going much easier without that!" she scolded, tugging at a leopard skin lapel.

"He's nae given to heedin' advice, lassie!" growled Jock, also having crossed. "Let's get walkin'," he added, striding off down the track.

"The – the car . . .! We can't leave it behind! I need it to bargain with the Skipper over our accommodation!"

"And the cat!" joined in Daniel. "Tiggy's still in the car! We can't leave him!"

The youth was ignored while Jock rejoined them and began belittling the Third over not having the nerve to drive the car through the ford.

But even if she'd negotiated the water, getting the electrics wet had always resulted in later problems during previous outings in the Morris, argued the officer.

"Yes, Mr Horton's Morris I told you about didn't like the damp," reiterated Daniel. "We used to stop on the way to school on Winter mornings to watch him pulling on the starter until the battery was dead. Then he'd insert the cranking handle and start cranking away, cursing and red-faced until the engine spluttered into life while clouds of thick smoke poured from the exhaust and we'd all cheer and beg for a lift if he was going our way cos sometimes he'd take another route to his works depending whether or not Mrs Horton happened to be going shopping which sometimes was the case on a Tuesday and Friday and quite often the car wouldn't start at all in which case . . ."

Mr Horton's Winter morning stress wasn't appreciated by Daniel's listeners, least Jock.

"Your Mr Horton never asked you to gi' a hand wi' the crankin' instead o' standin' aroun' gawpin'?" he enquired coldly. "Cos if I'd been in his shoes, I'd have found another use for that fuckin' crankin' handle!"

"Er – what like?" asked Daniel, guardedly.

"I'd have rammed the bastard...!"

"Enough of such vulgarity McLaughlin!" cut in the Third, if only to reassert his authority.

Thankfully, their particular Morris Eight surged easily through the ford and suffered no subsequent problems from damp in the electrics. The cat as usual, was fast asleep on the rear seat when they'd returned to continue their journey. All seemed to have enjoyed their cooling soak and other than Jock's animosity, Daniel was still quietly happy with his time ashore along with such unconventional characters, not least the delectable, unpredictable Heloise who, still carrying her frock seemed comfortable with rejoining him in the rear: a closeness he appreciated until tired, she leaned against him, her bodily warmth and sweet odour combined with the car's vibrating motion began arousing in him feelings more suited to the sheeted privacy of his cabin bunk: feelings he'd rather not have while dressed so inadequately causing him to be grateful for Tiggy having chosen *his* lap to sleep on, Heloise's repeated request to 'have him for a while' being refused causing her muttered annoyance but which to his immense relief, she drowsily accepted. Undoubtedly, had this situation been occurring in the back seat of a car perhaps borrowed from one's dad where it was common knowledge that many sexual liaisons were initiated these days, he'd have been unable to resist. But this wasn't such a situation even while Heloise had closed her eyes and rested her head on his shoulder, her lovely face so close to his, her pert, quivering breasts only inches away from being caressed and the sweet fragrance of her nakedness making resistance nigh on impossible, resist he must! This innocent sleeping beauty was trusting him not to touch. To be protective of such innocence. An innocence that he'd strive to . . .

Innocence? What innocence? This was Heloise! The nymph who'd apparently given herself in broad daylight on Pendine Sands! The insatiable river princess he'd witnessed but hours ago being taken on this very back seat . . .! Well, no. His limited view of the steamy embrace hadn't exactly enabled him to see *copulation* if it had at all taken place. And as for Pendine . . .? Well, the Third could certainly spin a good yarn . . .? Glancing down to where the cat's tail lay across partly open thighs, a thought approaching indecent crossed his mind and Tiggy emitted a sleepy mew of pleasure at being stroked; strokes that grew longer even though most cats don't appreciate their tails being groomed, this one simply purring contentedly while it was Heloise's light gasp that alerted her lover.

"I've been watching you, boyo!" scolded the Third with a chuckle and rearranging the rear-view mirror while Daniel snatched back his hand protesting, "I – was stroking the cat!"

"Did you hear that, McLaughlin? Our Cabin Boy's really taken to pussy back there and can't stop stroking it it seems."

The Third's vulgarity was shared by a cackling Jock and Daniel knew he was in for another roasting.

"Our prisoner's been touchin' up your lady, eh? Well, that'll be another charge he'll be facin' once we get back to the Skipper an' his day o' judgement is nigh cos the park is only a couple o' minutes away! Did you hear me, laddie, a couple o' minutes away."

Moments later, Jock's threats were troubling Daniel as they pulled up in front of tall, impressive wrought iron gates bearing the title *CWMDONKIN PARK*.

"Judgement day, laddie!" growled the Cook. "Judgement day!"

"Ise got a complaint to make, Sister! Dis boy's behaviour is makin' my nerves bad. One minute he's makin' love to his pillow, den next I'm tryin' to re-fix his drip an' he's suddenly reachin' for de hem of my skirt like he's got someting naughty in mind an' he won't desist till I smack his hand an' cos dat ain't no banana he's playin' wid under dem sheets, Nurse Furber an' Ise no longer comfortable givin' him a bed bath, dat's for sure!"

Cwmdonkin Park changed abruptly from Guiana's general flatness and profuse vegetation in that from the moment of passing through its gates, a grassy hillside bearing scattered trees rose steeply up as far as the eye could see. The gates had been opened by a short, elderly hunchbacked man of western appearance who'd spoken to the Third unsmilingly telling him that they'd have to park up and continue on foot.

The name Captain Roberts had been uttered frequently by the officer causing the disgruntled gatekeeper to eventually throw up his arms submissively and allow them to drive on. With its overheated radiator steaming heavily, the car crawled up the steep, winding pathway, the Third resting it at the fourth of several benched sites where they alighted to sit and take in the view of the large bay below. Sitting together in quiet contemplation, the Third and Heloise's mood was one of utter contentment. Even the cat sensed their ease and began to purr and seek fuss from the couple relaxing in the sunshine.

"We're home at last, my sweet," sighed the Third gazing into Heloise's moistening eyes. "We're home at last."

"Dinnae get too fuckin' comfy afore you've had a word wi' the Skipper," intruded Jock spitefully. "He'll decide whose home this is."

"Oh, he will, will he?" enquired an indignant Heloise. "We made this place our home long before your precious Skipper stumbled in. We've long been acquainted with every tree and bush of this place; a place where love is born and lives, not snooty, retired naval officers!" she continued passionately, gesturing out over the descending treetops to the shimmering expanse of the sea. "Only *one* other before us understood and felt the embrace of Cwmdonkin as we do!" she added with a knowing look at the man who held her.

"We'll see about that," muttered Jock sounding not quite so sure of himself. "We'll see what Captain Roberts has to say about . . .!

Booooooooooom!

"Edgar! That'll be Edgar by God!" yelled the Cook, looking genuinely disturbed as he pointed seaward to the obvious source of the siren blast, a solitary ship steaming along the horizon. All joined in the solemn observation of the spectacle, the quiet eventually broken by Daniel determined to lighten things up.

"He, er – Edgar must have got out of his box then? So as to, er – get the engine going and man the wheel: I, er – wonder how he managed that?"

"His box? What box?" asked the Third, still gazing dreamily out to sea.

"The box on the hold that you kicked onto the galley roof," replied Daniel, hoping that his intervention might make the daft lot see sense but getting blank, even hostile, looks he tried again.

"What, er – I'm trying to tell you, Mr Williams, is that it couldn't possibly be Edgar out there because before you went ashore in Mackenzie, something terrible happened to . . ."

"Dinnae let the boy pass on distorted yarns that the Skipper is waitin' only minutes away to pass on factually himself," interrupted Jock. "Only minutes away."

The bandstand stood at the base of a sparsely wooded hillside which they were now descending. It differed from conventional bandstands inasmuch as its open sides had been filled in with interwoven canes and its conical roof was of thatched straw.

"There's no sign of anyone having moved in, darling," said Heloise, hopefully.

"He has, I assure you, lassie," muttered Jock.

Heloise wanted to find out for herself moving faster down the incline, the others at her heels. Approaching the wooden steps leading to the bandstand's darkened entrance, she continued to voice her excitement.

"Our lovely home in the park, Ivor. How could I ever have left it?"

"You'll recall me saying that you'd regret it, my sweet," replied the Third in the same sentimental tone. "But there was no stopping you from flitting off to follow your precious dream."

"And you were so understanding, my darling," purred back Heloise as they embraced each other.

"You are my everything," declared Ivor. "Weren't my letters proof of that?"

"What letters, Ivor, darling?"

"The letters I gave young Daniel here to . . .?

The Third turned to Daniel looking puzzled.

"My letters, Daniel. What did you do with them?"

"Er – you never got round to handing them over, sir. But – but I found them and I, er . . ."

"Thank God for that! They were a declaration of my undying love for Heloise here! Where are they now?"

"Where are they now, er – exactly, sir?"

"Yes! Where are my letters *exactly*, boyo?"

"Er – about two hundred miles off Florida, sir. Or – or thereabouts, sir."

"Two hundred miles off bloody Florida did you say, Cabin Boy? Two hundred miles . . .?"

"Stealin' an' losin' an officer's property's one more charge he'll have put to him any time now if Captain Roberts is home," cut in Jock while writing something down in a suddenly produced notebook.

"If Captain Roberts is *home* did you say?" asked Heloise, her eagerness dissolving as she spoke. "I hope you're not inferring that Captain Roberts has taken up residence in our very own little love nest?"

"That's *exactly* what I'm inferrin', lassie," replied Jock smugly. "Had you nae noticed that?" he added, pointing to a painted sign over the doorway which read *ROBERT'S NEST.*

"He – he did mention it while aboard, my sweet," intervened her beau. "Now, er – lead on, McLaughlin. Let's see if Captain Roberts is in, shall we?"

"Yonder fleabag'll nae be welcome!" warned the Scot indicating Tiggy who'd followed from the car. With Jock leading, the troupe mounted the steps to enter the strange construction but were immediately entangled in a mosquito net suspended over the doorway.

"Who – who the blazes is that?" called out Captain Roberts from somewhere within the dark interior.

Curtains were quickly opened to reveal the Skipper seated on the edge of a large bed rubbing his eyes.

"Sorry, sir," apologized the Cook disentangling himself from the net. "I did a wee cough an' I'm sure you'll excuse my abrupt entry when I tell you that both absconders are in my custody."

"Good for you, McLaughlin. Let me pour myself a scotch and light up a ciggy and you'll have my full attention."

All but the cat were now free of the net and were studying the bandstand's homely interior which, to Daniel, closely resembled the Skipper's *Roundcape* accommodation in layout and opulence. In fact, what he was seeing, the Skipper now on his feet looking authoritative in his immaculate white uniform, scotch in one hand, cigarette in the other, was a virtual re-enactment of the day he'd been summoned to his quarters and quizzed over the Third Mate's disappearance.

About to address them, Captain Roberts suddenly became aware of Heloise who'd modestly slipped back into her frock before entering.

"Introduce me then, Ivor. The young lady I presume is the one rumoured to be involved in you losing your . . . er – in your illness?"

"Marbles! In him losing his marbles is what you were about to say!" interrupted Jock rudely. "Am I nae right, sir?"

"Quiet, McLaughlin!" retorted the Captain. "And show more respect for an officer if you will? Now," he added in the same serious tone, "I believe you've made a list of the charges to be put to our Cabin Boy here? And incidentally pray, why on Earth is he wearing that silly jacket which he would appear to be wearing back to front?"

"Recommended by myself, sir," explained the Third, "for the sake of common decency, sir."

"Common decency be fucked!" interrupted the Cook again. "If you'll ask the lad to turn aroun' you'll be faced wi' the same bare arse that I've been tempted to gi' a good kickin' these last few hours!"

"Not true!" offered the Third indignantly. "His arse . . . er – his bottom, sir, is only in view when he's forgotten to fasten the, er – last button, sir and – and . . ."

"It – it was like one of those peculiar dreams, sir," piped up Daniel. "If – if you've ever had one, sir? When you're out and about and suddenly you find you're . . ."

"When you're out in public inadequately attired, eh, son?" smiled the Captain. "Yes, I think most of us would have had that particular dream. Most embarrassing, eh, son? Most embarrassing. Now, let us get on with the business in hand. The charges if you will, McLaughlin. The charges."

"An' about fuckin' time too!" groaned Jock. "The first charge bein' that o' desertion which speaks for itself so I'll go straight to . . ."

"And if it's just your shirt you're wearing, young man," chuckled Captain Roberts addressing Daniel, "you keep tugging at the hem hoping to God that it's long enough to . . .?"

"So I'll go straight to the attempted murder charges!" bellowed the Cook, clearly not happy with the repartee between Captain and Cabin Boy. "The first one bein' the attempted drownin' o' Mr King, the Chief Cook an' meself by allowin' a hurricane propelled sea to invade our place o' work, the galley o' *MV Roundcape*."

"Blooming rubbish!" protested Daniel. "If you'd not lost your temper and tried pinning me against the bulkhead with the blooming door! No water would've got in!"

"You'll be given the opportunity to answer the charges later in the proceedings," advised a suddenly officious Captain Roberts.

"An' also, two attempts at murderin' the ship's Donkeyman!" continued Jock.

"He – he's not dead then ?" enquired Daniel, visibly relieved.

"The laddie's unwittingly revealin' his involvement it seems?" snarled the Scot. "An' his attemptin' to murder me a second time'll be easy to pin on the wee bastard, there bein' witnesses who'll say they saw him thrustin' the broken bottle at me that night in Mackenzie!"

"Good God!" gasped the Skipper. "Are McLaughlin's claims true, young man ?"

"I – I'm not used to alcohol, sir and it's all been a kind of nightmare which has sort of blurred things since going ashore with the Donkeyman. But I might well have had a go at the Cook, sir, cos the bully's had it in for me since Cardiff. He even knocked me unconscious for just whistling up the blooming wind, sir."

Captain Roberts's grim expression had Daniel regretting his not making an effort to join those other voices which now seemed to have given up on him. These regrets grew stronger as Jock continued.

"Captain Roberts, sir. You asked just now about the jacket he's wearin'. Well, sir, he stole it an' while theft cannae be ranked wi' attempted murder, it nevertheless, as you know, in the old days would, at sea, be a crime punishable wi' lashes or even a keel-haulin'."

"That's true, McLaughlin. From whom did he steal the jacket? A jacket, I might add, that I find so preposterously garish that, if mine, I'd be happy for someone to steal."

"The little thief stole it from me, sir!" declared Billy White negotiating the mosquito net while allowing the cat to enter with him unnoticed. Now dressed in vest and shorts, he joined the others confronting the Captain.

"That *preposterously garish* jacket is *mine* I'll have you know, sir and was designed by Bristol's top tailors whose elite clientele included . . .!"

"Beau fuckin' Brummel I shouldnae wonder!" interjected the Cook. "Now shut your gob, Billy, while we see that the Cabin Boy here gets his comeuppance!"

With Billy's arrival being accepted with the same indifference as any other bizarre happening, Daniel chose to concern himself with his immediate problems rather than to ask pointless questions, his main worry now being that with those other voices having ceased leaving him with no apparent escape route, he'd have to accept this surreal place until an option hopefully presented itself. In the meantime for his *health's* sake, he'd try to appease and play along with them.

"The, er – charges, sir," he began politely, "they can all be explained by the circumstances I found myself in at the time, sir. The, er – jacket for instance, I borrowed it to wear ashore after being stripped of my clothes while . . ."

"While pissed!" completed Jock vehemently. "He stole White's jacket in order to jump ship after beatin' the Donkeyman half to death! A *circumstance* any fool would be anxious to be away frae, eh, sir?"

"I – I came ashore because I was concerned about Mr Williams' welfare. I – I intended to come straight back," lied

Daniel. "Mr Williams went ashore in the mistaken belief that Edgar, er – Mr Reece had gone ahead of him to the, er – park as he told me. But – but, as most of us know now, sir, poor old Edgar was still, er – on board."

"Ah yes, son! I recall you telling me as much just after the event and I'd become interested in your exact involvement with Mr Reece and Mr Williams here: particularly in respect of what you may have overheard regards their complicated private lives which I'm told led to much bickering between them. Bickering which a certain crew member, namely seaman Ianto Morgan, suggested was attributed to the fact of Mr Williams being enamoured with Mr Reece's wife. Was this suggested association through your friendship with the said officers, known to you is what I'd like to know?"

"Er – en' what sir? An' – and Ianto had a reputation for spinning . . ."

"Enamoured, son. In your parlance *the hots*! Did our Third Mate Mr Williams have the hots for the wife of Mr Reece do you know?"

Daniel sheepishly glanced over to the Third who appeared as nonplussed as himself but who then mouthed an emphatic, "No!"

Confident now as to reply, the youth turned back to the Skipper.

"Oh no, sir! It wasn't Mr Williams who had the, er – hots for Edgar's missus! Mr Williams wouldn't spread himself around while he's got Heloise here! Ianto's just stirring things up like and he hasn't read all of the soppy, er – love letters from Mr Williams to his lady here as I did while convalescing in . . ."

He sensed the Third's accusing looks.

"I – I think that you'll find Ianto's got Mr Williams mixed up with somebody else who was said to be getting his bread buttered on both sides as was the joke aboard . . ."

"What are you sayin', son?"

The Skipper's ears had pricked up at this revelation.

349

"Are you suggesting, son, that a third party was involved in the alleged adulterous behaviour of Mr Reece's wife? If so and even if only to clear the name of our Mr Williams here, then please name that party?"

Daniel shuffled awkwardly, his eyes meeting the Third's once more but in vain.

"The name of this third party, son, if you please?" demanded the Skipper.

"I, er – well – it was mentioned that a, er – third party was mucking about with Mr Reece's wife, sir. But – but don't, er – take this as gospel cos . . ."

"Who, son?"

"Er – Crusty Lightfoot, sir."

"Crusty Lightfoot? Who the devil is Crusty Lightfoot?"

"Their, er – baker, sir. Mr and Mrs Reece's baker so I was led to believe, sir."

"I just knew it wouldn't be my Ivor mucking about with Mrs Reece!" cried Heloise tearfully. "One only has to read his sentimental letters to me for proof of that!"

"Please don't distress yourself, young lady," consoled the Skipper. "I'm sure those letters were as sincere as you would wish them to be. But in those written during his time aboard the *Roundcape*, might there have been anything *between the lines*, as it were, that caused you to be the slightest bit suspicious?"

"No. Not in those particular letters because I didn't receive them."

"You didn't receive them, young lady? Why ever not and where are they now?"

"Two hundred fuckin' miles off Florida's the answer to that one if you insist on pursuin' this pathetic twaddle!" interrupted an impatient Jock. "Your schemin' Cabin Boy's started this bullshit in order to distract you frae the matter in hand, cannae you see?"

"Is Mr McLaughlin correct, son?"

"No, sir and Mr Williams will back me up I'm sure, won't you, Mr Williams?"

"Well – in respect of Crusty Lightfoot's involvement, yes, Daniel," began the Third hesitantly. "But the gravity of those other charges is such that I daren't be seen as backing you up; especially your jumping ship because I was a witness to your doing so when you arrived ashore."

"But – but you jumped ship as well, so how come you're not being blooming-well charged? It's just not fair."

Because Mr Williams wasn't of sound mind when he took that action, son," sided the Skipper. "Wouldn't you agree, Mr McLaughlin?"

"Aye, sir, I couldnae agree more! The officer's prescribed delusory medication washed down wi' three large bottles o' jungle juice combined wi' the stress o' his nae gettin' his leg over the bonnie lassie here for a couple o' years could well have contributed to the malaise you describe."

"I – I'm not sure how to take that?" protested the Third.

"Don't take offence, Ivor," calmed the Skipper. "Our Cook and Cabin Boy aren't to blame for their lack of respect. Their inferior upbringings would have seen them develop clueless of the system."

"What fuckin' *system*?" ventured Jock.

"The system that gives a commissioned officer from whatever service, preferential treatment to that of his subordinates," replied the Skipper pompously. "The system that condemns and punishes a lowly Cabin Boy simply because of him being lowly and lets an officer off with a strongly worded caution followed by a gin and tonic in the mess; or at the worst, he's asked to resign and face the consequences of such a resignation."

"The poor sod!" sympathized Jock. "An' what kind o' consequences is an early retired officer likely to face?"

"He, er . . ." Captain Roberts began to reply less confidently, "if say, he were below the age, er – forty and not retired on full pay then he might have to purchase a 'house' rather than a 'residence' befitting his officer status and – and have to live with the ignomy of having lower class neighbours who, say when dining out, might confront and embarrass him with their lower class accents similar to those subordinates who . . ."

"Who got a hundred lashes or a keel haulin' for a lesser offence than the fucker he was asked to resign on full pay over!" completed the Cook with more than a hint of sarcasm. "An' forgive my curiosity, sir but these dinin' places where gentry would prefer not to sup wi' subordinates? The staff I presume would respect class an' nae get pissin' in the gravy or gobbin' in the mashed potatoes an' go draggin' one's steak about the deck wi' the ship's, er – establishment's cat in pursuit like I've seen happen when a stroppy officer's given a Table Steward a bad day?"

All eyes fell on the only Table Steward present.

"You'd not dare do as McLaughlin describes would you, White?" enquired the Skipper in disgust.

"Of course not, sir!" assured Billy. "But you know that fish pie that's been sittin' on your bureau waitin' your attention this last twenty minutes an' the ship's cat sittin' beside it lickin' 'is chops . . .?"

"Where – where did that animal come from?" yelled the Skipper. "Get rid of it!

"I'll get rid o' the bastard!" bellowed Jock but too late with his boot as Tiggy raced out. "I'll skin it alive!" he threatened. "Now, for fuck's sake, let's get yonder Cabin Boy's trial an' punishment over wi! It's gettin' more like the Mad Hatter's Tea Party than a session o' maritime fuckin' law!"

"I – I've got a compromise to offer, sir."

Daniel's bold intervention surprised even himself.

"If – if you kindly get my cards together, sir, I'll bid you all goodbye and head back to Ffokcuf where, to my utter delight, I discovered last night, Hilary, the love of my life now lives and has been waiting for me these last few months. And, sir, once reunited as is the total bliss of Mr Williams and Heloise here, we'll head for Georgetown and the embassy in order to be transferred back to Cardiff where I'll get a job in the docks and

352

get married. That, sir, will be the end of all our problems wouldn't you agree?"

All eyes stared blankly at the maturing Cabin Boy as the captain began praising his eloquent speech.

"Well spoken, son. A good old romance always goes down well in my book. I'll get your cards and you can be on your way with the blessings of us all."

A tense quiet followed his good wishes until an incensed Jock sprang to life.

"An' a fuckin' whip roun' to boot as soon as I lay my mitts on a fuckin' whip! The wee bastard's makin' a mockery o' the whole proceedings an' you're lettin' the fucker get away wi' it!"

"Well, you've maybe got a point, McLaughlin," condescended Captain Roberts, "but it was a bloody good speech wouldn't you agree? Oh well yes, he certainly doesn't understand the gravity of the charges," he added, while pouring himself another large whisky and lighting up a cigarette.

"Let us refer back to the most serious charge he faces which I'd say was the tipping of the pantry slops over the boarding Guianese customs officials or oh yes, there was that particularly disastrous morning when his inefficiency caused my kipper to be a good three minutes late. Or could it . . .?"

"Or could it mebbe that he caused the Chief Donkeyman to become a gibberin', sexual psychopath by hangin' his Y-fronts outside his boat-deck accommodation?" was Jock's sarcastic offering. "Just ask the schemin' wee bastard about the mornin' he tried drownin' the ship'sCooks!"

"I was coming to that dreadful occasion, McLaughlin," answered the Captain turning towards Daniel.

"Did you, young man, on that morning of hurricane weather, enter the galley intent on harming theCooks?"

"No, sir."

"What intent had you in mind, son?"

"To get your kipper, sir."

"The wee Sassenach bastard's at it again, sir! He's makin' a mockery o' the whole fuckin' business!"

"Try to answer without upsetting Mr McLaughlin, son. I'll repeat my question. Did you that morning enter the galley with murderous intent?"

"No, I entered with half of the blooming Atlantic, sir! And – and I nigh on shit myself I did, sir!"

Jock groaned loudly then bellowed, "I cannae believe you're lettin' him get away wi' such contempt! Ask him why the fuck he came to the *weather side* to gain entry? In layman's terms the *Dangerous* side in such conditions! Ask him that!"

"The blooming weather was all over the place and I couldn't tell weather from lea side, sir," countered Daniel. "It was, er – very stormy."

"Very stormy was it, son? But you still rather stupidly ventured out in such weather without assessing any possible consequences it would seem?"

"Well, er – I'd little choice, sir, cos the Chief told me that you'd throw a wobbly if you didn't get your kipper on time."

"He did, did he, son? A slight exaggeration but yes, I am a stickler for getting my meals on time, so credit to you for making an effort in such weather and, by the way, did you sustain any injuries by perhaps colliding with the bulkheads during your water-borne entrance to the galley?"

"Er – not by colliding with the bulkheads, sir but I did sustain injuries to the head by it colliding with a, er – frying pan, sir."

"What frying pan, son?"

"The biggest one old bully-boy Jock here could lay his hands on, sir."

"He's lyin' so as get your sympathy, sir!" yelled Jock. "He's been lyin' an' skulkin' since Cardiff has the wee stirrin' anti-Celt bastard!"

"Well, we are a largely Celt crew and he's certainly in the minority aboard but anti-Celt's a little strong, eh, McLaughlin?" remarked the Skipper.

"I'm not blooming-well anti-Celt!" spouted Daniel, eager to correct the suggestion. "Haven't I always headed aft for good company and found it with the Deckies? And Mr Williams here's been like a dad to me! That's why I followed him ashore cos I – I was lost without him. He used to have me in stitches with his tales about Heloise and himself shadowing this poet chap who he said came over to the masses as the Welshest intellectual of all time but who was happiest when having a pint and a joke with the lads. What a shipmate he would have been! An' – and there was old Donald Peers who me mom and sisters would sit swooning over around the wireless while I followed me dad out of the room at the very first note of *Babbling Brook* when really, I'd got my ear pressed to the door the whole half hour of . . ."

"I rather think you've convinced us that Mr McLaughlin's accusation can be disregarded," intervened the Captain. "but I'll have to refer to my dictionary with regard to the word *'Welshest'*!"

The Cook's resulting protests were overlooked once again and the Cabin Boy was beginning to sense that his pro-Welsh stand was winning the day. But Jock was determined to win over the Skipper by fair means or foul.

"Sir," he began, his eyes narrowed with malice. "The laddie's statement just now about him following Mr Williams ashore because 'he was lost wi'out him'? Well sir, never let it be said that I'm one for spreadin' vile gossip aboard but the Cabin Boy here seems to be convincin' you that he's as pure as the driven snow, I'd nae be doin' my duty under your command if I concealed frae you the true nature o' the Cabin Boy's prolonged visits to Mr Williams' accommodation as told to me by somebody in the know. Visits which were contrary to maritime law in that they were *sexually* motivated!"

"Absolute and utter tosh!" protested the Third, clutching Heloise tightly around the waist. "My *nature* is obvious to anyone!"

"Any port in a storm!" cackled Jock evilly. "An' to further open your eyes, sir, question the laddie about his lifelong companion, a certain Maurice Bloom who he pursued halfway across England through bein' emotionally distraught!"

"Such – such accusations!" gasped Captain Roberts. "I sincerely hope that they're strongly denied by you too, son? Does being *emotionally distraught* mean that you were in love with this Maurice Bloom?"

"That I . . .? How stupid can you get?" erupted Daniel. "Maurice is a *boy's* name and while I wish luck to those whose nature is otherwise, I was as much attracted to Maurice as I am to the great hairy haggis who's filling your mind with such rubbish!"

"You cheeky wee bastard, I'll . . .!" Jock, about to lunge at the increasingly angered Cabin Boy, hesitated as the Skipper delved further.

"So, if your fervent pursuit of this Maurice Bloom wasn't motivated by feelings of the heart, son, what did motivate it?"

"Not because of being emotionally distraught, that's for blooming sure, sir! I was peeved by Mrs Bloom rolling up the lino and doing a bunk with Maurice as she did! I'd never had a mate quite like him. We'd have these imaginary adventures around his place and along the Wharrage brook and not long before he left, this, er – young lady had begun visiting his field, so I was curious to know if she'd followed him to Coventry, me not having seen her since they'd vacated the place in such a mysterious way if, er – you understand what I'm saying, sir?"

"Of course I understand what you are saying, son. You were emotionally distraught over Maurice leaving you for this, er – mysterious young lady whom he'd likely found more attractive. Then on discovering the truth over at Coventry, you joined the Merchant Service in a state of rejection which resulted in you venting your feelings on your fellow seamen in a manner that brought about the charges that you face today. Am I correct?"

"Most certainly not, sir. But if I say yes, will you please give me a commission and accept my immediate resignation and we'll drink to it in the saloon with a gin and tonic?"

As to whether or not Captain Roberts accepted Daniel's resignation was lost in the following uproar which had Jock cursing the youth for his impudence; the Third and Heloise attempting to barter with the Skipper over what they claimed was *their* accommodation and Billy protesting about not having the theft of his jacket resolved. The man considering their arguments however, was looking tired of the noisy assembly who'd disturbed the tranquillity of his stay in the park and so began ejecting them with the threat not to return unless summoned!

Outside, it was the Cabin Boy they turned on for having none of their problems resolved until it was realized that blaming him was futile and ways of re-approaching the Skipper began to be aired. Daniel though, feeling the odd man out, said nothing and was now beginning to regret not answering the friendly voices which had surely abandoned him to face the consequences of his obstinacy. This regret was growing by the minute: he wanted a way out!

It was Heloise who unwittingly led him to a possible way out on becoming aware of his troubled look.

"Fancy some exploring?" she suddenly asked, taking him by the hand and leading him away from the bandstand, the others seemingly too absorbed in conversation to notice their departure.

"There's a small lake down in that far corner of the park," she told him. "Let's go and cool off shall we?"

He'd not seen any water other than the sea since entering the park but, surely enough, after pushing through a small spinney in the direction she'd indicated, they arrived on the banks of a small stretch of water.

"Let's sit for a while in the peace and quiet," she whispered, moving close to him as they settled in the warmth of a perpetual sun. "When did you first become fascinated with me, Daniel?" she asked, softly and unexpectedly. "Is it right that you spent a lot of time looking at my photos?" she continued, putting an arm around his shoulders and kissing his cheek.

"Mr, er – Williams told you that did he?" he asked shyly but quietly enjoying her sudden tenderness. "Well, er – yes, I did spend some time looking at . . ."

"And what were you thinking as you looked?" she chuckled, throwing her arms about him in a full embrace. "Tell me please. What were your thoughts?"

"I – I'm not as good as your Mr Williams with words but I – I wondered what it would feel like to kiss that lovely mouth because it looked so soft and, er – kissable and – and I wondered what it would be like to stroke that silky, black hair while looking into those lovely, smiling eyes which I knew would be the colour of the sea before . . ."

"Before a storm" she completed with a sigh. "Oh, darling Ivor does have a way with words but I wanted to hear *your* thoughts, Daniel. And why *that* lovely mouth and *that* silky, black hair when you have the real thing right beside you?"

He knew what she was saying but still hesitated to react should she be teasing?

"Maybe I can tempt you this way?" she cried, scrambling to her feet and slipping out of the frock. "I'm told you were so desperate to ogle me that you tried scratching off my painted bikini!" she taunted, posing brazenly for a fleeting moment before turning to dash headlong into the water.

"Come on in then!" she called out while splashing about childishly. "It's wonderful!"

He'd not miss out this time, was the lascivious thought that overruled his concern over Billy's jacket getting yet another soaking as he joined her in the water.

To take the drape off and engage with her in the buff would have been the obvious thing to do if only he shared her exhibitionist nature and it was no surprise when she began ridiculing him for not having the courage to take off his restricting attire and began teasing him by agilely evading his every attempt to fondle her nakedness before eventually swimming off to her right and disappearing beneath a clump of bushes at the water's edge.

A non-swimmer, he followed her by wading close to the bank until reaching the overhanging bushes. Ducking beneath them, he came across a slow-running tributary which he followed a short distance finding no trace of her but continuing on, fascinated by things pleasantly familiar to him such as the rippling sound of water at his feet, birdsong in the dense overhang of bushes and trees along the banks of this meandering waterway all giving him peace of mind and a sense of belonging.

"Daniel!"

She was concealed close by, her tone as she called friendly and inviting, causing him indecision. Should he seek her out and indulge in the mystery of sex as she had clearly been offering minutes earlier? Or should he search further into this waterway? About to settle for the latter, she emerged from the bushes so sexually alluring, her smile so promising that it overwhelmed all rationality and sent him blindly rushing from the water into the open arms of . . . Billy!

"This fuckin'-well belongs to me!" yelled the Assistant Steward who'd appeared from nowhere to retrieve his jacket which he swiftly peeled off Daniel's back then sprinted back in the direction of the bandstand leaving one startled and naked Cabin Boy to dash for cover in the handiest clump of bracken.

"Keep blooming-well away!" he yelled, as a grinning Heloise approached, his shyness having demolished his libido.

"We're equal now!" she teased, not helping his acute embarrassment. "So what's keeping you?"

"You – you've got to find me something to wear!" he appealed to her. "Anything, please!"

"Okay," she answered playfully while uprooting long grass and bracken from around his hiding place.

"Don't be blooming-well stupid! I can't parade around wearing . . .!

But he could! Hadn't he and the boys, while larking about in the woods stripped off and dressed themselves as primitive warriors utilising anything to hand?

"But – but I'll need string or something to, er – keep it together?" he found himself asking absurdly through sheer desperation.

Heloise had the answer to this too as she began unthreading the hem of her discarded frock until she'd enough strands of cotton to nimbly fashion a waistband strong enough to support the rudimentary garment which he gratefully and hastily donned just in time for Billy returning along with the Skipper, Jock and the Third. If the Steward had brought them along to poke fun at his lack of clothing, his new apparel was equally as funny judging by how all but the Skipper fell about laughing on seeing him. Even Heloise couldn't hold back a snigger as he confronted those mocking, angrily.

"What's so blooming-well funny?" he wanted to know, causing more hysterics.

"Noth' – nothin', Danny boy!" howled Billy. "Ev' – every Montague Burtons in the fuckin' Congo are stockin' that particular line!"

"That's quite enough levity for one day!" bawled the Skipper, much to Daniel's relief. "We're not here to poke fun at the boy! We're here to once and for all determine his mental state."

His authoritative intervention brought about an ominous silence as he turned to address Daniel.

"Yes, son," he continued, "in your absence this last hour, individuals have discussed their grievances with me and, after much debate, it had been concluded that your mental state while serving aboard my ship has been both indirectly and directly to blame for the said grievances."

"Which, er – individuals concluded that my mental state has been both indirectly and directly largely to blame for the said grievances?" enquired a bravely sarcastic Daniel.

"Well, er – Mr McLaughlin was very vocal in apportioning blame," replied the Captain sheepishly. "But I personally, before reinstating you in a straitjacket and locking you away, wish to ask your good self a few questions about your background which might explain your becoming, as Mr McLaughlin suggests, the scourge of the British Merchant Navy. He is also convinced that your mental state led you into becoming a habitual criminal and that you joined up in order to escape justice ashore. Is he correct in guessing that you have a history of criminality?"

"Er – not really. Oh, that is all but my handcuffing Dennis Skinner to the back of the greengrocer's cart then going in for my tea and forgetting about him," replied Daniel, determined to answer stupidity with stupidity. "But Dennis was only dragged a few yards until the greengrocer heard him screaming and covered in shit."

"Defecate himself through fear did he?"

"Oh no. It was the horse's shit that he was covered in because it was always inclined to drop a load outside our house which me dad used to get me to shovel up and mix with the chicken shit to help the celery on. I think that's why I've never been partial to celery!"

"Celery's a fine vegetable," commented the Skipper, "an' *umbelliferous* delight my wife calls it. Very partial to a stick of celery is Mrs Roberts."

"I'll bet she didn't shovel horse and chicken shit around it," came Daniel's less grand reply, goading Jock to intervene furiously.

"Why the fuck is the laddie allowed to bring chaos to order?" he remonstrated. "Cannae you see that he's got his canny way to change the run o' things when everythin's stacked against the cheeky wee bastard? I suggest we move back to your pad, sir, an' proceed in an atmosphere more in keepin' wi' a maritime court o' law."

"May I kindly remind you at this point just *whose* pad Captain Roberts is *temporarily* residing in?" enquired an indignant Third Mate, unhappy that the return of his accommodation had not yet been resolved. "So would you not waste any more time, McLaughlin and put the matter of the swop to Captain Roberts!" he added sternly.

"Did you hear that, sir?" the Cook enquired of the Skipper.

"Did I hear *what*, Mc Laughlin?"

"Mr Williams here, sir, has a suggestion to put to you concerning the venue of the boy's trial. A venue where charges o' theft, desertion an' attempted murder will be heard. Charges so grave as back home they'd likely be heard in the highest o' courts an' wi' that in mind, sir, Mr Williams, in the circumstances we find ourselves, wishes to offer you in return for your present accommodation, a venue considerably more salubrious an' suitable for such high profile proceedings to be conducted."

"Such as?"

"A pre-war Morris Eight in mint condition wi' a useable spare wheel, sir."

Predictably and as Jock had intended, the Captain for the second time in an hour launched a verbal attack which continued as he literally herded his irritating visitors back towards his accommodation."

"Not you!" he bawled at Daniel. "Not until you're suitably attired to face the charges!"

Heloise too was singled out and ordered to, "stay with him and see that he's dressed in a fitting manner!"

Where he might find clothes of a *fitting manner* was of little concern to the youth. He'd been on the verge of escaping this surreal pantomime and now had a second chance which he most certainly wasn't going to miss! He'd found the route home and once they'd moved off with the their backs towards him . . .

"Weird kinda coma dis boy's in! If de doc' hadn't done as we asked an' had him strapped down in a blessed cot, Ise sure he'd have bin out of dis place like a shot! Looked like he was runnin' in bed! Runnin' in bed I tell you!"

That they'd turned to see him in flight, caught up with him and as threatened, reintroduced him to the straitjacket, was his immediate thought on coming to. But curiously, he wasn't restrained in any way and then recalled the mad dash along the waterway he'd discovered earlier until reasonably sure he wasn't being followed, he'd flopped down exhausted at this particular spot. Not followed . . .? Well, that is except for the person instructed to stay with him. . .?

Heloise, hands on naked hips stood smiling at him from shallow water barely up to her knees.

"I slept a while myself," she yawned, striking the pose that had likely inspired someone to call her his *river princess*, that same someone who'd once enthused to Daniel that while clothes enhance most women, rare specimens of total perfection such as his Heloise need no enhancement.

"Why – why did you follow me?" he asked eventually.

"You heard the Captain tell me to stay with you," she replied, leaving the water to sit beside him on the grassy bank wearing that same flirtatious smile as earlier by the pool.

This time however, he would not be weakened by her charms. His mind was set on going home; the return of the voices just now had helped make the decision to be on his way: and alone.

"You must go back. You don't belong where I'm going. I – I think that you've been playing games with me and I've decided that you belong back there with . . ."

"With Ivor," she completed for him. "Well, I too have been trying to make a decision, Daniel," she continued minus the smile."I've never quite settled as I believe you gathered from what Ivor let slip while trying to impress you with stories about the perfect union. Perfect in his mind but not so perfect in mine while there were distractions which I also believe you learned about through his fanciful anecdotes and also through tittle-tattle fed to you by his supposed best shipmate . . .!

"Edgar . . .? You mean Edgar don't you? Like him telling me that you, er – dumped him for, er – somebody else which hurt him so much that he began making up yarns which he even started believing himself and – and . . .!"

Daniel faltered purposely. He was stupidly allowing himself to be sidetracked from his new resolve and if he continued he'd find himself delving back into the *as likely*, concocted tale about her fascination with the poet chap which saw her following him to New York and vanishing off the face of the . . . Oh no! He was done with the fantasy world of Mr Williams and co'! He was finished with all that crap and was going home! Better convince her of exactly that!

"I'm going home!" he announced loudly. "Right now!"

"Not before you've explained to me how Edgar arrived at the *dumping* notion?" she replied clearly hurt. "Nothing was further from my mind during our wonderful times together in the park, on Pendine and along the Gower! It was only restless me that disturbed the bliss. Even my parents called me a 'wild child', difficult to tame. I was barely in my teens when I lost myself to the Gower, that unspoilt gem that Swansea still tries to hide from the outside world. *Heloland* I named it on declaring that magical peninsula mine and before my sixteenth birthday I knew virtually every inch of its changing shoreline from its vast, empty beaches and remote coves to its spectacular headlands created for quiet contemplation as was discovered by . . ."

Heloise appeared to be in quiet contemplation herself but the pause only lasted seconds and she'd a suggestion to put to him.

"That's it, Daniel! You and I! Before you make for home let's both enjoy the Gower, eh?"

Her proposition, while tempting, had him worried. Why *him* and not . . .?

"Er – what about . . ?"

"Ivor? Oh he'll follow undoubtedly but in the meantime . . . I mean, you sometimes look at me as if you wanted to eat me while just now, back there in the bandstand you were off to marry somebody named Hilary? So, as I was about to say, in the meantime, you and I . . .?"

Well, yes . . . if she was game, why not? His mention of Hilary had only been a ploy to get him out of an unpleasant situation, so before those voices came back and made him rethink and spoiled his chances of frolicking on sun-kissed beaches with his own 'Flower of the Gower', he must be decisive and fully embrace what may never be offered again and was about to say 'yes', of course I'll come with you, the most beautiful woman I've ever seen both in photos and real life. Of course we'll go together to those Gower beaches and even to Cwmdonkin Park if our love dictates so because you'll obviously come to realize that there's more fun in the arms of a young . . . ?

"Looking forward to seeing your pal Maurice again, eh?"

Her question stopped his thoughts dead! Her tone suggested she knew more about this old friend than those stupid remarks uttered by the Skipper back there in the bandstand. His dream of paradise turned to uneasy suspicion.

"You'll be hoping that the Blooms saw sense and came back with Maurice to the cottage I guess?" she continued knowingly. "That would be icing on the cake for your homecoming would it not, Daniel? Would it not I ask?"

She was goading him into replying and appeared to be enjoying having rendered him speechless.

"You – you know about Maurice?"

He appeared stunned as he found his voice and struggled to put a question together.

"You – you know about Maurice and – and about the, er – Blooms?"

"Do I know about Maurice and his family?"

Her tone suggested that of course she knew the Blooms! Why ever should she not?

"I know about them and about you! You ought surely recall that I do, Daniel?" she stressed with a teasing grin that increased his discomfort. "At the Bloom's place and wherever you and Maurice chose to conjure me up? Two growing lads with vivid imaginations which made it easy for me to slip back to the holiday home of my early childhood where, until my accident and the war brought more permanent residents who . . ."

"Over there! I heard somethin' a wee bit upstream!"

Jock's shout startled Daniel almost as much as Heloise's curtailed revelation which, while intriguing, made his flight both, more urgent and that it ought be *'alone'*.

"I've left my frock under that bush over there!" she told him, sensing his panic and pointing to the opposite bank. "I'll get it and come with you!"

She was only halfway across when he slowed his pace briefly to glance back and then there was nothing stopping him as he drove on, sometimes in the water and sometimes where growth was sparse, along the banks; any route that put distance between him and anyone following! Some fifteen minutes on he paused and was relieved to hear no sound in his wake. He guessed that Heloise had had another change of mind, especially as he'd not waited for her which he felt a little guilty about but could certainly do without she further hindering his now positive objective. Yes, best to continue alone, alert to the chance of harm along the uncertain path a possibility while she, undoubtedly belonged back in Cwmdonkin, would likely be safe. So onward he must go along this watercourse which, from the moment of him discovering it, had offered hope and now had him certain that he would eventually come across things familiar such as oddly-shaped willows clinging precariously from sheer banks rising from the snaking water. Banks that he would climb and hopefully recognize as territory roamed and often claimed in the adventure of boyhood.

He pushed on, not so quickly now with no apparent pursuers but very soon, his initial optimism fizzled as the going became more difficult, the water murky and even swampy along some stretches. Even the overhanging tree branches so reminiscent of his own brook had reduced to a tunnel of rotting, smelly vegetation becoming smaller and gloomier with each arduous step. Much disheartened, on arriving at a small break in the meandering tunnel, he scrambled out of the now boggy crevice to find himself in dense woodland. Selecting the easiest to climb of the taller trees, he hauled himself up branch by branch to reconnoitre his surroundings.

What he saw confirmed his growing fear. No rolling Worcestershire countryside this terrain! An ocean of thick, green jungle stretching in every direction finally convincing him that this route was not the route home! Before descending, was a shout even worthwhile?

"Mauriiiiiice! Mauriiiiiice!"

"Dere ain't no Maurice in dis ward, young man, shout as you may an' dere's de other patients whose not too happy wid your noise so shut it before de doctor comes lookin' wid dat big needle what some says he's been stickin' in you when nobody's about."

❖ ❖ ❖ ❖ ❖ ❖ ❖ ❖

"Danieeeeeel!"

At last! Maurice had heard him calling from his own treetop perch just a couple of hundred feet away and was waving back! and he'd been about to climb down disillusioned and lost as what to do and now, his old chum Maurice was pointing. Pointing at . . . Yes! He was pointing to where the horizon was formed by the undulating humps of the Malverns, exactly as if they were viewing them from their old school playground! And – and just forward and to the west of the Malvern chain, Bredon hill! What a stroke of luck! Such a coincidence that he'd left the watercourse where Maurice just happened to be up to his old sport of tackling the loftiest of trees and having spotted him doing likewise, was welcoming him by indicating landmarks familiar to both! Good old Maurice! But – but Maurice had vanished as quickly as he'd appeared! Perhaps – perhaps he'd climbed down to rendezvous with him further along the watercourse which, because hereabouts bore some resemblance, must be . . .? Just had to be . . .? Their brook! The Wharrage brook!

"Yippeeeeeee!"

Invigorated, he literally tumbled from the branches and within seconds had resumed his upstream slog confident now that his route would lead him to familiar territory where Maurice would be waiting agog with questions to put to his seafaring chum!

367

Seemingly hours on and just when his spirits were beginning to flag again, his prayers were answered as the murky, static water as his feet became clear and flowing and he emerged from the dark canopy into a green, sunlit dell alive with Nature in her prime.

He was elated! No Maurice, but this was the place where they'd spent many carefree hours. Where they'd dammed the brook to indulge in a Summertime bathe and there, in the exposed roots of that large Ash, the foxhole they'd enlarged to form a hideaway from which to spy on the girls playing in the trapped water. A great place to linger but home beckoned as *Barwick Green* rang out full volume from the open window of a not too distant house. A quarter to seven. *The Archers* radio serial always commenced at quarter to seven weekday evenings. Tea would be over and mom would have sent dad out to potter in his shed in order for her to absorb fifteen minutes of 'the lives of everyday country folk'. Fifteen minutes for him to slip over and observe the Blooms busying about their newly-returned-to home. Mrs Bloom's face would be a picture of contentment he knew, on recalling her wistful look when he'd told her how cold and empty their old cottage in the field had looked following their leaving for Coventry. Yes, he'd slip over there and see their joy firsthand. Mr Bloom's beaming fixed smile as he turned over the rich, black soil in readiness for another bumper crop and Mrs Bloom cranking up a nice new shiny bucket filled with well-water more natural and cleaner than anything she'd got from her city tap.

About to venture forth to the happy, healthy Blooms, his unconventional attire made him hesitate. So dressed, he'd face ridicule should he meet anyone along the Walkwood road. His return from the training school wearing his blue serge, smartly pressed uniform, had been a proud one but turning up in the skimpy make-do skirt of a savage would be as inexplicable as it would be embarrassing! The answer was to be less visible by avoiding the road and houses which he did by sneaking along the brook where it ran through Mrs Bennet's smallholding, then under the Wharrage bridge and emerging into the meadow running behind Constable's and Batson's cottages, keeping low behind their garden hedges until he arrived at the one that bounded and overlooked the Bloom's domain and clambered through.

No sign of life from this point so he ventured closer using the orchard to shield his approach where his bare feet squelched on fallen fruit left to rot around neglected trees. Maurice's family couldn't have arrived back in time to harvest the orchard he guessed but on reaching the cottage his suspicions grew on finding the building as dilapidated as on his last visit! Dirty windowpanes and even a couple of them broken told of more neglect while its rickety front door was almost totally obscured by untended roses on its trellis surround. On touching the door lightly with his foot it creaked open wide enough to reveal a telling emptiness. His hopes were dashed! The Blooms weren't back in residence after all. But – but Maurice? The person aloft in the tree earlier on was most definitely Maurice.

He'd known the lad for most of his life and couldn't fail to recognize him. Perhaps he'd returned alone? At seventeen he was almost old enough to do his own thing and his parents weren't so mean as to deny him returning to where he'd been happy and he'd certainly not appeared exactly carefree when he'd visited him in his city home. So that's what Maurice had probably done. He'd returned home alone and would now be absorbed in doing what he'd loved most throughout a decade of fun alongside his number one chum. Enjoying himself in the territory around the brook which they'd claimed and vowed never to give up. And Daniel would prove that this was the case by finding his chum's belongings somewhere inside his old cottage home. He'd not have arrived back without a change of clothes and some kind of bedding?

And there'd be curtains! His mother, even in such seclusion had been very private and would insist that her son must have bedroom curtains. He stood back to check out the two upper windows and yes! The one to the right had drawn-back curtains and – and . . .? Was – was that Maurice who'd fleetingly appeared at that window? Was he so pleased to be back home that he was having a homecoming lark with him? Typical of Maurice to game about like that.

About to step inside the cottage and seek out his gaming chum, the sound of wood cracking, possibly underfoot, broke the uncomfortable silence. He turned to glimpse a figure on the far side of the orchard but it vanished as quickly as had the face at the window. Had his pursuers caught up with him or was it. . .? But Maurice, if it had been him at the window, hadn't had the time to perhaps leave from the back door and arrive at that point in the orchard, the quickest way being over Mr Bloom's vegetable patch where he'd have easily been spotted.

Daniel's gaze lingered where Maurice's dad had toiled to make his family independent of the local, travelling greengrocer with a dislike for field cottages, noting the damaged garden fork and Mrs Bloom's holed bucket were exactly where they'd been left. More evidence of them not having returned: Mr and Mrs Bloom that is but – but Maurice . . .? Well, Maurice's appearance at the window had been a split second too long and the game was up!

Stooping to negotiate the bramble-festooned entrance, he entered the miniscule, stone-floored kitchen and on into the dusty, cobweb-strung parlour. Cautiously, he approached the stairway leading off this empty room: cautiously because throughout his long association with the Blooms, he'd never once climbed those stairs to the upper floor. The stairway door was open, inviting him to be brave and go up which, after another moment of hesitation, he gingerly did and was almost at the top when *déjà vu* caused him to hesitate yet again! Yes! He'd lived this moment before! A darkened staircase leading to a small landing with two doors off . . .? Hilary . . . ?

The choice of which door on the Cardiff occasion had been answered by the young Welsh girl impatiently snatching open hers from within. Now, facing that door again, it was not the face of Hilary confronting him but the face of . . .? The face of Abu!

Pinned to the door was what he assumed to be one of Maurice's watercolour masterpieces. Like Augustus John, head and shoulder portraits were his forte and this one, remarkably like Daniel's old friend Abu, the Greaser, was proof of that. Just coincidence the resemblance to the heavily-bearded, elderly Somali who, for once, wasn't smiling. Much out of character, he must point out to Maurice. In fact Abu looked deadly serious, his eyes boring into Daniel's as if to tell him something. To warn him about something rather . . .? To warn him of what . . .? Not – not to enter that room perhaps? No, this was ridiculous! Reading something in an expression which, after all, was but paint on paper! Was he becoming so edgy that he had to interpret anything as suspicious? Why suddenly so cowardly when he'd survived hurricanes, drowning and all manner of abuse and now was too scared just to open a door? Was he hell!

Supine on the bed once graced by the young and innocent Hilary lay the *obligatory naked* Heloise.

"Did you think you'd seen the last of me, young man?" she smiled, while arranging her shapely limbs to benefit his spellbound perusal. "Why so shocked? Expecting to find someone else were you?"

"I, er – yes," he gulped. "Maybe – maybe I was."

Maurice or even Hilary, yes but – but not you, he was about to say but thought better of it.

"How, er – long have you been here?" he asked instead.

Anything to take his mind off how much he was drawn to her in that wanton pose.

"About an hour before you, you slowcoach," she grinned, her palms massaging firm nipples teasingly. "An hour of just lying here with nothing to do but dream about somebody coming through that door," she added, rolling her eyes invitingly.

"Er – Mr Williams is it you've been waiting for?" he asked tentatively, while hoping she'd say no, it was he *Daniel* she'd awaited on that bed.

"We've been over this ground before have we not, Daniel?" she replied with a hint of disapproval. "Ivor's a wonderful man but I believe Sara explained Heloise's fickle nature to you earlier today, so please let that be the end of it or fickle *me* might turn on you!"

That he'd misheard the name 'Sara' during her little outburst Daniel chose not to query because why escalate Heloise's brief change in mood when moments earlier things had appeared very much in his favour and that while Ivor wasn't exactly cast aside, being the free spirit that she now was enabled her to invite whom she wished to share her life and, presumably, even her large, comfy bed!

"It was always so difficult; almost like cheating at times," she insisted on explaining, making Daniel sorry for having mentioned Mr Williams. "Even while convincing Ivor that my infatuation was exactly that and my New York trip would be a fitting conclusion to, or at least, a winding down of my adolescent fantasy in order that I prepare myself for . . . Oh, Daniel, my sweet!" she interrupted her lament. "You've not the faintest idea of what I'm going on about have you? Or – have you?"

"I – I have heard the odd story about your, er – association with, er – Mr Williams," stuttered Daniel somewhat relieved at being distracted from his salacious observation. "And – and I learned a little more from reading the odd letter intended for, er – you. Well – that is from *glancing* through them while they'd been, er – left with me for safekeeping. Well – he had intended them to be left with me, Mr Williams that is but – but unfortunately they sort of, er . . . got mislaid."

"Never mind about the letters," she excused him, while sitting upright and throwing back her long, black hair. "These stories you mentioned, they came from Ivor I take it? What do you remember about them? Did he talk to you about my infatuation? The one that I was just beginning to bore you with? My infatuation with a literary genius? Did he talk to you about that?"

"Er, – yes, he, er . . ." Daniel faltered, now very much regretting having mentioned Mr Williams and just when things had begun to look promising sexually, but she wasn't about to revert back to the temptress while preoccupied with what the officer might have said?

"He talked about my admiration for the genius did he? About my constant desire to attend his recitals where and whenever, did Ivor?"

"Er – yes, he . . ."

"And my New York trip? Did Ivor tell you about my trip to New York? What exactly did Ivor tell you about that trip, Daniel? Every little detail you can recall about that particular trip? How he reacted to what developed, what did the poor man do when I didn't . . .?"

"When you didn't return you mean?" enquired Daniel quietly, hoping that if he was helpful in putting her mind at rest she might see fit to show gratitude by becoming as sexually inviting as when he'd entered the room. "I – I only learned about how he, er – reacted from somebody else," he told her, recalling Edgar's diatribe about the Third while at berth in Newport News. "It was his friend Edgar, Mr Reece who told me about how he'd become, er – strange and – and not able to work for a couple of years after you'd gone missing. Where – where did you get to by the way? There's a lot of people wanting to know the answer to that question."

"What is the general opinion about my disappearance, Daniel?"

Even while serious, the naked Heloise was still so sexually alluring that he found difficulty in applying his mind elsewhere.

"Have you been stuck dumb, young man? Why don't you answer?"

Would she please close her thighs first? he almost asked but she was demanding a reply to her question.

"I – I didn't take much notice of opinions myself but some rumours were that you'd, er – met up with somebody else or not even gone to New York but – but I, er – was told by Abu . . . er –

373

Abu's a Greaser on board, that – that something else was the reason for your not, er . . . for your not coming back."

"Oh – silly shipboard gossip," she smiled. "Ivor told me that it goes on all of the time. What gossip was there on board about my not returning? Come on, tell me. It wasn't as ridiculous as my taking off with somebody else I hope?"

"Er – yes . . . according to Edgar . . ."

This would make her laugh and laughter, it was said, would often pave the way to a woman engaging in sex, mused Daniel hopefully.

"But old Abu came up with the absurd notion that you'd, er . . ."

"That I had *what*? Don't keep me waiting, Daniel. That I had *what*?"

"That you had blooming-well died!" he replied, so sure of her finding the answer hilarious that he was already fumbling for the knot in the cotton supporting his make-do skirt.

"I died? That I had died?" she howled, causing Daniel confusion as to whether they were howls of laughter or distress?

"Oh dear! Oh dear!" she eventually collected herself enough to gasp between bouts of laughter, raising his hopes for an imminent invitation.

"What – what other nonsense did they dream up about me, Daniel? Not – not anything as absurdly creepy as our family joke about my premature rendezvous with the angels at age six, I hope? Out with it Daniel! What else did those silly sailors come up with?"

Spurred on by the laughter theory, Daniel, through his own chuckles replied, "And – and some on board actually had you in an intimate relationship with the poet chap! They came up with this daft suggestion that you and he . . ."

"An – an intimate relationship with . . .?"

Her tone was instantly *not* funny, her dark green eyes welling up with tears.

"An intimate relationship with . . .?" she repeated her incomplete response conveying utter refute of what had been

374

suggested. "It wouldn't have been Ivor behind such rubbish!" she snapped. "He'd have told anybody for nothing that it had all been a *game*! My infatuation with the *poet chap* as you call him! A game that not for one second had the genius been aware of! Didn't even suspect that admirers were so close other than maybe being surreptitiously photographed in Laugharne on one occasion when we couldn't resist the chance. Even then, it was only Ivor holding the camera that came to his notice while little me right by his side didn't get so much as a glance which always seemed to be the case in whatever circumstance, he didn't even once appear to acknowledge my existence!"

Now, sitting in a more seemly manner on the end of the bed facing him, she continued less tearfully and went on to say just how distraught she'd been over her final experience in the poet's presence, an experience clearly painful to recall.

"No, he didn't ever appear to acknowledge my existence," she repeated. "Not even at the last New York recital when I collapsed did he so much as look towards the disturbance in my section of the audience. Didn't even pause in his delivery or even glance toward my stretchered exit. I looked down on the scene and felt sorry: sorry for both him and myself that now we'd never confront each other, not even for one fleeting moment. Just one glance," she added quietly, "would have been solace enough in the hereafter."

The return of her tears had Daniel wanting to hug and console her but something in what she had just said caused him to hesitate. What she'd told him fitted well with the Third's and Edgar's accounts of her movements up until she'd 'disappeared' in New York; and then there'd been Abu's more disquieting explanation which had tallied with Heloise's even more disquieting disclosure moments ago! *'That she'd looked down on the scene'!* And as ominous the words *'solace enough in the hereafter'*.

"Come here!"

Heloise noting his hesitation to do what he obviously wanted to do, took the initiative by throwing her arms around him pulling him firmly down into what was surely the 'missionary' position! Instinctively, their mouths fused and he knew that *it* was inevitable! His hands began a clumsy exploration from breasts to groin and then clasped her buttocks causing her to arch forward while emitting a long sigh of readiness. The sensual, longed-for Flower of the Gower writhing naked beneath him was offering herself to him at last! His senses were reeling in anticipation of this, the most pleasurable act known to man! His flimsy skirt was no barrier and *it* was about to happen! But – but . . .? Something had dulled his senses in those last final seconds and she too, had paused. Had the crackling sound of the bracken in his attire spoiled the moment for her? And – and why was she so cold? She was freezing and – and stiff! Cold and stiff like a . . .! If a corpse, a very angry one?

"You've infected me! You've picked something up on the Demerara and given it to me!" she yelled. "I'm bitten, you little shit! You've infected me!"

"I – I haven't!" he countered. "I never did anything on the blooming Demerara! Honest! In fact I've never, ever . . ." He paused to examine his makeshift apparel. "It's – it's nettles! It's stinging nettles. I got stung myself on the end of my, er . . . finger while I was plucking . . ."

His protest ended abruptly as a half house brick struck the back of his head and he gave a delayed, "Ouch! What the . . .?

"It came through that window!"

Heloise paused from scratching her stomach to point at a broken pane.

"I – I'll nip outside and find out who chucked it!"

Any excuse to extricate himself was all Daniel needed. His urgency of minutes ago extinguished. His head throbbed painfully but he'd got an excuse to hastily remove himself from whatever in the sketch Abu had been warning him about in that room? Quickly proceeding to leave the place where moments earlier he'd been so happy to be, he made for the door only to find it locked! He was locked in that room with someone – something that now had him in dire fear!

"The – the key! What – what have you done with the key?" he stammered.

"So soon to reject me! A boy suddenly a typically selfish man!" she retorted, once more seated on the end of the bed but this time with a threatening scowl instead of the 'come hither' look.

"She complains of a few measly stings and in a flash she's not wanted? To become *non-existent*, eh? Well, Heloise is tired of being *non-existent*! Like him of Cwmdonkin!" she began to resume her unhappy diatribe of what had so hurt her. "I followed him halfway across the globe only to remain *non-existent*! Just a brief pause from his delivery to acknowledge something was occurring in that auditorium! That his number one fan had collapsed he'd never know! *Nothing* simply *nothing* would distract him from keeping their rapt attention! *Non-existent*, this Cwmdonkin Rose, this Flower of the Gower! My Ivor! My dear, sweet Ivor! He should never have let me have my selfish way to attend those recitals. He ought never have . . ."

Another brick through the window curtailed her spiralling lament. In shock at it narrowly missing her, she mysteriously produced the key and tossed it to Daniel, yelling an unladylike, "Go and get that mad bastard!"

Catching it, the grateful youth needed no further encouragement and within seconds, was out of that room and descending the stairs as fast as his still trembling legs would allow, not slowing across the downstairs accommodation and through the front door until some twenty feet clear of the Bloom's old home and whatever now inhabited it? In contemplation of this, the reason for Abu's warning, he stood gazing back at the cottage until it crossed his mind that he ought be looking out for the brick thrower? Moments later, his earlier suspicions seemed correct as he spotted Maurice at the top of the field near its exit! His old chum was up there nonchalantly flying his kite! They acknowledged each other simultaneously, Maurice beckoning him to come on up. Arriving alongside him, his 'forever best friend', being so preoccupied with handling his soaring kite, failed to grasp Daniel's outstretched hand, appearing as cool as on their last meeting in Coventry.

"Are – are your folks back as well?" enquired the newly-returned young seaman.

"Yes," replied the other, his eyes still trained skyward. "Or they will be this evening along with the rest of the furniture. I came ahead to receive and assemble some new beds which I've just finished and I'm just passing time waiting for them."

"How, er – long have you been up here?" ventured Daniel. "With your kite I mean?"

"Only about five minutes. I've been down by the brook for a few minutes as well. Remember? I spotted you from up that tree?"

"So – so it wasn't you throwing bricks at your windows?"

"Bloody hell no! I'd not be so daft as that even if we weren't moving back in!"

"Have – have you noticed any strangers hanging about since you arrived back?" asked Daniel, still trembling from the cottage encounter.

"Yeah, I have as a matter of fact. Down on the bridge. A bloke with a scar on his face who looked like he could use himself. There was something scary about him so I didn't hang around. Do you know him?"

"Yes, I blooming-well do and it's likely him who's been doing your windows in!"

"What! Me mom and dad'll be furious!" declared Maurice while observing Daniel for the first time. "What on earth is that get-up you're wearin'? Don't tell me that's what they're wearin' in the Merchant Navy these days?" he chuckled, grinning broadly.

Blushing, Daniel was about to explain but the cottage windows were Maurice's priority.

"Me mom and dad'll be none too pleased sleepin' in a draughty bedroom," he moaned, his attention back with his kite. "They might even blame you, 'specially when they see you dressed like a savage! You'd best nip off home before they get here."

The old chums' reunion was hardly as envisaged. In fact his airborne toy seemed of more interest than reminiscing, noted Daniel as Maurice sent the kite into a spectacular dive.

"There – there's more your mom and dad'll not be pleased about!" blurted the indignant 'savage', determined to worry the other into paying attention. "Those new beds? Some – somebody's been larking about on them!"

"Larking about?"

Maurice was all ears now, the kite left to wander aimlessly.

"Somebody's been larking about on our new beds did you say? You're making it up! I know you of old! Me mother always did say that you were over-imaginative! She said that the navy would knock all of that nonsense out of you!"

"Nonsense eh? Over-imaginative was I?" retorted Daniel. "That time in Coventry, remember? When you told me about the naked girl tailing me out of the very gate over there? Who was being over-imaginative then?"

The kite had crash-landed into the orchard below and Maurice made as to move off to retrieve it but hesitated.

"I – I didn't imagine it," he muttered. "Honest, I – I really did see her and I've never forgotten it cos – cos it was the only time I ever saw a girl, er – naked."

"Well – well, I've got news for you, me old mate!" continued Daniel, emphatically. "You've got a treat in store cos she's the one who's been larking about on your new beds down there!"

Maurice stared at him in disbelief then turned to focus on his old home.

"That bloke!" he suddenly exclaimed, pointing towards the orchard. "He's down there!"

Daniel had spotted Jock too! The reunion chat was over except for one last impart as he set off for home?

"Maurice! Tell your mother that she's in her bedroom! Oh and was there anybody living in your place just before you moved in during the war?"

"Er – only some Welsh family at summertimes, the landlord told me mom. But they quit after their daughter fell into the well. She died, it was said, but miraculously brought back to life in hospital, but suffered bad health for yonks afterwards, so me Mom was told by the . . . That bloke Daniel! He's seen us and is headin' this way!"

One glance towards the orchard and even at this distance, the Cook's eyes definitely met his and the chase was on! The route he'd come was the best bet, the bridge and adjacent brook familiar to him but foreign to his not-so-nimble pursuer who ominously, was now in possession of Mr Bloom's garden fork!

Maybe not so nimble but the Scot's powerful frame was enabling him to close in rapidly, the sound of guttural cursing becoming louder by the second; the pursued's jellying legs causing him to regret the long anticipated encounter with Heloise which, while hardly as pleasurable as fish and chips in the paper, might well prove to be the first and last carnal indulgence of his short life!

Another *"Bastaaaard!"* too close for comfort induced the necessary spurt to reach water; the cool, flowing water of his ubiquitous brook. The route was much to his advantage now! A route hollowed out by Nature alone with every bend and undulation of its steep banks, those of a once much larger watercourse, as familiar to him as every tree and bush alongside the meandering water. Just ahead of that root-exposed clump of willow leaning precariously from a tall, muddy incline made concave by Winter floods, crumbling red bricks still visible through creeping mildew; the bricks of a bridge where plans and promises had been made; a bridge where girls had kissed and cried; a bridge insignificant to many but significant to those who had lingered.

The Wharrage bridge.

Trust Eileen Bracewell to be hanging about with the hots at a time like this! Flash your knickers at the hot-tempered bully coming after me, Eileen! Flash anything to distract him from whatever he intends to do with that blooming fork? No such

380

luck! He hasn't even slowed! The truth is, Eileen, violence is his forte and he'll get more joy shoving that fork into me than shoving his . . . Oh God! He's nearly on me!

The bridge's shadowy cavern traversed, he arrived at two strands of wire beyond which Mrs Benett's large sow had just begun to disport herself in a vile, stinking ooze normally inhabited only by swine until Daniel's frantic attempt to vault the simple barrier failed and sent him sprawling alongside the surprised animal which then unwittingly helped matters by rolling into Jock's path giving his prey precious seconds to extract himself from the mire and begin the home run.

Daaaad! You were right about me not being suited for sealife! I'm back and if that job's still vacant at Lower Bentley Farm, I'll be up there first thing in the morning! Oh and tell mom to light the boiler so I can have a bath cos I'm covered in pig shit and – and there's a mad sea cook who – who's about to disturb the chickens close behind me an' – and he'll put 'em off laying for days! That'll grab his attention! The sound of squawking fowl never fails to get his back up!

"Find that last bit of reserve, eh, Brazier!" had yelled his sportsmaster as he'd laboured towards the finishing line in the only sport he'd ever shown promise. But his lungs had pained as they did now but through a much greater urgency because like himself, his pursuer hadn't the time of day to linger with the sow and was once again lunging through the water hot on his heels!

"I'll get you, you wee bastard!"

But Jock wasn't aware that around the next bend lay the clay steps shaped by his own hands leading up to their back garden where he might find his mother hanging out the washing while the racket being made by the fowl resembling that they made when a fox was lurking would ensure his father being quickly on hand to investigate with his brother's ancient Winchester .22 at the ready, and while Jock was capable of knocking a young Cabin Boy out with one blow, he'd certainly think twice when faced with that deadly weapon! *Ouch!* Mr Bloom's abandoned fork still remained sharp but Jock's ungainly thrust had fortunately sent the bully sprawling again as his quarry confronted . . .! Confronted the wire netting fence that his dad had said he'd one day annex that part of the brook and surrounds with in order to increase his poultry stock! Huge arms suddenly clamped about his upper body as he desperately attempted to climb the wire, told him that the bane of his short sea life was upon him, the fence about to collapse under their combined weight but other arms reaching out to soften his fall and help him back to where his journey along the brook had begun.

"Nurse Furber! I was jes' tryin' to rub some ointment into where this boy's bin scratchin' his self 'roun' his toto an' he clear scared de daylights outa me by tryin' to climb over de rails of his blessed cot! Oh, an' an' he seems to be comin' 'roun'! Best call Doctor Jessop I tink!"

The nurse's words went something like that as Daniel opened his eyes to the reality of a Trinidadian hospital ward. This time, he'd no desire to return to where he'd been for the last few days. His nurses were angels. Everything Heloise had promised then failed to be. Her physical beauty however, was stunning: such as had Daniel seeking to compare for many years. Beauty that belongs to mystical places and in the minds of men who find and are overwhelmed by such beauty. Alike to the man who penned the letter which Daniel received while awaiting a passage home from Port of Spain.

Third Officer I H Williams
c/o Central Infirmary (Salisbury Ward)
Georgetown British Guiana
September 19th 1955

Dear Daniel,
I'm requested by our agent here in Georgetown to contact you in relation to your hopefully soon passage home which has given me the opportunity to enquire as to your health after your recent hospitalization. Our agent says that I'm to be your chaperone and has stated that I should join you soon in Port of Spain. My own dalliance here in Georgetown had been due to heatstroke they tell me, from which I'm now recovered and soon to be discharged from the above address which I'm looking forward to because even after years of colonization, the Guianese are still ignorant as to the British palate! Fortunately a sweet little nurse has contacts in the ex-pat community here, through which she's ensured that I'm not losing any more weight. She, Daniel and I'm telling you this in confidence, has a brother who works on the river and is why I'll not be chaperoning you on any passage home. You see, part of her brother's work involves ferrying travellers who wish to go inland via the Demerara which should prove invaluable to me.
So my young friend and shipmate, having been subbed by our agent (and I've reminded him that you too will be in need of remuneration) I'll be taking a more leisurely trip back up that river of rivers with this young man who informs me that he's quite familiar with a certain stretch . . .

383

About The Author

Author Dan's work experience began in the fishing tackle industry, through to engine assembler and tester, sailor, soldier, drop-forging technician, sports-hall supervisor, self-employed graphic artist and outwork distributor, all helped greatly, he says, with his lifelong cartooning hobby.

Born of Welsh ancestry in the 1930s old district of Birmingham, Hitler's blitz caused his family to seek refuge in the county of Worcestershire where he spent his childhood.

Aged 17, he followed his two elder brothers into the Merchant Navy but

Author and children in Cwmdonkin Park, Swansea (Dylan Thomas's memorial stone behind to right) around 1975

home on leave he received his call-up papers and became a gunner/despatch rider in the Royal Artillery where he also undertook further education. He served his time in Malta, Cyprus but mostly under canvas in Aqaba, Jordan where, riding his ancient BSA motorcycle alone in the desert, engendered his fondness for large, uninhabited spaces such as his previous experience at sea. Cartooning however, was for the time being, suspended through tough army discipline but never out of mind, resumed following demob.

Following his army service, he worked as a component technician at HDA Forgings, Redditch. Not happily but to provide eventually for his wife and two children. While in this employment he began jotting down the seeds of *The Brook to Cwmdonkin*, while his main hobby was cartooning for the local media and friends. Separated in his early 40s, he became a single parent to his daughter Michelle, while son Stephen was brought up by his mother. Being a father, he says, still brings him great comfort and wishes that he'd had more to do with raising his son, while fully understanding that his own health at that time would have proved detrimental to looking after a small boy, a role much better suited to his kindly mother.

384

In his late forties while holidaying in Thailand, his cartooning hobby continued, his sketches over many years being published in the Pattaya Mail, Chiang Mail and the German language newspaper, the Pattaya Blatt. (Google Pattaya Mail). Aged 75, a long illness meant less travelling and more sedentary time during which he worked on bringing his long-nurtured idea *The Brook to Cwmdonkin*, to fruition.